THE MAGISTRATES OF HELL

A Selection of Recent Titles from Barbara Hambly

The James Asher Vampire Novels

THOSE WHO HUNT THE NIGHT
TRAVELING WITH THE DEAD
BLOOD MAIDENS *
THE MAGISTRATES OF HELL *

The Benjamin January Series

A FREE MAN OF COLOR
FEVER SEASON
GRAVEYARD DUST
SOLD DOWN THE RIVER
DIE UPON A KISS
WET GRAVE
DAYS OF THE DEAD
DEAD WATER
DEAD AND BURIED *
THE SHIRT ON HIS BACK *
RAN AWAY *

* available from Severn House

THE MAGISTRATES
OF HELL

Barbara Hambly

This first world edition published 2012
in Great Britain and in the USA by
SEVERN HOUSE PUBLISHERS LTD of
9–15 High Street, Sutton, Surrey, England, SM1 1DF.
Trade paperback edition first published
in Great Britain and the USA 2012 by
SEVERN HOUSE PUBLISHERS LTD

British Library Cataloguing in Publication Data

Hambly, Barbara.
  The magistrates of hell.
  1. Asher, James (Fictitious character)–Fiction.
  2. Vampires–Fiction. 3. China–History–1912-1928–
  Fiction. 4. Horror tales.
  I. Title
  813.6-dc23

ISBN-13: 978-0-7278-8158-8 (cased)
ISBN-13: 978-1-84751-422-6 (trade paper)

All Severn House titles are printed on acid-free paper.

Severn House Publishers support the Forest Stewardship Council [FSC], the
leading international forest certification organisation. All our titles that are printed
on Greenpeace-approved FSC-certified paper carry the FSC logo.

MIX
Paper from
responsible sources
FSC
www.fsc.org FSC® C018575

Typeset by Palimpsest Book Production Ltd.,
Falkirk, Stirlingshire, Scotland.
Printed and bound in Great Britain by
MPG Books Ltd., Bodmin, Cornwall.

For Mosswing and Moondagger

Special thanks to May Liang
Thanks also to
sorceror
ramlatch
maria bonomi
phaedre
catsittingstill
klwilliams
wmilliken
nestra
belanis
esc key
incandescens
badwolf10

AUTHOR'S NOTE

Since the normalization of Communist China's relations with Western countries in the 1970s, the system known as *pinyin,* by which spoken Chinese is transliterated into the Western, or 'roman', alphabet, has gradually superseded the earlier system of transcription – the 'Wade-Giles' method, which dates from the mid-nineteenth century. In 1982, *pinyin* was adopted as the 'official' method, and all Western books on China now use it.

This made for an awkward choice in writing a novel which takes place in China in the fall of 1912.

I eventually decided to use the old Wade-Giles system to transcribe the spoken Chinese of the story's characters – and all personal and place names – for two reasons. First, it was the system in use at the time in which *Magistrates of Hell* takes place: Englishmen would have referred to China's capital as Peking rather than Beijing, and the nineteen-year-old student laboring in the First Provincial Normal School of Hunan would have been called Mao Tse-tung (or Mao Tse Tung) rather than Mao Zedong. (The Chairman does not, by the way, appear in this novel.)

My second reason for using Wade-Giles was simply because most of my research was done from books published long before 1982 (or 1958, when the government of Communist China adopted *pinyin,* for that matter). Either way, I would be altering half of my transliterations from one system to the other, and as I understand it, neither system adequately transcribes Mandarin anyway.

That was my sole consideration in choosing one system over the other. I do not intend or imply any political meaning in my choice, and I apologize if I have offended those who were caught up in the horrors and conflicts of the past sixty years of China's troubled history. My choice was made purely for aesthetic and historical consistency, and my goal has been, as always, simply to entertain.

ONE

'James,' said the vampire, and let his long, insectile fingers rest on the keys of the Assistant Trade Secretary's piano. 'What are you doing in Peking?'

Asher had glimpsed him from the doorway of the long drawing-room, while attempting to ascertain firstly, whether the man whose testimony might well save his life was at the Trade Secretary's reception ('Yes, Sir Grant's about here somewhere,' his host had assured him, before being called away to more important guests), and secondly, whether there were any men present who might make arrangements to have him – James Asher – murdered on his way back to his hotel. On a visit to China fourteen years previously, Asher had encountered high-ranking officers of the Kaiser's Army in the German-held territory of the Shantung Peninsula who would certainly demand a reckoning for his deeds there if they recognized him.

And they probably won't believe me if I tell them I've retired from the Department and am here solely in my capacity as Lecturer in Philology and Folklore at New College, Oxford . . .

I certainly wouldn't.

Aside from the preponderance of men in both the drawing room and the parlor behind it – and the fact that the servants were all Chinese – the reception appeared little different from any large gathering in Kensington or Mayfair, to celebrate the engagement of the host's daughter. The champagne was French, the *croûtes* and caviar on the buffet entirely predictable.

Then Asher had seen him in the doorway between the drawing room and the parlor: a thin, pale gentleman slightly below average height, his long, wispy hair the color of ivory and his face not the face of a man from this newly-dawned twentieth century. A sixteenth-century face, despite the stylish black evening-clothes and white tie. In fact, Don Simon Xavier Christian Morado de la Cadeña-Ysidro had died in 1555.

And had become a vampire.

Asher took a deep breath and let it out. 'I think you know what

I'm doing here.' He reached for the inner pocket of his long-tailed black dinner-coat, and Ysidro moved one finger: *I've read it.*

Of course he's read it. It's what brought him here as well.

For a moment he looked down into the vampire's eyes, crystalline sulfur palely flecked with gray. *I should have killed him in St Petersburg, when I had the chance.* The fact that Ysidro had saved his life, and that of his young wife Lydia, should have made no difference. Asher had killed vampires, in the seven years since he'd first become aware of their existence, and had seen them kill. He knew Ysidro was one of the most dangerous in Europe. Probably the oldest and one of the most adept in that paramount skill of the vampire, the ability to seduce the minds and influence the perceptions of the living.

To the point that they don't feel they can kill him even when they're standing over him with a stake in one hand and a hammer in the other.

Ysidro turned to the young lady who was seated next to him on the piano bench. 'Know you anything of Schubert, mistress?' he inquired in the French that was nearly universal in the diplomatic community.

She nodded – Asher guessed her to be one of the Belgian ambassador's daughters. Even females slightly too young to be officially 'out' were precious additions to parties in the small world of the Legation Quarter.

'Can you play his "Serenade"? Excellent.' Though his closed lips hid the long vampire fangs, Ysidro had a beautiful smile. 'James,' he went on, rising. 'Let us talk.'

The hand he put on Asher's elbow to steer him through the crowd toward the parlor's bow windows was light as a child's, but capable – Asher knew – of crushing the bone within the flesh.

The chatter around them did not seem to have changed markedly since 1898.

'Honestly, there's no arguing with them,' declared a bracket-faced matron in lilting Viennese French as they passed, to an elegant dame in aubergine silk. 'Our Number One Boy will *not* leave the mirror above the mantelpiece in Freidrich's room, no matter *how* many times I order him to. He says it's *bad joss* to have it facing the bed . . .'

Dialects and accents were Asher's hobby and delight – his business, these days, as a Lecturer in Philology. His trained ear identified the schoolroom French of the British and Russians, the slurry Parisian of the French ambassador and his wife. Over in a corner he heard German: a harsh Berliner accent, and a countrified Saxon. Yes, there was Colonel von Mehren, whom he recognized from his earlier visit. *Is he still the Kaiser's Military Commissioner?* And with him old Eichorn, Chief Translator at the German Legation, who didn't seem to have aged a day. Von Mehren wouldn't associate Asher's current unobtrusive brown mustache and unassuming bearing with his previous incarnation as the shaggy, grumpy Professor Gellar from Heidelberg. No danger there. But Asher had always suspected that Eichorn – one of the long-time 'China hands' immersed in the language and culture – was running an information network for the *Abteilung*.

Keep clear of him . . .

Still no sign of Sir Grant Hobart in the crowded parlor. At six feet two, Asher's old Oxford acquaintance was difficult to miss. Asher followed Ysidro behind the velvet curtains into the embrasure of the parlor's bow window, the cold blackness of a bare garden on the other side of the glass. Naked trees fidgeted in the wind that swept from the Gobi desert, dry as the fawn-colored dust which was a part of living in Peking. Like the house, the garden was a brave pretense that living in China wasn't really so terribly different from being in England: the 'stiff upper lip' at its most defiant.

'I think you will find the Kuo Min-tang deep in error when they seek to give the men of China a vote, Sir Allyn,' proclaimed a voice just beyond the concealing drapes. Asher raised his brows as he recognized the speaker as the 'provisional' President of the new-formed Republic itself: the head of the largest faction of its Army. Yuan Shi-k'ai, stout and gorgeously attired in a Western uniform thick with bullion, watched the faces of the diplomats around him with cold black eyes. 'The people of China need a strong hand on the rein, as a spirited horse is only happy when it feels its rider dominate it. Without a strong man in power, only disaster can follow.'

Sir Allyn Eddington made the non-committal agreement expected of a host. A few feet off in the crowd Asher heard Sir Grant's name and craned to look: a slim woman in a very girlish white dress had caught Lady Myra Eddington by the arm – Asher could see the resemblance in their faces. She had asked, 'What does Sir Grant say?'

Lady Eddington replied soothingly, 'He promised Ricky would be here, Holly darling. That's all he can reasonably do.'

'It's an insult!' Holly Eddington's sharp cheekbones reddened. 'It's our own engagement party—'

'Dearest,' her mother said with a sigh, and she laid a kid-gloved hand on the young woman's shoulder. 'You know what Richard is. I'll tell Cheng to let us know when he arrives, but beyond that, pestering Sir Grant about his son isn't going to get us anywhere.'

She nodded toward the far corner of the room as she spoke, and at the same moment Asher heard Sir Grant Hobart's unmistakable voice bray, 'Poppycock!'

The crowd shifted, and Asher saw his quarry in conversation with two German officers whom Asher didn't recognize and a Japanese Colonel whom he did: a stout, diminutive, and heavily bespectacled little nobleman named Mizukami, who fourteen years ago had been the Meiji Emperor's military attaché to the German Army in Shantung.

Not the time to go over and ask a favor. Even had Asher not just encountered the one person – living or dead – who could tell him what he needed to know about the shocking thing that had brought him thirteen thousand sea miles to this farthest corner of Britain's influence, the newly-born Republic of China.

In the shadows of those wine-hued curtains, the vampire's eyes caught the glare of the parlor's electric lights, reflective as a cat's. Asher slid his hand into his breast pocket, found the article he had clipped from last August's *Journal of Oriental Medicine*. He had reread it a hundred times on the six-week voyage on the *Royal Charlotte* and still hoped it wasn't true.

'Last year in Prague you spoke to me of the nest of creatures there, undead things that weren't vampires,' he said. '*The Others*, you called them then.'

Ysidro's assent was a motion of his eyelids that if he'd been a living man would have been a nod. There was nothing dead, or static, about the vampire's stillness: it was as if after three hundred and fifty years he had become infinitely wearied of intercourse with the living world.

'Did you ever see them?'

'Once. Like the vampire, they can make themselves extremely difficult to see.' The vampire's gentle whisper still held the faintest traces of the sixteenth-century Castilian that had been his native tongue. It was typical of Ysidro, Asher reflected, that the girl at the piano – now rendering a very beautiful version of Schubert's 'Serenade' – hadn't noticed either the vampire's fangs when he spoke, or the fact that his nails were long, shiny, thick and sharp as claws. Such was the nature of the vampire's psychic power.

She probably also didn't notice that he wasn't breathing.

'Difficult even for vampires?'

Another flicker of assent. 'Nor can our minds affect their perceptions, as they do those of the living. This may be partly because the Others haunt the islands of the river in Prague, hiding beneath its bridges to take advantage of our – *incapacity* –' he seemed to sidestep an admission of weakness with aloof distaste – 'with regard to running water.'

'Which they don't share?'

'No. I did not, you understand, venture close to them.' Ysidro drew on his gloves, gray French kid, and smoothed the silk-fine leather over his long fingers. 'They devour vampires as they devour the living and, indeed, anything else they can catch.'

'You said then that they were to be found only in Prague.'

'So the Master of Prague told me. So too did I hear from the Masters of Berlin and Warsaw. Those of Augsburg, and Moscow, and of other cities, had never even heard of such creatures.'

'Yet now they've turned up here.'

A small line, like the trace of a fine-pointed pen, appeared for a moment near one corner of Ysidro's lips, then vanished.

'What else did the Master of Prague tell you?'

'Only what I then told you. That they first appeared in the days of the great plague, five centuries and a half ago. That they conceal themselves in the crypts and tunnels that honeycomb the ancient part of the town. They seem to reproduce themselves as vampire reproduce, through contamination of blood, though apparently without the phenomenon of death through which the vampire pass. The Others are not physically undead: merely very, very difficult to kill.'

'*Do* they age and die?'

'This the Master of Prague did not know.' The vampire turned his head sharply, as if at some sound beyond the windows, though the only thing Asher could hear above the chatter of the crowd in the room was the keening of the wind.

He's nervous, Asher thought, interested.

No. He's afraid.

'So far as Master of Prague can tell –' Ysidro recovered smoothly – 'the Others have a sort of consciousness, yet do not seem to retain that individuality which makes me Simon and you James. They move like herding beasts or fish in a school. Like the vampire, they seem to be destroyed by the rays of the sun, though the process takes much longer, and they seem to have the same adverse reaction to such substances as silver and whitethorn and garlic. Like the vampire, while they retain the physical organs of generation these appear to be otiose. Did not this old Jew, this professor of yours with whom you traveled to China, know these things?'

'Most of them.' Asher was interested that the vampire knew who his traveling companions were. 'Professor Karlebach's study has been primarily vampires.'

Whatever the Master of Prague might have told Ysidro about Professor Solomon Karlebach was reflected in another infinitesimal tightening of the vampire's lips.

'Whether there are masters and fledglings among them, as among vampires, he knew not, nor how they communicate amongst themselves. None has ever heard one speak.'

'Asher, old man!'

Asher turned at the sound of Hobart's booming voice and held out his hand.

'Eddington told me you'd showed up on the doorstep looking for me. More dark doings at the crossroad, eh?'

Asher laid a finger to his lips, his expression only half-humorous. The British Legation's Senior Translator grinned and shook Asher's hand as if he were operating a pump. Asher made no move to introduce Don Simon, as he was fairly sure Hobart was completely unaware of the vampire's elegant presence in the shadowed niche between curtains and window glass.

'I need someone to vouch for me,' said Asher. 'To tell anyone who asks – and I'm pretty sure that someone from the German Legation *will* ask after me – that Lord, yes, you knew me at Oxford and know for a fact that I haven't stirred from the place in twenty-five years.'

'Hah! I knew it!' Hobart's pale-blue eyes sparkled, and he bared his stained teeth again. 'All that sneaking about Shantung in ninety-eight, with a German accent and that moth-eaten beard—'

'I mean it, Hobart,' said Asher quietly. 'If you recognized me back then, there's always the chance that someone will recognize me now. And it is vital that inquiries be discouraged – or led as quickly as possible up the garden path.'

'You can count on me, old fellow.' The big man saluted, then sobered and cast a sour glance across the parlor at the uniformed Germans. They were now in conversation with one of President Yuan Shi-k'ai's aides, a sleek, rather ferret-like man with a beautiful Chinese woman of perhaps fifty supported on one arm. 'The Huns are thick as thieves with Yuan,' he added in a lower voice. 'I'll swear they were the ones who swung those loans he got from every bank in Europe. That's Huang Da-feng with them now, Yuan's go-between with the criminal bosses in the town. And that woman – you wouldn't think it to look at her – runs half the brothels in Peking . . . Not that Sir Allyn has an inkling, I'll go bail.'

Hobart nodded in the direction of the drawing room doorway, where their host and his sharp-faced hostess were conferring with the Chinese butler in his white coat. 'With that wife of his looking over his shoulder I doubt Sir Allyn knows what a sing-song girl *is*.' The big man grimaced: he was one of the old China hands, who had been in Peking for twenty years while ministers, attachés, and diplomats came and went. 'If you need a hand with anything, Richard or I – you know my boy Richard's out here with me now? Secretary – I needed someone I could trust . . . and needed to get the boy away from the company he was keeping in London, if truth be known. But if you need help . . .'

'Not my business.' Asher held up his hand. 'This time I really *am* here only in quest of verb forms and legends. In particular, a legend about rat-people – *shu-jen*, or *shu-kwei*. In particular I'm looking for a missionary named Dr Christina Bauer.'

'Oh, Lord, her!' Hobart made another face. 'Hand in glove with the Kaiser, if you ask me. Colonel von Mehren's been out to Mingliang Village half a dozen times this past year, and you can't tell me it's all to do with the Kuo Min-tang militias in the countryside. Mingliang's where the Bauer woman's got her church and what she *claims* is a clinic. But you could hide a regiment in some of those caves in the hills, and nobody in Peking would be the wiser. I'll send Richard out there with you—'

Lady Eddington's shrill voice reached them above the babble of the crowd. 'He knew the engagement was to be announced tonight! It's a deliberate insult!'

The red, wrinkled skin of Hobart's face seemed to darken with his frown. 'Told the boy he'd better show his face here tonight,' he grumbled. 'I don't know what else she wants me to do. Go down to the Chinese city looking for him?' He laughed rudely. 'Wouldn't put it past the girl – *and* her mother – to have made the whole thing up. But it's damned awkward. For all I know Ricky *did* ask Holly Eddington to marry him: the boy drinks too much. I got him out of a scrape in Cambridge when some harpy of a landlady'd got her claws in him over her so-called daughter—'

His gray-shot mustache bristled as he pursed his lips. 'You haven't got a son, have you, Asher? I heard someone say you finally pulled it off with old Willoughby's heiress. Never thought I'd see *that* happen.'

'Miss Willoughby did me the honor of accepting my hand, yes.' Asher kept his voice level, but remembered several reasons he hadn't liked Grant Hobart at Oxford.

'She here with you? I understand old Willoughby cut up to the tune of a couple of million.'

'Mrs Asher accompanied me to China, yes.' *If I break this ass's nose for him, I'm sure it would draw Colonel von Mehren's attention to me.* 'We arrived this afternoon on the *Royal Charlotte* and are staying at the Hotel Wagons-Lits. And yes, we have a daughter, Miranda, born at the beginning of this year.'

Even the mention of her name lifted Asher's heart.

Hobart dug him in the ribs with his elbow. 'Eh, you old dog . . . You just watch out when the girl grows up. If old Willoughby's shekels are settled on her, you're going to be for it, with fortune-hunters coming out of the woods all 'round you like Hottentots. Every girl in Oxford was after Ricky like the hounds of Hell on account of his mother's fortune. Not that the men here aren't ten times worse if there's an heiress to be had. Well, you know how it is: if a man's in the diplomatic he's *got* to marry money, even if it's only a couple hundred—'

His words were cut off by a woman's scream. *The garden*, thought Asher as he flung open the window behind him – Ysidro had vanished, he wasn't even sure when. Bitter night wind smote him, and in the dark of the garden a blur of white moved.

Another scream: horror and shock.

Asher was out the window and across the brick terrace in two running strides. Light fell through the drawing room windows behind him, through a door further along the house, enough to show him bare thin trees and a frozen bird-bath, and a gate in the garden wall at the far end. Two white-coated Chinese servants ran out with lanterns, followed by the first rush of guests. The jolting glare showed Asher a young dark-haired woman standing in the graveled path – he recalled her slim-cut pale gown from the drawing room – and, a few feet in front of her, the white form of a woman lying on the ground.

Ysidro—

Shock nearly suffocated him, rage and horror.

He'd never—

He knelt. There were two bodies, not one.

The woman who had screamed sobbed out, 'Holly! *Dio mio*, Holly—!'

It was indeed Holly Eddington who lay on the path. Asher recognized the dress – white tulle with pink rosebuds at the bosom, appropriate for a girl of seventeen but not for a woman whose age (when he'd seen her speaking to her mother) he'd guessed as mid-twenties. He'd have been hard put to recognize her face, so distorted it was with strangulation and unuttered screams. She'd been garroted with a man's necktie, the red-and-blue silk still twisted tight around her throat.

The man sprawled on his face a few paces from her snored drunkenly. Despite both cold and the wind Asher could smell the liquor on him. Tweed trousers and a well-cut jacket of the same material: wherever he'd been, he'd left for there in the afternoon. The gleam of the lantern picked out bronze-gold glints in his rumpled hair. When he stirred, and fumbled about him with his hands as if to rise, Asher saw he was young – probably barely twenty – and that his collar was open, his throat bare.

Sir Allyn Eddington pushed his way to the front of the crowd, cried, 'Holly! Oh, God!' in a voice that seemed to rip the words from his viscera.

His wife screamed, '*NO!!!*' and shoved Asher aside, fell on her knees beside the girl in white. 'Oh, God, is there a doctor—?'

The surgeon from the German Hospital struggled out of the

crowd, squatted beside Holly Eddington, whom Asher knew at a glance to be already dead.

The young man beside her struggled to his hands and knees, blinked owlishly up at the crowd before him, then threw up with alcoholic comprehensiveness.

Eddington screamed, 'Bastard! Bastard!' as if those were the worst words that he could produce, and flung himself on the young man. Asher and the Japanese attaché Mizukami grabbed him by the arms before he could reach his intended target. The Trade Secretary fought them like a roped tiger. 'You murdering young pig! You filthy beast—!'

Grant Hobart thrust past them, dropped to his knees beside the drunken youth.

'Richard!' His cry was the sob of one who has lost his final hope of salvation.

TWO

'**A** known killer attends a festivity, at which a young girl is killed.' Rebbe Solomon Karlebach's deep voice ground the words with a heavy-handed sarcasm that was almost relish. 'I am astonished! Do you suppose there is some connection?'

'There might be.' Asher refused to be baited. He glanced at the doorway which separated the parlor of his suite at the Hotel Wagons-Lits from the little hall which led to the servants' rooms and the nursery, where the widowed Mrs Pilley – twenty-two, sweet-natured, and wholly convinced that China would be a better place if taken over by England and forcibly converted to Methodism – slumbered with tiny Miranda.

Then he crossed to the other chair, took his wife Lydia's hands, and kissed her. 'On the other hand, *I* am a known killer – known in certain circles, which I trust do not include anyone here in Peking – in that I've murdered total strangers when no war has been declared between our countries.' *And not always total strangers . . .*

His mind flinched from that memory. 'Colonel von Mehren

has killed people, if he's been in the German Army for thirty years. I know – of my own knowledge, as the lawyers say – that Count Mizukami killed at least one man in the Shantung Peninsula fourteen years ago, because I saw him do it. And I'm sure he had his bodyguard on the premises somewhere—'

'You know what I mean.' The old professor leaned back in the deep-green velvet chair beside the hearth, folded the more mobile of his arthritis-crippled hands over the gnarled and frozen knot of the other. His dark eyes, far from the mocking tone of his voice, studied Asher with troubled concern.

'I know what you mean.' Asher tightened his grip on his wife's long, ink-stained fingers. After six weeks at sea together in the *Royal Charlotte*, she still wouldn't wear her spectacles in Karlebach's presence, and consequently – by the look of the cribbage board on the marble-topped table between them – was being annihilated at the game. Like a leggy, red-haired marsh-fairy in one of her astonishing collection of lace tea-gowns, and nearly blind as a mole, Lydia was unshakeably convinced of her homeliness and to Asher's knowledge had only been seen wearing her glasses by himself, their tiny daughter Miranda, *very* occasionally by her maid Ellen . . .

And by Don Simon Ysidro.

He went on, 'But I doubt Don Simon had anything to do with Miss Eddington's death. She was strangled with Richard Hobart's necktie, not bitten and exsanguinated.'

'It is death that the vampire feeds upon,' retorted Karlebach darkly, 'not the blood alone. This you know, Jamie. The energies released by the human psyche in death are what feed his ability to manipulate the minds of men. He was being careful. He knew he had been seen.'

'Yes, but in that case, why kill at all?' Lydia moved over to make room for Asher on the arm of her chair. 'Why murder the daughter of the Assistant Trade Secretary, of all people, in a public place, when there were probably Chinese beggars asleep in some alleyway twenty feet from the spot? No one would make a fuss if *they* died.'

Karlebach sighed deeply and regarded Lydia for a moment over the rims of his own spectacles, beneath a shelf of white eyebrows that seemed to curl with the strength of his vital personality. 'You defend him too, little bird?'

Lydia looked away.

Someone – probably Ellen – had, in the few hours that Asher had been gone, rearranged the parlor of the Ashers' suite with all the small comforts that Lydia had brought from home to adorn their stateroom on the *Royal Charlotte*: small red-and-blue silk pillows had been added to the green velvet chairs, favorite books placed in the shelves and on the room's central table. Even the familiar gold-and-sky-blue Royal Doulton tea-set was laid out, the pot gently steaming.

Though Asher always felt bemused when he traveled with his wife and his wife's staggering caravan of luggage, there was a good deal to be said, he reflected, for coming in from an icy foreign night to find all things exactly as they were at the house on Holywell Street in Oxford.

'Who knows why the Undead do as they do?' Karlebach held up one crooked hand, as if to stop an argument that neither his former student, nor Lydia, made any attempt to pursue. 'The vampires cease to be human when they pass beyond the realm of the living. Their thoughts are not like ours. Neither are their motives anything which the living can fathom.'

He lapsed into brooding silence, and Asher – who knew that Lydia tended to become absorbed in conversation, to say nothing of not being able to see across the table – fetched the teapot and refilled the old professor's empty cup.

Rebbe Solomon Karlebach had been old when Asher had first met him almost thirty years ago, an undergraduate already on his second tour of *Mitteleuropa* and eager to speak with one of the most respected scholars of the superstitions rife in the remoter corners of what had been the Old Holy Roman Empire. He had spent all that summer of 1884, and the following three, studying at Karlebach's feet in that moldering stone house in the Prague ghetto, and had come to love the old man as a father. Only the previous year, however – some years after he himself had encountered, in Undead flesh, what he had long believed to exist only in legends – had it occurred to Asher to ask his teacher whether he, too, had had personal contact with vampires.

Karlebach now plucked a sugar cube from the saucer Asher offered him, tucked it into his cheek behind its jungle of snowy beard, and sipped his tea through it, lost for a time in his own thoughts. 'And did he speak to you, this vampire of yours?' he asked at length. 'Did he tell you of the Others? Of whether the thing that this Bauer woman found is the same as the creatures that haunt the crypts beneath Prague?'

'He did,' replied Asher. 'But he could tell me nothing beyond what you and I already know.'

'Could tell you, or would tell you.' The old man's dark eyes glinted in the dim gleam of the shaded electric lamps. 'You cannot trust the vampire, Jamie. Even in the tiniest of matters, they deceive. It is their nature.'

'That's as may be. But before the killing was discovered, Sir Grant Hobart told me that Dr Bauer has a clinic in a place called Mingliang Village in the Western Hills, about twenty miles from here. There are bandit gangs in the hills, to say nothing of the Kuo Min-tang – Republican fighters opposed to President Yuan and the Army. I expect we'll need an escort. Hobart suggested his son,' he added drily. 'But it doesn't look as if that's going to happen.'

'Beast!' Lydia rapped his elbow with the backs of her knuckles as he returned to the chair arm at her side. 'Her poor parents – what a horrible thing! And poor Sir Grant! One would think, though,' she added reflectively, 'that if Richard Hobart had proposed to Miss Eddington in his cups, and truly couldn't stick going through with it, he *could* simply have fled the country.'

'That depends on what he was drinking. If he was down in the Chinese city, it could have been anything.'

Lydia winced, but nodded sadly. Despite the elfin features and her air, in company, of having never done anything in her life but attend dress fittings and Royal Flower Shows, Lydia had trained as a physician at a charity clinic in Whitechapel and had had ample occasion to observe the effect on human behavior of alcohol. She started to ask something else, glanced at Karlebach, and closed her mouth again; Asher guessed her question echoed his own thought.

What, if anything, did Ysidro see?

Evidently Karlebach guessed this as well. For later, when Asher walked him down the hall to his own small room, the old man brought up the subject of the vampire again. 'Trust not what he tells you, Jamie,' he rumbled in his thick bass. 'This vampire seeks to use you for the purposes of the Undead. Deception and seduction is how they hunt. You well know how they can manipulate the human mind to see things as they wish you to see them.'

It was late – the clock had struck midnight when Asher had first come into the parlor – and even Rue Meiji, one of the main streets of the Legation Quarter that lay below the windows of Asher's suite, had gone quiet. In the bright glare of the electric lamps, the corridor had the queer, dead look of such places very late at night; doubly disturbing, Asher had found, since he had learned what walked the dark hours.

'When first you spoke to me of this Spanish vampire of yours,' Karlebach went on, 'I feared for you, my son. I could see that he had placed you under the spell of the vampire mind: the spell whose first effect is to make the victim believe that he is not under a spell. Fear this. Fear him.'

'I do,' said Asher, quite truthfully.

'It is unfortunate that your friend Hobart will now be taken up with this shocking business. Quite aside from his personal agony, of course – but the truth is that we could have done with one who could help us, here in the Legations.' The old professor opened the door to his room, which was freezing cold. Asher pushed him into a chair, fetched every shawl he could find for him, and made up the fire, despite Karlebach's somewhat mendacious protests that there was no need to bother about him . . .

No matter how tough the old scholar was, he was still ninety – not an age at which a man should be obliged to journey to China to hunt monsters. Yet Karlebach, when he had turned up – to Asher's shock – in Oxford in September, had insisted, and would not be left behind.

As Asher set a pan of water on the hob to heat for the old-fashioned stone water-bottle, Karlebach continued, 'I could speak to mine own ambassador about an escort, but they will want to know why. And I fear who they might tell, if indeed we find these creatures here.'

'I'll speak to Sir John Jordan tomorrow,' promised Asher. 'Now that I have the assurance that there's someone in Peking who'll vouch for it that, appearances to the contrary, the man who was here in ninety-eight wasn't me.'

'You're very good to me, Jamie.' Karlebach caught Asher's hand, when he returned to the chair to help his old mentor to his feet. 'I would say *like my son*, if it wasn't that one of them is a good-hearted blockhead who can't tell Maimonides from the funny papers, while the other is a slick *momzer* whose heart begins with the law courts and ends at Accounts Payable. Bless you.'

Wind moaned around the hotel's Gothic eaves as Asher walked back down the corridor to his own suite. He wondered where Ysidro was staying and how the vampire had managed to procure the human assistance that the Undead needed in order to travel any great distance from their homes.

For that matter, he reflected, he had no idea where Ysidro called his home these days. Had he returned to London, after Asher had left him asleep in the crypt of St Job's monastery in St Petersburg last year? Had he chosen some other city as his headquarters, since Lydia had acquired such a disturbing adeptness at tracking down vampire nests through bank records and property transactions?

And if that were the case – his mind returned uneasily to the fear that never quite left him – what about the other vampires of London? Did the Master Vampire of London know that Lydia had ways of finding them? He had long suspected that the London nest only kept their distance from Lydia, and from Asher himself, out of fear of Ysidro. Would that fear hold, if the Spanish vampire left London for good?

For people who're in danger because we know too much about the vampires, we know damn little about them . . .

His hand was on the door handle when he heard Lydia say inside the parlor, 'He should be back any minute . . .'

Ysidro. Who else would it be, at this hour of the night? *Damn his impudence—*

Anger flared in him, and he thrust open the door.

Grant Hobart turned from where he stood before Lydia by the fire.

'You have to help me, Asher.' The translator paced a few steps away from the hearth, as if incapable of sitting down. His face, heavily scored with lines though he was only a few years Asher's senior, looked ten years older than it had five hours ago. 'Ricky didn't do this thing. He couldn't have. He's incapable of it.'

'You said he drank.'

'He gets stupid when he drinks, not violent.' Hobart took a

deep breath as if remembering where he was, inclined his dark, leonine head to Lydia. 'I beg your pardon, Mrs Asher. We shouldn't—'

'It's quite all right, sir.' Lydia rose, a slim tallish figure in ivory point-lace, the firelight picking threads of brass and copper from the auburn masses of her hair. 'I can retire if you gentlemen would like to be alone so you can speak more freely, though I assure you,' she added, her brown eyes wide, 'nothing much shocks me. Did your son habitually mix opium with liquor, Sir Grant? I only ask,' she went on, into Hobart's startled silence, 'because generally if one isn't accustomed to opiates, one just falls asleep . . .'

'He had used them together before.' The words came out stifled, shamed.

'Tell me about your son and Miss Eddington.' Asher pressed their new guest into the chair which Rebbe Karlebach had vacated and fetched a clean teacup from the sideboard while Lydia dug a notebook from beneath a pillow. 'You said you thought he might have proposed to her while drunk?'

'He could have.' Hobart sighed. 'It's what that—' He made himself swallow words descriptive but unwise. 'It's what that mother of hers hinted, when I went to her and Sir Allyn to try to see if there were a way of breaking it off, the more fool I. Myra Eddington had already put the announcement in the paper. Not just that little rag the Legations put out – she'd telegraphed it to *The Times*, da— curse her –' he glanced apologetically at Lydia – 'and sent word to the whole cursed family.' His hand, huge and heavy, as if he were a navvy instead of the scion of a well-respected diplomatic family, bunched into a fist on the polished marble beside the cribbage board. His mouth twisted in an ugly sneer.

'It's all because of Julia's money, of course,' he continued after a brief struggle with his anger. 'Julia and her damn money-grubbing father. I'll have to write to Julia of this in the morning. God knows what I'll say to her.'

He rubbed his face, as if trying to wake from nightmare. 'It's why I'm here, Asher. I have to be able to tell my wife *something*. She dotes on Ricky. I have to tell her that things are in hand, that someone's looking into it. You speak Chinese. You aren't a part of the Legation, a part of the whole Eddington set, which goes on tiptoe at the mere mention that something might disturb Yuan Shi-k'ai or upset their precious election – as if Yuan's going to let there *be* an election . . .'

'Chinese?' Asher raised a finger, and Hobart waved impatiently, as if even the question were obtuse.

'It was the Chinese that did it. Surely that's obvious.'

'Why would they do that?' protested Lydia.

'How the he— How the dickens would I know that?' Hobart retorted. 'You can't tell what's going on in their minds. I've served here nearly thirty years, and I've still never managed to figure out why the P'ei will only work for the Huang, and why a man who's sworn allegiance to the Tian Di Hui for half his life will suddenly turn around and kill the leader of the local lodge. Trust me, I see the hand of the Chinese in this.'

Lydia started to speak again, and Asher caught her eye, slightly shook his head.

'Any particular Chinese?' he asked mildly. 'Servants in your house—?'

'Good God!' cried Hobart. 'How should I know? They're all in it together – how would I know how they're connected?'

'May I speak to them? Your servants, I mean . . .'

Hobart hesitated, and his glance shifted at some afterthought. Then he said, 'Of course. I'd ask 'em myself, but they're too damn frightened for their own jobs to say *boo* to me.'

His hands shook a little as he lifted the delicate blue-and-gold china, and his powerful shoulders slumped, as if suddenly the only thing that was keeping him going was the comforting heat of the drink. 'Thank you for going over to the stockade with us earlier tonight, Asher,' he added quietly. 'I won't forget this, I swear.'

'Was your son friends with the girl? Before he proposed,' Asher amended, his voice wry.

'Well, you know how it is in the diplomatic. There's damn few single women out here, and even a shrill man-hunter like Miss Eddington starts to look good when all you've seen for a year is the local sing-song girls.' Hobart's face twitched again, as if at some memory. 'Ricky was friendly enough, but he certainly had no intention of proposing. The girl's four years older than he – *was* four years older,' he corrected himself, with a slight flush of shame at his own callous tone. 'Not an ill-looking

piece, but at twenty-four she hadn't had an offer in her life and
wasn't likely to get one. The Eddingtons have a fine family name,
but they don't have a pot to . . . they don't have a penny to bless
themselves with.' Another apologetic glance at Lydia. 'God knows
why they brought the girl out here. A man's got to have four
hundred a year guaranteed private income to get promoted to
attaché, and Sir Allyn's estate won't run to that. Not once he
gets his son settled.'

'You said your son went down to the Chinese city—'

'Eight Lanes.' He named a portion of the town notorious for
its taverns and brothels.

'Surely he didn't go alone.'

'Good God, no! I imagine he went with his usual gang of
good-for-nothings: Cromwell Hall, Gil Dempsy from the
American Legation, and Hans Erlich, von Mehren's clerk . . .
and yes,' he added wearily, 'I told the boy a thousand times not
to go about with Erlich, because Ricky could not keep his mouth
shut when he'd had a few *shao-chiu* . . . But since Erlich was
generally three drinks ahead of Rick, and too stupid to tell horse
artillery from a governess cart, I wasn't worried, even if Rick
had known anything of military importance, which he didn't. For
God's sake, Asher, this is China, not France. There's nothing *to*
know out here.'

He set the cup down, sat with his elbows resting on his knees,
his great head bowed. *Like a soldier when the heat of fighting
passes out of him*, thought Asher, who knew the sensation well.
When there's nothing left but cold, weariness and pain . . .

At length Hobart said, 'Thank you. Oh, I know you'll never
find the Chinese who did it, but at least establish that it *was* the
Chinese. That it wasn't Richard who did this – this frightful
thing. Do that, and I'll see to it that you get whatever you need
for your own little expedition to look for *shu-jen* . . . and whatever else you need,' he added, meeting Asher's eyes significantly.
'Just clear Richard of this charge. We don't need to know anything
beyond that.'

'For a man who's lived in China for nearly thirty years,' objected
Lydia as Asher returned from seeing Hobart out of the suite,
'Mr Hobart doesn't seem to have made the slightest attempt to
learn about the Chinese.' She dug behind the chair pillows and

extracted her silver spectacle-case, unfolded the eyeglasses with her usual deliberation and blinked gratefully up at him, the final reflections of the dying hearth catching in the round lenses. *'They're all in it together*, and *you can't tell what's going on in their minds* . . . I'd expect that kind of thing from Mrs Pilley, but not from a Senior Translator who's been in China thirty years.'

'True, o Best Beloved.' Asher knelt with poker in hand and made sure that the fire was well and truly out, while Lydia got to her feet and made a circuit of the room switching off lamps. Their house in Oxford was an old-fashioned one, still lit by gas and, in some rooms, by paraffin lamps, though as a result of the journey Lydia had begun planning how electricity could be installed in her workroom. At least gas, Asher reflected, would have kept a parlor this size relatively warm. Away from the hearth it was cold as a tomb, and the bedroom would be ten times worse.

'The odd thing is –' he stowed the poker in its rack – 'Hobart *does* know about the Chinese. At least, when I was here fourteen years ago, he read the *Peking Gazette* regularly and had dozens of contacts in the city. And if you'll notice, he seems to be up on who the local bosses are and who they deal with. Living through the Uprising might have changed him.' He took a bedroom candle from the little stand beside the door, scratched a match from the box that he always carried in his pocket as Lydia pressed the final switch to plunge the room into darkness. 'But if it brought about that much of a revulsion against the Chinese, he could have gone home.'

'Perhaps he doesn't get on with Mrs Hobart?' Lydia gathered an enormous cashmere shawl from the back of the chesterfield and draped it around her shoulders, something she would have frozen to death rather than do in the presence of anyone but her husband, for fear of appearing less than perfect in her lacy gown. 'Though I suppose in that case he could have transferred to India. I wonder how much of the Foreign Service is actually based on marital incompatibility? Though it would be very pleasant, I suppose, to have a nice house in England and be able to do as one pleased without having a husband cluttering things up—'

Asher put a hand over his heart. 'I shall take up rooms at the College again the moment we get home—'

Lydia looked startled, then flipped the fringes of the shawl like a whip against his arm. 'I don't mean you, silly. Sir Grant doesn't look like he can make tea *nearly* as well as you do. But if Richard Hobart didn't want to have Holly Eddington as his wife, all he had to do was send her home once they were married and stay out here in Peking. If he's going to inherit that much money, he could afford not to live with her.'

'True also,' agreed Asher. 'Which makes the whole thing doubly odd.'

Together by the light of the single candle they tiptoed down the glacial servants' hall to the door of the nursery. Mrs Pilley, a nameless mound of blankets, was a great believer in 'cold room, warm bed', but Miranda at least was tucked up under a number of eiderdowns with a warm cap tied over her soft fluff of red hair.

After ten years of marriage to Lydia – and two miscarriages which had devastated that matter-of-fact, curiously fragile woman who had been everything to him from the moment he first laid eyes on her – the birth of their daughter seemed to Asher a miracle. When Professor Karlebach had telegraphed him in August, asking him to accompany him to China, Asher had refused. Even when the old man had crossed to England, arriving on Asher's doorstep with the *Journal of Oriental Medicine* in his fist, Asher had had misgivings.

Asher had read the article himself when it had appeared, and had recognized the description of the creatures he'd glimpsed in Prague.

But it was Lydia who had said, *Of course we have to go.*

He slipped his arm around her waist now, gently closed the door.

Miranda. Tiny, red-haired, beautiful beyond belief . . .

And as safe here, he reflected, as she – or Lydia – would be back in Oxford.

Possibly safer. Since the Boxer Uprising in '01, the King's representatives kept a sharp eye on everyone who came and went in the high-walled Legation Quarter.

And curiously, he found his meeting with Ysidro that evening at Eddington's reassuring.

Deny it though Ysidro would, Asher knew that the vampire, in his curious way, loved Lydia. And he, James Asher, could ask no better protector for her than that yellow-eyed Spanish nobleman who had died before Queen Elizabeth came to the throne.

Died and become Undead.

The bedroom was arctic. Ellen had warmed the bed with a stone water-bottle, and it, too, had gone icy. By candlelight Lydia pulled off her tea gown and corset in record time and, night-gowned to the chin, scrambled beneath the feather bed, then immediately proceeded to use Asher's legs as a foot-warmer.

Later, as they were drifting off to sleep, she asked, 'Are you really going to look into things and question Sir Grant's servants?'

'It isn't my business,' said Asher sleepily. 'And, I have doubts about what I'm going to find. But yes. It's only his word that will shield me from suspicion, and there are several people who might very well recognize me from my previous visit. I can't really refuse.'

Silence, and the scent of sandalwood and vanilla, as she rested her head on his shoulder and stroked his mustache into tidiness with her forefinger.

'Did Ysidro say how long he'd been in Peking?' A trace of hesitation tinged her voice as she spoke the vampire's name. There had been a time when she had refused to do so – a time when she had turned her face from Ysidro completely. *You defend him, too?* Karlebach had asked, and she had had no answer.

'We were interrupted.' Asher spoke with deliberate matter-of-factness.

'Or whether there were vampires in Peking?'

'No,' said Asher softly. 'I wondered about that myself.'

THREE

From the Wagons-Lits Hotel it was a straight walk of a few hundred yards along the decaying banks of the old canal, to the gray walls of the British Legation, massive in the morning sunlight. Rickshaw men followed Asher and Lydia like persistent horseflies, with cries of, 'Anywhere Peking twen'y cent! Chop-chop, *feipao*—'

Asher stifled the urge to shout, '*Li k'ai*!' at them – *go away*! But it was always better when *abroad* – as His Majesty's Secret

Servants would euphemistically say when they were poking around in countries where they had no business being – to pretend total ignorance of the local tongue. One heard far more interesting things that way. And in any case, he, James Asher, had supposedly never set foot in China before. He laid a gloved hand over Lydia's, where it rested in the crook of his arm, and looked about him with the fatuous smile of an Englishman surveying a country that didn't come up to British standards of government, hygiene, morals, cooking, or anything else.

But he murmured to her from time to time. 'This canal used to be better kept up . . . Behind that wall, where the Japanese Legation is now, was Prince Su's palace . . . There was a lane over there that led to what they called the Mongol Market. The vegetable-sellers would arrive before dawn on market days with trains of camels, and the noise would drive anybody out of bed . . .'

Lydia, for her part, turned her head with a gaze which appeared regal but was in fact an ingrained battle not to squint at a world which was nothing to her but blobs of dazzling color in the brittle bright Peking sunlight. The sewagy pong of the canal water mixed with flurries of charcoal smoke from the dumpling man's cart, then sharp sweetness as they passed the vendor of sugared bean-cakes. She was longing to put on her spectacles, Asher knew, with a head-shake of regret. There were times when he wanted to go back and thrash the stepmother and aunts who'd told her she was ugly.

'The Chinese say that when people first arrive in Peking they weep with disappointment,' he remarked, 'and when they leave, they weep with regret.'

She smiled. 'Did you?' She had, Asher knew, been disconcerted at her first glimpse of it, from the windows of the train from Tientsin yesterday afternoon: stagnant pools around scattered congeries of pigsties, chicken runs, and clumps of low-built houses in the Chinese City. Even here within the towering walls of the Tatar City, and of the walled Legation Quarter tucked away in one corner of it, the impression was of dirt and desolation, gray walls, blind alleyways, and grinding poverty.

'I was hidden in a corner of a boxcar filled with raw cow-hides,' returned Asher, 'with a price on my head and fifteen German soldiers on my trail. So – no.'

Lydia laughed.

*   *   *

At the rambling old palace where His Majesty's Ambassador still had his headquarters, Asher sent in his card and gave Sir John Jordan the same story he'd given Hobart the previous evening: that he was here to look into a remarkable piece of ancient folk-lore which had resurfaced, for purposes of incorporation into a book he was writing on the transmission of rodent motifs in Central European legend. 'While I'm here,' he went on, after Sir John had inquired in a friendly manner about the book, 'might I visit Richard Hobart at the stockade?'

The ambassador paused in the act of signing an order for an armed detail to escort Asher to the hills on the following morning, his eyebrows quirked.

'I'm a cousin of his mother's –' this was another fiction, though Asher had met Julia Hobart on the occasion of her son's matricu-lation from Caius College – 'and I'm a bit concerned that poor Hobart might be . . . Well, that any letter he sends her now might paint a picture affected by his own feelings. As is quite natural.'

And, his eyes on the ambassador's face, he saw it: the flare of the nostrils and the way the lips compressed over words that the man would not say to an outsider.

He not only thinks Richard did it . . . but he also isn't surprised at the crime. He saw it coming.

No wonder Hobart wants to shove the blame off on to that unprovable mass of aliens outside the Legation walls.

'Of course, Professor Asher. Mr P'ei—?' Jordan's touch on the desk bell brought the dapper Chinese clerk in again. 'Would you take Professor Asher over to the stockade and tell Captain Morris he's to be given every accommodation in seeing Hobart?'

Lydia remained behind, for tea: everyone in the Legation Quarter was delighted with any new face, and even the married men would flock around an intelligent, well-spoken lady like pigeons to corn. Asher left Sir John showing her around the courtyard – this part of the original Legation still retained its scarlet pillars, green-tiled roofs and the gold dragons on its ceilings – and followed the helpful Mr P'ei down the bare yellow dust of the central mall to the newly-built barracks and the stockade.

'I swear I would never have harmed a hair of her head.' Richard Hobart raised his face from his hands, blue eyes sick with dread. 'No, I hadn't the slightest desire to marry

Holly – Miss Eddington – but for God's sake, I wouldn't have murdered her to get out of it! If I was fool enough to propose to her, the least I could do was go through with it, even if I was . . . was too stupid with drink to know what I was saying.'

Tears swam in his eyes. His face was longer than his father's and narrow. At Cambridge, Asher had been struck by the boy's resemblance to his lanky American mother. His cheeks glittered with stubble of the same bronze-gold color as his dirty hair, but his clothes were clean, and not those he'd had on last night. His father, Asher guessed, had brought them earlier that morning: the neat gray suit of a young embassy clerk, its starched, spotless collar adorned with a subdued green tie. Young Hobart's hands trembled convulsively where they lay on the scuffed table of the interview room, and under a wash of sweat his face was chalky. *He must have the hangover of the century, if not worse.* Asher wondered how much opium the young man smoked and how frequently.

'Do you recall anything of the night you proposed?' He had learned that a matter-of-fact tone would often steady someone on the verge of hysterics.

'Not a damn thing.' The young man shook his head in despair. 'Father was having some kind of ghastly whist-club over that night, so Gil and Hans and I made ourselves scarce. The Eddingtons would be there, you see, and I – well, I was rather avoiding Holly. I know it sounds frightful, Professor Asher, but she did *cling* so, and she was always going on about how much she loved me . . . A bit sick-making, really.'

A shudder went through him, and he pressed his hand to his lips. 'We stayed down in the Chinese City long enough, I thought, that they'd all be gone by the time I got back. But I must have been wrong about that, because I have a vague memory of meeting Miss Eddington as I came up the garden walk. I was feeling a bit wibbly in the morning and came down late, thinking Father'd gone by then, but he was sitting at the breakfast table with a face like Jupiter Tonans. He practically struck me over the head with the newspaper and asked me what the hell I meant, getting engaged to Holly Eddington. I guess her mother'd sent the announcement in, first thing, and it was in print by noon.'

'Were you angry?'

'I was bally well appalled. Well, Miss Eddington was a . . .

I'm sure you know, sir, how hard it is to avoid someone here in the Quarter. And the Eddingtons go everywhere. One doesn't want to hurt anyone's feelings. But I wasn't falling in love with her, as her mother kept hinting. I'd had enough of that at Cambridge – matchmaking mamas shoving their daughters at me . . . Father'd have it that I never proposed at all: that Miss Eddington and her mother cooked it up between them, knowing I wouldn't remember what I'd said. But she had a ring – the cheap sort of thing you'll find down at the Thieves' Market – and was showing it off all 'round the Quarter by that afternoon. It drove me wild, but what can one say?'

'When was this?'

'Last Thursday, the seventeenth. Just a week ago. That wretched mother of hers had invitations out for the engagement party the following day. Oh, dear God!' He sank his head to his hands again and whispered, 'I didn't do it. I swear I didn't do it, Professor. Look, can they get me out on bail, at least? I've been sick as a dog . . .'

'What about last night?'

'Could we talk about this later, please?' Richard swallowed convulsively. 'I'm sick—'

'You're going to be a great deal sicker, and this may be my last chance to get any sense out of you for days,' responded Asher. 'Tell me about last night. Where did you go?'

'The Eight Roads,' the boy mumbled. 'Just outside the Chi'ang Gate—'

'I know where it is. Who was with you?'

'Hans, Gil, and Crommy. We all had passes – for the gates, I mean, after dark. Crommy gets one of the rickshaw boys to take us; they all know the way.'

Asher shook his head, amazed that those four choice spirits hadn't been quietly murdered in a *hutong* months ago. 'Do you remember coming back?'

'Not a thing.'

'Or why you came back early? It was barely ten o'clock when Miss Eddington's body was found, and she'd only been dead a few minutes.'

'Ten—' Richard looked up again, his face now greenish with nausea. 'I say, I couldn't have got that drunk in three hours! Are you sure?'

'Absolutely,' said Asher. 'Did you in fact mean to insult your fiancée and her parents?'

'Good Lord, no! Crommy swore we'd only have a drink or two and – well, and a little jollification, just to brace me up for the ordeal . . .'

Asher reflected that Miss Eddington, had she lived, would have been fortunate to avoid a thundering case of syphilis on her wedding night.

'I swear I never meant to get really drunk! And I was going to go back to the Eddingtons'. But I honestly can't remember . . .' The young man turned a sudden, ghastly hue and pressed his hand to his mouth, at which Asher signed to the guard who stood beside the interview-room door. After the prisoner had been helped from the room, Asher sat for a time at the scarred deal table, looking at the shut door which separated the chamber from the lock-up without truly seeing it.

Seeing instead the Trade Secretary's narrow garden in the jerking lantern-light, the small gate that opened into the alleyway, which in turn led between the garden wall and that of the British Legation and back to Rue Meiji. The alley serviced half a dozen of the Western-style bungalows, allowing Chinese tradesmen and vendors of vegetables and meat to bring their wares to the kitchens, where Chinese servants would prepare them for those who had forced their trade and their religion on the country at gunpoint. At night the alleyway was deserted. Anyone could have come or gone. At ten o'clock, Rue Meiji was still alive with rickshaws – one had only to walk down the alley and lift a hand . . .

A known killer attends a festivity at which a young girl is killed . . .

Ysidro, sitting in the window bay of the Trade Secretary's rear parlor, thin hands folded, like a white mantis contemplating its prey.

How long has Ysidro been in Peking?

''Scuse me, Professor Asher?'

The young man who stood in the interview room's outer doorway had the slightly grayish look about the mouth of someone suffering a brutal hangover. Still, he held out his hand and introduced himself, though Asher had already deduced that this must be Gil Dempsy, clerk at the American Legation: 'They told me you were a friend of Sir Grant's, who he asked to look into this awful mess. I'll take oath Rick didn't do it.'

'Would you?' Asher followed the young man out on to the verandah that flanked this side of the garrison offices, shaded against the baking heat of the Peking summers but at this season blue and chill. 'Any thoughts on who might have?'

'It's got to have been the Chinese, sir.' Dempsy sounded a little surprised that there might be any alternative possibility. He took a bamboo box of home-made cigarettes from his jacket pocket, offered Asher one and then lit one up for himself.

'Why would they have done that?'

'Who knows why Chinese'll do anything, sir? It's not like Miss Eddington'd taken out a million-dollar insurance policy, or was spying for the Germans, or anything.'

Asher turned his mind aside from inquiring whether his informant was sure about these assertions and said instead, 'Tell me about last night.' Further inquiry as to Chinese motivations, he was well aware, would get him nothing but Sax Rohmer generalities about inscrutable Oriental evil. 'Why leave Rick at Eddington's in that condition instead of taking him home? How drunk was he?'

'That's just exactly what I don't know, sir.' Dempsy picked a fragment of tobacco from his lower lip. 'The thing is, Hans and Crommy and I were all – well, we didn't see Rick leave Madame Yu's. For streets around, you know, there's nothing but dives, and we were wandering from one to the next. I came out of one place, and Hans said that Crom had said Rick had gone off in a rickshaw, and blamed if any of us could find him. He was pretty capsized when last I saw him,' the young man concluded. 'But, drunk or sober, he'd never have hurt a white woman. Not any woman, really.'

Asher raised his brows. Dempsy looked a little conscious and added, 'I won't say I've never slapped a Chinese woman, Professor. Hans'd have it that the Chink girls don't respect you if you don't, but I never found that. Besides, I really don't care if they respect me or not.' He shrugged, uncomfortable despite his words.

On the parade ground beyond the verandah, an officer's whistle shrilled out a signal to a troop of khaki-clad Durham Light Infantry, whose every stride kicked up small clouds of yellow dust.

'Do you think Hobart actually proposed to Miss Eddington?'

Dempsy gave the matter some thought. 'He could have,' he said at last. 'Please don't think Rick gets hammered like that every night of the week, sir. His pa keeps him pretty busy. And anyone in the Quarter'll tell you, he won't drink at those little parties they're always throwing here, where everybody sips sherry and talks about Back Home. But about three times since he's been here, we've gone down to the Eight Lanes and he's wound up well and truly obfuscated, and he's said things to me then that he had no recollection of afterwards. So he could have asked her, yes. But equally, Mrs Eddington was so—'

His mouth tightened under its thin black mustache, and for a moment his eyes shifted. Not a lie, thought Asher, so much as a second thought: *is it wrong to tell him this?*

'He might have said something that Mrs Eddington pushed her daughter into believing was a proposal?' he suggested gently.

Dempsy looked embarrassed. 'The thing is, sir, Mrs Eddington was darn set on Miss Eddington marrying Rick. And I think Miss Eddington was . . . was darn set on marrying *anyone*. Well, she's twenty-four . . . She *was* twenty-four,' he corrected himself. 'When a girl gets to be that age—'

The door behind them opened. Asher smelled fresh vomit even before he turned to see the soldier who'd taken Rick back to the cells emerge with young Hobart's fouled gray jacket rolled up into a bundle with the shirt and green silk tie. In a carefully neutral voice, the soldier said, 'You'd best let Sir Grant know that his son will be needing fresh clothing, sir.'

Dempsy waved as if to dispel the reek. 'Jesus! And after all the fuss he made about getting his suits tailored, and his hankies to match.'

'Did he?' Asher signed the soldier to remain. Folded on top of the gray suit and green tie were the tweeds Rick had been wearing in the garden the previous night, including, grotesquely, the red-and-blue necktie with which Holly Eddington had been strangled.

'Oh, hell, yes.' The clerk made the whisper of a chuckle. 'I guess I'm an American, sir, and the others are always ribbing me, how I look like I got dressed in a high wind . . .'

Which wasn't true: Dempsy's jacket was old and the cut of

his trousers far from fashionable, but he had the well-scrubbed look common to many Americans. Despite his queasy pallor, he was freshly shaved, with a clean shirt and his tie done in a neat four-in-hand.

'Is Rick fussy about his clothes?'

'Not as bad as Hans Erlich.' Dempsy grinned. 'The two of them – Hans and Rick – will go on about what shade of tie goes with which socks like a couple of my mama's friends back home. But please don't think there's anything sissy—'

Asher's gesture disclaimed any such interpretation, and he took from the folded clothes the red-and-blue silk necktie – which the daylight showed to be entirely inappropriate for the muted mauves and greens of the tweed that Rick had worn the previous night. 'Was this the tie Rick was wearing last night?'

Dempsy studied it for a moment. 'No. The one he had on last night had spots, not stripes. The light wasn't real good, but I think it was sort of greens and grays.'

'That's what I thought.' Asher folded the tie up and tucked it into his pocket.

FOUR

'Twenty-four hours?' Professor Karlebach growled like a very old lion troubled by flies. 'Ach, and for what? These creatures multiply, Jamie! Each night's delay puts other victims in peril.'

Laughter from the party at the next table: the Austrian ambassador and two of his aides, chattering in Viennese French.

With a sidelong glance at them, Karlebach continued, 'And it increases the chances that these things – these *Others* – will come to the attention of some one of the powers here.' He gestured with the most recent issues of the *Journal of Oriental Medicine* and *Etudes Physiologiques*, pulled from the crammed pockets of his rusty, old-fashioned frock-coat. 'Dr Bohren from Berlin, and that cretin Lemaitre from the Sorbonne, have written letters decrying this Bauer woman as a hoax, but you know it's only a matter of time before someone in some War Department is going to start asking themselves how they might use these things. Surely we can reach this village this afternoon by motor car?'

'We can. Provided nothing goes wrong.' Asher sat back as the white-jacketed Chinese waiter brought green turtle soup and *petite sole aux tomates* to their table. The dining room of the Wagons-Lits Hotel was justly famous throughout the diplomatic community for the excellence of its lunches, and Asher had taken great care to obtain a table in the most inconspicuous corner of that elegant salon.

'Have you ever ridden in a motor car, sir?' Asher asked. 'The tires are rubber: on a good macadam road you can go twenty or thirty miles between punctures. But here?' He made an eloquent gesture with his eyebrows. 'The road ends at Men T'ou Kuo. We'd have to procure horses there – or donkeys, more likely – to ride on to Mingliang. Given the presence of bandit groups in the hills – and Kuo Min-tang militia – personally, I would rather wait till we have an armed escort.'

'I bow to your greater experience, Jamie.' The old man rumbled his discontent. 'It's just, when I think of those who will be placed in danger—'

'If someone will inevitably be placed in danger,' said Lydia, 'I would much rather that it not be you, sir, or Jamie.' And she laid a hand over Asher's wrist.

For this reason, with the conclusion of lunch, Asher passed the afternoon in giving his companions a Cook's Tour of the Legation Quarter, with its odd mix of modern European structures and antique gateways left over from the days before the Uprising. Parade grounds, barracks, and soldiers in the uniforms of most of the armies of Europe served to remind them that they were intruders in that ancient land, and unwelcome ones at that.

'Half this area was a regular Chinese neighborhood up till the Boxers shelled it into rubble,' Asher explained as they paused to marvel over the Gothic absurdity of the French Post Office. 'A maze of *hutongs* – those high-walled alleyways – and *siheyuan*, courtyard houses—'

'Like the Legation this morning?' asked Lydia.

'They make up most of Peking. Sometimes one courtyard per house, sometimes two or three or five or ten, all leading out of one another. You never knew what was in some of those

compounds. What the Boxers didn't demolish was burned by
Chinese mobs, or destroyed by the Expeditionary Force when
they came through.'

Karlebach listened, nodded, and growled, but made the observation that it wasn't to play Sherlock Holmes that they had come
to China. When they reached the end of Legation Street, and
looked out through the gate across the open glacis that surrounded
the Quarter's wall, he rumbled, 'So he could be anywhere out
there, could he not? Your vampire.' He surveyed the sea of
upturned tile roofs, the line of gaudy shops on the other side
of Hatamen Street. Rickshaws, laden donkeys, and lines of thick-
bodied, two-humped shaggy camels passed them, and endless
streams of blue-clad Chinese.

'He might.' Asher felt Lydia's silence beside him. Her anger at
Ysidro over the death of a traveling companion – three years ago
in Constantinople – had left her, and she would speak of the vampire
perfectly readily if the subject arose. Yet he noticed she never
brought up his name herself.

Except now and again, in her sleep.

As generally happened in any open space in Peking, the portion
of the glacis from the gate to the polo ground – some two hundred
feet – had been taken over by Chinese vendors of dumplings and
caged birds, cloth shoes and horoscopes, fried scorpions and paper
toys, as well as by the occasional acrobat, storyteller, juggler or
newspaper seller, and a long rank of rickshaws, the pullers of which
shouted their readiness to transport passers-by to anywhere in the
Republic for twenty cents. Thronging together, they smelled
different from English crowds. As he had on his previous visit to
China, Asher felt as if he had disembarked, not on another corner
of the planet, but on another world altogether, as different from
England as H.G. Wells's description of the civilization on the Moon.

You can't tell what's going on in their minds, Hobart had
protested – loudly. *How would I know how they're connected?*

He isn't far wrong, reflected Asher, listening to the babble
of voices, the curious sing-song effect of a language in which
changing tone is as much a part of the meaning of the word
as its consonants and vowels. Watching the gestures of hands,
the slight cues of clothing and demeanor that communicated
nothing to an observer who didn't understand the culture or
the city.

But, in fact, Hobart is lying.
And I wish I knew about what.

That night, after supper, and after Miranda had been put to bed
– impatient with parents who had been largely at her beck and
call throughout the six weeks on the ship and who now left her
with Mrs Pilley and Ellen – Asher returned to the Quarter's
eastern gate. He'd left Lydia and Professor Karlebach poring over
issues of the various medical journals which had appeared subsequent to Dr Christina Bauer's article about the creature whose
body she had dissected – journals which contained derisive letters
speculating on everything from the missionary's attempts to claim
undeserved credit in the scientific community by a fraudulent
'discovery', to the degenerate nature of Oriental races in general.
The night was still, and the cold piercing. He traded a cigarette
with the guards on the gate – Russians, tonight – and talked with
them a little in their own language before moving on.

Beyond the gate – across the open glacis – he could see the
massive towers of the Hatamen Gate, shut and barred now for
the night and guarded by a prosaic brace of blue-uniformed
policemen. The wide avenue was growing quiet.

Remaining within the Quarter's high wall – a city within a city
– he walked up Avenue Yamato and along Rue Hart, passing the
lights of the Peking Club and the elaborate gateway of the Austrian
Legation, then quartered back along Rue du Club past the customs
house and the rear of the French barracks. His footfalls echoed
on the pavement, though he was a silent-moving man.

Promenading oneself, Ysidro called it. What a vampire did
when he came into a city not his own. Vampires were ferociously
territorial, and no vampire would dare hunt on the grounds of
another without first speaking with the Master of the local nest.

Asher suspected Karlebach knew this, and knew where he was
going when he'd said, 'I'm going to take a walk.' As he'd gone out
the door of the hotel suite, he'd felt the old man's eyes on his back.

He knew the signs and guessed that Ysidro had not fed for many
nights. As Karlebach had said, without the energy absorbed from
the victim at a kill, a vampire's psychic skills – the abilities which
enabled them to pass unnoticed in a crowd, to make the living see
them as they wished to be perceived – waned. Throughout their
conversation last night, Asher had been disconcertingly aware of

dreamlike flashes of Ysidro's true appearance, skeletal and strange, like a vision that came and went.

The vampire, too, might be out promenading, placing himself where the vampires of Peking – assuming that Peking *had* vampires – would be aware of him. Giving them the option of where and when to accost him and ask him his business.

Always supposing they spoke English, or Spanish – possibly even Latin.

Always supposing that they didn't, like the so-called Boxers – religious cultists and practitioners of one of the several forms of martial arts, who had led the massive uprising a dozen years previously – believe that any European, even an Undead one, should be killed at sight.

For his part, Asher didn't believe for a moment that Don Simon Ysidro would go to ground outside the Legation Quarter. He certainly hadn't sufficient Chinese to make arrangements to hide his coffin – actually a double-lidded tan traveling-trunk with brass corners – anywhere in the 'Tatar city' that lay beyond the Quarter's walls, and the Chinese city beyond that. And ninety-nine one-hundredths of the population of that city actually believed in vampires and would have been more than eager to hunt them down and kill them.

Our strength, Ysidro had said to him once, *is that no one believes . . .*

But the rules were different, here.

So Asher walked, and listened, uneasily aware that there was a slim chance that European vampires might have survived the Uprising and the Boxer siege of the Legations and might still be hiding in the Quarter itself.

He had asked Karlebach once, *Do they know of your researches?* after the old man had admitted to him that he was indeed acquainted with the vampires of Prague.

Oh, yes, Karlebach had replied, with a grim glitter in his eyes.

Later, on the *Royal Charlotte* as it steamed its way through the Mediterranean and across the Indian Ocean, Asher had seen that, like himself and Lydia, Karlebach wore links of silver chain around his knotted wrists, enough to burn the hand of any vampire who seized him, even through the frayed linen of his cuffs. An instant's break in that superhuman grip could be the difference between life and death.

Around his throat he also wore silver chains – like Asher, whose neck was tracked with bite scars from collarbone to ear lobe. As Karlebach had said, a vampire could get the living to obey, but this was no guarantee that the other vampires of a given nest would approve of the knowledge that living servant might gain. It was a situation which seldom ended well.

Do all who have to do with vampires end up wearing those chains?

He turned his steps back toward the hotel just after midnight. The watergate at the southern end of the canal had been repaired since the Uprising: it was a proper gate now, which couldn't be slipped through by ill-intentioned persons. Still, Asher found himself listening, and he remembered the equivocal shadows below the bridges of Prague, the dank stone tunnels that led into the old city's maze of crypts and sub-cellars . . .

Peking – lying close to the deserts of the north – was a city of artificial lakes and marble bridges, of waterways built by emperors to cool and brighten their playgrounds and to thwart the dry spirits of evil. The sides of the canal had been embanked with bricks since last he was here, and the smelly water lay invisible in the shadows. The noises he heard he thought – he hoped – were rats.

Ysidro didn't accost him. If anyone – or anything – else watched him pass, he was unaware of it.

But later that night he dreamed that he was back on the banks of the canal, and that something was moving along the opposite side in the darkness. Something that stopped when he stopped, yet when he moved on again he heard footfalls scrunch softly on the gravel of the road verge. Once, in a glimmer of starlight, he saw that whoever it was, he – or she – or it – bore Richard Hobart's red-and-blue silk necktie in hand.

Peking's new railway line ran directly out to the village of Men T'ou Kuo, but the nearest ferry over the river Hun Ho lay some miles to the south. Thus it was almost noon on the following day before Asher and Professor Karlebach, accompanied by Sergeant Willard and His Majesty's troopers Barclay and Gibbs, reached the little town on horseback.

The Western Hills rose some fifteen miles from the walls of Peking, steep-sided, dry, dun with coming winter. Thin brush and an occasional straggle of pine or laurel grew in deep gorges, or around the sprawling half-empty temple complexes where Europeans would picnic in summer among the chanting monks. The unpaved track from Men T'ou Kuo to Mingliang Village wound along the main river gorge and then up over a ridge under sharp, heatless sun.

'Used to be a fair bit of traffic along this way, sir,' provided the sergeant, in the treacle accents of the Liverpool Irish. 'Back in the nineties when the mines at Shi'h Liu was still a goin' concern.' He pronounced it Shee-Loo. 'Like a picture book it was, with lines of camels and donkeys takin' coal down to the depot – coolies, too, some of 'em carryin' a hundredweight of tools or what-have-you just on a shoulder-pole. Tough little buggers.'

'And when did they quit working the mines?' asked Asher. Sergeant Willard looked about his own age, graying and sturdy. *One parent, probably his mother, from South Ireland*, he calculated by the man's pronunciation of terminal – *er*.

'Been quit for years, sir. Well, stands to reason – they been diggin' those mines back since God invented dirt. The new ones is over toward Tong-shan. Hardly anything left of Mingliang these days, now the mine's shut.' The sergeant turned sharply in his saddle to glance at the crests of the hills above them. He'd done this three or four times, Asher had observed, since they'd left Men T'ou Kuo.

And he was listening, as Asher himself had listened now for an hour.

Softly, he asked, 'What do you hear, Sergeant?'

'Could just be monkeys, sir,' spoke up Trooper Barclay, his glottal vowels putting his birthplace within a few streets of London Bridge. 'There's a deal of 'em in these 'ills, an' they'll follow riders sometimes for miles.'

Or it could be the Kuo Min-tang. Yuan Shi-k'ai's assurances to the contrary, not all Chinese felt 'happy and secure' with the heavy hand of the generalissimo of the Northern Army on the rein. Rumor was rife in Peking of the militia groups forming to protect the Republic should its 'provisional President' decide – as he was rumored to be contemplating – to found a new Imperial dynasty with himself as its first Emperor. But as Hobart had pointed out on Wednesday night at Eddington's, an army could be concealed in these empty hills. They were by all accounts riddled with abandoned coal-mines as well as natural cave systems, some of which ran underground for miles.

Lydia had protested that morning at being left behind to collect gossip about Richard Hobart ('Why do I *always* have to do that bit? You're going to need a medical opinion of whatever specimens Dr Bauer preserved . . .'), but when it came down to it, Asher had wanted to make the first reconnaissance himself. Every time he glanced over his shoulder at the brush-choked gorge below, or strained his ears to identify some fancied anomalous sound, he was glad he'd left her behind.

He would have left Karlebach as well, had the old man not refused to surrender his 'rightful place' in the party. 'I know about these things, Jamie,' he had insisted. 'I have studied them for decades.' He had grown more autocratic, Asher thought, since the death of old 'Mama' Karlebach – that bent, tiny woman who had welcomed Asher as a student to the house in the old Prague ghetto back in the eighties. She had spoken only Yiddish, but had been a formidable scholar in her own right. Since her death ten years ago, it had seemed to Asher, from Karlebach's infrequent letters, that the old scholar had relied more and more on his students, adopting one or another of them as he had adopted Asher, in preference to the company of a family with whom he had nothing in common.

The most recent of such surrogate sons, Asher had gathered, had been a young Hungarian equally devoted to the study of folklore and to the righting of his nation's wrongs at the hands of the Austrian Empire. His name – Matthias Uray – had vanished quite suddenly from the old man's letters, and Karlebach had not spoken it at any time on the voyage. Presumably, thought Asher, he had deserted Karlebach for the Cause, just as he, James Asher, had deserted him, first to serve Queen and Country with the Department . . .

And then to partner with a vampire.

Would Karlebach have come to China at all, Asher wondered, had his wife still lived? Had he not felt himself deserted and alone?

He considered his former teacher now, as the old Jew nudged his skinny Australian 'whaler' close to the sergeant's mount, and asked, 'Have you heard of other dangers in these hills, besides irate natives?'

'You mean bears or suchlike, sir?' Both troopers looked blank at the question, though the younger one – Barclay – cast a nervous eye at the double-barrelled shotgun that Karlebach carried in his saddle holster. 'There ain't been bears 'ereabouts for – Lord, not 'undreds of years.'

And Gibbs added, 'Ye'll scarce be needin' the 'eavy artillery, sir.'

'Ah.' Karlebach patted the smooth-oiled stock. 'One never knows.'

The shotgun bore the mark of Kurtz – one of the premier gunsmiths of Prague – and, Asher could see, its trigger and guard had been specially modified to accommodate the old man's arthritis-crippled fingers. For six weeks on shipboard, he had watched his mentor practice with this formidable weapon, and he knew that each of the cartridges that distended the pockets of that rusty old shooting-jacket were loaded, not with lead, but with silver deer-shot, enough to tear a man or a vampire to pieces.

Karlebach's pockets clinked also with a dozen phials of distillations which he had concocted from the grimoires that were one of his major occupations – silver nitrate combined with those things inimical to vampire kind: garlic, whitethorn, wolfsbane, Christmas-rose.

'Don't you worry, sir,' added the older trooper cheerfully. 'We'll get you there safe as 'ouses.'

Movement in the trees below the road drew Asher's attention, but as always, when he looked, there was nothing to be seen.

Mingliang Village lay some four miles back from the Hun Ho river, where a smaller gorge widened out at the foot of a shoulder of hills. The Lutheran mission stood at the top of the village, which was a maze of gray mud-brick *siheyuan*, the compounds bunched tight together with only a snarl of alleyways between. Many of these, Asher noted as they climbed the narrow ways up the hill, were deserted. Empty gates opened into courtyards filled with the dust of many winters. A number of the village shops, down near the bottom of the hill, were closed up.

Still, the terraced fields along the stream – wherever there was an inch of soil to spare – were all brown with the stubble of millet and dry rice; no land was yet gone to waste. The familiar stink of chickens and pigs, of charcoal fires and night soil drying, hung in the air above the smells of pine trees and the river; and a man who'd been checking bird traps in the woods, as the little cavalcade came around the last turn of the track, ran ahead of them, up the twisted streets and into the neat brick building beside the white church, calling out '*T'ai-t'ai! T'ai-t'ai . . .!*'

A woman who had to be Christina Bauer emerged, shading her eyes.

Asher dismounted at once and removed his hat. 'Frau Doktor Bauer?'

'I am she.'

Bavarian German, sing-song and slurred.

'Please allow me to introduce myself.' He extended the letter of introduction that Sir John Jordan had written for him the previous morning. 'I am Professor James Asher, of New College, Oxford. This is my colleague, Professor Doctor Karlebach, of Prague.' Sergeant Willard had sprung down immediately to help Karlebach dismount, and steadied him as he limped stiffly to Asher's side and extended his hand.

'*Gnädige* Frau . . .'

Had she remained in Germany she'd have been a stout *hausfrau* surrounded by young grandchildren. China had made Dr Bauer thin, and had weathered a pink complexion to dusty brown, but she still had the broad hips and shoulders of her ancestry and the smiling calm of a peaceful heart in her eyes.

'We are here to speak to you about the creature you found last spring in the hills,' said Asher. 'The thing you said the villagers called a demon, a *yao-kuei*.'

She closed her eyes, and her breath went out of her in a sigh of deepest relief. '*Du Gott Allmächtig*. Someone believed me.'

Karlebach frowned. 'I should think the remains would have convinced them.'

'Remains?' Her eyebrows arched as she turned to regard him. 'That's the whole trouble, Herr Professor. The remains are gone. Without them, no one will believe . . . Who would? But it means we can get no help.'

'Help?' Something shifted in Karlebach's eyes. Wariness. Readiness.

Not surprised, thought Asher. *Not even startled*. Afraid with the fear of one who's seen this coming.

Knowing it for the truth, he said, 'You've seen more of them.'

FIVE

'This is all that's left.' Frau Bauer shut the door of the workroom at the rear of her clinic building, crossed to the single window that looked out on the woods and closed the shutters, putting the room almost in darkness. Her dress was old and hadn't been made for her – the seams bore faded lines where they'd been let out. Somewhere in Germany, a congregation read her letters aloud at 'Missionary Week' and collected clothing for her and her flock.

'It weighed seventy kilograms when it was brought in. Whole, the relationship to humankind – *homo sapiens sapiens* – was obvious; it even wore clothing that I think it must have stolen from militia troops.' She struck a match, lit a candle in a tin holder.

Lydia was right. She'll have to come out here as soon as possible . . .

'After the dissection it took me two days to realize that sunlight was destroying the flesh and the bones.' Dr Bauer unlocked the wooden chest in the corner, lifted out a tin box, of the sort used to carry photographic supplies. 'When I opened the box the following morning all the flesh and soft tissues were gone. Like a fool I left everything on the table, locked up this room and went out to question everyone in the village. Herb-doctors will pay for old bones, you understand: old writings, fossils, anything ancient to make medicine with.' She shook her head. 'Everyone swore they had not touched them and *would* not touch them. The fear in their eyes was real, Herr Professor. The bones showed no sign of decay when I came back that afternoon, but crumbled in the box after I locked them up again.'

She raised the lid, whispered, '*Verflixt!*' and, with a pair of tongs, gently lifted out the contents on to the metal instrument tray. 'I'm sorry.'

'Not at all,' murmured Asher. 'This is fascinating.'

The skull reminded him of one he'd seen in London, when one of the fledgelings of the Master of London had been burned.

Shrunken and discolored, the very structure of the bone had been unable to withstand the terrible changes that sunlight wrought upon vampire tissue. *But slow this time*, he thought. *Slow and in darkness . . .*

Some of the facial bones had dropped off it, and those that remained attached seemed to have grossly shifted their position and angle. *A softening of the sutures? Is that possible?*

Lydia would know.

He flinched at the thought of her riding that winding track through the hills, with rustlings and whisperings in the gorge below.

The pelvis had shrunk also, and only almond-sized knobs remained of the long bones of arms and legs. Teeth remained in the upper jaw. Not only had the canines developed into fangs – longer than those of the vampire, but as far as Asher could tell exactly similar – but other teeth had burgeoned into tusks as well.

Frau Bauer stirred with the tongs at the fine blackish dust on the bottom of the box. 'Bits of the ribs remained, only last week,' she said. 'I put a few spoonfuls of the dust into two other boxes: one exposed for fifteen minutes to the daylight, one given no additional exposure. Both boxes were completely empty two days later. There seemed to be no difference between the rates of the dust's decay.'

'My wife is going to want a copy of your notes, if you're willing to share them.' Asher held up the tray, moved it about to further study its contents. 'She is a medical doctor and deeply interested in . . . cases such as these.'

'*Cases*?' Frau Bauer's eyes widened: shock, dread, eagerness. 'There have been other such, then? Do you know what these things are?'

'No,' said Asher quickly. 'My wife's interest is in anomalous deaths: specifically, in cases of spontaneous human combustion, which this rather resembles. You say you've seen more of these things?'

'Not I myself.' The missionary moved the lamp closer as Asher angled the tray. 'Liao Tan, the Number One of the village, saw one in the twilight, in the woods at the end of the valley, about three weeks after this one was found—'

'Where did you come by this one?' interrupted Karlebach.

'In your so-interesting article you speak of peasants bringing it to you . . .'

'Liao Ho – Number One's nephew – has a house beyond the others in the village, on the track toward the mine. His mother – Tan's sister – was a little mad, and in her later years she could not abide the noise of her neighbors. Ho kept the house after her death. He is something of an eccentric himself.'

She half-smiled at the thought of her cantankerous parishioner. 'He keeps pigs and shared the house with three very fierce dogs. Tan told me the week before that his nephew's pigs had been attacked in their pen by some animal: wolves, he thought. One night, Ho heard the dogs barking wildly out in the darkness and followed them to the edge of the marsh that lies below the old entrance to the mine. He found this thing there, horribly mangled. Later two of the dogs became sick and died as well.'

Asher's glance crossed Karlebach's and saw, behind the small, oval spectacles, the dark eyes fill with tears.

It had once been a man, thought Asher, setting down the tray with its fragmentary remains. *A man with a wife and probably a child – like Miranda. A man who had loved and been loved, wanting only to get through this life . . .*

And unlike the vampire, he had not chosen to make this change.

Contamination of blood, Ysidro had said. *They do not seem to retain that individuality which makes me Simon and you James . . .*

'Ho brought the creature back to me at once.' With the point of the tongs, Dr Bauer gently touched one monstrous fang. 'Ho has never believed in demons. He insisted that the things people said they saw in the twilight had some kind of natural explanation. He also insists that the stories that these *yao-kuei* can summon and dismiss hordes of rats from the mines are superstition—'

'Rats?' Karlebach looked up sharply.

'So the story goes. Such vermin are abundant both in the mines and in the marsh below the main entrance.'

'And how long,' inquired Asher, 'has the story "gone" like this, Frau Doktor? I've studied the folklore of Hebei Province, and nothing I've heard of has ever sounded like this.'

'No, this is very recent. The villagers call them *yao-kuei*, but most attribute their appearance to the misdeeds of the Emperor and the loss of Heaven's Mandate for his rule. I first heard stories of *yao-kuei* being seen not long before Christmas, so it has been almost a year.'

She replaced the bone fragments in their box and locked it up again. 'You understand, my people here go out very little once the sun is down. Aside from concern about ghosts in the darkness, for years now there have been brigands in these hills. Now that Kuo Min-tang militia are forming, it isn't unheard of for men to be kidnapped into their bands. Poor Mrs Wei swears that the *yao-kuei* took her husband, who was lame and of no use to either the bandits or the Kuo Min-tang.' She shook her head. 'One cannot understand people like that.'

Karlebach whispered, 'A year . . .'

'It is conceivable, is it not –' Dr Bauer carefully locked the box back into its cupboard – 'that a group of these creatures – a little tribe – has been concealed in the caves in these hills, all these centuries? The caves near Nan Che-Ying Village have never been completely explored, and the river that runs through the Kong-Shui caves goes for miles beneath the earth. Such creatures might well scavenge food from the mine workings and from the garbage heaps of the temples.'

'But in that case,' said Asher, 'wouldn't there be stories earlier than last year?'

'Let me see its clothing.' Karlebach's voice was hoarse.

Dr Bauer pulled back the window curtains, opened the shutters, and fetched another box. Good-humoredly, she said, 'I have to warn you about these.'

Asher flinched from the smell as she brought out the rags: the remains of a short *ch'i-p'ao* – the straight, baggy, coat-like tunic that for two hundred and fifty years had been standard dress for all Chinese, male and female – and the remains of a man's *ku* trousers. Both had been torn to ribbons by the dogs and were unspeakably soiled.

'You read my description of the thing,' said Bauer quietly. 'I wish you could have seen it. It must have observed how men wear clothing and put these on in imitation of what it had seen. You saw the skull. The face wasn't remotely human. It was almost hairless, its spine bent forward, and the hands bore claws rather than human nails. For twenty-five years I have worked here in Mingliang, calling these beautiful souls here to Christ, and never have I heard of anything like these: not in fairy tales, not in legends, not in the stories that grandfathers told the little ones to scare them from going into the old mines. I've heard a thousand fireside legends, Herr Professor, and I've talked to hunters who've been all over these hills . . .' She shook her head, her eyes filled with anger and fear.

'Now anthropologists from Berlin call me a faker, and my own bishop has accused me of trying to garner contributions to my mission by coming up with a "scientific discovery". And all the while my people here tell me they have seen more and more of these things. The village policeman saw what he thought was two of them together, only five days ago – and now I see by your faces that you are not shocked, not even very surprised. Where, and when, have you seen these things before? What can you tell me of them?'

'We can tell you nothing, *gnädige* Frau,' said Asher, before Karlebach could speak. 'Because we know nothing. But it would help us learn if you could have someone take us to the place where your policeman saw these things, and also to the marsh below the coal mine, where Liao Ho's dogs killed our friend there in the box.'

'It is them.'

Dr Bauer – pacing sturdily ahead of them along the steep, brush-grown trackway up the gorge – glanced back at the sound of their voices, but Karlebach breathed the words in the Czech which had been his childhood tongue, and which Asher had spoken on his wanderings through Central Europe twenty years before. The missionary had greeted Sergeant Willard and trooper Gibbs in halting English, and in that language had thanked them for accompanying the exploring party. And while Asher knew that thousands of Germans – possibly tens of thousands – considered the Kaiser's warlike aspirations as irresponsibly appalling as the English did, there was no guarantee that Christina Bauer was one of them.

And even if she did, Asher knew that in every foreign ministry in every country on the globe there was one clerk or secretary or minister-without-portfolio whose sole business it was to pick up shreds of information – from shopkeepers, from missionaries, from other peoples' servants – and sort through those shreds for something which could be used by the Home Country. He'd done it himself. He didn't know what use the German General Staff would think up for things that were deathless, predatory, and might or might not share the mental powers of illusion and deception that seemed to come with the vampire state. But with a colony of them as close to Berlin as Prague, he wasn't about to take chances.

'What are they doing here?' he asked softly in the same tongue. 'I asked vampires I met in Central Europe whether this . . . this *mutation*, this altered form, had ever been known to spontaneously appear . . .'

'And you believe what they told you?' His shotgun slung over one powerful shoulder, Karlebach leaned on a stick as he walked, but though the trackway was steep, his breath seemed as strong as that of the two soldiers who brought up the rear of the party.

'They had no reason to lie.'

'It is the nature of the vampire to lie, Jamie,' retorted the old man. 'Until you believe that, you will not know them.'

The gorge of the Mingliang stream had been severely deforested over the centuries. Here and there thin stands of pine trees remained, but mostly there was only brush along the water, and thin yellowed grass flittering in the icy wind. Chan – Liao Ho's remaining dog – stopped on the trail, a growl rumbling in his throat. 'What you see back there, eh?' demanded the little farmer, and he gently shook a handful of his pet's thick ruff. 'Somebody follow, not follow?'

Asher, too, scanned the bleak hill-slopes. All his instincts from seventeen years in the field prickled under his skin. *Not the* yao-kuei*, anyway* . . . It was mid-afternoon, the sun slipping from zenith to the western ridges.

But someone. On the hard dust of the trail he'd seen recent boot prints, enough to know that either bandits – endemic in China during periods of unrest – or Kuo Min-tang 'militia' had been in the area within the past few days. Bandits might not feel up to taking on two British soldiers with Enfields – young Trooper Barclay had remained behind in the village with the horses – but those Enfields would appeal strongly to a larger band.

The track ascended a rise of ground, then went down into what had been a level area in front of the Shi'h Liu mine entrance itself, perhaps a hundred yards in length, once given over to washing sheds, outbuildings, and slag heaps of waste rock. A ramp of rammed earth had been erected – who knew how long ago? – up to the cave mouth, which was a vast uneven oval set on its side, blue with shade in the yellowish rock of the hill's steep shoulder. Seepage had turned the whole area into a sodden wasteland, weed-clogged, black with coal-dust, choked with cattails and sedges and, as Dr Bauer had said, rustling with rats.

'The body lay here.' Dr Bauer motioned to the nearest of the rock heaps, a few yards from the track where it first began to descend.

'He was running back to the mine.' Liao Ho put a hand on Chan the dog's head. Asher let the missionary translate the little farmer's words into German, for Karlebach's benefit. 'Shun and Shuo had torn his throat out, and he had clawed them in return. In the dark –' he nodded toward the mine – 'I saw the eyes of others, like the eyes of rats, but man-high. Rats were everywhere in the marsh, squeaking and running about.'

'And was this near where your policeman saw them?' Asher asked of Bauer, in German still.

'No. Those were nearer the village, much nearer. No one comes this close to the mine in the twilight.'

'You want to be careful, sir,' warned Sergeant Willard as Asher picked his way around the worst of the pools toward the ramp that led up to the cave mouth. 'This's exactly the kind of place bandits'll camp in . . .'

Having neither German nor Chinese, the soldiers were under the impression that Asher and Karlebach were seeking a legend, rather like the yeti of the Himalayas: a belief Asher had been careful to foster by his replies to Willard's questions en route. 'Does it smell like there's men hidden inside?' he asked, and the sergeant's gray-blue eyes narrowed.

'It don't smell natural, sir, and that's a fact.'

This was true. The latrine-stink of men camped together – and the smell of smoke that would drift up even from fires built far back in the tunnels – was absent, and there was certainly no sign that horses had been anywhere in the valley. But there was a smell of some kind, which raised the hair on the back of Asher's neck.

They climbed the ramp, the packed earth dimpled where track had been laid for the mine carts, but the iron rails and wooden ties alike long ago carried away by thrifty villagers. The outer cave was roughly the volume of the church in Wychford where Asher's father had held his living, and was filled with the same soft grayish gloom. By the low narrow shape of the two tunnels that opened from one end of it, it was clear to Asher that the mining had been done in the old way: with picks, and the coal carried out in baskets on men's backs. At the other end of the cave the floor had subsided into a sort of sinkhole, where a suggestion of water glimmered far below.

Asher took the lantern from Sergeant Willard and lit it, and then walked to the nearer tunnel, six inches shorter than his own six-foot height and barely more than half that width.

Gray rats scurried away into darkness. Turned back to look with eyes like tiny flame.

The smell was stronger here, nauseating. Asher was aware of his heart pounding. Karlebach came to his side, his less-crippled hand curled on the trigger of the shotgun, the barrel resting lightly across his other wrist. The old man murmured, 'Yes. They're here.'

Eighteen months ago, when Asher had traveled with the vampire Ysidro through the eastern reaches of Europe, they had been in quest of information about whether it were possible – whether any of the vampires in Berlin or Augsburg or Prague or Warsaw had ever heard of it – for vampires to mutate spontaneously, without masters and without instruction in the ways of survival. The Others, however, had been whispered of only in Prague. It had been enough, at the time, to learn that the Others were not the creatures that he sought.

Staring into the endless black seam, Asher now regretted the questions Ysidro had not asked at that time of his fellow Undead. He started to make a comment to that effect, but the expression on his companion's face silenced him: a despairing intensity, as if the whole of the old scholar's being strained to pierce the midnight beyond the kerosene's glow. Beneath the luxuriant masses of beard his mouth was set, and Asher could see that he trembled.

Eighteen months ago he was content to live in Prague. Content to study the secrets of that ancient place in the full knowledge that vampires walked its streets . . .

What changed?

The knowledge that vampires existed elsewhere in the world had not sufficed to turn the old man from scholar to hunter. Yet when Asher had denied the request in that first letter, the old man had packed up and left the house where he had been born, where he had dwelled the whole of his long life, to journey first to England, then to China.

Why?

Why now?

What does he know that he has not told me?

Stirring, deep in the darkness. More eyes glittered, as if the floor of the tunnel were now carpeted with rats. Behind him, Asher was aware that the light in the outer cave was dimming as the sun moved beyond the valley's rim.

'I think this is all we can accomplish today,' he said, and Karlebach startled, as if Asher had fired off a gun. 'We've found the place; we've ascertained that these are indeed the creatures you know in Prague.'

Karlebach stammered a little, then said, 'Yes. Yes, of course you're right . . .'

'We don't know how many of them there are, or how deep in the mine they're hidden – or how much twilight in the world above suffices to wake them.'

Karlebach nodded. For a moment Asher felt that the old man would have said something else to him. But instead he looked aside, mumbled, 'That's true. We had best— We had best be going . . .'

As if, thought Asher, having come halfway around the world to find this place, he had no clear idea of where to go from here. Of what to do.

Of what he WANTED to do.

Odd.

He followed his old teacher back toward the cave entrance, where Sergeant Willard, Liao Ho, Trooper Barclay, Chan the dog, and Dr Bauer stood silhouetted against the fading daylight.

Karlebach stopped twice, to look back into the dark of the tunnels.

Asher wondered what it was that he expected to see.

SIX

'It's called the Temple of Everlasting Harmony.' Like most Russian ladies of good family, the Baroness Tatiana Drosdrova spoke fluent French, and it was in this language that she addressed Lydia as she climbed down and paid off the three rickshaw 'boys' who had hauled her party at a jogging run nearly two miles from the Legation Quarter. 'Stay here, all-same.' She pointed imperiously down at the hard-packed dirt of the lane – the 'boy' to whom she spoke was, to Lydia's estimation, sixty at least, old enough to be her father and far too old to be hauling stout Russian females around the alleyways of Peking. 'Ten cents.'

'Ten cents, all-same.' The gray-haired puller gestured from himself to the two younger men who'd ferried Lydia, doe-eyed young Signora Giannini – the other diplomatic wife of the party – and the Baroness's two sturdy Russian bodyguards to the head of Silk Lane, which stretched away to their right. 'Ten cents, ten cents.'

Meaning, Lydia assumed, that each of them wanted that modest sum to stay put while the three ladies investigated the Temple.

'Ten cents, ten cents,' agreed the Baroness affably. She spoke little English, but appeared to be conversant in the pidgin used by every servant and rickshaw-puller in the city. 'Of course he'll abscond the moment someone offers him eleven,' she added, switching back to French as she straightened the veils on her flat, outdated little hat. 'But there are always a dozen pullers just down Silk Lane, so we won't have lost anything much.'

Over tea at the Legation yesterday morning, Sir John Jordan had promised to arrange for Lydia to see something of the city in the company of one of the doyennes of the small European community. Lady Eddington, the senior woman in the British quarter, who would ordinarily have taken the newcomer under her wing, was incapable of seeing anyone in her grief, but in St Petersburg eighteen months ago Lydia had become acquainted with a cousin of the Baroness, who in any case would tolerate no interference with her right to overwhelm any visitor who came her way. To Lydia's inquiry if Sir John could perhaps find some way to include Signora Giannini in the invitation, he had given her his lazy, intelligent smile and replied, 'Leave it to me, ma'am.'

Paola Giannini was the woman whose screams had brought everyone to Holly Eddington's body in the garden Wednesday night. But having met the Baroness, Lydia realized that Sir John had assumed she'd been warned about her and sought to mitigate some of the impact of her company.

Guidebook in hand, the Baroness strode through the carved gateway of flaking green lacquer and into the courtyard beyond. 'You'll observe the post-and-lintel construction of the ceiling,' she commanded. 'The main building is called the *cheng-fang* and invariably faces south, and it contains the most auspicious apartments of the establishment.'

On the ship from Southampton, James had described Peking as a succession of mazes, like a series of puzzle boxes. Without her spectacles, which would have detracted fatally from her forest-green-and-lavender chic, Lydia found the city a sinister labyrinth of gray-walled lanes, brilliant and dirty shop-banners, brittle sunlight like white glass and the most astonishing cocktail of sounds and smells. Under the shadows of massive gateway towers, narrow cats' cradles of the *hutongs* alternated with wide, arrow-straight processional avenues jammed with traffic, hopeless to keep track of or to orient oneself in.

The rickshaw-pullers all worked for the men who owned the vehicles themselves, Paola had explained as the three rickshaws dodged nimbly between carts, porters, candy vendors, night-soil collectors and old gentlemen carrying birdcages: rather like cab drivers in London. Often the pullers slept in the rickshaw barns, and frequently they were in a sort of indentured servitude to the owners for other favors as well, a form of livelihood that merged into the criminal underworld of moneylenders, brothel-keepers, and men who bought guns illegally from the Army and resold them to the Kuo Min-tang.

'Thus the bodyguards, you understand,' the Italian girl had added, with a wave at the third rickshaw behind them, which contained Korsikov and Menchikov, immense mustachioed Cossacks who seemed to have stepped straight out of The Ballad of Ivan Skavinsky Skavar. 'In truth, I have never had the slightest trouble since I came here – the President of the Republic is most careful to keep friends with the powers of Europe. Even so, I should not wish to be set afoot in the city alone.' Like the Baroness – and everyone else in the Legation Quarter except the Americans, who in Lydia's opinion could barely cope with English – Paola spoke French.

Lydia had peered around her at the gray walls of the *hutongs*, the gates opening into courtyards full of children and laundry, trying to orient herself and failing. Now and then a particularly handsome roof would be seen over the walls, tiled in bright red or green and touched up with gold, but these were hidden almost at once by the next turning of whatever lane they were in. Both Paola and the Baroness had warned Lydia about the smell, but it wasn't as bad as Constantinople.

As far as Lydia was concerned, *nothing* smelled as bad as Constantinople.

The Temple courtyard was cramped and tiny, cluttered with pigeon coops and stone fish-tanks. Yet there was a curious calm to it, as if it lay silent miles from the din of the street outside. A couple of very old elm trees grew there, and in front of one of its side buildings a hulking young priest in a brown robe swept the packed earth with a twig broom. Beneath the weed-grown mass of a double roof, the main building was dark and rather grimy-looking. A yellow dog slept on the shallow steps. Inside, a ferocious image glared from a niche on the far wall, resplendent among embroidered banners, paper lanterns, and plates of offerings: candy, fruit, sugared watermelon seeds, sesame balls, rice. 'That's Kuan Yu, the God of War,' explained the Baroness. 'According to Sir John, he was an actual person at one time – fancy making a real general a deity! Like building a temple to Napoleon and preaching sermons in his name. Not that there aren't imbeciles who actually do that, over in the French Legation . . .'

'He must have made quite an impression.' Lydia considered the crimson-painted face, the huge eyes staring into hers under starkly black eyebrows. The smell of incense was suffocating.

'This is Kuan Yin, goddess of Mercy.' Paola gestured toward a niche on the eastern wall, where a tall lady in billowy draperies was depicted standing on what Lydia assumed was a lotus. Even at this distance, the sculpted lady's features had a serene beauty,

as if she saw far into the distance of time and knew that everything would work out all right. 'They say she was a princess
who achieved Nirvana through meditation and goodness, yet
turned back from the Gates of Heaven when she heard a child
crying in the darkness of the world behind her.'

Paola crossed herself. In the dim shadows of the Temple, the
sable of her collar set off her creamy brunette complexion, her
Madonna face. She was, Lydia guessed, a few years younger
than herself, and quiet-spoken, though that might merely have
been the effect of the Baroness's company. 'I like to think that
through her, they honor the Blessed Virgin . . .'

'Yes, and who else they honor shows you how they think.'
The Baroness returned to the two younger women, stout and
frumpy in her seedy furs. She gestured toward the images ranged
along the other wall, each in its niche: 'Behold the King of Hell
and the magistrates that govern each of its ten levels, keep records,
assign punishments, maintain order, supervise the workers and
direct traffic, I dare say. It sounds just like Russia – except, of
course, in Russia it would be totally disorganized – and *just* like
China,' she added thoughtfully. 'Imagine a people who conceive
of the afterlife as being divided into departments and operated
by bureaucrats. They have separate administrative divisions in
Heaven as well.'

She bustled off again, toward a small door that opened into
the rear courtyard beyond; Paola had returned to her contempla-
tion of the Kuan Yin. Quickly, Lydia sneaked her spectacles from
their silver case and put them on, to consider the ten fearsome
gentlemen ranged along the wall in the gloom: staring eyes, bared
fangs, draperies that swirled and curled in the hot winds of the
afterlife. The Magistrates of Hell. A couple of them were depicted
with damned souls crouched around them, or crushed beneath
their feet.

The rustle of crêpe and the sweetness of Rigaud's *Un Air
Embaumé* beside her made her whip the spectacles off as she
turned. 'Do they divide sinners up by sin, the way Dante did?'
she asked.

A trace of frown appeared between Paola's delicate brows. 'I
don't know. The Baroness would. She is fascinated by these
awful things.'

'I'm sorry.' Impulsively, Lydia grasped the Italian girl's hand.

'When the Baroness suggested that she take me around, I asked Sir John if he might arrange for someone else to join us, because the Baroness is a little – a little overpowering sometimes . . .'

'Sometimes?' Paola's Madonna face brightened with schoolgirl mischief. '*Dio mio*, she would seize away the scepter of her tsar and beat him over the head with it!' Her voice was low, and she glanced toward the lighted courtyard door, to make sure there was no possibility of the lady hearing. 'She is like my Aunt Aemilia: so good and kind, yet so *bossy*!'

'Perhaps Sir John had his own motives in hinting to her to take me about today.' Lydia also lowered her voice conspiratorially.

'*É verra*! To spare poor Lady Eddington . . .' Paola shook her head. 'You and I perform the poor lady a great service, Madame Asher. A diversion, as the soldiers say. For whenever anyone is ill or out of sorts, the Baroness appears on their doorstep, with her own servants and her own soap and her own brooms, and a tub of boiling vinegar, and food in crocks – her cook should be shot, Madame! He is Georgian and truly one of the plagues of this earth!'

'How did you happen to be in the garden?' asked Lydia, 'If you don't mind me asking . . .'

Distress clouded Paola's eyes. 'Holly Eddington and I were of an age, Madame. There are not many so young, among the Legations. Poor Holly. She was very lonely, and anxious, as women are who reach the age of twenty-four unwed and unasked. Bitter, too, I think, that women like that poisonous Madame Schrenk – the wife of the Austrian Minister's First Secretary – would say of her, *Poor thing . . .*'

The young woman sighed as she moved off along the line of those fearsome other-worldly magistrates who glared and scowled in the shadows. 'We both of us loved music, and birds, though we had in truth little else in common. At her invitation I would come to play on her mother's piano, for Tonio and I have none in our little house. Like her mother she saw the Chinese only as devils, whom she seemed to think chose their own condition in this world. And she was so – so *pleased* with herself, that Mr Hobart asked her to be his wife. And her mother practically gloated. But in a place like this, one makes friends where one can.'

'How did you happen go out to the garden Wednesday night?' asked Lydia. 'You must have been freezing . . .'

'It was only to be for a moment, I thought. Holly and I were arranging for the cake to be laid out, when one of the servants came in and told her that Signor Hobart had come to the garden gate and was asking to see her.'

'Asking to see her?'

'Even so, Madame. Since eight o'clock she was almost in tears, that Mr Hobart would have not come to the reception for their own engagement. She said, "If he is drunk, I will kill him!" and went out – though of course she knew and I knew that he would be drunk. I finished with the cake plates and the champagne. Then I realized it had been fifteen minutes, perhaps more, and Holly had not returned. I looked out into the garden and didn't see her – her dress was white, you remember, and would show up in the dark. I went out the French door of the drawing room and a little way down the path, before I saw something white on the ground.'

She turned her face aside, stared for a time at the statue of what seemed to be a disheveled poet with huge fangs and a scroll in his hand, and sinners screaming in torment beneath his feet.

'Did you hear anything?' asked Lydia softly. 'Or see any movement?'

Paola shook her head. 'I thought at first that she might have fainted. Then when I came near and saw Richard lying near her, and smelled the liquor and the opium smoke in his clothing—'

Even without her spectacles, Lydia heard the mingling of distress and guilt in her companion's voice.

'I'm sure she wouldn't have wanted a third party present . . .'

'I know she didn't.' The young woman turned back to her. 'Yet I should have at least gone out on to the step, to watch them from afar. Richard has always been a perfect gentleman, even when he is drunk; he would not hurt even a flea.' She sighed and folded her arms, as if against the Temple's bone-deep chill. And sadly, added, 'Yet everyone in the Legations knows about his father.'

'Please to get down from your horses. Be of no trouble.' The tall man in the gray-green uniform – the only one of the bandits mounted on a full-sized European horse rather than a shaggy Chinese pony – gestured with his revolver. His face was heavily scarred with smallpox, eyebrow-less and thin-lipped, his hair cut short. The men around him – some in peasant *ch'i-p'aos* and *ku*, others in Western-style uniforms – pointed their German and Russian rifles at the little party.

Sergeant Willard, hands raised, said quietly, 'Kuo Min-tang.'

'Can we run for it?' Karlebach's curling gray eyebrows had pulled into a solid shelf over the jut of his nose, and beneath them his dark eyes glinted. 'It will be dark in an hour.'

'We wouldn't make it twenty feet.' Asher – who had raised his hands like the others the moment the men had emerged, on foot and on horseback, from the tangle of rhododendron brush along the trail – dismounted and stood quiet while one of the Chinese stripped him of his greatcoat, then dug through the pockets of his jacket beneath. He added, 'Get down, Rebbe, please,' in a level voice when the old man hesitated. 'Or they will shoot you.' And when Karlebach obeyed and was, for his cooperation, relieved of his old-fashioned shooting-coat, his scarf, his watch (Asher had taken the precaution of leaving his own watch and money back at the hotel – he'd travelled in the Chinese countryside before), and his shotgun, he went on, still in the Czech that he knew no one around them would understand, 'They don't want trouble with the British authorities if they can help it. What they want is the horses and the guns.'

Personally, he was grateful that the Republican revolutionaries showed no signs of taking their boots as well.

'Ask them, please,' said Karlebach, '*please*, to give me at least the medicines from the pockets of my coat . . .'

Asher relayed this request, in his hesitant Chinese, to their captors. The men opened one of the little bottles, sniffed the contents in turn, tasted it, and all grimaced. 'What?' demanded one of them, and Asher replied:

'*Yi-yao.*' *Medicine*. 'For my father,' he added, laying a hand on Karlebach's shoulder.

Evidently satisfied that the stuff wasn't liquor or anything remotely like it, they returned the opened bottle with bows.

Sergeant Willard muttered, 'It's them who been followin' us all day, my next pay-packet to a copper cash.'

Asher made no reply. Someone had certainly been following them. But it made more sense for the rebels to have taken them in this place – on the bare ridge halfway between the railway town and Mingliang – outbound and in the daylight, to give themselves more time to get farther. Why wait till now when it was dusk, unless they had only recently picked up their trail?

The gorge was already filled with shadow. He heard one of the men snap in Chinese, 'Hurry up!' as the others shoved the rest of the tiny bottles into Karlebach's crippled hands. 'It'll be dark before we camp.' And he caught the words, '*Yao-kuei . . .*' spoken too quietly for the pockmarked commander to hear.

The commander himself remained mounted, but did not speak again. Dr Bauer had warned them, when they'd returned from the mine to the village to collect the horses and start back to Men T'ou Kuo, 'Ride quickly, but if you're stopped, remember that they don't want trouble. Give them the horses and the guns, and they'll let you walk back to the railroad in peace . . .'

Which would have been all right with him, Asher reflected as he watched the robbers move off up the trail into the thickening darkness, if he hadn't seen the skull in the box at Dr Bauer's mission.

Sergeant Willard muttered, 'Cheesus wept. We'll be till midnight, hoofin' it back to the railroad, lads – you be all right, Professor K? Need a hand, sir?'

And Trooper Barclay muttered, 'We'll all need a bleedin' hand 'fore this night's done! Christ Almighty, I'm cold as a nun's knickers! We'll be frozen stiff by the time we get back to town.'

Asher said nothing, though he too had started to shiver. He guessed what would be moving in these hills, once darkness fell, and knew that cold was going to be the least of their troubles.

SEVEN

'Please understand that Sir Grant has never been anything but a perfect gentleman to me.'

Lydia recognized the earnestness in Paola's voice and the expression in those enormous brown eyes, almost of desperation that Lydia should understand that what Paola was about to say wasn't to be taken as the malicious backstairs gossip that it would be if someone else were to say it. Lydia reflected, a little sadly, on the number of scandalous secrets communicated to her by cousins, by her beautiful stepmother, by the daughters of her aunts' friends and by the other young ladies at her very expensive Swiss boarding-school, prefaced by that devastating disclaimer.

She tucked the Italian girl's hand into the crook of her arm and bent her head to listen as they strolled along the shopfronts of Silk Lane.

'I think you know that only a very few men in the diplomatic corps bring their wives to China,' explained Paola, in a slightly constricted voice. 'The young clerks – and some that are not so young – er . . . *consort* with Chinese women . . . Yes, and some who have their wives here as well,' she added, with a trace of bitterness. 'Some – like Colonel von Mehren and Herr Knoller in the German Legation – even keep native mistresses! Others just go to the Chinese City, or make arrangements with the Chinese – er . . . *go-betweens –*' she fumbled again for the polite term – 'to have women brought to houses that they agree upon. This is what Sir Grant does.'

Ahead of them in the throng of Chinese – shopkeepers, soldiers, strollers and vendors of mousetraps and hats – the Baroness marched from counter to counter of the small shops that opened into the Lane, fingering lengths of silk and shouting at the merchants in pidgin or Russian, and discoursing on the various grades of the fabric and the descriptive nomenclature of its hues. Menchikov – or perhaps it was Korsikov – hovered no more than a foot from her elbow, but the Chinese around them did no more than stare, as if at an elephant or a funeral parade. Lydia was aware, too, that three times as many children, peasant women, and porters were following her – keeping a respectful distance from Korsikov (or Menchikov) – but pointing (a gesture done with the chin in China, rather than the fingers) and exclaiming, no doubt, that Westerners really *were* descended from devils because, like devils, this one had red hair.

Madame Drosdrova ignored them as if they were merely flies buzzing around her hat.

'I'm quite shocked to hear it,' exclaimed Lydia, who wasn't. 'But it's really a far cry from debauchery with Chinese – er – ladies, to murder . . .'

Paola shook her head violently. 'It is not just debauchery, Madame. It is . . .' She looked like she wanted to lower her voice, but the general noise of chatter in the street all around them put this discretion out of the question. 'I understand – I have heard – that Sir Grant likes to . . . to hurt the women he . . . he consorts with. Badly, sometimes. There are men like this,' she added earnestly, as if certain that this was something a respectable woman like Lydia had never heard of before. 'Not just slapping one's wife when one is drunk, you understand, such as all men do—'

Lydia opened her mouth to protest that *all* men did nothing of the kind.

'—but deliberately. And there are men in China who buy women – girls – from their families, to hire them out to men who . . . who take pleasure in this.'

Behind her hat veils, Paola's face suffused with a flush of embarrassment. Lydia recalled the relevant chapters in Krafft-Ebing's *Psychopathia Sexualis* – which she had read with a combination of clinical interest and baffled amazement at one point in the three years she had spent attending medical lectures and dissections at the Radcliffe Infirmary at Oxford – but forbore to mention this, to request more specific information, or to reflect on the information she had just received, not only about Sir Grant Hobart but also about the home life of the Italian Assistant Diplomatic Attaché.

She also stifled her next comment: that, given the extremes of poverty in China and the general Chinese attitude that anything and everything was marketable, the sale of these services didn't surprise her. That was also the sort of remark that would have sent her stepmother and aunts into an advanced case of the vapors . . . whatever 'vapors' actually were. (*Dr Charcot in France – or was it Dr Freud in Vienna? – would undoubtedly have an opinion on nervous causes of the vapors . . . I shall have to look that up . . .*)

She settled on, 'Sir *Grant*? I would never have thought it!'

Though according to Krafft-Ebing, a great many men did precisely that, and not all of them in Peking, either. Nor did it appear to be possible to tell who was a likely candidate for such behavior simply by looking at them.

'If I'd only heard it from Madame Drosdrova, or Annette Hautecoeur –' Paola named the wife of the French Legation's Assistant Trade Secretary – 'I would think, *this is gossip* . . . You have no idea the frightful gossip that one encounters here, ma'am, at every turn! But this my husband told me.'

'I have reason to believe,' put in Lydia tactfully, 'that men gossip among themselves every bit as badly as women do.'

The Italian girl shook her head again, 'No! Only women gossip, and even if men did, Tonio – Signor Giannini – is not that sort of man.'

They stopped outside the largest silk-shop in the street, before which a very old Chinese gentleman was stirring and mixing what looked like dough in a basin filled with white powder; he would lift it out, draw it between his hands to make it thinner and thinner, then double it on itself and drop it back for a quick roll in the powder again . . .

'My husband warned me,' Paola went on, 'in my first month that I was here, not to be friendly with Sir Grant, and when I asked him why, he told me about the Chinese girls and the house of Mrs Tso that Sir Grant visits in Big Tiger Lane. My mother would not have said that this was a proper thing for a man to tell his wife, but because we are all so much together in the Legations I am glad that I know this, so that I may keep a proper distance. Later I heard from Madame Hautecoeur that there had been a terrible scandal, and a girl was said to have died in that house.'

By this time the dough had been separated into bundles of individual strands no larger than stout sewing-thread, and the crowd around the old gentleman's wheeled bin had thickened until it nearly blocked the street. 'What is it?' asked Lydia in fascination, and Paola shook her head.

Lydia repeated the question to a man next to her, pointing, but his reply – 'Ah, *t'ang kuo*!' – conveyed little. When the dough had been reduced to a fibrous skein of powdery threads, the old man dropped it in a dusty *whoof* of whiteness on to the nearest shop counter and hacked it into short lengths with the razor-sharp cleaver at his belt, and seemed not to understand Lydia's questions as to its nature or price. When she finally offered him a copper cash he gave her four pieces, gathered his basin and its portable stand, and moved off to put on his show in the next alley.

'Don't you dare eat that!' Madame Drosdrova emerged from the silk shop and snatched the glutinous morsel from Lydia's fingers. 'It might be poison!'

'Nonsense, people bought them for their children,' retorted Lydia – and in fact four or five urchins in the street were devouring the *t'ang kuo* with enthusiasm. But Madame wouldn't have it. She wadded the paper around the *t'ang kuo* and flung it to the gutter, from which the children promptly snatched it up and ran away.

'What *is* it?'

'Good heavens, child, how should I know?' Madame herded the two girls back toward the rickshaws. 'It's probably opium!'

Menchikov (or Korsikov) trailed behind them, both laden with so huge an armload of paper-wrapped parcels from every shop in the lane that a fourth vehicle had to be hired to transport it all back to the Russian Legation.

'So you see,' concluded Paola as she climbed up into the high-wheeled wicker chair, 'though Richard Hobart seemed indeed to be a most polite young man – and was, I understand, coveted by all the ladies of the Legations who had daughters to dispose of suitably – when I heard that he had arrived at Sir Allyn's reception Wednesday night, late and probably drunk, I should never have permitted Holly to go down to meet him alone. He *is* Sir Grant's son.'

Lydia reflected that if her own conduct were assumed to reflect her father's, no man in his right mind would have sought her hand in marriage. As she put her foot on the step of the rickshaw a voice behind her whispered, 'Missy—'

The old rickshaw-puller held out to her a little white square of *t'ang kuo* wrapped in a bit of paper, with a conspiratorial grin.

It was candy, the white powder sugar, like Turkish delight. It covered Lydia's hands, and Paola's, with telltale evidence as they headed back toward the Legations at a breakneck trot through the blue evening streets.

'What is it?' Willard held up his hand for caution.

Asher had already stopped, listening to the deathly silence that had followed the chill keening of the wind.

Beside him, Karlebach's breath hissed sharply.

Damn it. Damn it, damn it, damn it . . .

'Bloody rotten luck if it's robbers, after that lot nicked the horses,' Barclay muttered.

'Can't be robbers,' returned Gibbs. 'They'll have seen somebody's already had a touch at us.'

'Well, I bloody well ain't givin' up my boots without a fight.' The younger trooper brandished his stout bamboo spear.

Asher – the only man of the party who'd had a hideout knife

in his boot – had, at the sight of a rare stand of bamboo in the gorge below them, scrambled down to gather makeshift weapons. It had been nearly dark even then. He'd cut five lengths of six feet apiece and carried them up to the road again to sharpen. The process had taken roughly half an hour, but he knew that even an extra half-hour wouldn't get them to Men T'ou Kuo or anywhere near it. It had been almost full dark when he'd finished, the moon not yet risen.

Now they stood straining their ears, each wondering if that actually had been movement they'd heard in the brush-choked gorge far below the track, or only some trick of the icy wind.

'How far is it until the trail turns off over the ridge, Jamie?' Karlebach murmured. 'We'll be farther from the stream then.'

'Do they stay close to water?' he returned. 'Or can they come on to drier ground if they want?'

'That I don't know. I've only seen them on a few occasions, you understand. Matthias—' His voice hesitated over the name of his latest protégé, the young man whose departure for some other cause had, Asher guessed, finally cut the old man loose from his accustomed ways.

'Phew! God!' Barclay gagged as the wind shifted, and for a moment the stenchy reek – like rotting flesh rolled in filthy garments – flickered in the air. 'Where the bloody 'ell 'ave them bandits been hidin'?'

'In the mine, you dumb berk,' retorted Willard. 'Didn't you smell 'em back there?'

Barclay took a few steps to the edge of the gorge, raised his voice to a shout. 'Hey! Chink-chink! We got nuthin', savvy? *Mei ch'iên*! Flat broke, y'hear . . . How'd you say "we ain't got a pot to piss in" in Chinese, Professor?' Starlight made smoke of his breath; the wind whipped it away.

So much, reflected Asher, for discretion about letting people know he spoke Chinese . . .

'Shut yer 'ole,' whispered Gibbs. 'See 'em there, against the sky?'

'There's boulders by the trail,' said Asher quietly, 'about a hundred yards back.' He had spent the past hour's walking identifying every scrap of cover or defensive terrain they'd passed. 'If we can cover our backs—'

'Too late.' Willard pointed. It was nearly impossible to see in the starlight, but behind them on the trail Asher thought he glimpsed the reflective glitter of eyes. 'What the hell—?'

'Keep in the open!' said Asher, and the five men set themselves back-to-back, spears pointing outward, as all the underbrush on the slope down to the stream crashed in the darkness with the sudden onslaught.

'How the hell many of 'em—?' Gibbs began, and then the scrambling forms sprang up on to the trail.

Asher struck with his bamboo, felt it sink into something that screamed, a hoarse awful noise, like an injured camel. The stink was nauseating. He heard Willard swear. Asher shouted into the crowding darkness, *'Na shih shei? Ni yao shê mo?'* but doubted he'd get an answer; he felt the thing he'd impaled still thrashing on the end of the spear, fighting to get at him. It lurched closer, and he felt its clawed nails flick his face.

Other screams. Barclay yelled, 'What the—?' and Asher heard the crunch of something – a rock? – impacting with flesh.

The darkness all around them seemed filled with shoving shapes – *Christ Jesus, how many of them are there?* Then a rifle fired from somewhere down the trail, and the thing on the end of his spear thrust at him again, its weight jerking at his grip, as if it cared nothing for the shot . . .

He saw its face then, and yes, it was *yao-kuei*, it could be nothing else: a dim impression in darkness of deformed features, a fanged mouth snapping at him, eyes gleaming.

Another shot. Then running feet and the screams of the Others – the *yao-kuei* – and a flash in the starlight of what looked, impossibly, like the blade of a sword. And an instant later on the round lenses of spectacles.

A man shouted, the bellowing bark of a Japanese war-cry, and *yes*, thought Asher, *that was a sword* . . .

The *yao-kuei* jerked, and where its face had been – pale and hairless and almost canine in its deformation – there was nothing. He smelled the blood that fountained from the severed neck. The pale glimmer of a man's white coat or jacket in the darkness, splattered with gore; another flash of sword-steel and spectacle-lenses. *Colonel Count Mizukami. He's the one who followed us.*

It's too dark to shoot without danger of hitting one of us.

He wrenched the bamboo free, drove it hard at another one of those dark, slumped forms, pinning it for the Japanese to slash.

He'd seen men torn apart in South Africa by shellfire, and had once had occasion to dismember the corpse of a man he'd killed with an ax in order to dispose of it discreetly – in the service of the Department, which was supposed to make it all right, though it had given him frightful dreams for years. But there was something horrifyingly fascinating about the archaic art of slaughter with cold steel.

He heard the *yao-kuei* shrieking and the crash of foliage below. *So they at least have some sense of self-preservation . . .*

''Ere, you watch where you're swingin' that chopper!' gasped Gibbs's voice.

Barclay only said, 'Gor blimey, it's the fucken mikado!'

Asher stepped forward, tripped over something that rolled slightly under this foot, and Karlebach gasped. 'Are you all right, Jamie?' He grasped his arm with his twisted hand. 'You are not injured—?'

'I'm fine. Is everyone all right? Is anyone hurt?'

'What the *hell* were they?' demanded Willard, and two pale forms emerged from the darkness and bowed.

'Ashu Sensei—'

Asher bowed in return, deeply. 'Mizukami-san? Are you well? Ten thousand thanks—'

'What were those things?' demanded the deep voice that he well recalled from his earlier days in the Shantung Peninsula. Behind the bespectacled little Japanese, his bodyguard – a broad-shouldered young man in his twenties – held a hand pressed to his side, his light-colored military jacket darkening with blood.

'We will speak as we walk, if this suits you, Mizukami-san? They will likely return. Is your man able to walk?'

Mizukami asked something in Japanese; the bodyguard straightened his shoulders and replied. Almost certainly, reflected Asher, he said that it was only a scratch . . .

'Colonel the Count Mizukami, may I present the Rebbe Dr Solomon Karlebach of Prague?'

More bows, but instants later they were moving off, the darkness in the gorge so intense that Asher was barely able to make out the dark notch in the land to the right where the trail veered and began to climb the ridge. The wind shifted, blowing colder from the north, and Asher smelled on it the unmistakable dry whisper of a coming dust-storm . . . *Please*, he thought wearily, *not until we get back to town* . . .

Willard swore. 'Just what we bloody need.'

Bringing up the rear of the party, Asher turned and looked back as the first light of the moon appeared over the hills. It was nearly full and showed clearly the slumped shapes of their erstwhile attackers clustered around the hacked pieces of the *yao-kuei* that Mizukami and his bodyguard had killed.

At that distance he couldn't be sure, but he thought that an arm lay on the pathway a few yards from the main scene of the carnage. The arm was moving, pulling itself along by its fingers, as if in dogged pursuit.

Beside him he heard a hiss of indrawn breath, and Count Mizukami whispered again, '*What are they*, Ashu Sensei? And why are you not surprised to find them here?'

One of the Others scrambled up from the shadows below the trail, caught up the arm, and trotted back towards its companions, tearing chunks from the flesh with its teeth, like an American devouring a turkey leg.

EIGHT

'And what did you tell him?' asked Lydia the next morning, when Asher related the events of the previous day in more detail than he'd had the energy for, in the small hours after half-carrying Karlebach up to the suite.

'Nothing, at the time.' Asher poured coffee rather gingerly from the bright polychrome pot that Ellen had set before them accompanied by scones (fresh), buttered eggs (excellent), extremely Scottish marmalade (tinned), and pungent commentary on heathen countries where the weather was enough to send a good Christian running for home. Asher got the impression that in the maid's opinion the dust storm currently wailing over the tiled roofs of Peking had been visited by a disgusted God upon an unregenerate population of idolaters. 'We had other things to worry about.'

The dust storm had overtaken them within sight of the lights of Men T'ou Kuo, after a stumbling race along the trail by moonlight, with no thought of anything but haste.

'Ito – Mizukami's bodyguard – was wounded, more seriously than he'd admit, I think. Mizukami had to help him most of the way back. And Karlebach was at the end of his strength.' Asher flexed his wrists, which ached from holding off eleven stone of homicidal impaled killer who should have been dead. 'Mizukami drove us back in his motor car – Karlebach, Ito, and myself – because there wouldn't be a train until morning. Even after the worst of the dust passed it was all he could do to hold the car on the road. He didn't explain his own presence, but I'm guessing that he and Ito had been following us most of the day. Mizukami must have recognized me and may still think I'm a German agent. I assume he will arrive shortly after we finish breakfast, to ask everything he had not the opportunity to query last night.'

Lydia glanced over her shoulder at the door of their bedroom, where the old professor had spent what had remained of the night. Though Karlebach had revived a little on the drive under the influence of the Count's French brandy, he had still barely been able to get up the stairs, and even allowing for the ghastly things electric lighting did to peoples' appearance, neither Asher nor Lydia had liked the chalky grayness of his face.

Since Lydia invariably traveled with both stethoscope and sphygmomanometer tucked into one of the dozen steamer-trunks of Worth and Poiret dresses, she'd made sure his blood pressure and heartbeat were normal, if weak, before mixing him a seda-tive. She'd spent the night in Miranda's little cubicle with Mrs Pilley, while Asher had dossed down on the parlor sofa.

Now, even with the windows shuttered, the drawn curtains bellied restlessly in the cold, dust-laden wind and the air was blurred with a gauze of suspended gray-yellow silt. In the nursery, Asher could hear Miranda crying fretfully at the dust in her eyes, nose, and porridge.

'You've heard nothing of Ysidro?'

Lydia shook her head.

Ellen appeared, starched and friendly, like a good-natured draft-horse in the spotless print cotton dress appropriate for maidservants before noon, to take away the tray, and through the open door into the 'service' half of the suite, Asher heard Mrs Pilley exclaim, 'Now, *there's* my good girl!'

'Miranda doesn't sound like she approves of her first dust storm,' he remarked, and Ellen chuckled.

'Oh, she's kept trying to scrape the dust off the porridge with her little fingers, and the Pilley –' Ellen had little use for the nurse, whose opinions on the rights of working men to picket ('They should be arrested!') and women to vote ('They should be sent home to their husbands, who should have kept them there to begin with!') she decried as barbaric – 'has been half-mad wiping her hands every two seconds. And it itches her eyes, poor sweet. How we're to bath her with this dust turning the water to mud I *don't* know. And how is poor Professor Karlebach?'

'I'm just going in to check.' Lydia rose, unobtrusively collected her glasses – which she'd whipped off at the first creak of the door hinges heralding Ellen's entry – and moved softly toward the bedroom: 'No, you sit there and finish your coffee, Jamie. I heard you get up and check on him in the night when you should have been resting yourself.'

Asher sat back and gazed consideringly at the half-open door of the bedroom after Ellen left, his coffee cup still cradled in his hands. *He that hath wife and children hath given hostages to fortune*, Francis Bacon had written. *They are impediments to great enterprises, either of virtue or mischief . . .*

When he glanced down at the cup he saw that a microscopic film lay on the surface of the coffee.

He was deeply glad that Lydia and Miranda were with him – were where he could protect them, or at least know what kind of danger they were in. But his dreams last night had been troubled by the reflective eyes, the deformed faces seen in starlight. The stink of rotting filth. Exhausted as he had been, he had waked half a dozen times, less from concern for his old friend than from the nightmare that he'd heard clawed hands scratching at the windows, seen those slumped shadows following him again along the stagnant waters of the canal.

How much intelligence do they have? Enough to know me by sight? To follow me?

To learn that there are those here I love?

Fear twisted somewhere behind his breastbone. His one failing, in his days as a field agent, had been his imagination. An agent's greatest gift, but a weapon that could turn in its wielder's hand, as it had turned in his.

And what about the vampires of Peking? He remembered
Ysidro's nervousness – remembered his own sensation, walking
along the canal's high banks two nights ago, of something
watching him, following him . . .

Months before Miranda's birth, Lydia had sewed lengths of
silver chain into the linings of the curtains of their daughter's
tiny bed, even into the bindings around Miranda's blankets. The
thought that she had to do this – the thought that the Master of
London, only seventy miles from Oxford, knew where he and
Lydia lived – still filled him with rage, terror, and guilt.

And though he had quit the Department before he'd asked
Lydia – at that time a penniless student disinherited by her disgrun-
tled father – to be his wife, he had done so with trepidation.
Spying was a bachelor's game, and even ex-spies spent the rest
of their lives glancing over their shoulders. In Asher's eyes, perhaps
the greatest of Ysidro's many sins was that, in dragging Asher
into the affairs of the London vampires seven years previously,
he had brought Lydia to the attention of those who hunted in the
night.

Lydia, and now the child she had borne.

She came back in, coiling up her stethoscope in her hands.
'He's still sleeping,' she said. 'Poor old gentleman . . . And I
must say, Jamie, that it was *infamous* of you to include poor old
Karlebach on yesterday's expedition and tell *me* I had to stay
back and try to get gossip out of the Baroness. Not to speak of
the fact that by the time I get out to Mingliang to have a look
at those bones they'll be crumbled to dust.'

'*Mea culpa!*' Asher raised his hands in surrender. 'But as long
as you *did* suffer an afternoon of the Baroness's company—?'

'Did you know in advance that she was like that?'

'I am innocent, Lords of the Court, of the charges directed
against me . . . though I had heard rumors.' He swiped his coffee
with a corner of his napkin, poured out the remainder of the
coffee pot's contents into Lydia's cup, and set a saucer over it.
'And speaking of rumors . . .'

'Yes,' Lydia said with a sigh. 'Speaking of rumors . . .'

And she proceeded to give an account of her own afternoon's
expedition to Silk Lane.

'I'm sorry to say,' said Asher when she had finished, 'that
your friend Madame Giannini wasn't wrong about Richard

Hobart's father. Grant Hobart had a smelly reputation even at Oxford. Of course, few of us were so green as to get ourselves entangled with the town girls, if all we wanted was a lark—'

'And here I thought you spent your college years in monkish seclusion with a Slovak lexicon!'

'Persian,' corrected Asher with a grin. 'And I'm afraid you're mostly right.' He removed the protective saucer from over his own cup, took a sip, and replaced it. 'Even before the Department recruited me I never saw the point of getting castaway five nights out of seven, like the other men on my staircase. And you can thank my parsonical upbringing for keeping me out of the clutches of those girls the others pursued when they went down to London. It would be hard to imagine behavior too gross for drunken undergraduates to stomach, but Hobart managed it. He'd excuse himself – usually say the girls asked for it. There was a rumor back then – this was in eighty-two – that he'd killed a girl, at some place in London.'

'Deliberately?' Lydia's voice was steady, but he could see she was genuinely appalled.

Asher thought about it. Remembered one spring afternoon in the Junior Common Room, and the silence that fell when Grant Hobart came through the door. Shortly after that, Hobart had come to him asking to be tutored in Chinese, a language Asher had been studying for two years. His father had given him three months, Hobart had said, meeting Asher's eye with steely defiance in his own, to get a hand on the language and set forth to make his career in the Far East.

Unwillingly, he replied to her, 'I think so, yes.'

She was silent, expressionlessly drawing tiny patterns with her coffee spoon in the dust that filmed the white tablecloth.

'I attended a lecture last year,' she said at length, 'by a Dr Beaconsfield, who claimed that such behavior is traceable to atavistic malformations in the nervous system. To my mind he didn't make a very good case for it. I'd be curious about Sir Grant's father.'

'Hobart spoke to me of his father exactly once, in all the time we were at Oxford together. I know Lady Hobart was a horror. And the fact remains that it doesn't matter whether the need for violence to achieve satisfaction with a woman is hereditary or not. Richard was set up. We did that kind of thing in the

Department all the time, to get a grip on someone we needed, though I never heard of a case where we used murder. The victim of this scheme isn't Richard, or even the poor Eddington girl. It's Hobart.'

Lydia thought about that for a moment. 'Then he's right. It really *is* the Chinese.'

'I think so. But for reasons that aren't inscrutable in the least.'

She added a neat series of boxes around her drawing.

He wondered if she were thinking about Ysidro, who had killed far more women than one or two.

'While we're in Peking I'll take you to the opera, Lydia,' he said after a time. 'There aren't any wings or flies, and when the scenery needs to be changed – or the hero needs to grab a sword – stagehands run out and do whatever is necessary in full view of the audience. But since they're dressed all in black, the audience simply pretends they're not there: agrees not to see them.'

'Like the servants in the Legation.' Her voice was sad. She understood who had had access to Richard Hobart's tie drawer. Who would know all about Holly Eddington's determination to wed him, and the fact that if someone – someone she must already have known – said, *He's asking for you at the garden gate*, she would go. 'Or the servants anywhere, for that matter.'

'Except that we don't know a thing about the servants in the Legations. Who they're related to or where they go on their days off. Nothing. They come recommended – but when they step through the gates they disappear. But I do know that here, family is everything. Cousins owe favors to great-uncles; second-cousins carry messages for aunts they've never met. Whole clans of people who earn in a week what we pay for a rickshaw ride will club together every copper cash they make for years, so that grand-nephew Shen, who shows such promise, can get a tutor and go to school and take the government examinations – with the understanding that if Shen *does* make good and ends up Inspector of Customs, he's going to let second-cousin Yao's boxes go through unexamined, even though he's never met Yao in his life.'

'Not so terribly different,' she observed softly, 'from home.'

'No,' he agreed. 'Except that Shen will almost kill himself to pass those exams, not for the sake of his own future, but because of what he owes his family. And we don't see them at all.'

She wiped her spoon clean of dust, used it to stir her coffee, replaced the protective saucer. 'So you think this girl that Sir Grant is rumored to have killed at this . . . this house he goes to on Big Tiger Lane is related to some of the Legation servants?'

'That makes the most sense of anything I've heard. A Chinese can't bring a case against an English diplomat, Lydia. This is the only way they could make him suffer: by having the son he loves disgraced and hanged.'

She said nothing. Thoughts turning, like her fingers on the table furnishings. Asher's thoughts, too, ranged back to those three strange months of spending four hours a day with that loud-voiced, hard-cursing young man who got himself violently drunk every night after the lessons were done. The fifty pounds Hobart had paid him then had been what had taken him to Central Europe that second time, to study with Karlebach.

And his familiarity with the less-known reaches of the Austrian Empire that he had thus acquired had been what had brought him to the attention of the Department in the first place.

He'd been the only one of the Balliol men who had been invited, five years later, to Grant Hobart's wedding to the daughter of an American millionaire.

Behind the closed bedroom door his quick ears picked up the creak of the bed springs and a rumbly murmur in Yiddish.

'I'll see how he is.'

Lydia wiped the dust off her spoon again and set it in her saucer. 'You know Sir Grant isn't going to want to hear that.'

'No. So, just in case of trouble, I've cached thirty pounds where I can get at it in a hurry, under a floorboard in the generator room of this hotel. He has a temper, and he may turn spiteful – in which case I may have to run for it. I wonder if old Wu is still willing to hide *ch'ang pi kwei* in his house . . .?'

'Old Wu?'

'A minor crook in the Chinese City. I think he works for the Sheng family, or he did fourteen years ago. He could procure anything from telephone wire to French champagne, and he'll certainly hide a *yang kwei tse* from the authorities – or irate Germans – if the price is right. But I'm hoping we'll be able to come up with a story of some kind that will exonerate Richard, cause minimal damage, and keep his father from killing again.'

He wondered, as opened the bedroom door and saw his old teacher propped up among the pillows, if he had learned to move so casually past the unavengeable murder of an unknown girl – barely more than a child, from what he knew of Grant Hobart's tastes – from his days with the Department.

Or was that something that had come on him since he'd known vampires?

'We have to go back.' Karlebach's left thumb – the only digit still mobile on that hand – curled down hard over Asher's fingers, as if he feared his former pupil would pull away at the murmured words. 'We have to go down into the mine, find where they lie. I saw shotguns for sale at Kierulf's store, next to the hotel, and there's a gunsmith attached to the British barracks—'

'I'll go.'

'No! I must—'

'*Why?*'

Karlebach turned his face fretfully aside. 'I know these things . . .'

'What more about them do I need to know,' asked Asher softly, 'other than that they must be destroyed? There must be maps of some kind of the mine. I'll find out from one of Sir John's clerks what the mining company was and how to get my hands on its records. If I tell them I suspect the Kuo Min-tang is using the mine for a hideout I should get access. It isn't as if it's a secret. Those medicines you made—'

He nodded toward Lydia's dressing table, where the phials stood in a glittering line. A minuscule drift of dust had settled along their bases.

'You don't know if they'd work against these things or not?'

'I was a fool to bring them.' Karlebach sighed. 'Had there been more remains at the German woman's mission I would have tried a drop here, a drop there, to see what effect they would have . . . Jamie, did you count them? Did you see how many there were? Dozens—' His lined face twisted with distress.

'There always seem to be more attackers in the dark,' said Asher firmly, though he himself had been appalled at their numbers.

'And we did not hear them, did not smell them, until they were almost on us. Matthias—' Again he hesitated on his betrayer's name. 'Matthias said they had something of the vampire power to shield themselves from the eyes and minds of the living.'

'Matthias made a study of them, then?' He wondered if that young rebel had had the opportunity to do so because the medieval crypts and tunnels beneath the Old City had been in use by the revolutionary groups of Hungarians, Czechs, and Slavs who plotted to free their various homelands from the age-long grip of Austria.

Karlebach lay motionless for a time, then nodded. In the dense gloom of the bedroom, tears gathered in the old man's eyes. 'Like me, he feared what would happen if some of these politicians, these generals, learn of them, seek to use them to control their enemies. Already there are too many evil weapons in the world, Jamie. And too many men who believe that some good can come from fighting what they perceive as evil with weapons of an evil stronger still. This is why I say, I have to go back to the mine. I have to see them for myself, with my own eyes that cannot be deceived.'

Asher was silent for a time. Then he said, 'Deceived?'

'Jamie—' Karlebach's voice sank to a whisper. 'These things are the kindred of the vampire. How can we tell that it is not the vampire that controls them? That commands them? These things have no minds of their own, but if a vampire rules over them, what can they not do? You have been deceived by a vampire before,' he added, deep sorrow in his voice. 'Your heart is good, Jamie, but in this you cannot be trusted.'

The arthritic right hand, with its crooked fingers, closed around Asher's, the grip still powerful as a young man's. 'The stakes are too high for me to risk the slightest error. So you see, it must be me.'

Maybe so, thought Asher, watching as the old man turned his face aside. *But something tells me I'm not the only one who can't be trusted.*

NINE

The winds did not abate until long after dark.

Shortly past noon, a message came from the front desk that Count Mizukami was asking for him. Such was the thickness of the atmosphere outside that the lights were on in the small private parlor to which the manager conducted him, and the electric brightness was hazy with floating dust. 'I am deeply thankful for your intervention last night, Mizukami-san,' said Asher, bowing. 'I and the men with me unequivocally owe you our lives. I trust that Ito-san's injuries were not of a serious nature?'

'My servant is resting. Thank you for your interest in him, Ashu Sensei.' The Emperor's attaché bowed in return, like a chubby, bespectacled elf in his trim dark-blue uniform. Asher hoped the changes wrought in his own appearance over the past fourteen years were greater than those that marked Mizukami: a powdering of gray at his close-cropped temples, and the deepening of the lines around his eyes. In 1898, Asher had been not only bearded and shaggy and masked with thick glasses, as befit his persona of an eccentric academic, but – whenever anyone could see him – irascible, ill-mannered, and fluent only in German.

Mizukami went on, 'My concern is that creatures which smell as those did will prove to carry some infection in their claws and teeth, so he is under observation from the Legation physician. Is Ka-ru-ba-ku Sensei recovered?'

'He is, thank you. Your arrival was fortuitous.'

'Perhaps not so fortuitous as that – Ge-raa Sensei.' Mizukami met his eyes as he gave his pronunciation of Asher's 1898 alias.

Damn it. And me traveling with an Austrian Jew can't help the situation . . .

'Please do not fear that that name will be spoken beyond the walls of this room,' Mizukami continued, into Asher's wary silence. 'I am a soldier. My country's former alliance with Germany, and its present one with Great Britain, are matters which concern me only when armies march. Yet because this Ge-raa Sensei – whom I now see you do not resemble in the slightest degree – was a German, and the Kaiser lays claim to lands which are within the rightful sphere of influence of Japan, I felt that I had to follow yesterday, to be sure. Please excuse me if my impression was in error.'

'I understand. I am grateful for the misunderstanding, without which my comrades and I would surely have been killed.'

There was silence then, save for the moaning of the wind outside, and those bright black eyes met Asher's in somber horror.

'What are they?' asked Mizukami at last. 'You had the villagers lead you straight to the mines, to the place where, I think, these – these *akuma*, these *tenma*, originated. Did you know they would be there?'

Asher hesitated. The fact that Britain and Japan were allies at the moment might or might not guarantee the help of this man, or his silence. 'I didn't, no.'

'But it was they that you sought?'

'Yes.'

'What are they?'

'We don't know. It's a form of pathology we haven't encountered—'

'Disease does not do what I saw last night. They took wounds no man could survive. Two of them we beheaded, and their bodies did not fall, but ran away down into the gorge. Ito cut the legs from several of them – in one case the arms also – and this did not kill them, did not even put them into shock. Without a word, they moved about you on the trail, like fingers of a hand, like dogs herding sheep. This is not disease, Ashu Sensei. Their faces were not the faces of men. Are they indeed devils, which science tells us do not exist?'

'I don't believe so, no,' replied Asher slowly. 'For all that the villagers call them that. But for this reason they must be studied, and studied in utmost secrecy. God only knows what the Germans would make of them – or do with them.' He watched Mizukami's face as he spoke, and though the Japanese remained expressionless, he saw the dark eyes move with his thought. He added, more quietly, 'And God only knows what my own government would decide to do with them – or yours. And what the results might be.'

Mizukami's breath whispered in a tiny sigh. But he only repeated, 'I am a soldier. My business is with armies, not with . . . with the things that come out of Hell. But the new Emperor of my land is . . . is not a well man. Since his accession this spring, nearly all the affairs of the Empire have found their way into the hands of the Diet – and of the High Command. I do not say that my judgement is better than theirs, yet I know that once the gates of Hell have been opened, it may not be possible to shut them again. You were not sent here by your government?'

Asher shook his head. 'The soldiers were detailed by the ambassador to assist in my investigation of backcountry legend. The night was dark; I told them our attackers were bandits, and they appeared to believe me. None of them saw what you saw.'

'And do any others know of these things? Ka-ru-ba-ku Sensei—'

'He has made a study of their legends,' said Asher carefully. 'It was he who recognized the description, when a missionary wrote of finding one of their bodies. My wife also knows. No others.'

'*Ah, so desu.*' The Count folded his hands over the hilt of his sword, studied Asher's face with those bright black eyes. 'So what now? Find how many of them there are, how long they have been there—?'

'According to Dr Bauer, they began appearing no more than a year ago. We don't know why. It's one of the things we need to find out, and quickly. In the darkness it was hard to judge their numbers,' Asher went on. 'At least twenty.'

'That was my thought. And more, I thought, remained in the gorge. You say they are in the Shi'h Liu mine—?'

'I think so, yes. They are creatures of underground, of darkness.'

'And yet not demons.' Mizukami regarded him thoughtfully. 'Would the records of the mining company be of use? This morning I sent to the offices of the Ministry of the Interior; I can have one of my clerks translate, if plans of the tunnels themselves exist.'

'That would be of great help.' Asher bowed again.

'I see that there are things about these – these *yao-kuei* – that you are not telling me, Ashu Sensei. Yet one thing I do ask – I must know. Have they spread into this city? Or into any other part of the countryside? I can see they are devils: they are creatures of Hell. Yet their bodies are like the bodies of men. Their faces—' He shook his head. 'You say they have been there no more than a year, and you know not whence they came. Yet they must have come from somewhere. So I must ask: are they multiplying?'

Asher thought of the moonlight on the Charles Bridge in Prague, the inky shadows of its Gothic towers and the stirring somewhere below its arches. *There is a strangeness on this city*, Ysidro had written to him . . .

He said, 'It's something we're trying to find out.'

Asher went walking when the wind died down, through darkness that smelled of the Gobi Desert beneath a smoke-red moon. Rickshaws passed with a hiss of pluming dust, their pullers laboring. On the steps of the hotel, and in the doorways of every shop along Legation Street, Chinese servants plied shovels and brooms, and he knew that in every Legation tomorrow soldiers – German, British, Russian, American, Japanese – would be doing the same.

His breath in the moonlight made a cloud of diamonds.

Are they spreading?

Asher shivered at the thought.

Karlebach had grumbled about taking the Japanese attaché into their confidence, despite the fact that the Count had seen their attackers clearly last night: better that he know, than that he make inquiries that would touch off other inquiries. *Once the gates of Hell have been opened, it may not be possible to shut them again.*

Lydia had asked him: was it possible for the Count to arrange for her to see records from the Peking police, about either mysterious disappearances during the past year, or murder in which the victims had been either exsanguinated or torn by what appeared to be animals? She wanted particularly to know about the vicinity of the old lakes of the walled Palace pleasure-grounds, or near what were called the 'Stone Relics of the Sea', the two unwalled artificial lakes in the northern part of the city. Given the political unrest that had gripped Peking since the Emperor's abdication – to say nothing of the Chinese troop riots in February and the roving 'beheading squads' which had followed in their wake – Asher guessed it was going to be very difficult to

determine any pattern that might point to the appearance of
Undead monsters in the city, but agreed to ask.

Peking was quiet now.

He reached the north wall of the Legation Quarter. Wind
swirled dust around him, brought him the scent of tobacco from
the gates, where the guards sneaked a cigarette. In the open
glacis, vendors who dwelled within the Tatar City were taking
down their barrows: candied fruit, second-hand shoes, scorpions
skewered on sticks and fried in oil. Voices chattered in the brisk
sing-song of the Peking dialect. Beyond that – beyond the wide
Tung Ch'ang An Street – the roofs of the real Peking rose: the
Tatar City that surrounded the Imperial City that surrounded the
Forbidden City – more puzzle boxes, each locked behind its
massive gates – where the young ex-Emperor still lived among
half-deserted courtyards and pavilions going to ruin. *And who's
sweeping the dust from his doorstep tonight?*

On his way back, Asher turned down the service lane that ran
between the Legation wall and the lower wall that defined the
back gardens of the line of brick bungalows where the Legation
officials had their homes. Through bare branches of garden trees,
he made out the roofline of the Eddington house, one lamplit
window.

Is Myra Eddington able to sleep yet?

Would I be, if it was Miranda who lay dead?

His heart contracted inside him at the thought of that red-
haired child, whom he had left crawling busily around the parlor
in quest of the blocks Lydia had hidden everywhere (including in
Karlebach's beard).

Holly Eddington – shrill-voiced, nervous, awkward in her
girlish white gown and ready to trick a man into marrying
her, for the sake of his money . . . She had been a child like
that once.

And so had the girl – whatever her name was – that Grant
Hobart had killed because he couldn't climax any other way.

'James,' a voice murmured in his ear. 'A pleasure to see you
well.'

Asher turned sharply.

A trace of wind stirred the vampire's long white hair, lifted
the skirts of his greatcoat. 'Don't look at me,' Ysidro added,
seeing his expression. 'I had nothing to do with the girl's death.'

'You heard something in the garden, though, when we spoke at Eddington's?'

'I did.' The vampire turned at once down the Rue Meiji, away from the gate, and Asher fell into step. 'When interrupted by your so-charming friend I went out and found the girl dead – only by minutes – and the young man in an advanced state of drunken unconsciousness. Had I been such a fool as to taste his blood I couldn't have found my way back to my own coffin. Does your Professor think me that stupid?'

'That greedy for blood.'

A line appeared – briefly – at the corner of Ysidro's mouth, then vanished. 'When the only thing in your life is a hammer, all problems look like nails. In an unknown city, where the presence of the vampires imbues the very stones, it were madness to drink without leave.'

It was clear, to Asher's eye, that he still had not fed. There was a look to him, skeletal and a little inhuman, as if he had trouble maintaining the illusion of life that made his victims trust him. The scars on his face were now clearly visible, white ridges over brow and cheekbone. He had gotten them in Lydia's defense.

'I suspect,' Asher said, 'that Karlebach, for all his studies, doesn't know as much about vampires as he thinks he does.' *Or I don't know as much about them as I think I do . . .*

'I have observed before this,' Ysidro commented. 'That vampire hunters become obsessed with their prey, to the exclusion of all else: family, friends, the joy of study or of love – everything but the hunt. In this they become like the vampire themselves. Their worlds narrow and focus, until they become a perfect weapon . . . but a weapon is all they are. I take it you did indeed find the Others in the Western Hills.'

Asher raised his brows. 'If you tell me you were present and didn't lend us your aid—'

'*Dios*, no! The dead travel swiftly, but I had errands of my own last night – which did not prosper, I regret to say. The first I knew of your adventures was when I saw you return to your hotel in the small hours, looking as if you had been to the wars. And this evening in the barracks quarter, your Soldiers Three spoke feelingly of an encounter with the foulest-smelling gang of brigands this side of Hell. Drugged, they said, or practitioners of mysterious techniques, like those of the *amuk* warriors of the Philippines.'

'Just as well. The last thing we need is for anybody's network of gossips to send word of their existence back to the species of bastards who invented phosgene gas.' Briefly, Asher recounted the events of the previous thirty-six hours as they walked, including the theft of their horses and the behavior of Dr Bauer's medical specimens when exposed to sunlight. 'I'd have liked to see the effects of a few drops of silver nitrate on some of those bones, and Karlebach has a whole pharmacopoeia of distillations, though how you'd convince the things to drink them is beyond me. I gather Dr Bauer believes them to be some kind of atavistic survival from prehistory, like the apemen in *The Lost World*, and hopes to prove this to the scientific community.'

'*There are more things in Heaven and Earth than are dreamt of in your philosophy*,' quoted the vampire. 'It is in fact no less reasonable than to believe in vampires.'

They reached the wall of the Imperial City, black and towering thirty feet above them on the opposite side of the street, its crenellations outlined dimly against the lights of the railroad yard. A street vendor's voice somewhere on the other side wailed hoarsely the virtues of pancakes and watermelon seeds.

'What have you learned from the vampires of Peking?'

'Naught.' Hands in the pockets of his long black greatcoat, Ysidro was barely visible in the night. 'Not even their shadows have I seen. Yet their presence hangs in the air like smoke. I promenaded myself along the glacis, and a little distance into the city, listening for their voices. I heard nothing. But when I sleep, I dream of being watched by something I cannot understand. Something terrible, silent, and cold.'

It was the first time Asher had ever heard him speak of dreaming.

The vampire countess Anthea Farren – gone now, burned up in a holocaust of flame in Constantinople – had said to Asher once that it was as if God had chosen, as the punishment for those who killed in order to steal more life, to make them seek every attribute of death except peace. To be vampire was a condition predicated upon always having somewhere to hide; always having inviolable control over one's environment. Thus as the years passed their un-life grew smaller and more rigid, and they sought to control every atom of the world that might be some threat to them. Most never dared travel. Many ceased to venture more than a few miles from where their coffins were hidden, lest they be somehow caught from home by the unforeseen.

Like that fairy book, she had said, in the darkness of a Vienna night, *where a man's limbs are replaced, one by one, by magic with limbs of tin, until suddenly he realizes he has no heart and is no longer a man. I'm afraid*, she had said, *and I know I should be more afraid than I am. I could die in moments, just because I don't know the right place to hide, the right turning to take . . .*

Her death, when it came, had not taken moments.

All of this echoed in Ysidro's stillness.

'Would it help you,' Asher asked, with a certain diffidence, 'if I went with you when you sought them? At least I could speak to them, if they appeared.'

'You would die,' said Ysidro, quite simply. 'Maybe I also, for allying myself with the living. I know not even if speaking to you thus tonight dooms you at their hands. I have no sense of their presence here in the Legation Quarter, yet this, too, may be an illusion wrought by them upon my mind. I cannot tell. I can say only, *walk carefully, and take all possible precautions*, for in my bones I feel they can strike with the speed of thought. I am sorry,' he added, and it sounded like he meant it.

Dust blew in Asher's eyes. As he wiped them he became aware that he had been standing for some time on the bank of the canal alone, where it ran beneath the city wall. In the sickly moonlight, only his own tracks marked the dust along Rue Meiji, back toward the hotel's yellow lights.

TEN

P'ei Cheng K'ang, Sir John Jordan said, was the most reliable of the British Legation's Chinese clerks, a young man whose parents had emigrated to India when K'ang was eight and who had subsequently been educated at Cambridge. He had family in Peking, however, and had recently married a young woman of their choosing, so he was grateful for Asher's offer of ten shillings per evening, to help him go over the maps and diagrams compiled by the Hsi Fang-te Hsing Sheng Company of its mine in Mingliang. The company itself had gone bankrupt years previously, and no wonder, thought Asher as he drew the musty sheaf of yellow paper from the envelope Mizukami had sent him. A glance told him the maps were incomplete. Even when he'd ascertained which portion of it was supposed to represent the Mingliang gorge, he could see it wasn't to scale, nor did it resemble much the terrain he had passed over on Friday.

'No, that's Mingliang, all right, sir,' the clerk reassured him, when Asher slid the map across to him. 'I suspect the man who put this map together had never been near the place and was trying to make the earlier maps all fit.'

They worked in the Legation offices – Asher had a deep mistrust about anyone knowing any more about his family or place of residence than was absolutely necessary – in a room of the original old princely palace that hadn't even been piped for gas, let alone wired for electricity. Paraffin lamps threw strange shadows over the red-lacquered pillars that rose between the prosaic desks of the clerks, caught glints of peeled gold and faded polychrome among the maze of ceiling beams. As he studied the maps, Asher found a great deal of his long-neglected Chinese returned to him, though he was glad of an assistant: 'Is that *incline* there? Does that *ten* mean degrees of slope?'

'That's *keng* – pit. I assume ten *bu* deep, unless – when was this made? Unless they were using meters.'

'When did the company switch over to meters? Does it say?'

P'ei shook his head. 'If a mine was getting its equipment from Germany or France they'd sometimes switch over to meters – even as far back as 1880 – but it depended on whether they kept foremen who were more used to measuring things in *chi* and *bu*. And then some of the foremen came from parts of the country where it was five *chi* to a *bu*, and some from where it was six *chi*.'

'Hmn.' Asher reflected that it was no wonder the unfortunate Emperor Kwang Hsu – before he'd been locked up by his ferocious old aunt the Empress Dowager and poisoned – had wanted to reform measurements. 'And where does this lead? It says *old tunnel*.'

'*Old tunnel* could mean something that was dug in the time of the T'ang emperors, sir. That part of the hills is riddled with old mines. Some of the tunnels are caved in or flooded. Others go Heaven knows where. The Company got cheated when it bought the diggings and tried to get its money back out of its workers' wages. They never put up enough shorings, or bothered to keep their pumps working properly.'

Asher glanced across the table at the young man, neat as any Cockney clerk in a blue suit and starched collar, with a little close-clipped French mustache. 'Have you ever been to the mines?'

P'ei shook his head. 'But one of my mother's neighbors worked in the Shi'h Liu mines, both before and after the Hsi Fang-te Company bought them. He said the galleries would sometimes connect with older diggings – from back even before the . . .' He stopped himself from saying *Long-Nosed Devils*. 'Before the Europeans came to China.'

'Did he ever scare you with stories of things hiding in the mine?'

The clerk grinned. 'You mean demons? He used to scare the daylights out of me and my brother telling us about a *kuei* like a giant catfish, with six pairs of men's arms and eyes that glowed in the dark. It would haul itself along the tunnel singing in a woman's voice and devour miners.'

But no *yao-kuei*. That would be – he tried to estimate the young man's age – maybe twenty years ago? And his instincts told him that Dr Bauer was correct. That the *yao-kuei* were of very recent appearance.

But how? Where did they come from? And why?

ARE the vampires of Peking behind it somehow?

During these three days of examining maps, Asher also paid visits to the other friends of Richard Hobart – a Trade Ministry clerk named Cromwell Hall, and the dandified German translator Hans Erlich – and confirmed what he already suspected: that on the evening of their disastrous expedition to Eight Roads, young Hobart hadn't been wearing the tie with which Holly Eddington had been strangled. It was clear to him that the young man had been very neatly separated from his companions that night, drugged – the rickshaw-puller must have showed Hobart's pass to the gate guards – and dumped in the garden beside his fiancée's dead body. The Department at its finest couldn't have done better.

On the third evening, Asher brought up the subject of where

a *yang jên* gentleman of moderate wealth and specialized tastes might go to seek entertainment in Peking.

'A friend of mine asked me to make inquiries,' he explained.

'You mean a boy?' P'ei didn't turn a hair. 'Or children?'

Waiters in Peking eating houses used the same tone to inquire: *All-same want steam rice, want fry rice*?

'Girls,' Asher said. 'Young girls. Who would I speak to about that?'

The clerk was silent for a moment, studying his face, though Asher himself had learned long ago that it wasn't always possible to judge a man's tastes in the bedroom by looking at him. In time he replied, 'I would go to Fat Yu, or An Lu T'ang. Yu, if your friend likes his girls very young. An, if he does not wish to be troubled by the law, if it should so happen that the girl gets . . . hurt.'

'I'll speak to my friend.' Asher saw in the young clerk's eyes the glimmer of wary disgust, as if he suspected that no such 'friend' existed. 'I'll ask him what he prefers. Thank you.'

P'ei turned back to the company records and unfolded another sheet in the pool of brightness cast by the lamp. 'Watch out for An,' he added. 'He works for the Tso family – they've become one of the biggest gangs in the city. Generally, An – and the Tso – provide the house. Your friend may find himself paying blackmail.'

'I'll warn him. Thank you.'

It was close to eight o'clock when he locked up the maps in the cupboard that Sir John had set aside for him in the Legation offices, gave P'ei his ten shillings – the clerk refused with a quiet head-shake the extra crown that he offered – and went out to Meiji Street in quest of a rickshaw. He had arranged to meet Lydia, Karlebach, the Russian attaché the Baron Drosdrov and his wife, and a Belgian professor of Chinese literature for dinner at the Peking Club, and he barely had time to stop at the hotel and change. Lydia and Karlebach had already departed – 'The old professor took himself off just after five, sir,' provided Ellen, with a note of disapproval in her voice. 'Said he had to buy some ties, but *I* say that's no excuse for leaving poor Mrs Asher to get herself to the Club without an escort.'

It was five hundred yards from the front doors of the Wagons-Lits Hotel to the Peking Club, along two of the best-patrolled streets in China, but Ellen had read – Asher suspected – far too many novels about the Yellow Peril to believe her lady could make the journey in anything resembling safety. 'Ties are a critical component of a man's survival in a foreign country, Ellen,' he replied gravely. 'I only hope Rebbe Karlebach set forth on his quest in evening dress, because the maître d' at the Club isn't likely to admit him if he isn't, no matter how many ties he has purchased.'

As it happened, he was given the opportunity to judge Karlebach's attire for himself. As usual – the habit of vigilance never left an old field agent, vampires or no vampires – Asher took note of every doorway, vehicle, and passer-by along Legation Street and Rue Marco Polo as his rickshaw bore him at a brisk trot toward the Peking Club. In the same fashion, over the past three days, he had thoroughly familiarized himself – and Lydia – with the hotel itself, until he knew every stairway, every attic, every cupboard, six different ways of getting to the money cached in the generator room, and most particularly every exit . . . just in case.

It was an old saying in the Department: that time spent in preparation is never wasted.

The night was a cold one, and he kept his own coat-collar turned up and the brim of his top-hat tilted down. Still, he identified people glimpsed in passing: Colonel von Mehren and sly old white-haired Eichorn emerging from the gates of the German Legation; Trade Secretary Oda-san – very trim in his London-tailored suit – crossing the street from the Japanese Legation to the Hong Kong and Shanghai Bank. He noted the old Chinese named Mian who peddled newspapers and bamboo baskets all around the Legation Quarter and who Asher suspected of being a letter carrier for at least one spy network and maybe several. Thus, when he stepped down in front of the lighted bronze doors of the Peking Club and paid off his puller ('Twenty-five cent anywhere in city, chop-chop . . .') he observed, a few hundred feet down the Rue Hart, the Rebbe Karlebach emerge from the gateway of the Austrian Legation.

Even at that distance, the old man's wildly outdated overcoat, white beard, and low-crowned hat were unmistakable. Instead of walking back to the Club's doors, Asher strolled along the street for a few yards, observing the tall, stooped figure by the lighted gateway: Karlebach turned to speak to someone still inside for a moment, then bowed and touched his hat brim before making his way toward the club. He carried no package.

Asher watched him for a few moments before turning himself and climbing the Club steps, to where Lydia – gorgeous in green-and-amber silk – awaited him in the lobby, in company with the Baron Drosdrov and his loud-voiced Baroness, and fragile old Professor Feydreaux. When Karlebach arrived, Asher made no mention of the Austrian Legation, and during an excellent supper of York ham and petits pois, Asher noted that his old teacher made no mention of it, either. Nor of purchasing ties. Lydia asked the old man about his visit to Silk Lane and whether he'd found a guide to show him the Temple of Everlasting Harmony – he said he hadn't – and hoped he hadn't had to rush from the hotel.

Karlebach, Asher observed, was a terrible liar.

If the Auswärtiges Amt was recruiting agents, they'd certainly have done better.

In any case, he couldn't imagine his friend letting any government – particularly his own, now that it was in close alliance with Germany – hear so much as a word about the Others . . .

Still, it was something to be noted.

Ysidro was waiting for him at the hotel.

Karlebach, Asher, and Lydia had taken two rickshaws back. A Chinese servant handed Asher a note as he and Lydia walked through the door of the Wagons-Lits. He made himself frown for Karlebach's benefit when he recognized the sixteenth-century handwriting, said, 'Yet more gossip about Richard Hobart,' and followed the servant to the same blue-curtained private parlor in which he'd met Count Mizukami four days previously. Ysidro sat beside the fireplace, studying a popular guidebook of Peking.

'I have spoken with another vampire,' he said as Asher closed the door.

'They – or at least one of them – know English, then?' Asher drew off his gloves, held his hands to the fire. 'Or Spanish – the Jesuits have sent missionaries here for three hundred years . . .'

'Father Orsino Espiritu was one of them.' Ysidro looked considerably less haggard than he had the last time Asher had spoken to him on the night of the windstorm – he guessed he had fed, probably far outside the city – but the haunted watchfulness remained in his eyes. 'He sleeps in the crypt of a deserted chapel near the old French cemetery.' He wore, Asher noted also, his usual spotlessly clean linen and a different suit, charcoal-gray tonight and not black.

So where is HE staying?

'The chapel was burned during the Uprising,' Ysidro went on. 'It is little more than rubble now. Father Orsino goes in mortal terror of discovery, and I had to chase him halfway across the old palace pleasure-gardens, only to discover when I caught him that he is quite insane.'

'That doesn't sound helpful. Did he speak of the other vampires of Peking?'

'He says they have all been transformed into gods.' Ysidro considered the low-burning fire in the grate for a time, long white hands folded on the small, square bone of his elegantly-trousered knee. 'He seems to have them confused in his mind with the Magistrates of Hell who rule the damned, and he regaled me at tedious length with questions about whether the mountain of knives was in the first or the fourth hell, and whether sinners in the second hell were fried in oil or steamed. There were, he informs me, originally a hundred and thirty-four hells, but there was a reorganization during the T'ang Dynasty and the number reduced to eighteen. Did I know how that came about? A most disconcerting interview.'

Asher settled in the opposite chair, fascinated. 'Who did he think you were?'

'A representative of the Inquisition, evidently, come to bring him back to Spain. I fear I did not disabuse him. Rather I warned him that I was working with the Pope's secret representatives – yourself and Mistress Lydia, as I hope you will remember, should you ever have the misfortune to encounter Father Orsino. He has been hiding, for most of the past three centuries, in the coal mines of the Western Hills—'

Ysidro paused as Asher straightened sharply from the hearth's warmth.

'He only left them this summer, because, he said, stinking devils had begun to breed there, and he feared that he was not safe.'

'This summer?'

'He saw, he said, the first one last winter. He said he thought it was a bandit who had gone insane and been thrown out of his gang, but he did not attack him because the man was a Catholic. How he ascertained this fact I am not sure. Then later, he said, the man began to deteriorate into a monster and attack the bandits himself, or the villagers if they walked abroad after dark. Father Orsino kept away from the *yao-kuei*, fearing that they would tell the Magistrates of Hell where he was hiding. Later he said they became so numerous he feared they would kill him and eat him, as they did the villagers' pigs – the villagers, too, if they could get them.'

'But he was hiding in the hills before that?'

'From the Magistrates of Hell.' Ysidro's yellow eyes caught the glint of the fire as he moved his head. 'They seek to kill him, he says, because as Christ's servant he had converted so many Chinese that Hell was becoming depopulated. One can only presume that the Magistrates were being paid on a commission basis.'

'Or lost face.'

'As you say. He made a hideout deep in the mines, with bars and locks of silver, which he says they cannot touch. He cannot touch them either, of course.' Ysidro shrugged with a gesture of a finger. 'I presume he hired the work done and then made a meal off the workmen – they were stealing the silver, I dare say, and deserved it. In any event, he begged me to take him out of China, to get him back to the Pope, who will – he says – keep the Magistrates at bay. He evidently feels that they have it in their power to take him straight to Hell for his sins.'

Asher said, 'Hmmn. And I suppose he wasn't able to tell you who made him a vampire in the first place?'

Ysidro moved his head slightly: *No.*

'Nor whether there is or was any connection between the *yao-kuei* and the vampires of Peking?'

'It was, as I have said, a disconcerting interview. He did say that the Magistrates of Hell no longer create more of their own kind, but rule the world through human intermediaries. He then gave me such abundance of details about the ranks, titles, and position in the hierarchy of the Afterlife of each Magistrate as to make me doubt his words. Yet clearly he spoke of vampires. They drink both blood and the spirit – the *chi* – he said, and through those gain power; moreover they sleep in the daytime. And of a surety, one of them made him.'

'*They would tell the Magistrates of Hell where he was hiding.*'
Asher rose and paced to the window, parted the curtain – heavy
peacock brocade from the mills of Manchester – and looked out
at the darkness. The Legation gates were closed. Rue Meiji had
fallen quiet. Only the moonlight – a few days past full – glimmered on the stagnant waters of the canal.

A patrol of the Legation police walked past, lantern-light
winking on the brass of their uniform buttons. At the end of
the street, the wall of the Tartar City towered forty feet
against the stars.

'*I hear their voices speaking in my mind*, he said. I could not
tell if it was the Others he meant, or if it was the Magistrates.
Perhaps he did not know himself.'

'You remember,' Asher said slowly, 'how, three years ago, the
master vampire of Constantinople lost the ability to create fledglings? The flesh of the new vampire changed and mutated, but
the soul – the spirit – could not enter the mind of the master, to
render the transformations complete. So the body of the fledgling
deteriorated, half-transformed, with the virus of vampirism still
within it . . .'

'And if that fledgling tried, in such a state, to make a fledgling
in his turn?' The vampire's pale brows pinched together over the
aristocratic curve of his nose. 'What then? I admit I am curious,
as to whether I could hear the thoughts of these creatures, as I
listen to human dreams . . . but if indeed they are the servants
of the Peking vampires, it may be foolish of me to make the
attempt. I would fainer keep my distance from them, until I know
at least a little of their intent.'

Asher returned to the hearth, stood for a time, arms folded,
looking down at that slender gentleman in gray. 'Do you think
they'd kill you? The Peking vampires, I mean.'

'I think they *could*,' replied Ysidro simply. 'Certainly, Father
Orsino has a lively fear that they would kill *him*. But then he is
a priest – and mad, as I said. And therefore, almost certainly, a
danger to them.' The vampire was silent then, contemplating the
fire as if the sable turrets of ash and ember were indeed the gates
to the eighteen departments of Hell, and by study he could probe
the dreams of those within.

'I do find it troubling,' the vampire went on at last, 'that with
a single exception, every vampire I have encountered of mine own

years or older – and Father Orsino has been vampire since 1580 – is insane. If this is something which befalls our kind after three centuries, I should like to know it . . . and also I should like then to know, how old are the Magistrates of Hell? And, are *they* sane?'

Asher was still sitting beside the fire, staring into the amber jewels of the dying grate, when a knock on the parlor door roused him from what he realized – to his annoyance – had been reverie long enough that his knees were stiff when he stood. *Damn Ysidro* – because of course the chair opposite his own was not only empty, but its cushions also returned to the pristine state of cushions which have borne no weight for a considerable time.

It was Lydia at the door. She still wore the evening dress she'd had on at the Club, olive-green satin trimmed with amber and black, but had taken off her jewels and her gloves. In the lobby behind her, Asher heard the clock strike midnight.

She sneaked a glance at the lobby to make sure she was unobserved, then put on her glasses. 'Is everything all right?'

Asher nodded, and took her hands in his to kiss. 'It was Ysidro,' he said, 'not anything about poor Hobart's son.' He dipped in the pocket of his evening jacket, but Ysidro's note was gone. 'I'm sorry—'

'Is he all right?' She caught herself up a little as she asked the question, and he remembered his own observation that Ysidro looked better . . . which meant that someone, somewhere, had died.

He answered, non-committally, 'He looked well. He said he had found another vampire here in Peking – a Spaniard like himself, not Chinese. I'll tell you later. I didn't mean to make you wait.'

She shook her head and held out a note in her turn. 'I wouldn't have bothered you,' she said. 'Only this came about an hour ago.'

Asher Sensei,
 Please come to my residence in the Legation, at your earliest convenience in the morning. Bring also Karlebach Sensei, if he would be so kind as to consent.
 Sincerely,
 Mizukami

ELEVEN

'I have not yet sent for a doctor.' Count Mizukami crossed to the cushion on which the bodyguard Ito sat, knelt beside him and rested an encouraging hand on the younger man's bare shoulder. He spoke softly, though the young samurai gave no indication of hearing what was said. Asher suspected he spoke no English. 'His fever came on suddenly yesterday, though he complained the day before that natural light hurt his eyes, and that his face and his body pained him.' These small brick bungalows at the rear of the Japanese Legation had been built after the Uprising and were equipped with electricity, incongruous beside the spare furnishings of tatami mats and braziers.

The windows of Ito's little chamber were shuttered. The samurai's futons had been wedged into the tops of the windows, to shut out even the little morning daylight that leaked through.

'I remembered what you said,' Mizukami went on, 'about what the Germans might take it into their heads to do, if they learned of these things – whatever they are – in the Western Hills. The ears of enemies are everywhere. Yet a doctor must be sent for.'

'My wife is a physician.' Asher walked over to the cushion, stockinged feet sinking very slightly on the woven matting, and knelt. 'Would you consent to it, for Ito-san to be seen by her?'

Ito shuddered when Asher put a hand under his chin, raised his head very slightly and touched the swollen flesh of his cheekbones and jaw. He could feel the fever that burned in the young man's flesh and see – around the bandages that wrapped his upper left arm and side – the angry inflammation spreading.

Blood stained the bodyguard's mouth. A little basin beside him was filled with red-soaked squares of gauze.

Karlebach, standing beside the door, buried his face in his hands.

'I will have her sent for.' Mizukami went to the door and gave some instructions to a servant in the hall, then returned to Asher's side and knelt again. His voice sank to a whisper. 'You see how Ito-san was wounded, the flesh of his arm and shoulder torn

open. When he beheaded the *tenma* –' he used the Japanese word
for a demon – 'he was doused in its blood. I feared infection
from their teeth and nails. Is this what comes of it, that his blood
has been infected, his very body turning into these things? Is this
how they multiply?'

Contamination of the blood, Ysidro had said. Like vampires.

Asher glanced back at Karlebach. The old man groaned softly,
but made no reply.

'I have heard so.'

'Heard from *whom*?' Anger flashed in the little Count's eyes.
'You spoke of legends – *what* legends? Where do these things
exist, where *have* they existed—?'

Ito groaned, and spoke as if to himself, a stifled handful of
words in Japanese. Blood dribbled down from his lips, where
the growing fangs cut them. Mizukami put his arms around the
young man's shoulders, held him tight, his face like a mask. 'Ito,'
he whispered. 'Ito-kun . . .'

'They've existed in Prague,' said Asher, 'for five hundred years.
They live in the medieval sewers, as far as anyone's been able
to tell, and in the maze of underground tunnels below the Old
City. They've appeared in no other place, until last winter.'

Mizukami raised a hand, very gently brushed the bodyguard's
face, which was horribly swollen and discolored where the sutures
were softening, elongating it. 'I heard him last night, walking
back and forth across this room,' the Count whispered. 'Yesterday
morning he said there was a muttering in his mind. Not voices,
but like the vibration of moth's wings, the songs of ghosts, driving
him from one place to another, demanding that he kill, or flee,
or just let them into his mind. *Ki o tsukete, Ito-kun.*' His grip
tightened around Ito's shoulders. *Keep your spirit strong.*

Asher half-turned his head, spoke over his shoulder to the old
scholar, who had not moved from beside the door. 'Can nothing
be done?'

Karlebach's voice was hoarse. 'No.'

'Not to slow the process? Or to arrest it for a time? The solu-
tions you made, the distillations—'

'*NO!*' Karlebach shouted the word, yanked open the door
behind him, and blundered from the room. In doing so he nearly
ran into Lydia, who was being ushered down the hall by a servant;
he pushed past her, almost fled.

Lydia said, startled, 'Professor—?'

'In here,' said Asher. 'This man needs your help.'

She hurried into the room and immediately donned her glasses, regardless of the presence of a stranger. 'Oh, my God—' Petticoats rustled as she knelt, opened her medical bag.

As she did so, Asher said, 'Count Mizukami, may I present my wife, Dr Asher—' and the Count and Lydia exchanged perfunctory bows. While Lydia examined Ito's face and mouth, Mizukami recounted to her in a low voice what he had already told Asher, and the events of Friday night. She checked Ito's heart and blood pressure, looked at his hands – bleeding also from the cuticles where the nails were beginning to thicken into claws – and into his eyes. The electrical light angled into them from her mirror didn't seem to pain the young samurai.

Only daylight.

When she moved to untie the bandages on his arm and shoulder, however, the young man suddenly pushed her away with a violence that threw her to the floor mats and lurched to his feet. He staggered to a corner of the room, and when Mizukami followed him, he rounded on his master and shouted something at him in Japanese.

Mizukami only faced him, compassion in his eyes.

Ito whispered something else, desperate, his whole body trembling.

When his master replied, Ito poured forth a couple of sentences, agony in his voice. The last things he would say, Asher understood with a rush of sickened pity, as a man with thought and volition of his own. Then Ito turned and faced the wall, and sank, first to his knees, then to a curled-up position in the corner farthest from the windows, his knees drawn up to his chest.

Her face filled with shock and grief, Lydia made a move toward him, but Asher held her back. Mizukami knelt at the bodyguard's side, then rose and returned to them, where they stood beside the cushion on the floor, the little basin of bloodied gauze.

'He sleeps.'

Silence stood between them for some minutes. The attaché's face was a well-bred mask, but for a time he could not speak.

'What did he say?' Lydia asked softly.

'*They call me*, he said. *They fill my mind. I cannot keep them out any longer.*'

Asher's gaze crossed Lydia's. They had both had experience with the ability of some vampires to read and to tamper with the dreams of the living. To whisper into living minds.

'Once it grows dark he's going to try to get out,' said Asher quietly. 'If not tonight, tomorrow. He'll be seeking to join them. I'm so sorry.'

Mizukami moved his head a little. 'There is nothing that can be done.'

'With your permission, Count, I would like to follow him when he does. To see if they're in the city as well.'

'This is wise of you, Ashu Sensei.' Mizukami's voice was suddenly flat with weariness.

'Until that time, I think it's better that he be kept confined.'

'Of course. It shall be as you say. Thank you.' He bowed deeply. 'And you, Dr Ashu.' He bowed again, to Lydia. His black eyes behind their heavy spectacles seemed opaque, guarding all thought, all feeling within.

'I'm so sorry—' Lydia began, and Mizukami shook his head again.

'There is nothing that can be done,' he repeated. 'I apologize in my servant's name for his striking you. He would not have done so had he been in his right mind. He has grown up in my household,' he added, 'the son of one of my father's samurai. Thank you for coming to do what you could.'

Karlebach waited for them in the parlor – the only room in the little house furnished in Western style with couches and chairs – staring through the window into the cold sharp Peking sunlight. Mizukami spoke to a servant, and Asher caught the words for 'two rickshaws' – *jinrikisha ga nidai* – and said, 'If you will excuse me, Count, the Professor and I would prefer to walk back to the hotel.'

Lydia – who had taken off her spectacles before stepping through the door of Ito's room – looked for a moment as if she were going to ask why, then caught his eye and only inquired, 'Shall I see you for lunch, then?'

Mizukami helped Lydia up into his personal vehicle at the door of his house, handed her the carefully-wrapped parcel which contained the bloodied pieces of gauze. When the rickshaw darted off down the neat, barracks-like street of the Japanese compound, the Count walked Asher and Karlebach to its rear gate, and bowed to them as they stepped out into Rue Lagrené.

As soon as he left them, Asher put his arm through Karlebach's and asked quietly, 'Is it Matthias?'

In his heart he already knew.

Karlebach's breath went out of him in a sigh. 'Matthias,' he whispered, and in his voice Asher heard the echo of King David's cry, *O my son Absalom, my son, my son . . . would God I had died for thee . . .*

From behind the high rear wall of the French barracks, the sharp blast of whistles rose for morning drill, the barking shouts of officers. Across the street, the white-painted brick of the customs yard threw back the sun's glare. Asher thought of that young man curled up against the wall in his white loincloth, sleeping the dead-still sleep of one who would not wake until darkness.

When darkness fell, would Ito – who had saved his life, and Karlebach's, there in the hills – even recall his own name? His family, and the islands of his home?

There is nothing to be done, Mizukami had said.

Asher walked in silence for a time.

'He came to my lectures on folklore,' said Karlebach, as if they had been speaking of the matter for an hour, 'because he wanted to "know the people" in order to "set them free" – as if they would rather have political representation than the assurance that they wouldn't be taxed into penury and their sons wouldn't be drafted. Matthias Uray . . . He was a law student, you understand. The sort of roughneck who riots with political clubs and demands independence for Hungary, and glories in the thickness of the file that the police have on him.'

'You told me he was in the movement for an independent Hungary,' said Asher. 'I often wondered how he came to you.'

'That was how.' The old man's head was sunk on his chest, as if he carried some terrible weight. 'Since first I learned of the vampire, I have watched the newspapers, read every account and traveler's tale, searching for word of their doings. The vampire, and latterly the Others as well. I used Matthias to gather information from sailors and soldiers, and from the workers down on the river docks, the people I am not able to speak to – men who would call me Jew and knock my hat off and kick it down the street for sport. Matthias wanted to know what I was looking for. Why I asked about these things.'

'Did you tell him?'

'No, the wicked brat.' The dark eyes sparkled suddenly with the memory. 'He went to the oldest newspapers in the city and looked up records, just as your beautiful Lydia does. And then, when he began to see patterns in the disappearances and rumors and things seen and whispered, he went further. He sought out old broadsides and ancient decrees, and letters from the great old banking-houses of the Empire that would send each other whatever strange tales came their way. *Then* he came to me, asking about the vampire, and about these degenerate cousins of theirs, these Others. He said I was old. Me. Old!' Karlebach sniffed. 'He said I needed protection, if I were to go poking about among the affairs of those who hunt the night. And under the sweaty muscle of a ruffian, I found the heart of an ancient knight.'

He closed his eyes then, as if he saw his ruffianly knight before him again, in a student's cap and three days' worth of beard, and the tears he had not been able to shed glittered in the chilly light.

'I told him – again and again I told him – to leave the Others alone. It is the vampire who is our enemy, I said. The Others are merely . . . merely animals, like the rats to whom they are allied. He asked me, "How do you know this?" And when I answered him, that one of the vampires told me this, years ago, he would throw back at me, "But I thought you say they always lie?" The truth is that learning was like a hunger in him, a yearning that nothing could sate.'

Two French officers passed them as they turned on to Rue Marco Polo: blue jackets, gold braid, the crimson trousers of which the French Army was so proud. On the other side of the street, old Mr Mian called out on his see-saw note, '*Pao chih*! *Pao chih*! Finest kind new-paper *pao chih*!'

'So he went down below the bridges one night?' Asher could almost see the dark figure silhouetted against the water's gleam, the splinter of light from a shaded lantern. Could almost smell the stench of the Others, against the foul pong of sewage and fish. It's what Lydia would have done. Or he himself.

'He came to me the following morning,' Karlebach whispered. 'He had been bitten, clawed – and had wounded them in return with the sailor's knife he always carried. His clothing was all soaked with blood, his own and theirs. The vampire Szegédy had told me once – the Master of Prague – that the condition of these creatures seems to spread by the blood, as the physical state of the vampires is spread. Matthias joked about it, as it was his way to do, but he was frightened. He knew what it meant, that their blood had mingled with his. He – we – knew already that the same elements inimical to the vampire would also destroy the flesh of these other Undead: hawthorn, whitethorn, wolfsbane, silver. And there were those before me who had used them in elixirs and distillations in the hope of reversing the physical effects of the vampire's blood . . .'

'Did they work?'

'Yes.' The old scholar's voice came out thin, like wire stretched to breaking point. 'We watched – we waited . . .' He walked on for a time, crippled hands jammed into the pockets of his long teal-green coat. Asher heard him trying to steady his breath.

'When was this?'

'August of 1911. A few months after you came through Prague. Then one morning Matthias didn't come to my house. A few days later I heard there had been an arrest of the Young Hungary group. He escaped, his friends told me. Escaped and fled the country.'

'So you started watching,' said Asher, after long silence. 'Watching in the medical journals, in newspapers, for some mention of a creature somewhere in the world that could have been him.'

'What could I do?' Karlebach stopped on the pavement, flung out his arms, his voice a cry of despair.

'Did you hope to be able to help him? To reverse the process?'

'I don't know what I hoped, Jamie.' They crossed the street to the hotel doors, absurd in their neo-Gothic splendor in the cold sunlight. 'I only knew that I could not desert him. And that I could not seek him alone.'

Liveried footmen sprang to admit them. At the desk the clerk handed Asher a note from P'ei Cheng K'ang, with an enclosure – duly translated – proposing a meeting with An Lu T'ang in two days' time in the Eight Lanes district. Another note, from Sir Grant Hobart, asked to see him at three that afternoon.

Asher turned back to his companion. 'Was this what you were asking about last night at the Austrian Legation?'

'Shipping records.' Under the heavy white mustaches, Karlebach's lips twisted. 'So you see I did pay attention after all to all your talk of spying, my old friend. And yes, a man who could have been Matthias "jumped ship", as I believe the phrase is, from the *Prinz Heinrich* at Tientsin last November, after signing on in Trieste in September.'

They paused at the foot of the stairs.

'When the Greeks said that Hope was one of the things that came out of Pandora's Box, Jamie, with all the other griefs and woes and pains that are the punishment of humankind, they never meant to describe it as the single ray of light in those clouds of stinging darkness. That was a myth invented by nursery maids, so they could tell that story to children without breaking their little hearts. Hope is the worst of those devils, the cruellest thing that the gods could think of to give to man.'

He turned in silence and preceded Asher up the stairs.

TWELVE

'Damn it, Asher, what the hell are you playing at?' Hobart looked up from his papers the moment the Chinese manservant closed the study door behind Asher. 'When I said get Rick off this damnable lie, I wasn't giving you carte blanche to go poking your nose into backstairs gossip!'

P'ei? Or had one of Richard's three jolly companions mentioned to Richard that he – Asher – had been asking about Hobart Senior's diversions . . . and about his servants?

'A British court isn't going to let your son off a murder charge if his only defense is "it must have been the Chinese".'

Hobart still had the same quarters he'd occupied before the Rebellion: eight rooms around what had been a minor courtyard in the rambling old palace that the Legation had originally taken for its own. The red pillars had been repainted and some of the soot stains removed from the ceiling, but the gold on the ancient rafters had never been touched up. The courtyard outside, spotlessly tidy, was bare of the flowers, trees, caged birds or kongs of goldfish that so many old China hands adopted to transform this strange architecture into a semblance of home.

The Senior Translator jerked to his feet and flung his pen down on the desk. 'They would if you'd do your job instead of swanning around the hills chasing ghost stories!'

'The job you gave me is to clear your son,' Asher returned calmly. 'Part of that process is to find out who would want to implicate Rick in so hideous a crime, and in order to learn *who*, one has to ask *why*.'

'*Why*?' It was a fair imitation of someone who didn't understand what Asher was talking about, but Asher could see fear widen Hobart's eyes. The harsh voice stammered a little: 'What d'you mean, *why*?' Then he waved his arms, raised his voice to a shout. 'You can't tell *why* a Chinese will do anything, you bloody imbecile! They don't think like we do! This is a people who believe magic headbands will make them invulnerable to bullets, for God's sake! Who believe their dead ancestors will arrange favors for them from the afterlife!'

'I suggest you attend a spiritualist seance in any corner of London,' said Asher, 'if you want to see people having conversations with their dead ancestors. And talk to the French High Command if you want to hear about how military elan is going to trump German machine guns. Police work is police work whether you're in Peking or London, and unless one or the other of us can come up with a specific reason why some particular Chinese would want to see your son hang for murder, what a London judge is going to see is your son's tie around the throat of a girl who was forcing him into a marriage he didn't want.'

Hobart opened his mouth to shout something further, but Asher held his eyes, familiar with his temper from those months of tutoring. Determined not to lose his fifty pounds – and with it, all chance of completing his studies – Asher had dodged thrown books, sidestepped physical violence, and plowed head-down through a near-constant deluge of profanity. The curious thing had been that in his calmer moments, Hobart didn't seem to recall clearly what he had said or done. He'd excuse himself in the most general of terms – *that's just my way, you know* . . .

Was strangling a fourteen-year-old girl in the bedclothes while you sodomized her '*just my way*' as well?

'You know Eddington isn't going to be satisfied with "it must have been some Chinese".' But unspoken between them hung the words *YOU tell ME why the Chinese want to see your son hang*.

Or why they want YOU to see your son hang.

Hobart cleared his throat. Blotches of red stood out on his cheekbones, like badly applied rouge. 'You're right, of course.' He sat again at his desk. 'Problem is, you can't tell – no white man can – which of those Chinks is working for which tong or gang or Triad or family or for the bloody Kuo Min-tang. Sure, they may give you some story about . . . oh, I don't know, revenge or protecting someone or . . . or family honor . . . But how can you tell it's true? The only thing I'm asking you to do is find some kind of hard evidence – something a judge will believe – that it wasn't and couldn't have been Rick. It doesn't have to be the truth—'

He waved impatiently when Asher opened his mouth to speak.

'Just do *something*, understand? And don't waste your time with the Chinese.'

Asher had heard that tone any number of times from his superiors in the Department, upon those occasions that he'd asked for permission to look into what had later turned out to be some murky Departmental jiggery-pokery. He knew he wasn't going to get any further.

'And it isn't my business,' he said to Lydia later, holding Miranda in a corral formed by his legs while Lydia sorted through the pile of notes – execrably translated – that Count Mizukami had had sent over that afternoon from the Peking police department. Arranged in neat stacks on the parlor's marble-topped table, they concerned all cases of disappearances or unexplained deaths in Peking from March – when the last of the 'beheading squads' had finished their post-riot rounds – up through May of that year, which was as far as his clerical staff had gotten to date. And, to date, they had proved nothing except that Peking had too many beggars, too many peasants flocking into the city from an impoverished countryside, and too many criminal gangs waging war upon one another for the police to keep adequate track of.

He went on, 'I honestly don't think Hobart's going to go to the Germans and peach on me. He's a beast – and I suspect, mad nor'nor'west where women are concerned – but my experience of him is that he's never been anything but steadfastly loyal to the Empire.'

'Will you go visit this An Lu T'ang who got Sir Grant his girls for him?'

Asher was silent for a time, while Miranda pulled herself up to an unsteady standing position, clinging to his knee. 'I don't know. Ten to one if I acquired proof of Hobart's activities, it still wouldn't clear Richard. I'd only be told to shut up and sit down by Sir John Jordan. Not because he thinks Hobart has the right to give rough handling to Chinese girls, but in the interests of diplomatic respectability. To say nothing of the fact that Hobart probably isn't An Lu T'ang's only customer in the Legation quarter.'

Lydia made a face. 'But you can't let the boy be punished. And you can't leave Hobart at large.'

'I won't.' He heard his own voice say the words, with a slight sensation of surprise at how completely he meant them.

'Do you think Richard knows about his father?'

'I'd bet almost anything I own that he doesn't. Why would he? *How* would he?' Asher disengaged Miranda's small fingers from his watch chain and dug in his pocket for a copper Chinese coin. 'Hobart came out to China in 1884 and went home just long enough to court, marry, and inseminate Julia Bunch. He left England three weeks after Richard was born and returned once every five years thereafter. Much of that time the boy would have been at school. I'd be surprised if Richard has spoken to his father above fifty times in his life.'

About as many times as I spoke to my own, he reflected, with a wry regret that wasn't precisely sadness. It was the way most people he knew had been raised. Presumably, if his father had known he and his wife were both going to die while their only son was thirteen years old he'd have made a greater effort to spend more time with him, if only to more firmly inculcate into him the vital importance of not letting down the standards expected of the Better Classes, and the paramount necessity of knowing all the Right People in order to further one's career.

That pedantic, fastidious scholar – whom Asher still thought of as 'old', though he'd been just forty at the time of the accident – could have secretly been Jack the Ripper or the King of the Cannibal Islands when he'd go 'up to Oxford' or 'down to London' from Wychford, and no whisper of it would have reached his children's ears.

All those children he saw in the *hutongs*, who darted in and out of courtyards full of laundry and goldfish and uncles and grandmas . . . Asher shook his head, prey again to that curious sense of visiting another planet.

'Do you think Hobart will make some other kind of trouble for you?'

'I hope he's not that much of a fool.' He held the coin between his fingers, made it vanish, and sat gravely while Miranda investigated every finger separately and probed with her tiny hand down his cuff. 'If he takes it into his head that *I* might peach on *him*, he may try to do something that will get me thrown out of China – hence the thirty pounds hidden in the generator room. I might have to go lie doggo at Wu's.'

'I knew I should have married Viscount Brightwell's son.'

'You're the one who insisted on coming to China . . .'

At that point Karlebach knocked on the suite door, bundled in his long old-fashioned coat and bearing a satchel which contained a dark lantern, branches of wolfsbane and hawthorn, and a dozen of vials of his arcane potions. Over his shoulder he carried the discreet case of his new shotgun, and his pockets rattled with ammunition.

Asher glanced at the clock. A little past four. In an hour it would be dark.

Ito would be waking up.

'If this samurai does not flee there tonight,' Karlebach asked as they crossed the lobby to the hotel's front doors, 'might this Japanese – or your own ambassador – gain us entry to the old palace pleasure-grounds around the – what are they called?'

'The Golden Sea,' Asher replied. 'President Yuan's taken over that whole enclosure for his own palace, so I doubt his guards will look with favor on two *ch'ang pi kwei* wandering around peering into grottos with a shotgun. But by the same token, they'd probably kill – or try to kill – any *yao-kuei* they saw . . .'

'If they don't try to hire them,' said Karlebach grimly.

'In any case, didn't you say that the Others – at least in Prague – avoid lights and people? Right now Lydia is concentrating her research around the "Stone Relics of the Sea" – the two lakes that lie to the north of the enclosure. They're open to the public, but many of the temples and tea houses around them have been deserted since the Revolution.'

'It would be worth my time to visit them, while you finish making your map of the Shi'h Liu mine.' Karlebach reached back to touch the leather-wrapped shotgun with the affection of a lover. 'How much longer until you have enough of a map for us to go down and find where these things sleep?'

'*If* they sleep as vampires sleep,' corrected Asher. 'We don't know that they won't wake up the moment they hear us coming – or *feel* us coming, as the vampires feel the living, even in their sleep.'

And if the *yao-kuei* had taken up some kind of residence near Peking's lakes, reflected Asher as the two rickshaws spun their way toward the rear gate of the Japanese Legation, what would the vampires of Peking make of that? Always supposing that the Magistrates of Hell weren't behind these creatures to begin with.

He folded his hands within their gloves, watched the shop-keepers lighting the first lanterns of the evening against the autumn's early twilight. *Their presence hangs in the air like smoke* . . .

And fear of them had driven the old Jesuit vampire to hide underground for nearly three hundred years.

Asher and Karlebach left their rickshaws at the rear gate of the Japanese compound on Rue Lagrené, followed the narrow line of neat brick bungalows: a tribute to the determination of the Japanese to become a Western power rather than be subjugated and chewed up piecemeal as China had been. The dwellings of its diplomats and attachés had nothing in them of the horizontal architecture and encircling verandas of Japan. They could have been imported whole from London or Berlin or Paris, like the solid walnut chairs that decorated Count Mizukami's parlor. Electric light streamed from sash windows; men in royal-blue uniforms, or the discreet gray or black mufti of European suits, climbed front steps, knocked at doors . . .

'Something's wrong,' said Asher.

Karlebach looked around him, then counted the bungalows and realized that all those officers, all those officials, were going to, or coming from, the fifth dwelling along the little street.

Count Mizukami's.

No sign of haste, or panic. Yet when Asher and Karlebach

arrived, it was to find the wall of the foyer lined two-deep with shoes, and when a servant conducted them to that blandly Western parlor, Asher saw the little shrine to the left of the door was closed and covered over with white paper. 'Someone has died,' he said.

His glance sought Mizukami, standing in a small group near the inner door into the rest of the house. Like a sturdy elf in his black suit, the attaché exchanged bows with the men who crowded around him. All Japanese, Asher noted.

Not someone whose death would be noted in the other Legations.

Karlebach's eyes widened with horror as he guessed whose death it must be. 'Then they do pass through death,' he whispered, 'they are indeed more like the vampire than we had thought. Will this Count of yours understand, do you think, if we tell him that we must see this man's body? We must cut the head off quickly and stake the heart—'

Asher gestured to him for quiet. Together, they made their way through the crowd to the Emperor's military attaché, and when he turned to them and bowed, Asher asked, 'Was it Ito-san, sir?'

'It was.' The Count's coffee-black eyes met Asher's, steady and deeply sad. 'The physical effects of his illness were more than his body could bear. He died a little before sunset.'

'I am deeply sorry to hear it. We owed him our lives, and it grieves me, beyond what I can say, to realize that our lives were bought at the cost of his own.'

'He was samurai,' replied Mizukami. 'He understood that it was his duty.'

'If you will excuse us, Count,' put in Karlebach in an urgent whisper. 'It is necessary – vitally so – that we be permitted to see the body. The head at least should be severed, lest—'

'It is custom,' returned the Count, folding his hands before him, 'that when a man commits *seppuku*, the friend who assists him onward severs the head. You need have no concern for that. I have made arrangements for Ito-san's body to be burned tomorrow, and his ashes will be sent back to his family in Ogachi.'

When Karlebach's brow grew thunderous – Asher could almost hear him demanding: how they would locate *yao-kuei* in the city now? – the Count went on, 'Some here in the Legation knew that he was ill, and I have put it about that it was of his illness that he died. He made a good end. A samurai's end, with courage and honor.'

Asher murmured in Czech to the furious old man beside him, 'What would you have done, sir?'

Ysidro had a point, he reflected, about the Van Helsings of the world.

They walked back to the Wagons-Lits Hotel through the early darkness. 'Ito's family had served the Mizukami for three centuries,' said Asher, and he drew his brown ulster more closely about him. His breath smoked in the light that fell through the gateway – massive and slightly absurd – of the French Legation. 'Of course the Count would assist him.'

He glanced across the street, with the casual air of one whose attention has been flagged by the cries of the old woman selling cricket cages on the other side of Legation Street, but didn't break stride. Nor did he see whatever it was – half-familiar flash of color or style of movement, a face he'd glimpsed somewhere before? – that had touched that old part of his soul, the part which had kept him alive in Berlin and Belgrade and Istanbul . . .

But his whole being – every instinct he possessed – shouted at him: *Run now and run fast. You're being followed.*

DAMN it.

And of course there was nothing behind them, or anyway nothing that looked dangerous. Too many shadows, the electric glow from the more modern buildings bright against the older softness of paper-lantern-light. A couple of rickshaws spun by; a little group of home-going Chinese – servants, presumably, but who could tell?; and three American soldiers striding along arm-in-arm singing 'Marching Through Georgia':

Hurrah, hurrah, we bring the jubilee,
Hurrah, hurrah, the flag that makes you free . . .

Had someone run across the street behind him, seeking cover in the doorway of the Chinese post-office, or behind the gateway of the German Legation? Had he half-recognized one of the peddlers? Or one of the German soldiers on the other side of the street? Someone who'd turned around after passing him and was now coming back the other direction? He didn't know, and being seen examining his surroundings would only make the situation worse. *They made one mistake. If they're not put on their guard they'll sooner or later make another.*

Unless, of course, they plan to do something about me tonight.

He didn't even know who 'they' were. *Abroad* one often hadn't the slightest idea.

Mentally, he mapped escape routes. A vampire wouldn't let himself be seen, unless it was a new-made fledgeling, or a vampire who had been starved for a sufficiently long time as to be losing his powers of concealment. If it was the Germans – or just possibly the Austrians, though he hadn't seen anyone he recognized from the Auswärtiges Amt here – it might only be a preliminary observation. *I've been around the Legation for over a week now. Anyone who wanted to find me, could . . .*

I'll have to tell Karlebach to make some kind of arrangement for Lydia . . .

IS old Wu still on Pig-Dragon Lane?

Windows, coal chutes, storerooms at the hotel . . . There was a kitchen service-door that opened into an areaway on Rue Meiji, about a hundred yards from the watergate that led out into the Chinese city.

Asher ascended the shallow steps of the hotel with a sense of relief. Karlebach had been haranguing him since they'd passed the French Legation on the subject of their next expedition to the Western Hills, and he'd barely heard a word. 'Once we get the other entrances to the mine blocked, we should be able to go in by daylight. The main thing is to locate where they sleep and—'

Karlebach broke off to return the greeting of the English doorman, and Asher crossed the lobby to the desk for messages. A gentleman who'd been reading *The Times* in one of the lobby's deep chairs got up, and Asher instinctively turned. Another, standing at the desk, advanced on him.

Here it comes . . .

The man who'd been reading *The Times* made his mistake. He addressed Asher before his confederate got within grabbing distance.

'Professor Asher?' *Sussex. A European's English would-be Oxonian . . .* 'The name is Timms. I'm from the Legation Police. There's been a most serious allegation brought against you, for selling information to the German Legation.'

Asher said, with a slight note of surprise, 'That's ridiculous.' He gestured – *wait just a moment, I won't make trouble* – and moved as if to go say something to Karlebach . . .

Then cut swiftly to the right, dashed for the windows that overlooked Rue Meiji, toppled a chair in the startled Timms's path, opened the window, and dropped through into the darkness.

He was pleased to see he'd calculated precisely; he was within a yard of the areaway to the kitchen. All the windows on that side were curtained against the icy night. He was stripping off his overcoat even as he sprang lightly over the railings, stepped back into the hotel and crossed the kitchen, overcoat slung over his arm – 'I'm here about the generator,' he explained to the one person who even gave him a glance in the bustle of preparing dinner – then walked straight to the doorway that led to the generator-room hall, stopped long enough to pick up his money, and climbed the service stair to the roof.

They'd assume he'd run straight for the watergate – it was a hundred yards from the window he'd escaped through – and would probably send a man up to watch Lydia's room just in case.

Hobart. His feet sought the risers of the stair as he climbed, silent, up fifty-six steps in the dark. Possibly the Germans – old Eichorn might have recognized him after all – but the Germans were hardly likely to accuse him of selling information to them-selves. *Mizukami* . . .? His instinct told him that the Japanese attaché was a man to be trusted, which of course might mean nothing. Vampires weren't the only ones who buttered their bread by getting people to believe them.

But Hobart had every good reason to want him deported quickly and a closet that fairly rattled with skeletons.

At this time of the evening, every room on the floor relegated to the personal valets and maids of the guests was deserted. Above that was the attic, pitch-black and crammed with trunks: the smell of dust as he came up the narrow stair was suffocating. A bare slit of a hall, a dozen small rooms, each labeled with the number of the floor to which the luggage within belonged – he'd identified the location of the light switch on an earlier reconnais-sance, but knew better than to give his position away by using it. From his overcoat pocket he took the candle he'd brought to go *yao-kuei* hunting with, lit it, and made his way to the ladder at the end of the hall which led to the roof.

By the light of the waning moon, Asher strode along the hotel's low parapet till he found a fire-ladder. The roof of the Banque Franco-Chinoise lay two floors below. The Chinese houses that had been here in 1898 had mostly been destroyed in the Uprising, and had been replaced by modern buildings with modern iron fire-escapes. A narrow alley separated the Franco-Chinoise Bank from the old Hong Kong bank – one of the few older buildings on the street still standing – and the fire-ladder came down almost at the alley's end. Still holding his ulster over one arm, its gray lining turned outward to foil the obvious question – *did you see a man in a brown overcoat . . .?* – he checked to make sure he had his pass for the city gates, walked up the alley, and found a rank of rickshaws, as usual, in front of Kierulf's Store.

'Silk Lane,' he said.

THIRTEEN

'They said Jamie was *what*?' Lydia stared in disbelief from Karlebach to the bulky tweed shape who had introduced himself as Mr Timms of the Legation police.

'No one's said anything, ma'am, begging your pardon,' corrected Timms stiffly. 'Mr Asher was alleged to be selling information to the German Legation—'

'Alleged by whom?' She got to her feet and stepped closer to her visitors, though she'd have had to stand on the policeman's toes to see his face clearly. She had an impression of saggy blue jowls and pomaded hair the color of coffee with not quite enough milk in it. 'And what sort of information could Jamie possibly learn in *Peking*? Troop dispositions on the parade ground?'

'The specifics of the charge aren't my business, ma'am. But he sure-lye had something on his conscience, the way he took to his heels.'

'That's preposterous.' She opened her mouth to add *Jamie would NEVER admit to the Germans, of all people, that he was a spy* . . . and realized this information probably wouldn't help the situation. Instead she let her eyes fill with tears and sank into the nearest chair, from which she stared up helplessly at the two men. 'Oh, who can have invented such a lie?'

Her stepmother, she reflected, couldn't have played the scene better.

Well, actually, she probably could.

'We'd hoped, ma'am—' Timms's voice wavered in its gruffness.

Good, I've shaken him . . .

'—that you'd have no objection to letting us search these rooms.'

Since Lydia knew that Jamie never wrote anything down except notes on linguistic tonalities and verb forms, she buried her face in her palms, nodded, and let out a single, bravely-suppressed sob. Had Karlebach been any sort of actor he'd have taken that as his cue to fly to her side and execrate poor Timms as a beast and a brute – increasing his anxiety to leave quickly and cutting down the number of things he was likely to notice in the suite – but the Professor only stammered, 'Here, Madame—'

It was Ellen who flew to her side. She must have been listening at the nursery door.

'Don't you *dare* set a foot in these rooms!' The maid brandished Miranda's damp bath-sponge under the man's nose. 'Not without a warrant, properly sworn by a judge, which I wager you *don't* have—'

'It's all right,' whispered Lydia. *We have nothing to hide* would undoubtedly create a better impression than: *Where's your warrant?* 'Would you please show the gentleman around, Ellen? And . . . and fetch me some water—'

She was pleased to note that Miranda, usually the most equable of babies, burst into howls the moment Timms opened the nursery door.

As the door shut behind Timms, Lydia got to her feet, gathered up the police notes, and handed them to Karlebach. 'I'll be quite all right,' she whispered and steered him into the hallway. *No sense having them confiscated . . .* Then, sorely puzzled and more than a little frightened, she walked to the window and stood, listening to Ellen scolding, Mrs Pilley having hysterics, and Miranda shrieking, and gazed out into the darkness of the alien

night. And wondered what there was for her to do, besides wait
for word.

Asher had intended to switch rickshaws at Silk Lane, but didn't
make it that far.

He heard the man at the side of the Hsi Chu Shih – one of
the main streets through the Chinese City – call out to his puller,
but didn't understand the words he used: Hakka or Cantonese or
one of the other dozen Chinese 'dialects' that weren't dialects
at all, but separate languages. So he was ready – almost – when
the puller turned from the wide avenue into a narrower *hutong*,
of gray walls and deep-set gateways, and from there into an
alleyway barely five feet wide, stinking of fish heads and human
waste. He called out, '*T'ing!*' – *Stop!* – but the puller kept going,
and at that point Asher slipped his knife from his boot and his
revolver from his jacket pocket, leaped out of the rickshaw, put
his back to the wall, and got ready for a fight.

Men had been waiting on either side of the alley, just within
its mouth. How many, he wasn't sure at first, for only the barest
whisper of lantern-light leaked through from the *hutong*. The
puller, the moment he felt Asher jump clear, dashed around
the corner deeper into the alleyway, taking the rickshaw and
its lantern with him: Asher spared a curse for him but didn't
really blame him. Faced with the prospect of being accidentally
murdered in the course of an affray that had nothing to do
with him, he suspected he'd run, too. He guessed more than
actually saw the shadows of two men blocking the mouth of
the alleyway where it ran into the *hutong*, and fired at them,
more to let them know he had a gun than in the hopes of hitting
either one. Then he ran for the alley mouth with all the speed
he could muster, hoping fear of another shot would keep them
back.

It didn't. His legs collided with something in the blackness,
and as he staggered, trying to catch his balance, he heard the
whistle of what he guessed was the Asian version of a blackjack.
Something clipped his shoulder with numbing force, knocked
him off-balance – *a flail*, he thought, tried to get up, and then
they were on him. He kicked, twisted as someone tried to grab
his head, slashed with his knife, nearly blind in the darkness.
Twisted again, and the flail – two short oak sticks joined in the

middle by chain – hit hard against his back. Someone had his wrist, wrenched at the gun in his hand—

Then let go, very suddenly.

He smelled blood. A lot of it. And the voided waste of a dying man.

One of his attackers cried out, and Asher scrambled free of the melee.

Feet pattered frantically. His eyes had adjusted to the darkness enough to see two men's forms flee up the alleyway and away. Darkness still hid nearly everything in the narrow space, but he glimpsed a pale glimmer of colorless face, colorless hair, just where the fight would have taken place, like a misty glimmer of wraith-light.

A soft voice remarked from the darkness, 'I did not think you were acquainted with any Chinese, James.'

Asher leaned against the wall, shaking. His shoulder throbbed as if it had been broken. He'd seen men who'd been beaten with rice flails and guessed how near he had come to death.

'Have these gentlemen anything to do with your attempted arrest?' The vampire was next to him, with the eerie suddenness of encounters in a dream. Asher could smell blood on his clothes. 'Or have you two separate sets of foes?' Ysidro took his hand, pressed the flail into it, and Asher transferred it to his greatcoat pocket.

'Can the rickshaw-puller be trusted?' Ysidro said, then handed him his knife, which he'd lost in the fight, and steered him back toward the *hutong* and – a few yards further – toward the lanterns and clamor of the Hsi Chu Shih. 'It's a dead-end alley. He's crouched at the farthest corner of it. Or shall we hire another?'

'I'll hire another.' Asher was a little surprised at the steadiness of his own voice. 'I'm not sure I could find my way to Pig-Dragon Lane on my own, and my friend back there –' he nodded behind him, down the alley – 'would tell the gang he works for where I am.'

'Here.' Ysidro halted a few yards short of the end of the *hutong*, where its shadows would still hide them, and held out to Asher a worn and rather dirty blue cotton *ch'i-p'ao*, taken, Asher knew, from one of the dead men they'd left behind. Without a word, he transferred the contents of his ulster and jacket to the pockets of his trousers, then stripped off the outer garments and donned the long, quilted coat. There was a black cotton cap in one of the pockets, and this he also put on.

'What lies in Pig-Dragon Lane?' Ysidro took the discarded clothing over one arm. 'And what, if I may so inquire, is a Pig-Dragon?'

'It's a creature that supposedly lived beneath some of the bridges of Peking.' The dead man had been nearly Asher's height and burly for a Chinese, to judge by the way the quilted garment hung on him. 'In Pig-Dragon Lane I hope to find a man who'll offer me safe lodging and tell me which gang it is that's after me, and why. I think they followed me from Mizukami's this evening.' He double-checked his pockets, slipped the knife back into his boot. 'Whether this has anything to do with my questions about who to go to if one's tastes are unorthodox, or—'

Ysidro turned his head sharply, a movement so out of character with him that Asher thought, *I wasn't the only one who felt himself followed* . . .

'What is it?'

'Naught.' But the vampire's yellow gaze quested sidelong, giving his words the lie, and it occurred to Asher that his companion had not fed upon the men he'd killed.

Dared not.

He laid a hand on the jacket and coat, felt the skeletal arm beneath. 'Might I impose on you to smear these in blood and dispose of them in such a fashion that whoever is after me – whether it's Hobart or Mizukami or the Germans or the Austrians or Uncle Tom Cobbley and all – will be reasonably sure I've come to a bad end? Nothing discourages pursuit like proof of one's demise.'

A flicker of a smile touched the vampire's eyes. 'Two hearts with but a single thought.'

'And would you tell Lydia that I'm well? Tell her also that she's not to let anyone – not Ellen, not Professor Karlebach, no one – know that she knows it. She must convince whoever is watching her – waiting for me – that I'm dead.'

'I will tell her. You do not trust the good Professor?' The flex in Ysidro's tone would have been a raised eyebrow, a cocked head in another man.

'Not as an actor.' They stepped out into the Hsi Chu Shih; it was the gesture of a moment to signal a rickshaw. 'I'm sorry to do this to him,' he added. 'And to Ellen. I know they will grieve. But Hobart wouldn't try to have me killed. This is someone else – something else. And it's beginning to look to me like someone doesn't want me poking around at the Shi'h Liu mine.'

'I will bear your words in mind.' The vampire stepped back as Asher sprang up into the rickshaw. 'And I trust you will not have the bad taste to request me to keep these same assassins from murdering the good Professor Karlebach.'

Asher laughed. 'I wouldn't ask it of you, Don Simon. But I will ask that you warn them. And that you look after Lydia.'

What a lunatic thing to say to a vampire, reflected Asher as the puller picked up his poles. *To a man who has for three hundred and fifty years prolonged his own life by killing others . . .*

Yet when Ysidro inclined his head and murmured, 'Such has always been my endeavor,' Asher felt not the slightest fear or doubt that the life of his wife – and of his baby daughter – was safe in the vampire's hands.

The rickshaw slipped into motion. When Asher glanced back, Ysidro was gone, as if he had never been.

No wonder Karlebach doesn't trust me.

When Lydia was ten years old her mother had died, after a lingering illness. She'd been sent to live with her Aunt Faith, who, among the five sisters, had been closest in age and temperament to her mother, and a concerted effort was made to 'protect' her from all knowledge of the disease that was ravaging her mother's body. Driven nearly to distraction by the sugary untruths, the smiling euphemisms and blatant attempts to divert her mind from 'unpleasantness' (*do they really think taking me to the pantomime is going to make me stop wondering what's HAPPENING to Mother?*), Lydia had finally slipped out of the house in the early hours of the morning and walked the two miles to her father's town house in Russell Square, to find the place closed up and her parents gone.

In real life she'd returned home in time to retrieve and tear up the note she'd left before her Nanna had found it – Nanna had very strict ideas about discipline for rebellious little girls. In her dream tonight, in the strange cold bed in the Wagons-Lits Hotel in Peking, she had somehow gotten into the house and was

moving through its shuttered rooms, as she always wandered in
the recurring dreams that had begun after that day. The parlor
with its ultra-fashionable gilt-touched wallpaper and Japanoiserie
– even the smell of the potpourri was the same. Her mother's
bedroom, the pillows on the quasi-Moorish bed – all the rage
that year – an undisturbed blue and crimson mountain, as if her
mother had never lain there. The stillness, in which her own
stealthy tread on the carpets made a distinct silvery crunch.

Sometimes in her dreams she was alone in the house.
Sometimes she knew her parents were there somewhere, only
she couldn't find them.

In her dream tonight someone else was there.

Someone she had never met. Someone terrible, and old, and
cold as the darkness between the stars. Someone she couldn't
see, but who listened to her breathing and smelled the blood in
her veins.

He knew her name.

Frightened, Lydia tried to find her way downstairs again – in
her dream she'd picked the lock on the kitchen door, though
in fact she hadn't learned to pick locks until James had taught
her, at the age of fifteen . . . But the rooms kept changing. She
went through the spartan chamber she'd shared with that frightful
German girl the first year she'd attended Madame Chappedelaine's
Select Academy in Switzerland, whatever her name had been –
Gretchen? Gretel? *How did I get here?* But there was Lake Como
outside the window, shining in the moonlight . . . Only, when
she opened the door there wasn't the hall outside, but the Temple
of Everlasting Harmony, with an endlessly long line of statues
stretching away into the gloom. The Magistrates of Hell: only,
some of them weren't statues, but followed her with eyes that
reflected the single candle-glow like cats'.

She picked up her skirts and hurried, hurried, knowing
somehow that in some finite span of time they'd be able to move
and would come after her . . .

She stumbled through the garden door beside the altar, which
opened into the upstairs parlor of her own house on Holywell
Street in Oxford.

Ysidro was sitting at Jamie's desk. 'Mistress,' he said.

Lydia woke. The oil lamp that illuminated the bedroom still
burned. By its amber glow she saw the litter of books and

magazines that strewed the blue-and-white counterpane around
her. The curtains of the window opposite the bed billowed and
stirred, to the discontented threnody of desert wind. The air
smelled of dust.

She found her glasses, got to her feet, wrapped herself in her
robe – the bedroom was freezing, Heaven only knew what time
it was – and, as she crossed the room, she made an effort to find
enough hairpins still in the thick red braid of her hair to fix it
up into a knot again. As surely as she knew her own name, she
knew who would be in the parlor.

And he was.

'Mistress.' Don Simon Ysidro rose from the chair beside the
hearth, inclined his head.

Lydia stood still in the doorway. *You knew he was in Peking*,
she reminded herself. And there was nothing between them, *could*
be nothing between them. Could never be anything between the
living and the dead.

Except there was.

'Simon.'

He'd built up the fire. Just minutes ago, to judge by the way
it was burning and the chill that still gripped the room. His fingers,
when he took her hand to guide her to the other hearth-side chair,
were cold as marble, but without the mollience of the dead
flesh with which Lydia was familiar from the dissecting rooms
of the Infirmary. She could not keep herself from noting he had
the drawn look that he did when he hadn't fed in many nights.

She fought the impulse to hold his fingers as they slipped from
hers.

'James instructed me to tell you that he is well.'

She took a deep breath, let it out. *He is what he is.* Held her
hands to the fire. They didn't shake. Part of her was aware of
him, wildly and completely, and yet . . . *It's only Simon.* 'You've
seen him?'

'I followed his rickshaw to a place in the Chinese City which
rejoices in the name of Pig-Dragon Lane.' The firelight traced
the aquiline curve of his nose, the shape of his cheekbones; gave
a warm counterfeit of human coloration to his flesh. 'I lingered
only long enough to assure myself that the man with whom he
sought refuge did indeed admit him, and did not murder him out
of hand. I dared not tarry.'

His head tilted a little, listening for something: a very slight distance in his eyes. Even at this hour, echoes of passers-by and rickshaw bells drifted from beyond the high city wall.

'He made it safely, then?'

'Not entirely. He was set upon by Chinese assassins, sent – he is well, I assure you, Madame – sent, he believes, not by this Hobart, whose tiresome son may rot in prison for all I care, but by those who would rather he did not interfere with events at the Shi'h Liu Mine. He is unharmed,' he reiterated, seeing the look on her face. 'Bruises only. Yet whether those behind the attempt are German or Chinese or – I may add – Japanese, I know not, and neither does he.'

'Is he still in danger?'

'He will be, should he be discovered. Thus he bade me arrange it that his bloodstained clothing be found tomorrow, and that word go out that he is dead. His hope – and in this I believe he is wise – is to go to ground until he can learn who it is who pursues him. Thus he asks of you, Mistress, that you make a great outcry that you know in your heart that he is dead. Can you do this?'

She nodded, chilled inside. *What if I do it wrong—?*

The strange eyes regarded her, gauged her; then he smiled and took her hand again. 'Good,' he said. 'Karlebach is not to know, he says, nor your maid nor any others whosoever they may be.'

'It will break the old man's heart!' exclaimed Lydia, though she knew absolutely that her husband was right. 'He loves Jamie like a son. And coming on top of the loss of his friend Matthias – it's a horrible thing to do to him. But it's true,' she added sadly, 'that he's a dreadful actor. Nobody would believe him for a minute, if he didn't really think it was so. And he can't do what a woman can, and just cover up in veils and stay indoors – oh, dear, I suppose this means I'll have to go into mourning. I wonder where one can purchase . . .? They hired *assassins*?'

'The blood that will be on his coat and jacket when they're dragged from the old palace lake is theirs. Your husband is a doughty fighter.' The smallest flicker of a smile touched one corner of his lips, a human expression, rueful. 'More so than ever I was in life.'

'Did you get in duels?' Lydia tried to picture him as he had been then, before a variant strain of the vampire state had bleached

the color from his eyes and hair, before long years of concealment and observation had taught him their dreadful lessons about
the nature of humankind. The scars on his face and throat, left
by the claws of the master of Constantinople, after three years
were as ghastly as ever, though he had spoken to her once of
having been burned by sunlight and having healed. 'I'm sorry,'
she added quickly. 'It's none of my business—'

'As a Spaniard and a Catholic in England, I could scarce help
it. And like a fool I thought t'was my right to walk where I chose
in London. I look upon myself in those days and wonder that I
lived to be taken by the Undead.'

Lydia was silent, studying his face in the firelight, aloof as
the image on a tomb. What had he looked like, she wondered,
as a living man? That rush of consciousness of his presence had
passed, and what she felt toward him now mostly was comfort,
and trust. 'Can you take a message to him?'

'I will if you ask it of me, Mistress.' Ysidro got to his feet,
gathered his long greatcoat from the back of the nearby chair.
'Yet my every instinct tells me that to step outside the Legation
Quarter is to step beneath the hanging blade of a sword. The
vampires of Peking watch me, invisible; even within its walls I
am not safe. You would laugh, I dare say, to see me tiptoe like
a thief from the watergate to the train station, to hunt in peasant
villages with unpronounceable names, in terror lest I miss my
way back before daylight.'

'Well,' pointed out Lydia practically, 'it *does* serve you right.'

'Indeed it does.' The cold, thin fingers closed around hers.
'Father Orsino – the Spanish priest – passed three centuries in
the Shi'h Liu Mine in composing a refutation of Luther's teach-
ings, which he begs me to collect for him from his hideaway
there, that he may take it back to the Pope, to whom it is dedicated . . . truly a frightful thought, when one considers how long
it must be by this time.'

'Are you going to the mine?' she asked, and she shivered at
the recollection of what Jamie had told her of the things that had
attacked him. At the memory of Ito's bruised and swollen face.
They whisper in my mind . . .

'I shall at least draw close enough to see what may be seen.
At the moment what we most lack of these Others is information:
their numbers, their movements, the shape and nature of their

minds. Your husband is not the only one who has worked for his country in this fashion, Mistress, and from the first, when I read of these creatures, it crossed my mind that there may be things of them that only the Dead can learn.'

The words *be careful* stuck in her throat. *I CANNOT ask him to take care, since he'll probably conclude his investigation by murdering some perfectly innocent person.*

And she felt overwhelmed again by the despairing knowledge that Ysidro was right. There could be no friendship between the living and the dead.

Not as long as the dead chose to prolong their stay on Earth by taking the lives of others.

Yet when her eyes met his, and saw in the pleated yellow depths that he was familiar with all those thoughts, her heart ached for him.

He bowed and kissed her hand. Cold lips like white silk, which covered killing fangs. The clock on the velvet-draped overmantle chimed, four sweet notes.

'To wake you thus each night were little kindness, Mistress. Therefore leave one curtain of your bedroom window open when it grows dark, if conference is required.'

Lydia felt the touch of his mind on hers, a crushing velvet sleepiness, and tightened her grip on his skinny fingers. 'Did you come in my dream? Not about being in this room, I mean, but in Papa's house?'

The weight of sleep withdrew. His colorless brows knit very slightly: 'The house of your father?'

'After Mother died,' whispered Lydia. 'I was trapped there, looking for her from room to room. I often dream that. But this time there was someone – something – in the house with me.'

'No,' said the vampire softly. 'That was not me.'

FOURTEEN

Wu Tan Shun – a little fatter and a little more gray than he'd been in 1898 – welcomed Asher, took his money, and guided him through a maze of courtyards strung with washing and crammed with pigsties and pigeon cages, barely visible by the faint orange lamp-glow that leaked through shuttered windows, to a *siheyuan* in a far corner of the rambling compound, its buildings drifted with dust and littered with broken roof-tiles. He was given a couple of US Army blankets, and the following morning a young man – possibly an inhabitant of one of the other courtyards – came in and left a pail of water, a bowl of rice and vegetables, Chinese trousers and shoes, and hurried away without even looking around. In the course of the day Asher investigated the other buildings around his own particular courtyard and of those nearby and collected a brazier, two buckets of coal balls – coal dust mixed with hardened mud – and a couple of straw mats. In the process he found that Wu had guaranteed his concealment simply by paying everyone in the other courtyards to give him what he asked while ignoring him completely.

It wasn't the Hotel Wagons-Lits, but Asher had no complaints.

On the second evening, as he was consuming the supper that had been brought to him – still without a word or a glance – by another man who looked like an impoverished farmer, a Chinese girl came around the screen wall into the courtyard, glanced around at the ruined buildings, then crossed to the doorway where Asher sat.

'Honorable sir cold?' she inquired when she reached him. 'Extra blanket?' she added and started to remove her *ch'i-p'ao.*

Asher got to his feet – he'd been expecting something along these lines, knowing Wu – and took the girl's hands, halting the disrobing process. '*Pu yao, hsieh-hsieh,*' he said and inclined his head in thanks. 'I most grateful, but honorable father of my wife forbidden me have congress other ladies during hiding. Can not dishonor his request.'

The girl – Asher guessed her age at seventeen or eighteen – smiled dazzlingly to hear him speak Chinese and bowed. 'Is there another service that I can do for the honorable gentleman?' Her voice was startlingly deep for a girl's, her Chinese the Peking dialect and somewhat removed from Mandarin, but at least, Asher reflected, intelligible. 'If I do nothing and go straight home,' she explained when he shook his head, 'my husband's mother will be displeased, because Mr Wu has paid her already and she'll have to give him the money back. May I *say* I spread for you?'

Asher smiled. 'What tell husband honorable mother not my business,' he replied, and her answering smile widened. 'Tea?' And he gestured toward the extremely pretty celadon pot – which he suspected had been stolen – that had arrived a few minutes previously with the noodles and the soup.

Her eyes brightened as she knelt on the straw mat in the doorway and poured out the first cup: 'This is Grandpa Wu's good *p'o lai*,' she exclaimed. 'He must really like you! You're sure there's nothing I can do for you?'

'Tell me story,' he said and sat cross-legged again on the other mat. 'Tell me about *yao-kuei* by Golden Sea.'

It was a bow drawn at a venture, but he saw dread darken her eyes. 'The Golden Sea? Is that true, then?' she asked worriedly. 'My younger sister's husband says there are devils in the Western Hills – horrible things that stink, which you cannot kill with guns . . . My younger sister's husband is in the Kuo Min-tang, you understand. The leader of his unit says there is no such thing as these devils because we now have science and are breaking free of the imperialist superstitions of the past . . . Are they indeed now in the city?'

'Don't know.' Asher accepted the tea, Green Snail Spring from Tong T'ing. 'You learn for me? Learn, not tell them—' He gestured to the courtyards beyond the wall, then touched his finger to his lips. 'I am not here.'

'I'll ask my brothers. We live only over in Crooked Hair Family Alley. That is, my family lives – my husband's brothers also. Why does the Tso Family want to kill you?'

Asher rubbed his shoulder. 'Tso Family, eh? And what is your honorable name?'

'Ling.' The name meant Good Reputation. 'Ch'iu P'ing Ling. My husband's honored mother is Grandpa Wu's niece.'

'Ling. Not know –' which wasn't quite true, Asher reflected as pieces began to fall into place – 'why Tso want to kill.'

'It isn't like the Tso,' Ling said thoughtfully, 'to go after a Long-Nosed Devil. Even though they're the enemies of the Republic and plot with the vile reactionary Yuan, *nobody* wants your armies back shooting everyone in sight. So you must have done *some*thing.'

She was, Asher guessed, very much a child of the *hutongs* – only an extremely lower-class girl would have escaped having her feet mutilated – and by Chinese standards not particularly pretty, with her long, horse-like face and wiry build. 'But why hide with Grandpa Wu?'

'Fear Tso family has sons, has cousins, work servants in Legation?' suggested Asher. 'Servants kill while sleep?' He made a throat-cutting gesture.

'No, you don't need to worry about that – are you going to eat that dumpling?' She pointed her chin at the one he'd left on his plate. 'The Tso don't have family in the Legations. It's mostly the Wei, the Hsiang, and the K'ung – the old families that have run things for hundreds of years here in Peking – or the families that work for them, like the Shen and the Shen –' there was a different tonal dip there: the one spoken high meant *gentleman*, the other on a descending tone meant *cautious* – 'and the Miao and the P'ei. And the Hsiang all hate the Tso, and the Wei owe too many favors to the Hsiang to go against them, if the Tso tried to sneak anyone in. The Tso only started making themselves a big family twenty years ago, my mother-in-law says: upstarts. Madame Tso gives herself airs now, my mother-in-law says, but her father was only a night-soil collector in the Nine Turns Alley, after all. My mother-in-law says the Tso are paying Yuan Shi-k'ai to try to get their people in, but it hasn't happened yet. You can make a lot of squeeze, working in the Legations.'

'Not during Uprising?' He lifted an eyebrow with a quizzical look, and Ling grinned.

'Not in the Uprising, no. I was only little then, but I remember Grandpa Wu had six or seven whole families of the P'ei hiding in this very courtyard, because the Boxers would have killed them. But of course now Grandpa says that never happened. A lot more hid in the coal mines in the Western Hills,' she added. 'And I never heard any of *them* say there were devils out there.'

'What about girl Ugly English Devil kill in Madame Tso house?' asked Asher casually. 'She was Miao? Or Shen?'

'Shen,' Ling corrected, using a different tone, and her long face clouded. 'You mean Mi Ching? Bi Hsu tells me – my husband's younger brother, who works over in Big Shrimp Alley – Bi Hsu tells me her brothers were nearly distracted with anger when they heard about it. But the family's really poor. When An Lu T'ang offered money for Ching, their father would never have sold her if he'd known what An wanted her for. But An Lu T'ang

works for the Tso, so you can't really say no to him, any more
than you can bring an English Devil to justice, no matter what
he does. This is the kind of exploitation that the Kuo Min-tang
seeks to rectify, but as long as Yuan Shi-k'ai continues to enslave
China to the foreign economic interests, nothing will get done.'

'Shen Mi Ching brothers, servants in Legation?'

'No, but all their cousins are.' Ling licked a final morsel of
dumpling from her fingers. 'Bi Hsu said to my husband that Mi
Ching's brothers should just wait outside Mrs Tso's house for
the next time Ugly English Devil comes for a girl. He goes about
once a week, though usually he just hits them or cuts them. But
Bi Wang – my husband – told him not to be stupid. As long as
our nation is enslaved to Western imperial interests, no justice
will be possible for the people of China, and you can't just kill
an English Devil in the street.'

*Well, not unless he's a traitor selling information to the
Germans*, reflected Asher. Though Ling was clearly parroting the
harangues she'd heard from her sister's husband and his friends,
he saw the sparkle of genuine anger in her face: anger at the
lines of men who'd marched along the Chien Men Ta Chieh in
1901, at the German soldiers who now occupied Shantung, and
at the Japanese who'd taken over Formosa and had their eyes on
Manchuria, with its coal and iron, as well.

He recalled the pockmarked militia commander in the hills,
the ragged men who'd helped themselves to his second-best
greatcoat and the British Army's scrawny Australian horses:
farmers driven from their land by taxes and starvation. Recalled,
too, the sleek young aide Huang Da-feng at Eddington's reception, hobnobbing with the Western officers, with that elegant
madame on his arm. *Runs half the brothels in Peking . . .*

No wonder this girl was angry.

Shen Mi Ching. Hobart probably didn't even know her name.
Asher felt rage at the man pass through him, a slow red wave,
and thought about what he'd arrange for any man who harmed
Miranda, or Lydia – or even his obnoxious, whining, spoiled
nieces and cousins, for God's sake! – if by some happenstance
or turn of events he was unable to prove such a crime on the
perpetrator . . .

And he shivered at the first thought that went through his
mind: *I'd speak to Ysidro.*

He'd do it. And he wouldn't care.

And that, Asher thought, after Ling took her departure and he retreated from the bitter cold of the courtyard to the nearly as cold corner of the *cheng-fang* where he'd installed the brazier and his blankets, *is the true reason Karlebach seeks to destroy the vampire, wherever and however they exist.*

For the sake of the souls of the living whom they do NOT kill.

For the sake of every soul in the world, if the living begin to use the Undead for their own ends outside the law.

Was that the reason Ysidro himself had undertaken the perilous journey to China, when he'd learned of the spread of the Others? It was difficult to tell with Ysidro, for whom the game of mirror and shadow went far deeper than the mere hunt. Was it simply that, as a chess player, the vampire saw ahead to what the governments of the living might do to acquire control of such creatures? Or was there something else?

Don Quixote, Asher found himself remembering, had been a Spaniard, too.

He had hoped Ysidro would visit that night, with word from Lydia, if not word about the Others, or the vampires of Peking. For a long time he lay awake, watching the moonlight where it came through the broken roof; then slid into unremembered dreams.

The hardest thing, Lydia found, was not telling Karlebach and Ellen.

The police found Jamie's blood-soaked coat and jacket in the north-western district of the so-called Tatar City, not far from the shallow lakes locally known as the 'Stone Relics of the Sea', late in the afternoon of Thursday, the thirty-first of October. On the following morning the nude body of a man was found in a nearby canal, so shockingly mutilated that it was impossible to determine even if he had been Oriental or European, though he was of Jamie's six-foot height. Lydia locked herself in her hotel bedroom in a simulated paroxysm of grief and refused to see either the old Professor or her maid for almost twenty-four hours.

She knew they would comfort one another. She couldn't face either one.

Nor could she face the question that kept recurring to her mind: *was the man they'd found already dead, by coincidence*

*and of some other cause? Or did Simon kill him for the purpose,
only because, whoever he was, he was six feet tall?*

And would Simon tell me the truth if I asked him?

Miranda she kept with her for a good deal of that time. She
read to her quietly, played little games with her, and while the
child slept, she continued to work her way through notes from
the Peking Police Department. The last thing her baby needed
was Mrs Pilley's lamentations and tears.

At breakfast the following morning – Saturday – she quietly
requested that Miranda be spared as much of the displays of grief
as possible. 'I'll tell her myself, when she's able to understand,'
she said, firmly, to the old man and the two women of her shattered household. 'But I beg of you, don't burden her with this
now.'

Ellen and Mrs Pilley both hugged her, something Lydia hated.
An hour later the Baroness Drosdrova appeared on the doorstep
with a complete mourning costume – donated by the very fashionable Madame Hautecoeur, the French Trade Minister's wife – a
platter of blinis (Paola had been right about the Drosdrov cook),
two hours of unsolicited legal advice about dealing with the affairs
of a spouse unexpectedly deceased, another forty-five minutes of
anecdotes concerning the various bereavements of everyone in the
Drosdrov family including Aunt Eirena whose husband had fallen
into a reaping-combine on a visit to the United States, and an
invitation (although it sounded more like a command) to accompany herself, Madame Hautecoeur, and Paola Giannini to her
dressmaker's to be fitted for still more mourning clothes.

She and Madame Hautecoeur had evidently gone to Silk Lane
yesterday afternoon and purchased sufficient black silk for all
necessary costumes. 'We wanted to spare you that.' They were
already being cut and basted by Madame's Chinese seamstress.

Lydia returned from the fitting (and a late lunch at the French
Legation) on Saturday evening to find that Karlebach's grief had
taken the form of plans for an expedition to the Shi'h Liu mines
on the following day.

'It is only the excursion of an afternoon, little bird.' The old
scholar patted Lydia's hands, made his haggard face into the rictus
of cheer. 'I will hire me a couple of soldiers from the American
barracks, and I will follow this so-excellent map.' He gestured to
the one Jamie and the Legation clerk P'ei had been working on.

'I will see for myself the entrances to these mines, to know how many must be sapped with explosives and what each looks like. Then we will be out of the hills before the sun is out of the sky—'

'It's what you thought was going to happen last time!' Lydia objected. 'You were nearly killed . . .'

His face grew grave. 'These things must be hunted in their nests, Madame. Hunted to their destruction.' And, when Lydia began to protest again: 'It is my fault – the stupidity of my weakness – that loosed these things into this country, these things that killed him. I owe him a debt. Mine must be the hand that atones.'

How on EARTH would you come to the conclusion that the Others killed him? She had to put her hand over her lips to silence the words that rose to them. *If the Chinese killed a Westerner they'd have made sure to mutilate the corpse to prevent identification . . .* Definitely *not* the sort of thing a genuine widow would say.

Instead she blurted, 'You can't go out there by yourself! You don't speak any Chinese!'

'I shall hire this man P'ei as well, this clerk whom . . . This clerk who helped with these maps.' Karlebach brandished the scribbled papers in his crooked fingers, and he avoided her eyes just as he avoided speaking James Asher's name. 'As for not knowing . . . little bird, I know my enemies. You have found solace for your heart in searching for them in your way.' His wave took in the fresh stack of police reports which had arrived, care of the Japanese Legation, while Lydia was away being fitted for six black walking-suits, four day-costumes, and an evening dress. 'Let me seek mine.'

Lydia felt a pang of regret that she'd let Karlebach see her note to Mizukami: *I find the exercise relieves my mind of the repetitive circling of grief, and I would like to think myself still able to help in my husband's quest for the truth behind this shocking affair.*

Did that sound too much like the intrepid heroine of a novel? she wondered.

Would a Real Woman – her Aunt Lavinnia was extremely fond of the expression, as if the possession of a womb and breasts was not quite sufficient to qualify Lydia for the title – *be so prostrate with grief at the murder of her husband that all she could do would be to lie upon the bed and howl?*

Lydia didn't know.

When her mother had died, she'd been so confused by her family's efforts to 'soften the blow' by lying to her that she found it, even now, difficult to think clearly about that time or to recall exactly how it had felt. Her father had died suddenly, of a stroke, about eighteen months after she had married Jamie: at that time she had not seen the old man for almost three years. He had disowned her when she'd entered Somerville College – terrifying at the time, but miraculous in its way, for the removal of her father's fortune had opened the way for Jamie to marry her. Her first letter to her father after her expulsion from Willoughby Court had been answered by one of the most spiteful documents she had ever read; subsequent communications, including the announcement of her marriage, had received no answer at all. She had been shocked and startled to hear of his death, but those feelings, too, had been whirled up together in bemusement over the fact that to her own astonishment – and to the howling chagrin of her stepmother – her father had in fact never changed his will, and Lydia had gone from being an impoverished outcast to being an extremely wealthy young woman.

How would a Real Woman react to grief, she wondered, *if she came from a Real Family and not a grotesque circus fueled by money, social climbing, and a self-centered autocrat who wanted to control his daughter's every breath?*

The poor old Queen had gone into complete seclusion at her husband's death and had worn deep mourning for the remaining forty years of her life. The eight-year-old Lydia's observation that this sounded like the most boring existence she'd ever heard of had earned her a smart slap from her Nanna.

In the end, after nearly an hour of arguing, Lydia managed to talk Karlebach down to a daylight expedition to the Golden Seas – the enclosed pleasure-grounds around the three large lakes immediately west of the Forbidden City's high pink walls – as soon as Count Mizukami could arrange passes through the gates. To his grumbles about the Japanese attaché's 'perfidy', Lydia had asked if he really thought he could answer for the discretion of 'a couple of soldiers from the American barracks' when they got in their cups. 'At least German spies won't know any Japanese,' she pointed out. So far as she could tell, *nobody* in the compound knew any Japanese.

Along with the day's police reports, Mizukami had sent her a note. She unfolded it and read it that night, when she finally settled into bed, with a splitting headache from the effort of remembering to periodically burst into tears throughout the afternoon and a deep feeling of sickened weariness and guilt.

Guilt for Ellen's reddened nose and bowed shoulders, and for the driven glitter in Karlebach's eye. Guilt for that unknown tall Chinese. Her whole skin had prickled when Karlebach had spoken of atonement: *if his grief drives him into doing something stupid, Jamie will never forgive himself. And neither will I.*

The note said:

> Dr Asher,
>   Please accept the expression of my deepest feelings of sorrow for you at this time.
>   Your strength to pursue these inquiries is a sword blade that will, I hope, cut grief. Might I ask of you, to communicate with me of what you find?
>   Please consider me at your service.
>   Mizukami
>
> Black shadow, black ice.
> Shadow warrior pursuing shadow,
> Unto shadow returns.

And Karlebach was right. There would have to be another expedition to the Shi'h Liu mines, and soon. And she knew Karlebach could not be kept away.

In addition to Mizukami's plump envelope of reports, Lydia had picked up at the desk four other notes, all of them from bachelor diplomats at the Legations, begging her to permit them to be of service to her. Given what Hobart had told Jamie about most of the men in the diplomatic corps needing to marry money, she wasn't precisely surprised, but she groaned inwardly at the thought of the scramble that would ensue when word got around that her fortune was her own and not in any way entangled in Jamie's affairs, alive or dead. She wanted to kick herself for having slipped that information into the conversation over lunch with Madame Hautecoeur and the Baroness, in reply to tactfully worded queries as to whether she would need financial assistance: both women, she did not doubt, had too-ample experience with women who came out to the East with husbands and then lost them there.

She leaned back against the pillows, closed her eyes, and wondered if fainting when the subject of her widowhood was brought up would discourage the likes of Mr Edmund Woodreave, the Trade Minister's Chief Clerk: *'If at any time you need the solace of a loyal friend . . .'*

Indeed! From a man I met precisely ONCE at the Peking Club . . .

He was the man who had also referred, rather tactlessly, to *'your poor husband's appalling death'*. Lydia wondered again about the man who had actually suffered that 'appalling death'.

If I asked Simon he would say, 'Nothing of the kind, Mistress. The man was dead when I found his body.' Or perhaps, 'He was a wicked man, and I killed him as he was cutting the throat of an innocent child . . .'

She slipped from beneath the coverlets, hurried – shivering – to the window, and opened one side of the curtain. Peking lay dark beyond the glimmer of lights on Rue Meiji, a mass of upturned roofs against distant stars. She lay long awake, reading in the neat, rather German handwriting of Count Mizukami's clerk all about disappearances, deaths, and strange things seen around the Stone Relics of the Sea.

But Ysidro did not come.

FIFTEEN

Wind from the north sliced Asher's padded *ch'i-p'ao* like a razor. The moonlight made a cloud of his breath. All around the shores of the Stone Relics of the Sea, ice formed a rough crystalline collar, and the crowding roofs of fancy tea-houses, ancestral temples, pleasure pavilions and dim-sum parlors shouldered black against the sky.

Not a fleck of light in all that shuttered darkness. Curious, Asher reflected, considering what Grandpa Wu and Ling had both told him: that the empty pleasure-grounds along the lake-shore were haunted these days by thieves, gunrunners, and killers-for-hire. From the humpbacked marble bridge where he stood, the smell of smoke from every courtyard around this side of the lakes came to him, in fierce competition with the refuse dumped on the lakeshore near the mouths of every *hutong* that debouched there – impossible to tell whether anyone had built a hidden fire along the lake that night.

Then the wind shifted, and for an instant he caught the stink he'd smelled in the mountains, below the Shi'h Liu mines.

Yao-kuei.

They're here.

That was the short of what he had come to learn. He could go home now . . .

Do the Tso know it yet?

He stepped from the bridge to the muddy verge of the frozen lake itself.

In addition to his knife, his revolver, and a tin dark-lantern, he'd brought with him a sort of halberd that Grandpa Wu had sold him for three dollars American, the kind of thing that gang enforcers carried on late-night forays, like a short sword-blade mounted at the end of a staff. For two nights now he had waited to hear from Ysidro, but the vampire had either gone to ground or, like Father Orsino, was hunting far from Peking. That afternoon Ling had said a friend of her mother's had smelled 'rat-monsters' by the lake. A beggar-child, the woman had said, had disappeared, the third in two weeks.

The Tso family had their headquarters in the triangle of land between the northern and southern lobes of the lake, away to his left across the water. Everyone in this neighborhood worked for them. In daylight, despite the Chinese clothing, Asher knew he could never pass unnoticed. He supposed the sensible thing would be to declare the evening a success, go back to Pig-Dragon Lane, and wait until he heard from Ysidro.

IF I hear from Ysidro.

And if I hear from him before Karlebach looks over Lydia's shoulder at her police reports some evening and decides to make inquiries here on his own. The old man would have the freedom to come here during the day, but if the Tso were trying to keep inquiries away from the mine, the danger to Karlebach would not be less.

He is obsessed.

Long service in the twilight world – where love of country and duty to the Queen were the only landmarks – had taught Asher what obsession did to men's judgement. *They see what they want to see*, his Chief had once said to him. *They convince themselves things are safer than they are.*

The stench – barely a whiff – disappeared as the wind veered to the north again. *From the west*, thought Asher. Along the long axis of the northern 'sea'. Giving the western shore – and the maze of *siheyuan* that made up the Tso family headquarters – a wide berth, Asher picked his way down counterclockwise along the southern lobe of the lakes, boot soles squeaking in the frozen mud. Movement ahead of him and to his right: he almost jumped out of his skin. But it was only a rat, fattened with garbage to the size of a half-grown cat. Here away from the pleasure pavilions, the waste of soap- and paper-making in the *hutongs* above him was dumped, as well as the flayed debris of butcher's stalls that even the ever-hungry poor of the city were unable to use: skulls, shells, cracked horns and the boiled-out husks of hooves. Knowing the Chinese capability for converting the tiniest scraps of waste into something that could be eaten or sold, Asher could only pity the rats trying to make a living off this.

To his right the shore bent away, toward a bridge and another of the city's canals. The ice on the lake wasn't thick enough yet to take a man's weight, and he scanned the black mass of wall and roofs at the top of the bank, searching for the entrance to another *hutong*. Judging by the filth heaped on the shore just here, it wouldn't be far. Another rat made the reeds rattle close-by. He saw a third, and a fourth, dart across the open ice, the moonlight so strong that it made little blue shadows around their feet.

Asher moved to the left to skirt the worst of the rubbish – moonlight catching on the lugubrious shapes of skulls and pelvic bones – but his boots broke through the ice. He staggered, the water freezing his feet even through the leather, and waded back the yard or so to the mud and reeds. When true winter came, of course, every child in the city would be out here, skating on the ice . . .

Always provided things haven't come to shooting by then between the President and the Kuo Min-tang.

The wind that raked his cheeks slackened a little. He smelled it, clearly now despite the cold.

At least one of them, under the bridge.

He turned, to pick his way back along the shore.

And stopped, his breath sticking in his throat. All that formless dark slope, from water's edge to the wall at the top of the bank, moved with rats.

Shock took his throat like a cold hand. He had never seen that many rats in his life. The silvery-dark scuttering among the reeds was literally like a carpet, alive with a foul, bubbling animation. When he turned they sat up, all of them. Eyes like a spiderweb dewed with flame.

Oh, Jesus.

Looking at him.

The smell of the Others grew stronger behind him. In the moonlight it wasn't easy to be sure, but he thought he saw something move along the lakeshore, a hundred yards from where he stood. *There* . . . Black, and man-high against the cold glimmer of the ice. Asher started to edge back, but the rats were moving, too, streaming down behind him. The thought of being swarmed brought nightmare panic.

The thought of being wounded – of wounding the *yao-kuei* in a fight and getting enough of their blood into his own veins to turn him into one of them – brought the instant conviction: *No. Not as long as there's a bullet left*. There really were worse things than death.

He waded out into the lake, ice breaking before his legs and the water excruciating. Plowed his way back toward the mouth of Big Tiger Lane, which led south toward more populous streets. A *yao-kuei* came down the slope toward him at a shambling run, from another *hutong* somewhere ahead along the wall in the dark. Asher backed further into the water, almost to his waist. Debris underfoot slithered and rocked, and he cut at the first of the rats with his halberd, struggling to keep his balance.

The next moment the *yao-kuei* flung itself at him, floundering in the water, clawed hands grabbing, fanged mouth gaping to gouge. Asher had sufficient experience with quarterstaff and single-stick to know how to leverage the halberd blade to deadly effect, and his first blow took the thing's head three-quarters off . . . but only three-quarters. Head dangling by a flap of flesh, arteries fountaining blood, the *yao-kuei* staggered, threshing its clawed hands to find its prey. Asher stepped in as close as he dared and severed the hamstrings of both legs, then turned and stumbled through the water, scanning the banks.

He was in luck. Something – a dog pack, he thought, though in moonlight and the black shadows of the bank it was impossible to tell – had scented the enormous multitude of rats on the bank and charged in for a hunt. Asher had an impression of scuttling black forms, of red eyes sparking as the smaller animals fled. He pulled the slide from his lantern, hurled the tin light into the thick of the rats that swarmed between him and the dark rectangle that he hoped and prayed was the opening to Big Tiger Lane. Everything on the bank was wet with slush, but the scant oil in the lantern's reservoir flared up as it hit the ground. The rats scurried from the flame, and Asher ran upslope as he'd never run before.

From the corner of his eye he glimpsed two *yao-kuei* running up the bank far behind him, moving as if coordinated by some unheard communication. His mind logged the phenomenon even as he threw himself into the indigo chasm of the alleyway, as he fled, stumbling, one hand on its wall to guide him.

He didn't stop running till he reached the back gates of the Forbidden City; skirted its massive walls, taller than the average London house, clear around, to pass it on the eastern side rather than go anywhere near the walls of the Palace Lakes to the west. The Palace Lakes connected with the 'Seas', as did the Forbidden City's moats and the canal that flowed a little further east. Soaked to the waist, shivering and numb, Asher finally hailed a rickshaw near the new University, but he flinched every time they passed over another canal.

At this hour the streets were empty. He thought of Lydia, safe among lace-trimmed pillows in the Wagons-Lits Hotel, and wondered if she were being watched.

Probably. By the Tso Family or those who might work for them – who might or might not be riding Grant Hobart like a horse on a curb bit. Or by the Legation police, who wanted nothing more than to do their duty and slap a suspected traitor in a cell where some employee of the Tso would have a good chance to get at him . . .

Asher rubbed his frozen fingers and wondered how long his hideout in Pig-Dragon Lane would be safe.

And whether Karlebach would stay out of trouble until it was safe to get word to him.

And if Lydia was safe.

And what had happened to Ysidro . . .

It was three days before Lydia realized that Ysidro was missing.

On Sunday – the day after Lydia received Mizukami's packet of further police reports – the Count himself called at the Wagons-Lits Hotel, to extend to her whatever help he was capable of giving and, a little to her surprise, to offer to arrange her journey home.

'Thank you.' She leaned across the hearth of the blue-curtained private parlor off the hotel's lobby, pressed the Colonel's white-gloved hand. 'I feel that I can be of some use here. The task Jamie set out to accomplish is unfinished.' Her eyes met Mizukami's – slightly blurred even at a distance of two feet. She put back the veils of her hat, an elegant confection of sable tulle and plumes, to see him more clearly. 'And it is something which cannot be walked away from.'

'I honor you for wishing to continue it, Madame. You are willing, then, to go on as you have begun with the reports? For I begin to suspect that these *tenma* – these creatures – may indeed be in Peking as well.'

'I am, thank you,' said Lydia. 'Though it's rather difficult to pick out patterns in a foreign country, a world not my own. Could you – would you . . .' She hesitated. 'Is it possible that it is within your powers to get me access to banking records as well?'

'Nothing simpler.' He took a small tablet from the pocket of his plain blue uniform jacket and made a note to himself. 'You understand that the Chinese – particularly the more traditional families – use a different system . . .?'

'This would be Western banks,' said Lydia. 'The Franco-Chinois, the Hong Kong Specie Bank, the Indochine . . .'

'It will be my pleasure, Dr Asher.'

She was aware that something she'd said had sparked his curiosity. His head tilted a little, and she felt, though she could not see his expression clearly, that behind his own thick lenses he was studying her face.

Crossing the lobby to return to her suite, she was accosted by the most persistent of her would-be suitors, Mr Edmund Woodreave: tallish, stooped, pot-bellied and wearing a coat which

had seen better days. 'Mrs Asher,' he said, striding so quickly
to cut her off from the stairs that she would have had to break
into a run to avoid him, 'I beg of you to give me the opportunity
to express to you how sorry I am . . .'

'Please . . .' She made one of her Aunt Lavinnia's best
I'm-going-to-faint gestures.

'Of course.' Woodreave took her hand. 'I quite understand. I
only mean to tell you how deeply I appreciate the position in
which you find yourself now, and to place myself entirely at your
service.'

'Thank you,' said Lydia, in her most frail and failing accents.
'If you will—'

He tightened his eager grip. 'I hope you know that you can
call upon me, at any time, for any service whatsoever. I know
we're not well acquainted, but I know also how difficult it is to
be suddenly left on your own—'

'I'm quite—'

'—and any service that I can render you, at any hour of the
day or night, you have only to send a note round to my lodgings
at the Legation . . .'

Only the rigor of Lydia's instruction by her Nanna, four aunts,
and a stepmother prior to being brought 'out' in London Society,
that she could not, must not, ever *ever* scream at anyone: *Would
you go away and let me alone?* no matter how much they deserved
it – and the knowledge that to do so now might announce to
someone that she was not truly a widow and that Jamie was
hiding somewhere – kept her silent for the next thirty minutes
while Mr Woodreave explained to her how terrible it was to be
a widow and how much he would like to help her.

Returning to her suite, she then had to deal with a stream of
callers who arrived to pay their respects. Madame Hautecoeur
and the Baroness turned up first – indeed, it was the Baroness
who finally drove Mr Woodreave from the lobby – and presided
over the tea table, bearing the brunt of the conversational duties
while Paola Giannini stayed, loyal and blessedly silent, at Lydia's
side. Lydia felt sick with dread that Lady Eddington would appear.
Much of the talk, in fact, was of that bereaved lady, who was
preparing for the terrible task of accompanying her murdered
daughter's body home to England on the *Princess Imperial*. The
women who came to comfort Lydia in her supposed grief spoke

with genuine sorrow of Holly, and for the most part she hadn't the courage to even open her mouth.

She finally pleaded a headache, and for the remainder of the day she stayed in her room, reading stories to Miranda and tallying police reports . . .

And scanning through banking records that were delivered at supper time, for any of a dozen names she had encountered in previous research.

On the following day she found one.

Esteban Sierra of Rome (*does he REALLY have a house in Rome?*) had made arrangements not only to open a substantial account in the Banque Franco-Chinoise, but also to rent a storage room in its underground vault. For 'antiquities and *objets d'art*' said the application, in that strong, vertical handwriting with its odd loops and flourishes. Current contents: a single large trunk.

Don Simon had told Jamie once that vampires knew when the living were on their trail. People who lingered once too often on the sidewalk opposite a suspect house. Faces seen in neighborhoods where the vampires, with their hyper-acute awareness of human features, knew every face. By showing even an interest in the underground bank-vault, the 'antiquities and *objets d'art*', Lydia was aware she had committed the paramount sin of bringing 'Esteban Sierra' to the attention of anyone. She – and Jamie – had only lived this long because Ysidro understood that they knew the rules.

She left the curtains of her window half-open, half-closed yet again, as she had last night and the night before.

In the morning she sent Count Mizukami a note.

The Count was the soul of discretion. He had watched events in China long enough – and had sufficient familiarity with its current 'acting' President – to understand the danger of a single wrong word, the smallest misplaced whisper, flying to official ears. He accepted without question Lydia's word that nothing must be spoken of her visit to the bank vault. He must acquire permission, and the keys, but only Lydia would be permitted to enter.

The aplomb with which he made these arrangements – with which he *could* make such arrangements – caused Lydia to wonder a good deal about the contents, and renters, of the bank's other strongrooms.

Just before closing time on Wednesday, the sixth of November, Mizukami and Ellen conducted Lydia two doors down the street to the bank, and a clerk escorted them as far as the stairs. Her veils over her face, the rustle of her black silk skirts like the scraping of silver files in the stillness of the underground hallway, Lydia made her way by the bright electric glare to the vault door marked 12. The clerk had explained the procedure for opening it, and she guessed she would be very politely searched by a female bank employee the moment she emerged. She was aware of her heart pounding: he would be furious, she knew, when he learned that she had violated the secrecy with which he surrounded himself.

It might lose her his friendship: that queer, shining shadow that shouldn't exist but did. If he heard her – felt her – through his dreams, he would be cursing her now.

But he might be in danger.

When last they had spoken, she had seen the fear in his eyes.

As the application said, there was only one thing in the vault: a huge tan leather travel-trunk with brass corners, easily large enough to hold the body of a man. *He's keeping his clothing and books somewhere else . . .*

It was like him, she thought as the door shut behind her, to rent a bank vault next door to their hotel.

From her handbag she took her silvery spectacle-case, lifted her veils aside and donned her glasses.

The trunk was closed. She knew it could be locked from the inside. The outer locks were just for show. It was daylight outside, though not a ray of it penetrated to this room. He would be asleep. With the door closed the silence was like a weight, pressing in on her eardrums. She'd asked him once how much vampires were aware of, during their daytime sleep, and he had only said, 'The dreams of vampires are not like the dreams of men.'

Forgive me . . .

She took a deep breath, put her hands on the trunk's lid, and pushed.

It opened with soundless ease.

The trunk was empty.

SIXTEEN

The ruined chapel, Ysidro had said, near the old French cemetery.

The rickshaw-puller knew the place. Asher left the man by the steps of the new Cathedral, with instructions (and an extra fifteen cents) to wait for him there. The district had been hammered mercilessly by Boxer cannon, so many of the buildings hereabouts were new and built in the Western style. The chapel ruins looked as if they'd been shuttered up for years.

The moon was dwindling, and at this hour few lamps remained in any of the shops along Shun Chih Men Street. Once dark fell on Peking, the blackness in the *huntongs* had to be experienced to be believed. The feeble glimmer of his tin dark-lantern barely showed Asher the other side of the alleyways as he made his way on foot toward the chapel. He understood that he was taking his life in his hands, but his life had been, in a sense, a mosquito sitting on the arm of Fate ever since he'd come to China.

On the chapel steps, he paused and put around his neck the silver crucifix he'd purchased early in his association with vampires. He had quickly learned that the holy symbol was only as good as its silver content, at least as far as protection was concerned, but under his collar and scarf he wore the silver chains that never left him. On this occasion the crucifix served another purpose.

He took also from his pocket the little tin box that Karlebach had given him on their arrival in China: crushed, slightly gummy herbs, the bitterness of which was accompanied by a quickening of his heartbeat and a heightened clarity of mind. Vampires hunted by sleepiness and inattention. Even a half-second could make a difference.

Inside, the building was littered with debris. Everything wooden had long since been carried off by the neighbors for fuel. Fury at Western missionaries had left only a single statue of the Virgin still standing, in a niche to the east of the main altar. Raising his lantern Asher saw that her face had been blackened, her nose chipped off, her eyes gouged out. Someone had recently repaired them with new plaster, carefully painted. Her lips still smiled.

He took a candle from his pocket and lit it at the lantern's flame. This he set on the altar; then he knelt, hands folded. '*In nomine patrii, et filii, et spiritu sanctii, amen. Pater noster, qui es in caelis, sanctificetur nomen tuum . . .*'

His father would be turning in his grave.

But then the old man would be used to the exercise by that time.

And if Father Orsino Espiritu was listening, the Latin prayer – and the unspoken lie that the supplicant was Catholic – might just save his life.

A Jesuit, Ysidro had said.

When the Order came to China in the sixteenth century every country in Europe had been broken on the rack of religious war. To accomplish their conversions in the East, the Jesuits had clothed Catholicism in the trappings of Buddhism, learned the language – almost the only Westerners to do so – and dressed themselves in the robes of Buddhist monks. Later, when the greed of Western merchants had sought to tap China's riches, they – and the men and women they had converted – were seen as traitors, lackeys of the West.

He has been hiding for most of the past three centuries . . . Ysidro had said of Father Orsino. '*I hear their voices speaking in my mind . . .*'

Asher whispered the Latin of every prayer he could remember, aware that any vampire entering the ruins would be able to hear the pounding of his heart.

Of course the vampires of Peking would watch a Jesuit. So what would they make of the appearance of a second Spanish vampire, save that they were in league? Was that why Ysidro had not been in contact with him since he'd taken refuge in the Chinese City, a week ago now? What would they make of a living man, in the Chinese garb that the Jesuits assumed, whispering Latin prayers in the darkness?

'*At te levavi animam meam: Deus meus, in te confido . . .*' *In you I will place my trust . . .*

Gray sleepiness crushed down on his mind, stealthy and over-whelming. He thrust himself away from the altar rail in the instant before a clawed hand seized his throat. The hand jerked back, and he heard a curse in antique Spanish; ducked, turned his body as a blow brushed his face. 'Padre Orsino!'

In the candle's light he glimpsed the thin white face, the reflective glimmer of eyes. A hand seized his arm and hurled him out on to the stone floor of the nave with an impact that knocked the breath from his body. The vampire pinned him, caught his wrists and again pulled back with a hissing scream of pain and rage. Asher rolled, scrambled clear and shouted, '*In nomine Patrii*, Orsino! I'm here from Ysidro!'

The words weren't out of his mouth as the vampire slammed him against the ruined altar-rail, clawed hands gripping his shoulders with brutal power.

But Asher felt him hesitate, and he said into that moment's stillness, 'Simon Ysidro sent me.' He spoke Latin. At a guess, Padre Orsino wouldn't understand modern Spanish.

The vampire tilted his head. Regarded him with eyes that were, in the candlelight, dark as coffee and had clearly not been sane in centuries. Straddling his body, he held Asher without effort against the broken railing and the floor. When he pressed a clawed hand to the side of Asher's face, it was warm. His clothing smelled of blood.

'You are his servant?'

'I am. I am called Asher.'

'Where is he?'

'I came to see if you knew that. I have heard nothing of him for seven days.'

'He is vanished.' Father Orsino rose. He stood over Asher's body, a small man whose hair, like his eyes, seemed very dark in the dense gloom of the chapel against the pallor of his skin. He wore the long Manchu *ch'i-p'ao* and *ku* trousers, but his hair was sleeked back into a bun on the back of his head, after the fashion of the Chinese before the conquest by the Manchus. 'Come,' he said. He glanced around him, held down his hand to pull Asher to his feet – Asher guessed by the pain in his side that the vampire's violence had cracked a rib or two. 'They cannot hear us, beneath the earth,' Orsino whispered conspiratorially. 'They cannot listen – cannot find me.'

He took Asher by the elbow, picked up the lantern and led the way past the main altar to a broken doorway and the ruin of a vestry. Most of its roof and part of a wall was gone, but there was no sign of rats or other vermin. Another doorway opened on to a stairway down to the crypt, two full turns down into a Stygian abyss that smelled of mold. A new door had been installed at the bottom. There were bolts on its inner side, a hasp with a padlock. The stone vaulting of the crypt beyond barely cleared the top of Asher's head, and by the lantern's feeble glimmer he made out piles of dug-up earth, and straw baskets for moving it, among the fat wooden pillars.

Presumably Father Orsino was in the process of making a more secure lair for himself deeper down. Asher wondered where he planned to dispose of the dug-out dirt.

The vampire shot the bolts and turned to face Asher. Though Ysidro was too wary to risk a kill anywhere in the city, Asher knew that the weight of the earth blocked vampire perceptions. Father Orsino might consider it safe.

'Don Simon told me that I could find you here,' he said, to remind his host – in case it had slipped whatever was left of his mind – that he, Asher, was supposedly a good Catholic and working for the Pope.

'He said you could take me back to Rome.' Orsino set the lantern on a corner of the huge old chest that lay, half-hidden, by the low pillars at the nearer end of the crypt, and he folded his heavy, thick-fingered hands. 'He said His Holiness would forgive me my sins, because I have in all these years killed only the damned. God save me . . .'

'I know nothing of what His Holiness said to Ysidro. It is only my task to serve him.'

'What, none of you know?' The hushed voice had a twisted shrillness to it, the gleaming eyes narrowed. 'Are you lying to me? Trying to trap me?' Orsino seized Asher again by the shoulder of his coat, shoved him back against a pillar. 'Is that what happened to Don Simon? That you betrayed—?'

'I know nothing.' Asher kept his own voice steady with an effort. 'Truly. It's why I must find him.'

The Father's lip lifted back from his fangs. 'I find it hard to believe that none in your company knows the mandate of His Holiness.'

'There is no company. Only myself and my master. Did Don Simon tell you otherwise?'

Father Orsino passed a hand over his forehead, his brow suddenly tightening with confusion and pain. 'They are gods,' he said. 'You cannot . . . A man cannot fight against gods.' He blinked at Asher, dark eyes filled with terror. 'I've done everything I can, but hundreds worship them, you see. Thousands. The living bow down to them in their pagan temples, bring them sacrifices. And they have, each of them, a thousand and ten thousand and a hundred thousand prisoners, dead men, dead women, flesh burned off their bones but walking still. These they call up out of Hell . . .'

'Have you seen them?'

'Every day.' Orsino's voice sank still further, hoarse with terror. 'I sleep, and I see them, surrounded in flame with their flayed worshipers all burning around them.'

Truth? Dream? Madness? A recollection of his days trying to convert the Chinese? 'And they trust their worshipers?'

'They are gods,' the priest repeated. 'Of course their worshipers must obey. Else they themselves will be dragged down to Hell by the bailiffs, Ox-Head and Horse-Face, down a thousand and ten thousand and a hundred thousand black iron steps to the gates of the First Hell, which is called Chin-kuang. The living must obey them because their ancestors are in Hell, where all unbelievers go. They dare not disobey. Their families will not allow it.'

His face convulsed, and his grip tightened on Asher's shoulder. 'Did he send you to trap me? My father . . . and the Pope . . . The monster that first came to the hills was Catholic! Did the Pope send him? I heard him pray . . .'

'The Pope has not betrayed you.' Even cold with fright, Asher felt a queasy shiver of enlightenment. 'The Devil speaks Latin as well as the Pope, Padre. It was the Devil who sent you a monster out of Hell, to try your spirit and your faith. His Holiness would never betray you.'

Father Orsino released his hold, almost threw Asher from him. 'What you say is true.' His eyes were ravenous, riveted now to the shoulder of Asher's *ch'i-p'ao* where hot blood soaked through the padded cloth.

Get him thinking of something else quickly. 'Do the vampires rule over their living families here? Is that what it is? That some of them are the ancestors that the family venerates?'

'No. Yes.' The vampire stammered as the words disrupted his attention. 'I–I have never seen them. I don't know. Not one. Ever, ever in all these long years . . .'

'Not he who made you?'

The question seemed to confuse Father Orsino, who shook his head. 'They don't make others like themselves any more,' he said. 'Nor do they suffer one another to make them. They trust no one, do you understand? Not their families, not one another.'

He stepped forward again, put his palms against the sides of Asher's head, drew him close, his words a frightful halitus of blood. 'They told me it is the children that lead vengeance to their doors. When we come up out of Hell we are helpless, like snails ripped from their curly armor. It is why they all had to become gods, you see. They wouldn't let me, because I had sinned. The Yama-King gave them a choice about which Hell they would rule, once he'd reorganized. There used to be twelve thousand, eight hundred hells under the earth, eight dark hells, eight cold hells, and eighty-four thousand hells located on the edges of the universe, though I should imagine some of them were quite small. When I was a man I used to study them.'

He frowned, gazing into Asher's eyes as if hypnotized. 'When I was a man—'

'Is that why he made you vampire, then?' asked Asher steadily. 'Because you were not of his own family?'

'He wanted—' Father Orsino blinked, trying to call memory back. 'I no longer remember what he wanted. There was a reason then.' He pressed his palms hard against Asher's skull, struggling with some thought.

'He is—?'

'Li. Li Jung Shen. He is insane now. His family brings him prey, that he may do their bidding. Except . . .' He fell silent again, losing the thread of his thought. His hands slackened their crushing grip, only stirred through Asher's hair, absent-mindedly, as a man might stroke a dog. But his wandering gaze returned to Asher's shoulder where the blood darkened his coat.

'Except—?' Asher reminded him gently.

'Except when I waken sometimes at fall of dark, I hear him screaming.'

He stepped back a little then, and Asher slipped out of his reach, half breathless with the pain in his side, and gauged the distance to the doorway and the stair. His every instinct told him to flee, but a terrible suspicion was growing in his mind, and he asked instead, 'Can you tell where?'

The vampire shook his head, a slight gesture, reminiscent of Ysidro's stillness. 'Near here,' he said. 'A thousand miles straight down beneath the ground. A thousand miles and ten thousand and a hundred thousand miles, beyond the Third Hell, which is for bad mandarins, forgers, and backbiters. The forgers are made to swallow melted gold and silver, to the extent that they forged those metals in life. And the Fifth Hell is the Hell of Dismemberment, where the lustful, murderers, and the sacrilegious are torn into pieces, ground into pulp between rocks, run over by the red-hot iron wheels of spiked vehicles. Bao is the Magistrate of that Hell, Bao Cheng, who used to be a warrior in the time of the Sung emperors: a fearsome man, they say, but a writer of drinking songs and love songs. You are not sacrilegious, are you?'

He caught Asher's arm again, stared intently into his face. 'Your father prayed for you. Wanted you to enter the Church. You disobeyed him.'

Did he read that in my thoughts? Or is it of his own father that he speaks? 'My father wanted me to serve the Church,' said Asher, quite truthfully . . . *Though we won't go into the subject of which church.* 'I trod my own path, until I came into Don Simon's service.'

The vampire's brow twisted again. 'We are all prisoners of our families,' he said in a much quieter voice, and his eyes, yellowly reflective in the candle gleam, suddenly seemed to focus. 'They are the true Magistrates of Hell. Even when we flee them, they live on in our dreams. My mother—' He stammered on the words. 'My mother and my uncles wanted me to join the Society of Jesus, because I had a God-given talent for tongues. My father had died fighting the heretics in Holland. It was hard – it was very hard – to tell Christiana that it was not to be between us, Christiana whom I loved – or thought I loved. My uncle told me I would learn to love God more and to see Christiana's body for what it was, a sack of guts and blood, as are the bodies of all women. But it was hard.'

Very gently, Asher disengaged his arm from the gripping claws. 'I will ask Ysidro, when I find him, exactly what arrangements

His Holiness has made to get you back to Rome. Since I am the one who must make them, and carry them out, I will bring you word here when I hear.'

'Arrangements—?'

'To get you back to Rome.'

'Of course.' Father Orsino shook his head a little, like a man who realizes he does not remember what he has said. 'Who is Pope now? I made myself a refuge in the mines, behind bars of silver, behind gates the Magistrates cannot touch. A thousand and ten thousand and a hundred thousand black iron steps down into the darkness . . . My book is there. Ysidro said he would go get it for me. It is dedicated to His Holiness, but I hear so little of the world.'

'His Holiness Pius X,' replied Asher. 'A most sanctified and resolute man.' *And stubborn and reactionary* – the sixteenth-century Inquisitors would probably have regarded him as a Milquetoast for merely declaring Protestant-Catholic marriages 'religiously invalid' instead of demanding the lives of those who dared participate in them.

'And you will speak for me?'

'I will speak for you. Ysidro, too—'

'Oh, he has been eaten by the monsters in the mines.' Suddenly like a friendly priest guiding his parishioner into a confessional, Father Orsino waved Asher toward the stair. 'This is why I say that you *must* have some other member of your party who knows the arrangement.'

'Eaten?' Asher thought for one instant about going back and picking up his lantern – on the opposite side of the crypt – rather than ascending that long, narrow stair in pitch darkness with a vampire at his elbow, but discarded the idea at once. Not if it meant letting the vampire get between him and the door.

'He said he was going to the mines. Didn't I tell you? He went to fetch my book for me, my life's work, my refutation of all the works of the heretic Luther . . . I told him how to open the silver doors. So they must have eaten him.'

Asher put his hand to the wall of the stair, to guide him up, and – presumably in friendliness – Father Orsino laid a hand on Asher's back.

'I've given it a good deal of thought, and I think what happened must have been this,' the priest went on. 'The First Hell

– Chin-kuang, the one closest to the surface of the earth, where Chiang Tzu-wen, who used to be a warrior monk in the days of the Han, is the Magistrate – that is where the cases of the sinners are heard and punishments assigned. But I think that in fact the Second Hell, Chujiang, where Li is the Magistrate, is the Hell of Beasts, where dishonest intermediaries and ignorant doctors are devoured, gored, trampled, torn apart by demons in the form of beasts. And if that is so, then that's what these creatures are: *shou-kuei*, beast-devils, who got back into the First Hell through the carelessness of the Magistrate of Chin-kuang, and then managed to get through a hole in the wall of the First Hell and into the mines. That would account for his coming to the mines . . .'

'Ysidro?'

'No, no, the Magistrate of Chin-kuang! He's been there. I thought at one time it must have been Li, the Magistrate of Chujiang, but I don't think he'd dare. I have heard his footfalls in the dark.'

The priest's hand tightened on Asher's arm. He felt Father Orsino move past him. Heard the creak of the broken door, and a moment later – bright after the total blackness of the stair – faint starlight showed him the outlines of the holes in the vestry roof, the dense flat shadows of the broken walls.

'The *shou-kuei* will have eaten Don Simon by this time,' the vampire went on sadly. 'That is why you must help me, you and your family, to get my book and take it to the Pope. Can I count on you?'

A little breathlessly, Asher said, 'You may count on me. On us.'

'God bless you.' The Jesuit traced before him in the air the sign of the cross, then took Asher by the shoulders and very lightly kissed him on either cheek, lips warm with someone else's stolen life. 'And God speed you.'

A moment later, though the chapel was drowned in indigo and starlight, Asher woke with a gasp, as if from a dream, still standing in the ruined vestry before the black hole of the crypt stair. Silvery dawn light filled the room. His ribs hurt as if he'd been hit by a train. Outside in the alley, a woman was shouting the virtues of steamed dumplings.

SEVENTEEN

Two notes awaited Lydia when she returned to her suite. One – from Sir Grant Hobart – she simply put into the fireplace, as she had done two others he had sent her, behavior completely to be expected from a new-made widow, she thought. Anger at him still flushed heat behind her breastbone. *If Jamie HAD died, it would have been his fault.*

Whatever excuse he'll offer, I don't want to hear it.

The other – accompanied by a gaudy bouquet which must have come by rail from the south of China at considerable expense – was from Edmund Woodreave. Under Mrs Pilley's accusing gaze Lydia didn't feel she could very well dispose of the note, much less the flowers, as she'd disposed of Hobart's. And Woodreave's courtship, much as it exasperated Lydia, also amused her in its way: *does he really think ANY woman whose husband was murdered last week is going to find this attractive?*

Evidently he did.

Or is he so desperate to further his career that he's willing to try anything?

'He's such a very nice gentleman,' said Mrs Pilley, watching Lydia's face anxiously, 'and so devoted to you.'

'He barely knows me.' Lydia removed her hat and gloves and gathered Miranda into her arms. 'He met me exactly once, before I—' She bit off the words *came on to the market*, gave her head a little shake, and in her best imitation of Aunt Faith's die-away voice said, 'I find his importunities in the very worst of taste.'

Mrs Pilley sighed deeply, the expression on her face making it clear to Lydia that the little widow had what schoolgirls called a 'crush' on Mr Woodreave herself, though of course he would have no use for a woman who had no money of her own. A bleak and unfair world, reflected Lydia sadly, that condemned a young mother to looking after someone else's child (and in China, no less!) so that she could scrape enough money to keep her own son in school in England, simply because no man of her own class would take a woman without a 'portion' to sweeten the bargain.

She carried Miranda into the bedroom, to keep her company while Ellen helped her out of her dress and brushed her hair; put on her glasses and played little games with her daughter, cheered as always by the infant's curiosity and love. But when Mrs Pilley came in to carry Miranda off to bed, Lydia felt an uneasy qualm as she said, 'Professor Karlebach and I are going out to the Western Hills first thing tomorrow morning. We probably won't be back until after dark.'

'Yes, ma'am.' The nurse's large blue eyes were both puzzled and accusing: *how can you possibly do anything at all, with poor Professor Asher dead and in so terrible a fashion . . .?*

If Jamie were really dead, WOULD I be able to do nothing but stay in my room and wail?

Lydia didn't know.

She lifted her chin, made her voice tremble a little as she added, 'This is something Professor Asher would have wanted me to do.'

Instantly, the nurse's eyes flooded with tears. Ellen, coming in with a cup of cocoa and an extra scuttle of coal, gazed upon her mistress with such pity and sympathy that Lydia writhed inwardly. It was shame, not grief bravely borne, that filled her own eyes with tears as her two loving handmaidens made their exit with the sleeping Miranda in their arms.

Jamie, thought Lydia, *I know this is all to keep you from being hunted down and murdered, but as soon as you're home safe I'm going to shake you till your teeth rattle, for doing this to me.*

She had already spent an exhausting evening – after returning from the bank – arguing with Karlebach over how trustworthy Count Mizukami actually was, and then about whether she was really sure she was 'able for' tomorrow's reconnaissance expedition to the Western Hills, to locate all the lesser entrances to the Shi'h Liu Mine. The Count had sent three soldiers out to Men T'ou Kuo by train that afternoon, to arrange horses for the party. God knew what the Baroness, and Madame Hautecoeur, and that poisonous beldame Madame Schrenk at the Austrian Legation, would have to say about *that*.

Jamie, wherever you are, I hope you appreciate what I'm doing.

But the thought was like a child's cry in the darkness. And as she sat at the dressing table, and let the stillness of the night finally close around her, the thoughts returned that all her activity that day, and all her researches into bank records and police reports and maps of the Western Hills, had been designed to hide: that it had been six days since Ysidro had come to give her the news that Jamie was safe.

Six days is a long time.

Jamie . . .

Lydia pressed her hands to her face, trying to still her sudden trembling.

And the worst of it was that she didn't know exactly for whom it was that her breath came short and tears suddenly poured down her cheeks.

For her daughter's father, for unbending strength and wry humor, for the warmth of his arms around her?

Or for the expressionless whisper and cool yellow eyes of a man who'd been dead since 1555?

Her mind returned to the bank vault she had entered that afternoon. To the tan leather trunk with its brass corners and elaborate locks.

Empty.

Keep walking forward.

This was what her friend Anne had told her – that steady and pragmatic Fellow of Somerville College – back in the days when Lydia's father had disowned her, when Jamie had disappeared into the wilds of Africa and at seventeen Lydia had been tutoring medical students in order to pay her board bill. *Keep walking forward. You don't know what's beyond the next rise of the ground.*

She dreamed that night that she was looking for Pig-Dragon Lane. Darkness was falling, and something was terribly wrong about the rickshaw-puller: she kept trying to lean forward, to see his face. He was naked save for a white loincloth such as the bodyguard Ito had been wearing when she'd seen him at Mizukami's house, and like Ito he had bandages on his left arm and side. In the twilight she thought the man's thinning hair was falling out in patches, the way Ito's had been.

She abandoned the rickshaw in terror, but found herself afoot in lanes that all looked alike, with silk shops and paper lanterns and jostling crowds of Chinese. She asked the candy-maker at the corner of Silk Lane if he had seen Ysidro, and he answered her – in perfect English – 'He apologizes for being detained, ma'am, but he's left a message for you at the Temple of Everlasting Harmony.' He gave her some candy and pointed her the way through the crowd. As she made her way toward the Temple, she kept half-recognizing someone in the crowd, someone who wasn't there every time she turned around. Someone whose face she knew.

Jamie?

Simon?

The rickshaw-puller Ito?

A single lamp had been kindled in the Temple. By its glow, the eyes of the statues were reflective, vampire eyes. They followed her as she stepped into its darkness.

Whoever she'd seen behind her in the crowds of the street, she thought, was in the Temple somewhere. She could see him move. She knew she should be mortally afraid of him, and she wasn't.

The knowledge that she should have felt fear and didn't was what remained with her when she woke, heart pounding, to the sound of the hotel chambermaid laying the fire in the parlor and the voices in the street of a couple of American soldiers coming off patrol.

'Tell about Stone Relics of the Sea.'

Wu Tan Shun bowed deeply and signed to Ling to bring the bamboo tray of dim sum – small tidbits of shrimp rolls, 'phoenix claws' (which bore a suspicious resemblance to chicken feet), egg tarts, and dumplings big and small, steamed and fried – to the small table beside Asher's makeshift brazier on its section of matting. Four tiny pots of tea were already lined up. Since everyone in the surrounding courtyards continued to ignore him – including the doctor who had arrived that morning to strap up his cracked ribs – Ling had stepped in as cook and housekeeper, occasionally assisted by her three-year-old daughter Mei-Mei.

Mei-Mei was with her today, gravely bearing a smaller tray with a single plate of *bao* on it, her black eyes sparkling at the honor of serving both Grandpa Wu *and* Yin Hsing Jên: Mr Invisible.

'A city must have water,' said Wu, when Ling and her daughter withdrew. 'The lakes themselves are very ancient, dug by the

first of China's emperors. The presence of water mitigates the
influences of wind and dryness here, and provides a barrier over
which demons cannot cross. This is, of course, of paramount
importance, in a place where the Son of Heaven himself resides.'

Asher said, 'Of course.' As a folklorist he'd been long familiar
with the legend that vampires cannot cross running water, and
Ysidro had revealed the more complex truth of the matter last
year as the first-class railway carriage they'd shared had sped
across the Elbe. *I assume 'tis a sort of tidal magnetism*, the
vampire had said in his whispering voice, his long fingers shuf-
fling the deck in one of their endless games of cards. *Its effect
on our abilities slacks for brief periods at midnight. Yet in fact
none of us knows why: only that it is so.*

Asher guessed that the sluggish movement of the water from
the Jade Fountain outside the city and through the lakes was too
slight to discommode a vampire much, but it interested him that
the principle remained. 'What there now,' he asked in his clumsy
Chinese, 'Stone Relics of the Sea?'

From pouches of fat, the dark gaze rested speculatively on his
face. 'It is not a good place these days, Mr Invisible. Not a safe
place, once night has come.'

'When start? People—' He fished for a moment, trying to
recall the word for *disappear*. 'When *yao-kuei* under bridges?'

'Ah.' Wu managed to look sad and thoughtful while tucking
into egg tarts and 'chicken-velvet' with the relentlessness of a
machine. 'You have heard those tales? They began only this year,
a few weeks after the riots. It may be that while the Emperor
reigned, some order was retained and the *kuei* kept their distance
in fear. The Tso family lives by the side of the Sea, and what
they think of it, they do not say, though I admit to being most
curious about it. But people disappearing—'

He paused, a cup of mild-scented chrysanthemum tea suspended
in his chubby fingers, and in that stillness anger glinted suddenly in
his piggy eyes. 'That is a story that goes back twenty years.
Everyone knows the Tso pimps and child-merchants buy more
girls and young boys than any other family in the city. People
say Madame Tso set up some kind of arrangement with brothels
in other cities – that that's where these young people disappear
to. But why would a madam in Shanghai send all the way to
Peking for her stock? There are poor men with daughters in the

south as well as in the north. And many that the Tso buy are not
pretty; the daughters of beggars and laborers, with big, ugly feet.
These they can procure very cheap.'

He gulped his tea, wiped his fingers fastidiously on a napkin
which bore the monogram of the Peking Club.

'Tell about Tso.'

'Ah.' Wu nipped up the last bean-paste sesame-ball from the
plate. 'Madame Tso . . .' He gazed into the shadows of the half-
ruined chamber, swept clean now and tidied despite the holes in
the roof. 'Tso Shao Hua. They say these days that her father was
a night-soil collector, but that wasn't all he did. He worked for
Shui Ch'ia Chu, who used to be the *kuan ye* – the *grandfather
of money* – in that quarter of the city. Shao Hua married Chen,
who was the son of one of Shui's toughest enforcers. But she
was the real brains of the family, and beautiful as the sky with
stars. They still call the family Tso, though her sons are all actually Chens of course.'

'What happen Chen the enforcer?'

'The rumor is that she ate him alive for breakfast one morning.'
Wu chuckled richly. 'Chen Chi Yi is the Number One son. He
runs the brothels and the gambling, and procures guns from the
army for their enforcers to use. Madame Tso ousted old Shui
twenty years ago, and men you'd think would have stayed loyal
to the old man went over to work for her: afraid of her, everyone
says. No one in that quarter will breathe a word against her. Her
sons took over Shui's house, his rickshaws, his gambling parlors
and "chicken nests" . . . They opened into specialty houses,
working with people like An Lu T'ang, but even during the worst
of the Boxer troubles, nobody would touch the Tso property.

'When one of her *yin mei* puts an offer on a girl – like An
did with that poor child Shen Mi Ching – nobody dares say no,
though they know what it means. It gives An an advantage, that's
for certain: they say the Ugly Englishman saw Mi Ching at her
father's shop and asked specifically that she be brought to the
Tso house for him. Shen was very poor, but not that poor.' Wu
fell silent, heavy face creased with sorrow and distaste.

'Power come quick,' said Asher softly. 'Shui weak? No sons?'

'His sons were all killed.' Wu poured him another cup of tea.
'Yes, power came very quickly, once Tso came along. I'd like
one day to hear the true story behind it. They say she's a witch—'

He shrugged. 'Maybe such a thing is true. The Hao used to run things in the north end of the city, across Kuo Tzu Shih Ta Street from Shui territory. All their enforcers and pimps went over to Madame Tso within the same month. The same story with the whole area west of the Imperial Enclosure. Rumor has it she and her sons have been invited into the Golden Lakes, to visit with the President himself.'

'When?'

'A month ago? Two months? With the election coming up, that isn't a surprise. All the same—' Wu grimaced and discreetly poked among the dishes with his chopsticks, to see if a scrap of anything had been missed. 'She isn't a woman I'd like to see with more power. And she isn't a woman I'd like to see getting the same kind of power – whatever it is – over President Yuan Shi-k'ai that she has over the Hao and Shui's old gang.'

Asher thought the matter over, turning his teacup in his fingers. Remembering the beautiful Chinese woman who had come to Sir Allyn's on the arm of President Yuan's aide Huang Da-feng: *Yuan's go-between with the criminal bosses of the town*, Hobart had said, pointing them out. *The woman runs half the brothels in Peking* . . . 'What look like? Still beautiful?'

'Going to chance the displeasure of your wife's father?' The dark eyes sparkled grimly. 'Ling's a better bargain, Mr Invisible, for all she has ugly peasant feet and will talk you to death about the Republic. Yes, Madame's still beautiful, though she's getting on. She's grown a little fat, and the daylight isn't kind to her wrinkles no matter how much raw veal and strawberries she puts on her face. One story I hear is that all those girls she has An buy, and the beggar-children who disappear, she devours. I've heard the stories about evil women in the past bathing in blood to retain their youth – and I certainly wouldn't have put it past the old Empress! But it's not her youth or beauty she retains, but her energy. Her power.'

The fat man's voice lowered, and he leaned across the table to whisper. 'Sometimes I wonder if she drinks their *chi* – their life force – the way it's said the *chiang-shi* do.'

Asher said quietly, 'Indeed?'

The *chiang-shi* were the spirits of the Undead – the spirits that in the west were called vampires.

EIGHTEEN

At Mingliang Village the following morning, Lydia introduced herself and explained to Dr Bauer that the University of Tokyo had hired Professor Karlebach to continue her husband's investigation into the possibility of an atavistic tribe hiding in the Western Hills. The missionary thanked her, but though her sympathy for Lydia – in a skirted black riding-costume and a hat festooned with mourning veils instead of the jodhpurs she'd have preferred – was genuine and warm, there was reserve in her manner, almost fear.

When Lydia inquired, in her schoolgirl German, whether she might see whatever remains were left of the creature to observe if there were any cellular changes in the bone tissue, Dr Bauer replied, 'I believe that there were. My microscope here is not powerful. I doubt that anything is left of them by this time, but you would have to inquire with Dr Chun.'

'Dr Chun?'

'Of the Peita University.' Her voice was expressionless. 'A man came here Tuesday from the office of the President – a Mr Huang Da-feng – and offered me three hundred pounds for the remains and for my notes, which he said would be turned over to Dr Chun at the University.'

'Who is Dr Chun?' broke in Karlebach. 'And what does he—'

'There is no Dr Chun at the Peita University,' said Lydia. 'At least, not in the Medical Faculty – is there?' She turned back to Bauer. 'I looked through their catalogs on the boat coming out here.'

In that same constrained tone, Dr Bauer replied, 'Not that I know of. But naturally, I did not wish to disoblige President Yuan. He could close this mission altogether and destroy twenty years of my work here. And we stand desperately in need of money. And as no one – other than your poor husband – ever paid the slightest attention to the story of this thing in the hills, I felt . . .'

'I don't see that you had any choice,' Lydia reassured her. 'This Mr Huang—'

'Huang Da-feng certainly has no connection with the University,' put in Mizukami, who had stood quietly by the infirmary door while this discussion went on. 'His title is attaché to the President, but he began his career as a bully boy for one of the criminal gangs in the city. A gang which I believe contributed greatly to the President's treasury this year.'

Dr Bauer sighed and pushed the loose strands of her graying fair hair back into their bun. 'I have lived in China for twenty years,' she said. 'And I never thought I would ever have a single good thing to say about the Manchu emperors. Yet it seems to me that those who have replaced them – and everyone in the village seems to believe that it is only a matter of time before President Yuan will proclaim himself Emperor – are no better and, if possible, worse. Certainly, the men with Huang had more the air of thugs than of soldiers.'

'Did they go up to the mine as well,' inquired Lydia, 'after taking the remains and your notes?'

'They did. They hired Liao Ho as guide – and cheated him of his pay, so I'm sure he will be glad to guide you as well. Huang, too, seemed interested in finding all its various entrances.'

'Liao says, no one knows all the entrances to the mine.' Count Mizukami drew rein where the trail crested over the little ridge and looked across the marshy expanse of the old mine-camp toward the great irregular oval of the cave mouth. Even in the daylight it had the look of a gate into hell. Slag heaps, broken bins, and the few surviving fragments of sheds added to the dismal air of the place, and the Chinese ponies – surer-footed than the taller Western horses, and shaggy as teddy bears in their winter coats – tossed their heads at the smells that whispered from the mine.

Chan, Liao's big yellow dog, pressed close to his master's legs, the hair along his spine darkened with the lift of his hackles. A growl rumbled in his throat. Behind them, Lydia heard the three Japanese soldiers murmur to one another in their own tongue. The bodyguard Mizukami had brought out with them in the motor car from Peking that morning, a young man named Ogata, sat his mount little apart, his hand resting on the hilt of his sword.

The little guide, pointing, said something else to Mizukami, who added, 'Huang Da-feng had a map also, but two entrances that Liao knows about weren't on it.'

With the air of a man half-hypnotized, Karlebach slipped from his saddle, unshipped his shotgun from his back, and moved down the slope. Lydia sprang down and hurried after him, and when she touched his arm he almost started at the contact.

'It wasn't your fault,' she said.

He laid his other hand – his useless hand, bent completely in on itself with arthritis – over hers. 'Little bird,' he murmured, 'it was *all* my doing. They were like sons to me. Matthias, and Jamie.'

'What else could you have done?'

He only shook his head.

Leaving Ogata and Liao with the horses, Mizukami and his men descended the slope behind them, the three soldiers scouting through the marsh on both sides of the path, their rifles ready. The pools had frozen hard in last night's bitter cold; the touch of the noon sun hadn't melted them. Lydia's trailing black skirt caught on what had been a half-submerged branch, and she muttered an imprecation against Mrs Pilley and Ellen, who had begged her with tears to 'show respect' and 'consider appearances' by wearing this ridiculous costume.

At least with her face swathed in veils it was possible for her to wear her glasses without it being obvious. She had a feeling, as they climbed the packed-earth ramp up to the cave mouth, that she was going to need to see as clearly she could.

At the top of the ramp the soldiers lit the lanterns they carried. The floor of the outer cave – some sixty feet by thirty – was sheeted across with ice, and away from the opening the cold blue twilight deepened to the point that Lydia, exasperated, pushed up her veils so that she could see the openings of the two tunnels that had been cut into the mountain. *I don't CARE if I look like a goggle-eyed golliwog* (that was what her cousins had called her): it was simply impossible to see details through all that mourning. Pieces of broken carts, looted of their iron undercarriages and wheels, lay along the sides of the cavern.

'How much explosive will we need –' Lydia took her notebook from her jacket pocket – 'to close these tunnels? Jamie always says – *said* –' she corrected herself quickly – 'that gelignite works best, if it can be transported safely.' She turned to scan the great archway behind them, then looked at both tunnels and the shadowy well of subsidence to her right and did some swift mental arithmetic. 'I think what we really need here is some kind of poison gas – chlorine or phosgene – that's heavier than air and will sink.'

'Chlorine would be easiest to obtain.' A glint of something like amusement flickered behind Mizukami's thick spectacles. 'The liquid is produced in Shanghai and Hong Kong both, for purposes of disinfection. It will volatilize with air.'

'If containers of it could be placed deep in the mine – as close as possible to where the creatures sleep – and then detonated with a small charge to blow them up, just before the mine entrances are sealed—' She looked over at Karlebach, who was regarding her with deep compassion and something like awe, as if he would have said how brave and strong she was being . . .

As if he saw his own grim obsession reflected in her triumph over her supposed grief.

Oh dear, all that didn't sound awfully grief-stricken . . .

But how DOES one plan to blow up a mine filled with monstrosities in a grief-stricken manner . . .?

Beside her, Mizukami was giving orders to the three soldiers, two of whom moved off down the mine tunnels, the light of their lanterns dwindling in the darkness.

'We'll need to come up with some good reason for ordering all that chlorine,' added Lydia, a little worriedly. 'Not to speak of getting it up here. It would be ghastly to have either Yuan's troops or the Kuo Min-tang confiscate it—'

'I trust that you, Madame, will devise a reason sufficiently pressing to justify a strong guard.' Again Mizukami's eyes twinkled in a hidden smile. 'Leave the issue of its transportation to me. What troubles me most is President Yuan's inquiries.'

'Yes . . . Obviously somebody knows something. *Would* President Yuan go to the trouble of scouting the mine and securing the remains of the *yao-kuei* if he didn't think he could find some way to use them?'

'Use them,' said Mizukami grimly, 'or to rent them out to his friends. And if he can control them, or thinks he can . . . or thinks he will be able to do so in the near future . . . I fear he is the kind of man who will then seek a way to make them multiply. Yabe—' He signed to the third soldier – barely a boy

– to bring the lantern, then turned toward Karlebach, who had moved a few steps off, staring into the abyss of the nearest tunnel. 'Is there some way, Sensei, that these things can, or might be, controlled?'

Karlebach's dark eyes glinted suspiciously behind the small oval chips of his spectacles. She went quickly to his side, lowered her voice to a whisper: 'Did your friend Matthias learn anything of this? Or did the vampires of Prague speak of it—?'

'Anything a vampire says is a lie. Or a half-truth aimed to some ulterior purpose, to buy your trust for some still greater lie to come.'

'What did they say?'

Karlebach shook his head. 'Upon my honor, Madame, I know of no way that the living – those of us who are still whole men, with souls and minds – can have any influence upon these . . . these things. And if it were possible . . .'

The shriek that cut through the dark of the tunnel was picked up by echoes, magnified: horror, agony, shock. Lydia strode toward the tunnel mouth, and Karlebach caught her back and thrust her behind him. As Mizukami rushed past her toward the black square of darkness, the dog Chan set up a wild salvo of barking.

The next second the soldier-scout blundered into the light of Private Yabe's lantern from the tunnel's depth, falling into the walls as he clawed wildly at the rats that covered him: face, body, legs. Lydia sprang back – she had hated rats from childhood – then looked down as something brushed her ankle, gasped, and fled in earnest to the entrance of the cave.

Rats streamed out of the tunnel around her feet. Mizukami whipped his scabbarded sword from his belt and, keeping the blade covered, strode in and used the scabbard as a club to knock the rats from the soldier's face and body. The other men stomped, kicked, crushed at the rodents underfoot – the second soldier rushed past Lydia from the other tunnel and joined in the horrifying process. Lydia saw the subsidence at the east end of the cave also disgorging a river of rats, shouted, 'Watch out!'

Mizukami and Private Yabe grabbed the bleeding soldier by the arms an instant before he would have fallen and dragged him at a run toward the mouth of the cave, Karlebach and the other soldier at their heels. The guide Liao dashed up to Lydia's side, grabbed her by the arm and dragged her back down the earthen ramp: *'Hsiao hsing!'* he shouted.

The slag heaps, the naked bushes, the blackened reeds of the frozen swamp all threshed with scurrying life. But when the dog Chan charged barking into their midst, the rats scattered, as if, once in the daylight of the gorge, the urge to swarming attack was less commanding. They merely rushed agitatedly here and there, torn between their instincts and whatever it was that demanded of them that they kill.

Sick with shock, Lydia scrambled back up to the ponies, dug in her saddlebags for bandages and carbolic. She knelt beside the wounded soldier as his comrades lowered him to the ground. The stiff collar of his uniform had protected his throat, but rat bites covered his face, one eye and one side of his lips a chewed ruin. She wiped and mopped and washed, and paused long enough to hold out the brandy flask to Karlebach, who sank down on to a heap of rubble nearby, his face nearly green with shock.

'Take his pulse,' she ordered Mizukami. 'Sit him on something – tree stump will do – and get his head between his knees . . . please,' she added, remembering belatedly that Japanese men, even more so than English, were unused to taking orders from a woman. As she worked on the stricken soldier she spoke over her shoulder: 'Professor, can you hear me? Can you hear what I'm saying? Please answer—'

Faintly, Karlebach replied, 'I hear, little bird.'

'Can you breathe? Does your chest hurt you?'

'I'm well.' His voice was a little muffled, for the Count had obeyed Lydia's orders with great promptness and had lowered the old man's head down as instructed. 'I am – dear God . . .!'

'Count, have one of your men get this man – what is his name?'

'Takahashi.'

'Please have one of your men get Takahashi-san back to Dr Bauer. He'll need to be started on rabies treatments as soon as we get back to Peking. Mr Liao—'

She looked around for the guide, who was helping Ogata hold the frantic ponies.

'Count Mizukami, would you ask Mr Liao if he's up to guiding us to the remaining mine-entrances that he knows about? I realize it's a horrid thing to have to do.'

'No, honored Madame,' the Count replied quietly, 'it is not horrid. At least, no more horrid, as you say, than war. And this is war: something for which, in times past, women in my country have been as trained and ready as men.'

He stood back as Lydia went over to kneel beside Karlebach. 'Are you feeling better, sir?' she asked softly. 'I think you should go back with Takahashi-san to the village.'

'No.' He waved weakly, groped for his shotgun. 'No, the more of us who know the land – who know the places where explosives and gas must be placed – the better. Anything could happen to any of us . . . The old legends, the old accounts, said they could call rats to their bidding. In the catacombs beneath Prague Castle, in the wells and tunnels and chambers that all connect . . . Matthias was sometimes turned back by the rats. But never like this . . .'

Never that you knew about. Lydia looked back up at the mine entrance. *Or was that one of the things the Master of Prague told you that you thought he was lying about?*

From here she could see, in the shadows of the outer cave, hundreds of rats still darting around the crushed and battered corpses of their comrades. The cold breath that seeped from underground brought her their sweetish, frowsty stink. One of them, running back up the icy slope nearby her, made her almost jump out of her skin.

She realized she herself was trembling, with shock and cold that seemed to penetrate to her marrow.

Mizukami held out to her the brandy flask. 'Now at least,' he said softly, 'we have a good reason – a logical reason – for ordering hundreds of cylinders of chlorine and as much explosive as it will take to cave in the mine. Moreover, you know and I know now what it is that President Yuan seeks to control, if he can achieve command over these devils. Yabe—?'

The young soldier – who looked younger than most of Jamie's students, thought Lydia – was almost green with shock, but he stood stiffly to listen to his Colonel's instructions.

'*Hai.*' The young man saluted and helped his bleeding and half-conscious comrade on to one of the ponies. Chinese ponies being what they were, he led it down the trail toward the village, rather than risk riding. Karlebach got to his feet like a man half-stunned, looked around him for his lantern; it lay on its side just within the entrance to the cave.

Bracing herself with loathing, Lydia climbed back up the half-dozen yards that separated her from the gaping darkness in the hillside. The sound of rats squeaking and scuttering in the cave raised the hair on her nape. *Chlorine gas*, she thought. *Seal the mine, detonate the containers . . .* It would eat away most living tissue.

She bent quickly, picked up the lantern, straightened.

And, like a breath, a thought passed through her mind.

A whisper that seemed to come from the darkness; not physical sound, but something deeper, as if someone had breathed her name.

Only, it wasn't her name.

A single word passed through the back of her mind, leaving her shocked and cold and aghast and filled with horror.

Mistress . . .

And then was gone.

NINETEEN

Despite brutal cold and a cutting wind that kept everyone on Peking's dark streets wrapped in as many scarves as they could obtain, Asher felt as exposed as he would have had he been wandering the Tatar city in tweeds and a homburg. Even in the early-falling autumn twilight he kept instinctively to the smaller *hutongs*, avoided crowds and the lights of shops. There were Han Chinese six feet tall, especially from the north; with his hands gloved in cut-out rags and the lower half of his face swathed, he was no more conspicuous than any other passer-by in a faded, quilted *ch'i-p'ao* and padded trousers tucked into felt-soled boots.

But, years ago, Don Simon Ysidro had said to him, *We usually have warning of their suspicions*, when the talk had turned to the friends, lovers, and bereaved families of the vampires' victims who might guess how their loved one had died. *Most of us have good memories for faces, for names, and for details . . .*

Even locked in the irresistible sleep of the daylight hours, the vampire was not truly unconscious.

Asher knew he'd have only one chance to get a look at the

outer walls, to identify the various doors and gates, of the Tso compound. On a second pass, even in daylight, one who slept within might well turn in his sleep and think: *I have heard that unfamiliar stride before, smelled that flesh.*

He was fairly sure, now, what was in the Tso house and why the family had risen so swiftly to such power.

And felt like the world's supreme idiot, for not having thought of it before.

That is our strength, Ysidro had said to him once. *That no one believes, and not believing, lets us be.*

Yet at the moment he walked the streets of a city in which ninety-nine men of a hundred believed in the Undead and would be perfectly ready to hunt them and kill them . . .

Or use them for their own ends.

Or be used by them, for mutual benefit.

So you have become their servant? Karlebach had asked him, a year and a half ago. *His day man – like the shabbas goy my granddaughter employs to light the fires in the stoves here on the Seventh Day . . .*

They kill those who serve them . . . he had said.

And Asher thought now: *But what if they didn't?*

What if they employed, not one 'day man', but – as Father Orsino had said – an entire extended family of them: grandfathers, uncles, daughters, cousins? What if they helped and enriched and protected that family, in exchange for protection during the daytimes . . . and a steady supply of weak or confused or very young victims? *They rule the world*, Father Orsino had said . . . The spirit hidden in the cellar, the secret at the heart of the family, the ruler of the enclave – the Magistrate of Hell.

The thought was monstrous, but not nearly as monstrous as machine guns or phosgene gas or the staggering, horrifying stupidity of generals who remained convinced that an army's 'will to fight' and 'patriotic spirit' was going to carry a bayonet charge against a line of Vickers guns.

He turned off the Te Ching Men Street, worked his way east- ward past the Catholic University, glancing now and then at the hand-drawn map Ling and her brothers had worked up for him. A line of camels passed him, laden with coal; a rickshaw bearing two daintily-bedizened prostitutes nearly ran him down. This whole district was the domain of the Tso family. From the Tatar city's western wall almost to the old granaries on the east side, rickshaw-pullers worked for them, hawkers of hot soup and fried watermelon seeds rented their pitches on the street corners from them, small shopkeepers paid them for 'protection', gambling parlors gave them 'squeeze'. Everyone passed them information. Everyone wanted to be on their good side. It was a situation far from exclusive to China or Peking.

He counted turnings, looked for landmarks. In the cold twilight the narrow gray-walled *hutongs* seemed all very much the same to a foreign eye. But there he noted the shape of a gate with green-and-gold pillars instead of the more common red. At that intersection was an enormous, gaudy banner announcing THE EMPRESS'S GARDEN beside the gate of an eating house, tiers of open galleries around a central paradise. (*And what do the local Republicans make of THAT?*) Here was a *hutong* that made ten turns inside of two hundred feet and another that ran straight as a railway line for nearly that distance, and Asher's mind, trained to detail, logged these individual minutiae as he would have noted exits from a house in which he planned to meet an enemy.

He'd heard vampires speak of their fellow Undead who grew timid, shrinking in on themselves: afraid to leave their houses, afraid to go beyond what was familiar. Afraid lest some accident somehow trap them out of doors, in the burning horror of the rising sun. Sometimes they'd get their vampire compatriots to hunt for them, to bring them prey . . . But on the whole, Ysidro had told him more than once, genuine friendship among vampires was rare.

But the living they could use: through illusion, through dreams, through fear.

Even through loyalty, as Ysidro had used him.

The *siheyuan* of the Tso spread over thousands of square feet, on the little peninsula between the two north-westerly lakes. Roofs rose above the gray walls like dark masses of cloud in the twilight. Asher noted those where weeds had sprouted in the mud that held the tiles. Gates and doorways, some flanked with brightly-painted pillars, or fanciful beasts: lions, dragons, birds. He saw where paint had not been refreshed, where hinges bore rust and the accumulated gray-yellow dust of many winters. There were compounds in Peking where the courtyards, like the one he currently occupied, went uninhabited for decades; where weasels and foxes, geckos and stray cats and even *yang kwei tse* spies might dwell in perfect safety. The Tso walls backed on to the long northern arm of the Sea, across from a pleasure ground of ancestral temples and fancy tea-houses; looking back along the wide verges of ice-rimmed water toward the bridge, Asher shivered at the recollection of how nearly he had been himself surrounded the night before last.

Their families worship them, Father Orsino had said. *They are gods . . .*

But a moment later he had said, *They trust no one. It is hundreds of years since one of them created a vampire. They fear even their children.*

So what was the truth?

He turned back along the *hutongs* away from the water. In the lane that everyone called Prosperity Alley he was nearly crushed against the wall by a very long black Mercedes car, driven along the rutted way with little more than a foot of clearance on either side. Through its rear windows he glimpsed the woman he'd seen at Eddington's, and sure enough, the car halted outside the main gate of the Tso compound – the gilding and red-lacquered lattice-work of which would have done credit to a palace – and the Presidential attaché Huang Da-feng climbed out.

Half-hidden by the turn of the lane, Asher watched as Huang bowed and handed the lady out. Like many of the President's staff, Huang favored a European suit beneath his well-cut camel-hair British overcoat, but Madame Tso was all Chinese in her dress, the bulky, square-cut *ch'i-p'ao* of blue silk delicately embroidered, her coal-black hair oiled and smoothed close to her head and looped up into an ebony roll decorated with fresh gardenia blossoms that made expensive mock of the frozen season. Asher placed her at about his own age – forty-seven – with the round face and slight air of creamy stoutness that would cause a Chinese to liken her beauty to the sky with stars. She tottered elegantly on her bound feet, each of her blue silk shoes – the length of a schoolboy's finger – wrought of enough pearls and gold wire to purchase a farm.

So you have become their servant . . .?

He wondered how they had met, and what she had offered him – this vampire, whoever he was – that had convinced him

to become the god of her family. Ysidro had told him that few
vampires cared anything about their own families, once they
themselves were vampire. For most, all that existed was the
hunt.

Was it just that this woman knew a way to make the hunt
easier or more entertaining?

Or had the vampire, whoever he was, simply been drawn to
her? As Ysidro, deny it though he would, was drawn to Lydia
– a friendship that filled Asher with foreboding. It was not jeal-
ousy, nor yet fear for his wife's immortal soul: Lydia was mildly
disinclined to believe in anything she couldn't locate in the
dissecting rooms, and she would have greeted the idea that she
might one day run away with the vampire with a whoop of
laughter and a question about the sleeping arrangements.

Yet he feared for her, nevertheless.

The porters shut the gate, leaving the black Mercedes to block
the lane. Its driver glared at Asher as he squeezed past it, with
an expression that implied he would murder him should his
buttons scratch the lacquer of its doors.

What am I doing back at the Temple?

Lydia looked around the cluttered, shabby courtyard, aware
that she was dreaming but puzzled: *why am I dreaming about
the Temple of Everlasting Harmony instead of about rats?*

They had returned to Peking shortly after full darkness.
Exhausted and trembling, Lydia had insisted on accompanying
Takahashi to the clinic at Peita University, to have his horrible
injuries treated and to begin the long and painful course of treatment for rabies. Throughout the endless winter afternoon, as she,
Mizukami, Karlebach and the remaining two warriors had
followed Liao Ho through the rough terrain of the hills, again
and again she found she had to force her mind aside from what
had happened at the mine. She had made notes, matched prob-
able tunnels on the map with the subsidiary entrances Liao showed
them. Climbed old trails down which the coal had once been
carried in baskets, now overgrown with laurel and weeds, while
Private Nishiharu and Ogata the Bodyguard had scanned the
horizon with their rifles.

At every entrance – some of them mere holes in the hillside,
save for the slag heaps around them – she had gone as close

as she dared and listened. Because Karlebach was there, she could not speak, could not call down into that darkness. But each time they'd climbed up toward those inky pits, those long-overgrown piles of dirt and stone, frantic fear had clutched at her, frantic horror.

Simon . . .

They had covered something like twelve miles on foot and horseback, and Lydia was certain they'd have to go back to locate the rest of the entrances. At no point had a second whisper passed through her mind, nor any indication that the first had been anything more than illusion. And all the while the under-brush in the gullies, the withered brown grass on the deforested hill-slopes, had rustled with the constant, restless, horrible move-ment of rats.

Stricken with guilt over her fraudulent mourning, upon her return to the hotel she had consented to have supper with Karlebach, to make sure that the old man was all right. But she had barely listened to his tales of the iniquities of the vampires of Prague over the centuries of his research, had been unable to touch more than a spoonful of her food.

Only Miranda cheered her. Only in the hour she'd spent holding her daughter against her and reading aloud – watching the still-wordless thoughts chase each other through those lovely brown eyes – did she feel at rest.

But falling into bed, sick with weariness and shock, she had been positive she was going to dream about rats.

Or, worse, about that single, dying whisper in the back of her mind: *Mistress . . .*

Yet here she was in the courtyard of the Temple of Everlasting Harmony, listening to the muffled yammer of voices from Silk Lane and the soft brisk tap of passing donkey-hooves on the dirt lane outside its gate.

It was cold, and she was glad of her coat. (*Thank goodness it's the pink merino with the chinchilla collar! But I thought I left that back in Oxford, and in any case I shouldn't be wearing pink with black . . .*) The stone kongs where goldfish had swum only last week were frozen. The wind that had whipped and wailed over the hills all day sobbed around the Temple's upturned eaves and filled the air with the smell of dust.

From the dark of the Temple, eyes gleamed like a line of

terrible dragons: the ten Magistrates of Hell, surrounded by the writhing damned. Movement in the shadow – a pale flicker near the back of the long hall, where a door opened into a narrow garden, Lydia advanced a step to the threshold, her every instinct telling her: *Don't . . .*

But not afraid.

'Simon?'

Not a sound from within, save the moan of wind in the rafters. It was all exactly as she recalled it from her excursion with Paola and the Baroness, down to the yellow dog, curled up asleep in the corner by the God of War's altar, and the tattered banners of cut paper that swayed and groped like spirit hands overhead. Lydia walked forward over the worn flagstones, caught the heel of her shoe in a crack – *drat it, I really do need a lantern . . .*

And, as she often was able to do in dreams, told herself: *there's one over by the altar of that Fifth Magistrate, the one in charge of the people-chopper-upper machine . . .*

And so there was. And a box of matches on the corner of the altar.

She lit the wick, closed the glass slide, achingly grateful for the warmth of the small flame on her frozen fingers . . .

Turned back to the dark of the Temple, raising the lantern high.

But there was nothing there. No one, where she had been ready to swear that someone had stood, just moments before, just to the right of the God of War's altar, in the moving seaweed shadows of the hanging scrolls. Someone thin and old, who had watched her patiently. Who had known her name.

There was no one there now. Determined not to let the dream go, Lydia proceeded to search the Temple with her lantern, probing every dark corner and startling spiders and crickets.

She found nothing. The Temple of Everlasting Harmony was as empty as Ysidro's brass-bound trunk had been, in the rented safety of the bank vault next door.

TWENTY

As the following day – Friday – required the presence of the Japanese military attaché at one of the regular meetings of the Legations Council, Lydia had accepted an invitation for coffee and elevenses with the Baroness. For all her overbearing ways (she was widely rumored to beat her servants with a riding whip), the Baroness Drosdrova was capable of both kindness and sensitivity, so the only other company that morning was Paola Giannini. Lydia had had a headache planned, should she have walked into the Russian Minister's conservatory and found Madame Schrenk there.

There was a good deal of talk of opera, over an assortment of too-sweet jelly-cakes and rubbery blini. Madame Drosdrova had newspapers sent to her from every European capital and could chatter knowledgeably of what was on at La Scala and the Paris Opera. And there was a good deal more said about the Eddington murder, which would be arraigned the following week.

'Has nothing further been discovered?' asked Paola. 'Poor Sir Grant must be distracted!'

'Poor Sir Grant my foot.' Madame dusted powdered sugar from her fingers. 'I hear he goes in and shouts at Sir John and tears his hair and weeps, yet it doesn't seem to have stopped his visits to that house of accommodation he goes to, in the native city.'

'Surely, he wouldn't . . .'

'*Ma chère*,' said the Baroness, 'the innocence of your heart gives me the greatest admiration for your husband's character . . . or his tact. Only yesterday, when one would think Sir Grant Hobart would have nothing on his thoughts but conferring with the Legation solicitor – though anyone who would trust that slick little piece of Hibernian *canaille* is simply asking for what he'll get! – Hobart took a rickshaw out of the Quarter, all muffled up in a fur coat and scarves, as if everyone in the Quarter doesn't know those *frightful* yellow shoes of his at sight . . . *And* didn't return until the small hours of the morning, flaming drunk and shouting at the gate guards to let him in, Hans Erlich tells me. Is he still sending you notes, my dear?' She turned her lorgnette in Lydia's direction. 'Considering everything the man has to feel guilt about . . . And what's this, that nasty cat Hilda Schrenk was telling me about you going riding with Count Mizukami, of all people?'

'And did Madame Schrenk think to mention that I was accompanied not only by the Count, but also by Professor Karlebach and about half a regiment of Japanese soldiers as chaperones? I didn't think so.' Lydia caught herself up, set down the thumb-sized fragment of rock-dry toast on which she'd been spreading and re-spreading caviar for the past five minutes, and added, with a little quaver in her voice, 'I hope Madame Schrenk will never have the occasion to discover what it's like to . . . to feel trapped, and closed-in, so that *anything* will be preferable to staying in the hotel.'

She had heard her school friend Mary Teasborough say something of the kind, shortly after her brother had died, and hoped it would serve. But the memory of the rats in the mines, of the voice in her head whispering, *Mistress*, returned to her with such sudden force then that her hands shook and she pushed the toast-point aside. *At least new widowhood excuses one from eating the productions of the Drosdrov cook . . .*

'Darling—' Paola took her hand. 'You know you could have called upon either one of us.'

Lydia nodded, struggling to put that whisper from her mind. With what she hoped was a convincing-sounding catch to her voice, she murmured, 'As Professor Karlebach has been employed by the University of Tokyo to continue the Oriental portion of . . . of Jamie's work, he very kindly asked me to go along. I felt it was for the best . . .'

'And so it is!' The Baroness leaned across the table to grip her other hand. 'Hilda Schrenk is a spiteful old cat, particularly since you turned down that imbecile Alois Blucher's offer to go walking with you – he's her cousin, you know, and *frantically* in need of an heiress to marry. And Mr Woodreave was saying to me only yesterday—'

'If you speak of Edmund Woodreave to me,' said Lydia, 'I shall scream. But on the subject of taking the air – and I am much better today, thank you – I wondered if perhaps we might return to the Temple of Everlasting Harmony near Silk Lane this morning? I had a dream about it,' she added as the Baroness opened her mouth to point out that the Temple of Heaven, with its nine terraces and its curious round structure, was greatly superior architecturally to some forgotten shrine lost in the middle of the *hutongs*.

'What did you dream?' asked Paola, but the Baroness interrupted her.

'Dreams are nonsense. I'm forever searching the maids' rooms to get rid of those idiotic horoscope charts and dream books they all pore over, as if there weren't far more elevating literature in the world. I try to educate them, but the stubbornness of the Lower Orders is quite astonishing.'

Nevertheless, she rang the bell, ordered the servant to send for the rickshaw-pullers, and for Menchikov and Korsikov, and proceeded to take charge of the expedition.

Lydia wasn't certain what she hoped or expected to encounter at the Temple, but through the morning her anxiety had grown, both for Don Simon and for Asher. She wasn't a fanciful woman, but she was, in her own way, an imaginative one. It wasn't difficult to picture a situation in which Ysidro could have become trapped in the Shi'h Liu Mine, where the weight of the earth would prevent him from making any kind of clear contact – as she knew he could – in her dreams.

And though she knew that he could not be other than what he was, she'd seen the effects of chlorine gas on human tissue. The thought of him being still in the mines when hundreds of liters of chlorine were dumped down to form gas there, and the mine sealed, was a hideous one. It took no fancy or imagination to nauseate her with dread, and to send her to a place where she was fairly certain she wouldn't have dreamed about – much less twice! – on her own.

But when they reached the Temple, all things were very much as she had seen them in her dream, except that now the hall was filled with gray, prosaic daylight, and there was not the slightest trace of anyone untoward there. Only a fat, middle-aged priest, vainly sweeping at last night's dust on the floor, and the yellow dog scratching for fleas by the War-God's altar. For the sum of ten cents, Lydia was conducted over the entire building, including the back garden – choked with pigeon coops – and the cellar and sub-cellar, which seemed to be filled with broken birdcages, sacks of potatoes, anonymous crates, torn oceans of tattered banners, and the remains of a set of faded puppets.

She thanked the priest, tipped him, and took her departure – the Baroness discoursing at the top of her lungs on the subject of rafters, doweling, and the history of tile roofs in China – with the deep sense that she'd missed something. That she'd looked right at it – whatever it was – and had failed to notice it. As she crossed the courtyard to the gate she glanced back, but saw only, in the shadows of the Temple, the line of grimacing devils that were the Magistrates of Hell. Ancient local gods, dead warriors of forgotten dynasties, personified variations of Buddhist saints, trampling on the bodies of the meticulously catalogued sinners.

Employees in the service of the King of the Damned.

And they probably had to take Civil Service Examinations to get the post.

At the hotel, a note awaited her at the front desk from Count Mizukami. Takahashi-san was resting more easily, the note said. He had had to have four fingers amputated, but retained the sight in one eye. He would be returning to Japan as soon as the course of rabies treatment was complete. *Please do not take blame upon yourself, for the expedition in the course of which this terrible thing came to pass*, the Count wrote.

How did he know? she wondered as she sank into the chair by the fireplace in her suite.

> *As I said yesterday, this is war, and in war men sustain such injuries and far worse. It is a soldier's duty and his honor to bear them, as one day it will be mine. I have written to the proper authorities to report swarms of rabid and aggressive rats in the mine, and have made arrangements for the shipment of 1,000 liters of chlorine. Within days I believe I shall receive authorization to use explosives to seal the mine.*
>
> *On Monday I return to the Western Hills to complete reconnaissance of the mine entrances. You and Professor Karlebach are most welcome to accompany me, should you choose to do so. Yet, do not feel obligated, should you wish to spare yourselves – and particularly the good Professor*

*– the hardships, exhaustion, and shocks of yesterday. Believe
that the interests of the human race are in good hands.*
  Sincerely,
  Mizukami

When Karlebach – clearly the worse for *the hardships, exhaustion, and shocks of yesterday* – read the letter a few hours later, he only sighed deeply and nodded. 'I will go, of course.'

Lydia wondered how much of this resolve was undertaken to keep an eye on Mizukami. The old scholar had – Ellen had reported – spent much of the day in his bed: she had gone to his room three or four times, to make sure he was well. Now, resplendent in a stunningly outdated blue tailcoat and a tie which could only have been described as antediluvian, he looked a little better than he had last night, but there was a gray haggardness to his skin that Lydia didn't like.

She put her hand on his arm, said gently, 'It isn't him any more, you know. If he . . . If your friend . . . is still alive at all. That is . . . *Do* they die?' She had changed for dinner, into yet another lugubrious costume that she felt wasn't helping the old man's mood any. 'If they aren't killed by Mr Liao's dogs, I mean, or beheaded by poor Ito-san. Do they just . . . *die?*'

'I think so. Eventually.' He rubbed his gloved hand over his face. 'Else they would have spread beyond Prague ere this. And believe me, Madame, since first I learned of their existence, I have watched the newspapers and every account and traveler's tale that circulates Europe. And I know,' he went on, 'that Matthias – if his body still lives – would not recognize me. And that all these things I have brought –' he patted his pockets, where he usually kept his little phials of herbal decoctions – 'would not bring him back.'

No, reflected Lydia sadly. *But you carried them to the mines yesterday all the same.*

And it was for him that you were looking, hoping against hope . . .

And last night you had nightmares that when the chlorine gas is released into the sealed mine, it is the Matthias Uray that you knew – your ruffianly knight, your substitute son – who will choke his life out, and not some mindless Other who wears his flesh.

As even in waking I have nightmares about Simon.

They descended to the lobby, Lydia veiled and clinging to the old man's arm. As usual with the approach of the dinner hour, the handsome room, with its wood paneling, its Wilton carpets and the curlicued majesty of its Venetian chandeliers, buzzed softly with the conversations not only of the hotel's guests, but also of the various ministers, attachés, senior clerks and translators of the Legations who sought the talents of its chef and the clubby, friendly atmosphere of its dining room.

As Karlebach crossed the lobby to collect his mail from the desk, Lydia scanned the crowd, listening for voices that she knew, identifying French Trade Minister Hautecoeur by his silver-streaked leonine mane and by the color and shape of his wife's gown: Annette Hautecoeur, for all her crooning catlike tact, was a tall broad-shouldered woman whose silhouette was unmistakable . . . to say nothing of the fact that she was always surrounded by men, who were fascinated by her. And over there that splotch of green and blue had to be little Madame Bonnefoy from the Belgian Legation with her two daughters. With men it was more difficult. Lydia had to listen for their voices, watch the way they moved . . .

'I mean-ter-say, honestly, Colonel Morris—'

Lydia's blood ran cold at the plummy Etonian accents, followed – inevitably – by a maddening little giggle.

'—what earthly difference does it make whether Yuan's elected or t'other chap?'

Edmund Woodreave. She picked out his stoop-shouldered outline near the door, handing coat and overcoat to the Chinese porter – and Karlebach was deep in conversation with someone or other by the desk . . .

'You know we're going to have to blast the Germans out of Shantung sooner or later . . .'

He'd turn in a minute, and clothed in black as she was Lydia knew she'd be identifiable across the room even to someone as unobservant as Woodreave. She stepped back quickly into the open door of one of the lobby's private parlors and closed it almost to behind her.

'Oh! I'm so sorry—' she said an instant later. '*Tui-bu-chi,*' she added laboriously and hoped that what she'd said was actually *I'm sorry* and not something horribly indelicate.

'Nothing.' The Chinese gentleman bowed and waved a staying hand when Lydia would have slipped from the room again (and not, she prayed, straight into Edmund Woodreave's arms . . .). 'Mis-sus Ashu?'

For an instant Lydia was too startled to do anything but say, 'Yes.' She wondered in the next instant how he'd got in there. The management of the Wagons-Lits Hotel generally admitted only the best-dressed and most socially prominent Chinese to its lobby and parlor, and then – in the most tactful fashion possible – it did not let them linger.

And this old gentleman, though clearly not of the laboring classes, was shabbily, even raggedly, dressed . . . which was why he looked familiar, Lydia realized. His flowing robe wasn't the nearly-universal Manchu *ch'i-p'ao*, but the simple brown garment, rather like a Japanese kimono, worn by the priests at the Temple of Everlasting Harmony. Like the fat priest who'd showed her around the Temple from rafters to sub-crypt this afternoon, this frail old gentleman wore his long white hair in the fashion of centuries ago, before the Manchu had conquered China (as Madame Drosdrova had pointed out, at length). The hand he held out to her, with a folded piece of paper in it, was like a bundle of broken chopsticks.

'Dream.' He touched his high, domed forehead. 'Last night, other night. So sorry, speak not, write not. Dream. This hotel, red hair—' He gestured at his own white hair where it flowed down over his shoulders, his nails long, like an old mandarin's. 'Black gown. *Ashu*, he say. Not any other.'

Feeling as if in a dream herself, Lydia took the paper.

The words had been written with a brush – drawn rather, as if carefully copied – but the up and down strokes, the strange loops and flourishes, were reproduced with eerie exactness.

Mistress,
    I am in the mine, trapped. They cannot reach me, nor can I pass them. I have counted forty here. They sleep in the central chamber of the original mine, at the bottom of the first down-shaft, a hundred seventy feet deep, all together. Twice I have heard the voices of the living: two men, at least, and a woman, Chinese. I know not what they said, but they come and go in the day.

Remember me kindly, should it come to pass that we
meet not again.
    Unto eternity,
    Ysidro

TWENTY-ONE

Last year, as they had traveled through Eastern Europe together, Ysidro had said, *There is a strangeness in Prague . . .*

Heart racing slightly from the last of Karlebach's stay-alert powder, and cracked ribs gouging him at every step, Asher slipped through the courtyards of Grandpa Wu's compound, feeling a little like a ghost himself. Beyond his own deserted courtyard, most of the lamps had been put out already. He passed by men belatedly fastening shutters over their windows and women trading talk in doorways after their children had been put to bed. But they all looked aside from Mr Invisible. He stepped past a screen and so out by one of the compound's several subsidiary gates into Big God of Fire Temple Alley without garnering so much as a glance.

Deep night lay on Peking.

With any luck, by the time he reached the Stone Relics of the Sea, the Tso vampire would be out hunting and the Tso themselves asleep.

Get in and get out, he told himself. *You can't learn any more just watching the place from the outside.*

Yesterday's twilight reconnaissance had identified three areas of the Tso compound which the state of the roofs had led Asher to believe were deserted. One of these had a gate, the old-fashioned bronze lock of which Asher was fairly certain he could pick. He carried a dark-lantern and kept his revolver in the pocket of his baggy *ch'i-p'ao*. It would be death to use it, since a shot would waken the household.

There was, almost certainly, a vampire in the Tso compound. Maybe – the thought made him flinch – a nest of them.

And there might be *yao-kuei* as well. Karlebach had spoken

of the enmity between the vampires and the Others in Prague: *the vampires fear them . . . more than they do any of the living . . . Sometimes they will kill a vampire: open its crypt, and summon rats to devour it while it sleeps . . .*

But the rules were different in China. He had no idea what he would find, behind those tall gray walls.

But whatever it was, he had no desire to see it fall into the hands of President Yuan Shi-k'ai, who had proved already that he was willing to make any alliance, use any means, to keep his power.

And whatever had befallen Ysidro, Asher knew that he was now on his own.

In Shun Chin Men Ta Street he signaled a rickshaw – the one commodity one was virtually certain to find on the streets at literally any hour, outdoing even the prostitutes – and, after flashing his pass at the gate guards, had it take him as far as the old palace of Prince Ch'ing. From there he crossed the Jade Fountains canal on a footbridge and worked his way back along the dark *hutongs*, watching and listening for what he guessed he would not be able to either see or hear. Even at this hour, in the larger streets there were wine shops open, amber oil-light outlining the open gates of courtyards from which the rough voices of men spilled like gravel. He heard the rattle of *pai-gow* tiles and the sweet, nasal wail of sing-song girls. When he passed the Empress's Garden he saw the courtyard – and the encircling galleries within – filled with soldiers: Russian, German, Japanese.

He crossed into the darkness on the other side of the *hutong*, used the reflected light to check his map again. He was close. The new moon was barely a thread and the alleyways pitch-black. Anything could be watching him, listening to his breathing . . .

In Big Tiger Lane a rickshaw passed him, driver panting. The dim gold lamplight of a gate opening was like a bonfire's blaze in the dark. Asher flattened against a wall as a tall man emerged, wrapped in a black European overcoat. The Chinese who came out a moment later said, 'My threshold is honored by your honored foot, sir.'

Grant Hobart's unmistakable bray responded, 'You mean your money belt is honored by my honored money! Say what you mean, you damn pander.'

The Chinese bowed – a small man, gray-haired, in a dark *ch'i-p'ao*; presumably An Lu T'ang. 'It is as your honor pleases.'

Hobart grunted. 'Slippery bastard,' he said, in English, this time, and got into the rickshaw. 'Not that way, idiot,' he added in Chinese as the puller started away.

'Best you go over the marble bridge and past the Drum Tower, honored sir,' added An, with another bow. 'There are western soldiers at the Empress's Garden. Better to avoid Lotus Alley tonight.'

Hobart swore, and the rickshaw maneuvered awkwardly in the narrow lane. Asher turned his face to the wall as it passed him again, though he was fairly certain that, coming from the lighted gateway, Hobart would be unable to see him in the alley's darkness. *Damn it*, Asher wondered, *does a riot mean the Tso will have more guards out? There'll be stragglers all over the neighborhood . . .*

But not around in the back of the compound, he reminded himself. *If anything, a fight among the soldiers will draw whoever is awake to the front of the siheyuan . . .*

He found Prosperity Alley, which led, after several windings, to the lakeshore. So deep was the darkness there that he had to count his steps, his hand to the plastered brick of the wall, to find the doorway he had earlier marked. He opened the slide on the lantern barely enough to show him the lock, and while coaxing the rusted, old-fashioned wards he kept having to stop and re-warm his numb fingers against the hot metal of the lamp. He told himself, a dozen times during this process, that it was rare – unheard of – for the Others to come anywhere near lights and people.

In Prague they'd stayed down in the river bed and on the shallow islands that broke the stream. *If you don't go looking for them, you are generally safe*, Karlebach had said.

He was nevertheless aware of the pounding of his heart. *Now if only this is one of the nights when the vampire goes hunting . . .*

A shot cracked, barely sixty yards away. Asher's head jerked around, tracking the direction of the sound . . .

Dim shouts, muffled by the turns of walls and alleys. The shrill screams of women.

The Empress's Garden.

The soldiers.

Asher whispered a prayer of thanks. Every guard in the Tso household would now be at the front of the compound, close to what sounded like a spreading riot . . .

He pushed open the gate. With any luck the brouhaha would last long enough for him to get a good look around, always supposing he didn't encounter a vampire that had become too timid to venture out of its lair. But even that was preferable to running smack into a squad of Madame Tso's bully boys by day.

Behind the shelter of the screen wall Asher surveyed the courtyard in the thin blue starlight. Dust lay in drifts from last week's storm. Crippled weeds had flourished and died along the foundations of the surrounding buildings. Clearly, no one had been there in months.

He slipped around the screen, ducked through the nearest door: the *tao-chuo-fang*, the north-facing building which received the least sunlight. Inauspicious, a kitchen or laundry . . .

He slipped the slide from the lantern again: tall cupboards with their doors open, empty blackness inside; dishes on slatted wooden counters covered with dust. A few torn sacks. In one corner a trapdoor opened on to a ladder and led to a tiny root-cellar, cold as an icebox and damp with the proximity of the Seas. Splintered boxes, rat-chewed baskets, and stacks of cheap dishes, the kind one gave servants to eat off.

He scrambled up the ladder again, made a circuit of the buildings around the court. Under the *cheng-fang* – the main building, large and south-facing and generally given over to the formal reception room and the bedrooms of the master and mistress of the house – he found a larger vault, this one brick-lined and accessed by narrow steps, clearly a strongroom dug at some earlier period and containing forgotten treasures: bronze incense-burners of an antique pattern, a small chest which proved to hold hundreds of age-brown silk scrolls with the formal paintings of someone's ancestors, an exquisite *p'i-p'a* inlaid with shell. Reascending, he could find no evidence of a cellar beneath the 'backside house' behind the *cheng-fang*, so strode swiftly down the covered walkway to where he calculated the next deserted courtyard would lie.

Drifted dust, empty goldfish-kongs, stacks of tubs for orna-mental trees . . .

And the fishy, rotten, pervasive smell of the Others, which prickled the hair on the back of his neck.

It was strongest near the *cheng-fang*. Rats scuttled around the building's padlocked door. The lock was brand-new, bright in the sliver of Asher's lantern-light. When he opened it and gently pushed the doors, from somewhere in the building – somewhere below him – he heard a voice call, '*Ma-Ma . . .*'

The meaning the same, curiously, in English as in Chinese. *Mama.*

He closed his eyes. Sick shock flowed over him as he understood what Madame Tso planned, and what she had done.

It is our families, Father Orsino had said, *who are the Magistrates of Hell.*

Had he known?

In a former bedchamber that flanked the *cheng-fang*'s main hall, a trap door stood open where, logically, a bed would once have been. Next to the black square of the hole stood a small table, half-covered with empty pottery cups and bottles that sent up a queasy metallic reek. Like Karlebach's experiments, he thought, with the drugs that he'd given his student Matthias, in the hopes that it would stop the virus from consuming his body.

Or, in this case, maybe only with the intention of slowing down some of its effects?

Dark spatterings, like the stains of dripped blood, marked the edge of the table, the floor around the trapdoor.

When he bent over the square of blackness a voice from below called softly, 'Is it you, Aunt?'

And a bleating cry, like the bray of a goat: 'Mama—'

Asher rested his forehead briefly against the wall. A metallic clink from the abyss: hinges or bars. The smell of human waste mixed with the fishy nastiness of the *yao-kuei*. Asher didn't imagine there was much competition for cleaning whatever cells the two men – or former men – occupied down below in the darkness there. He moved soundlessly across the bedchamber to the door of the main hall . . .

. . . then flung himself sideways as a sword flashed in the lantern-light, inches from his face.

The blade jerked back mid-stroke. Round spectacles glinted. 'Ashu Sensei—'

Count Mizukami held out his hand for silence.

Asher caught him by the elbow, steered him across the hall and so to the starlight outside. The Count sheathed his sword, an oiled whisper. His face showed not so much a flicker of surprise to see Asher alive. 'They are down there?'

'Caged, I think,' whispered Asher. 'Being taken care of, and still human enough to talk and think. One of them's Madame Tso's son, another's her nephew.'

Mizukami's breath hissed sharply. Then after a moment's silence, 'They could have met the *tenma* on the shore of the Seas. Could have been infected by them there. Your most extraordinary wife found evidence of disappearances in this district, beyond what the rioting last spring could account for – and even the fighting among the criminal gangs. And yesterday, when we rode into the hills to survey how best to blow up all entrances to the mines, Dr Bauer said that she was given money by President Yuan, for all remaining evidence of the things in the hills.'

'I've seen Madame Tso twice with Huang Da-feng,' returned Asher grimly. 'Yes, her son *and* her nephew could have stumbled into the *yao-kuei* on their way home across the marble bridge some night and been accidentally infected in the course of defending themselves, but I don't think that's what happened. Is Mrs Asher all right? And Dr Karlebach?'

'They are well. You have married a samurai, Ashu Sensei, and one who keeps her secrets well. She has gone into deep mourning on your behalf and is being courted by every bachelor diplomat in the Quarter.'

Asher grinned in spite of himself. 'She'll murder me if we ever get out of this alive . . .'

Mizukami smiled. 'I have seen your love for this woman, Ashu Sensei, and hers for you. She veils herself in black and weeps where people can see her, but her eyes are not red. Nor are they the eyes of a woman who has lost that which she most treasures. And she told me that you speak well of gelignite for blowing up the tunnels in the mines.'

Asher rolled his eyes.

'She does well,' insisted Mizukami. 'And the grief of your friend Ka-ru-ba-ku Sensei is genuine and terrible to see. His heart and soul are now given to vengeance.' He nodded toward the blackness of the *cheng-fang* behind them. 'So you think that, to gain some advantage, this monstrous woman has had her own son, her own nephew, deliberately infected by these creatures. Why? What would it gain her that she could sell to Yuan? Surely she does not think they will be able to control them, and the rats at their command as well?'

'Not her nephew and her son,' said Asher. 'We have one more thing to find.'

TWENTY-TWO

Shots ripped the windy night; a woman screamed. Still away to the south-west in the direction of the Empress's Garden. Asher breathed, 'We'd better hurry. God knows how long we have till the police arrive.'

Mizukami consulted his watch. 'I paid the district captain for two hours,' he said. 'Ogata can be trusted to keep the riot going at least so long, particularly with Russians there.'

'Remind me,' said Asher with a grin, 'to recommend you for work in the Department . . . Not that I have anything to do with them . . .'

'Of course not,' agreed the Count. And added, 'Ge-raa Sensei.'

'Never met Professor Gellar in my life.' He led the way swiftly along a covered walk – cluttered with boxes, two parked rickshaws, and a bicycle – and through a small court, orienting himself by the double roof of a two-story 'backside house' that dominated the cold stars of the skyline. Through the latticed windows of a pavilion he glimpsed an empty bedchamber, lamplit and furnished in a half-Western fashion: perhaps the house of assignation, the gate of which opened on to Big Tiger Lane, where An Lu T'ang arranged for Grant Hobart to enjoy specialized pleasures? The bed was disarrayed, and the walls sported two Western-style oil paintings on its walls, graphically depicting some of the more violent loves of Greek gods. Chinese pornography, Asher knew, ranked as some of the least erotic in the world.

The courtyard beyond this one was deserted. There was no street gate, but the side building on the east – the *hsiang-fang* – was, unusually, two storied, its upper room shuttered fast, and

Asher knew from his daylight reconnaissance that this was in fact a sort of terrace which overlooked the narrow strait that ran between the two lobes of the 'Sea'.

This court, too, was littered with debris and dust, but there was none before the shuttered-up *cheng-fang*. Though the place had not been swept in decades, a pathway had been beaten clear among the tufts of weeds before its door. The lock was a Yale, about twenty years old.

Asher handed Mizukami the lantern, directed the narrow beam on the lock. 'Do you believe in the *chiang-shi*, Mizukami-san?' he asked softly. 'The *kyonshi*?'

He did not look up from his lockpicks, but he heard his companion's breath hiss.

'Two weeks ago,' said the Count at last, 'or a month . . . I do not know what I would have said to such a question. The *tenma* we saw in the hills – the terrible thing that befell poor Ito—'

'Those aren't the *chiang-shi*.' Asher held his breath, manipulated the delicate probes in the lock until he felt the mechanism give. Gently tested the handle. If there were a vampire within the building, it would have heard their breathing and the clicking of the tumblers as Asher's tools shifted them one by one. He could have sung 'Rule, Britannia!' at the top of his lungs and the only ones who would have learned something they didn't already know were whatever residents of the Tso compound weren't either preparing to defend the house against the rioters or out engaged in looting themselves.

He pushed the door open, took the lantern and directed its narrow beam, carefully, around the salon within. 'The *chiang-shi* are real,' he went on. 'I've spoken to them – I've traveled with them – I've killed them and seen them kill.' His gaze followed the sliver of yellow light as he spoke: a doorway at either side of the big room, the one on the east open, on the west, shut. The steely glint of another Western lock. 'In Europe – in the West – they don't trust the living, though they sometimes need our help. I think what's happened here is that one of them – maybe more, for all I know – has employed the whole Tso family to keep it safe, in return for its help in their criminal endeavors. I think its lair is what we're going to find downstairs.'

He handed Mizukami the lantern again when they reached the shut door, knelt with his picklocks.

The little nobleman looked around at the darkness of the shuttered chamber. 'Can this be so?'

'Can the other things you've seen? Will you wait up here and guard my back? You'll probably be safer if you come down with me.'

'I am samurai,' replied the Count quietly, his hand on the hilt of his katana. 'Yet I am not stupid. What is your judgement? You know these things. I do not.'

'Let's find the trapdoor down. But watch and listen. You may have no more than a heartbeat's warning – maybe not that. It'll try to make your mind sleepy before it strikes.'

The trapdoor, as Asher had suspected, descended from the locked western room. Like the other he had found, it was fairly wide, in a part of the room which in earlier times would naturally have been covered with a cupboard or a bed, and its darkness breathed the same dank cold. 'Will you remain at the top?' he asked softly. 'It may be out hunting at this hour, but there's no telling when it will return.'

Mizukami's blade whispered from the scabbard.

Asher descended, the lantern held high. The vault was deep, like the one in the French cemetery chapel; the brick stair made two complete turns, thirty steps. The faint foulness of old blood pervaded the clinging darkness. Things had died there, that no one had been willing to linger long enough to properly clean up.

He opened a door. The lantern beam caught the glint of reflective eyes, not three yards from his own.

A man's low giggle filled the dark of the chamber.

Mouth dry with shock, Asher yanked the slide fully open.

The vampire sat enthroned on cushions, facing him. Unmoving, except for the trembling of the belly muscles as it laughed, the twisting of its face. Long hair, longer than Lydia's even – a streaming black river of it – flowed down over its shoulders, coal-black against the death-pale ivory of its skin. Black eyes caught and reflected the lantern's light, stared into his: utterly and unmistakably mad.

And no wonder, thought Asher, so aghast that for a moment he could not breathe. *No wonder*.

The vampire – a man in his prime – was nude, a blue silk sheet draped over its lap. His arms had been cut off just below the head of the humerus, his legs, guessed at beneath the folds of the sheet, a few inches below the trochanter of the hip. Vampire flesh does not heal like human flesh, and there was no way of guessing how long ago this had been done. But amid the glazed, waxy glisten of the scabs over what had been the armpit, Asher could see the tiny buds of baby fists growing from the flesh, smaller than the helpless hands of a newborn . . .

And easy to snip off again with no more than a razor.

Twenty years. His mind stalled on the thought, dizzy with horror and shock. *Maybe more . . .*

There was a little dried blood on the silken sheet, on the pillows near his head.

They must bring him his kills . . .

For a time Asher could do nothing but stare as the vampire bellowed with laughter, fangs flashing. Blood dribbled from its gums, and bruises discolored the silk-white skin where the facial sutures would be. The bruising was precisely as Asher had seen on Ito-san.

They've infected him with the blood of the Others. There was no way he could have stopped them from doing so, even if he'd been awake for it.

Which means he can probably summon them.

Asher bolted up the stairs, pursued by the vampire's roars of mirth. Mizukami was flattened against the wall at the top, eyes straining at the darkness of the room beyond his small slip of lantern-light, but he flicked his glance sidelong as Asher emerged.

'Run!'

Without a question or a sound, Mizukami caught up his lantern and fled at Asher's heels, across the side room and across the main salon. They emerged from the door into the courtyard, and shots cracked out, not distant now but just across the court. Bullets tore the wood of the door frame next to Asher's face. Three men ran toward them, one of them with eyes that reflected the lantern-light like a cat's. Asher dodged left, returned fire with his revolver while Mizukami kicked the desiccated wood of the door of the two-story side-building. Asher ducked in after the Japanese into the darkness, up an open stairway to the shuttered terrace above.

The shutters on the upper floor were bolted from the inside but not locked; Asher jerked open a section, dropped both lanterns beside it, then dragged Mizukami to the farthest corner of the room where screens and chairs had been stacked, covered with sheets against the winter's pervasive dust.

Both men rolled behind them as feet shook the stair. Moments later their pursuers entered, dashed to the open section of shutter which looked down – Asher knew – on to the narrow ground between the compound wall and the strait that joined the Shih Ch'a Hai – the long northern lobe of the 'Sea' – to its southern partner. It was a few hundred yards from where the *yao-kuei* – and the rats – had nearly cornered him, and he knew how far it was to the entrance to the nearest *hutong*.

One of the men swore. '*Kou p'i!*'

'You see them?'

'Get them,' said a third voice, cold. 'Go after them.'

'We didn't see which way they went, Chi T'uan—'

'Then you better get down there and figure it out.'

The men crossed the room again toward the stair. When the man called Chi T'uan turned his head, in the moonlight Asher glimpsed again the reflective glitter of his eyes. *Vampire?* Or infected, like the other two down in the cellar, with the blood of the Others in the hopes of mentally controlling them? Of using them: unstoppable soldiers who would never listen to treachery, who wouldn't have to be paid in anything but living food . . . who wouldn't run away from a losing fight, and who would be very, very hard to kill.

Or both?

When the men had gone, Asher and Mizukami emerged from hiding, crossed to the ghostly rectangle of star-pinned heaven. Enough wind remained to sting Asher's cheeks and numb the end of his nose. Looking down from the terrace he saw men emerge from Big Tiger Lane on to the lakeside pebbles, some running north, some south, boots crunching in the ice. The pursuers clung together, looked fearfully around themselves . . . So presumably the fact that Madame Tso's son and nephew had become *yao-kuei* didn't mean that the other *yao-kuei* could be controlled to the point that they wouldn't attack Tso enforcers.

In the courtyard behind them and below, a woman's voice rose, sharp with anger. Asher crossed the room silently, opened one of the shutters a crack in time to see Madame Tso, still in her embroidered robe of blue silk, slap Chi T'uan smartly across the face.

'Lump of dog meat!'

'We'll catch them, Aunt.'

'Are your brother and my son all right?'

'I'm going down now to see.'

'And Li?'

'Aunt, I—' Chen Chi T'uan pressed a hand to his temple. He was, as far as Asher could see, tall for a Chinese and dressed and barbered in the Western fashion, his coat a flashy double-breasted American style. The hardness in his voice dissolved, and he said, much more quietly, 'I can't always hear him.'

She slapped him again. 'You're not trying, then! Ungrateful brat!'

'I am trying.'

'It should be growing easier.'

'But it's not! Aunt, I don't think it was a good idea to infect him with the blood of the *kuei*. What if it drives him crazy, the way it has Chi Erh—?'

'My son has been stupid all his life and hadn't the strength to resist. And, we hadn't learned the right combination of herbs then, to keep the mind strong. Chi Fu is all right—'

'Chi Fu is not all right! Chi Fu is turning into one of those things too, no matter how many herbs and medicines we give him! When I try to find my brother's mind, it's like trying to pick up the fragments of a rotting body—'

'You're a coward and a fool. Chi Fu will be well. He is recovering. As for Li – Li is *chiang-shi*. His body is like a diamond, stronger than the blood of the *kuei*. If he wouldn't do what is needful to turn you into *chiang-shi*, what other course was open to us? Don't be a baby, and give me your arm.'

Chi T'uan held out his arm, steadied his formidable aunt's mincing steps as he led her toward the door of the main pavilion. Toward the stairway that led down to their prisoner's lair, where the vampire Li could live in safety and darkness forever.

Asher and Mizukami descended the stair, crossed the courtyard swiftly, their breath clouds of silver in the excruciating cold. There was no one, now, in this part of the compound – everyone being presumably out combing the lakeshore or repelling rioters. They followed the walkway to the small courtyard where An Lu T'ang's pleasure pavilion stood, and so out into Big Tiger Lane.

The sounds of riot around the Empress's Garden had died

away. As they turned down Lotus Alley, broken shopfronts, smashed shutters, and fragments of furniture and bottles bore witness to the magnitude of the disorder. The lanterns of shopkeepers bobbed in the darkness as they took stock of shattered boxes and looted goods. Here and there bullet holes punctuated the thick walls, and the air reeked with spilled liquor and vomit.

Outside the gate of the wine shop itself, Mizukami stopped a blue-uniformed policeman and asked, 'Was anyone badly hurt?'

The representative of Peking's Finest expiated for some minutes on the subject of big-nosed foreign-devil stinking sons of slave girls and hoped their commanding officers would flog them with rusty chains until the skin was stripped off their backs, and no, nobody had been killed. Mizukami handed him a few coins and signaled a couple of rickshaws.

When Asher climbed into one, the Count said to the puller, 'Japanese Legation.'

An hour and a half later – it was by this time nearly three in the morning – Asher, pacing the sparely-furnished four-mat room at the back of Mizukami's cottage, heard the cottage door open and the soft scrunch of running feet on the tatami. A moment later, the door of the room was flung open and Lydia threw herself into his arms.

TWENTY-THREE

'Forty.' Asher turned Ysidro's note over in his fingers.

Though the cottage was wired for modern electrical lamps, Mizukami clearly preferred the dimmer glow of paraffin. An oil-lamp stood – incongruous with its pink-flowered globe – on the small Chinese table in the corner, and by its honey-colored light the queer letters – drawn with a writing brush as if they were pictures – were clearly readable on the stiff yellow paper.

Other than the lamp and its table, the room, like all those in the house, was furnished in the Japanese style, which to a Westerner's mind meant not very furnished at all. When Asher and Mizukami had returned there, servants had brought out quilts for Asher to sleep on, a neat dark square that took up two-thirds of the floor.

He now sat cross-legged on the floor mats beside a low table, Lydia perched on a cushion at his side.

A servant had brought tea, and then left them alone.

It was nearly dawn.

'Forty isn't so very many.' Lydia spoke in the neutral tone that Asher had observed her use when she was deeply troubled about something.

He knew what it was: what she wasn't saying.

'It is when there's only five or six in the defending party,' he replied. 'And when you know that if you're wounded – if enough of their blood gets into the cut – you'll be one of them within days.'

Lydia looked down at her hands. Not saying – because she could not say it, not even in her own heart – *we have to get him out*.

The words stood between them as they discussed the explosives, and chlorine gas, and how to keep the rats at bay long enough to plant the gelignite charges. ('Do the German regiments have any *flammenwerfer* they'd lend us, I wonder?')

Asher understood. It was one thing to say, *He is what he is, and he cannot help what he is*. The same was true of Grant Hobart. Karlebach had said to him once of Ysidro, *Every kill he makes henceforth will be upon your head*, and Asher knew that this was the truth.

The fact that Don Simon Ysidro had gone to the mines in the first place to help Asher's investigation of the Others – to keep the threat from spreading further – made no difference.

Nor did the fact that he had saved Asher's life, and Lydia's, and that of Miranda before she was born.

The fact that Asher had himself killed, repeatedly, over the span of nearly twenty years in the service of the Department made no difference, either. He had walked away from it. Ysidro could not, and never would.

To do him justice, the vampire was probably not expecting rescue. Nevertheless, Asher felt like a Judas, the pain of betraying and deserting a comrade grinding in him like the poisoned barbs of an arrow.

'She really deliberately infected her son, and then her

nephew – *two* of her nephews! – with the blood of the Others, for . . . for the sake of *power*?' Lydia shook her head disbelievingly, when Asher told her of what he'd found in the Tso compound, and what he'd overheard. 'How *could* she? How could *anyone* do that?'

He knew she was thinking of Miranda. Tiny, perfect, like a red-and-white flower . . .

'She's a woman who had her feet mutilated by her own mother before she reached the age of six,' replied Asher, 'so that she'd be "beautiful" enough to sell to someone whose influence would help her family.'

Lydia started to say something else, then couldn't, and only shook her head.

'A woman whose feet are bound lives in daily pain for the rest of her life, Lydia. I wouldn't say it gave Madame Tso a hatred for her family, but I can't see how it wouldn't give you a rather specialized view of what a family can reasonably ask its members.'

'And I thought Aunt Louise was bad . . .'

'I don't know how Madame Tso found herself in the position to mutilate the vampire Li and make him her prisoner,' Asher went on quietly. 'Whether it was chance, or whether he trusted her enough to let her know where he slept.'

'Well, I must say it certainly explains why the Peking vampires don't trust the living.'

'Or anyone. My guess is, once she had him at her mercy, she starved him—'

'It's what I'd do,' agreed Lydia reasonably. 'That is, if I were – um – that kind of person . . .'

Asher brought up her hand and kissed it. 'I've seen you in the dissecting rooms, Best Beloved, and you *are* that kind of person. You just haven't had her motives. There's nothing I wouldn't put past you, if Miranda were in danger.'

'Well, no.' She blinked at him behind her spectacles, as if his observation were self-evident.

'Later she had victims brought to him, in exchange for his using a vampire's ability to read dreams – and plant dreams – to give her husband and his enforcers an edge over other criminal families in Peking.'

'And reading dreams,' went on Lydia, 'and being able to . . .

to touch the minds of others, the way very old vampires can do, he would have become aware of the minds of the Others. Or the hive mind, anyway, which is what it sounds like they have.' Her brow furrowed briefly. 'I certainly wouldn't want to have had Madame Tso's dreams for the past twenty years . . .'

'No. But if he's been sending her wake-up-screaming night-mares every night for two decades, it's still a price she's willing to pay. She's willing to pay any price for power for herself and her family – including her sons and her nephews. It sounds as if she tried to force Li into making them into vampires, and when Li wouldn't cooperate, infected him – and them – with the blood of the Others, in the hopes of controlling the Others through Li. I'm guessing that not everyone in the family knows about Li.'

'Well, it's not a secret I'd share with some of the people in *my* family.' Lydia shifted her weight on the cushion. She had arrived, Asher was hugely amused to observe, fastidiously turned-out in a black silk mourning costume glittering with beads of jet. Her red hair, now unloosed from its careful chignon, stood out against the dark cloth like a river of lava. '*Can* the mind of a contaminated victim be preserved by those potions you saw in the Tso compound?'

'Matthias Uray's was, as long as he was able to take them.' Asher shivered at the thought. 'But whether the nephew I saw – Chen Chi T'uan – will be strong enough to control the vampire Li is another matter.'

'It's a scheme which may turn on her,' went on Lydia thought-fully, 'if Li becomes able to control these *yao-kuei* with any kind of accuracy. I wonder how precise his control will be, once he gets the hang of it? If it doesn't make him insane first, that is. I must say,' she added, 'it does serve them all right.'

Asher hid a grin, then sobered. 'It would,' he said. 'But it doesn't serve those around them right. And the innocent in every country on earth, if President Yuan decides to sell the secret to buy himself alliances. Those are the ones who'll suffer. This man who brought you the message –' he touched it again, on the table beside them – 'this priest . . .'

'Chiang – I *think* that was what he said his name was. He's one of the priests from the Temple of Everlasting Harmony. At least, he wears the same kind of robe.'

'A *yi*,' said Asher. 'It's the type of clothing the Chinese wore before the Manchu conquered them and made them wear *ch'i-p'ao* and queues. The Japanese adopted it from them, way back in the days – you'll usually see it only on temple priests. He said he dreamed this?'

'Copied it from a dream.' Lydia turned the paper around, studied the characters again in the lamplight. Even the idiosyncrasies of Ysidro's handwriting had been reproduced, the characteristic sixteenth-century loops on the Fs and Ys, the flourish on the end of each S.

'He must have a high degree of psychic sensitivity,' said Asher thoughtfully, 'given that Ysidro is trapped beneath the earth. Would he agree to be hypnotized, I wonder?'

'We can ask. His English isn't good, though. Do you know how to hypnotize people, Jamie?'

'No,' he admitted. 'But he may agree to put himself into a meditative state that would allow us to communicate with Ysidro in the mine.'

She met his eyes then, opened her mouth – and closed it. Only looked at him, her eyes, behind the thick rounds of glass, filling with tears.

And what? she would have asked him, he guessed. *Ask him to help us even though we're going to abandon him? Seal him in a grave – a grave filled with corrosive gas, skin and eyes burning away, conscious, blind, and without hope of ever escaping – forever?*

Yes, and yes . . . and yes.

Like playing chess, reflected Asher wearily. *Or more simply, like playing Patience. When you know five moves ahead that you can't win and there's nothing you can do about it . . .*

Remember me kindly . . . Ysidro had written.

He gathered her into his arms. She took off her glasses, laid them on the table beside Ysidro's note, and pressed her face to his shoulder, shivering as if with bitterest cold.

'Voice in dreams.'

The priest Chiang passed his hand across his high, balding forehead, white brows contracted with pain.

Lydia had not left Mizukami's bungalow until almost daybreak; Asher had slept until past noon. Mizukami's dwelling stood near the end of the grassy mall in a corner of the Japanese Legation, not far from the small service-gate that let on to an alley off Rue Lagrené. The military attaché's servants (and, surprisingly, his mistress, whose voice Asher heard through the thin walls but whom he never saw) were loyal, quiet, and treated Asher as if he were simultaneously very honored and completely invisible. It was not difficult to slip out of the Legation Quarter and meet Lydia in Silk Lane at two.

'I trust we're going to clear your name completely in short order,' she had said as they'd walked briskly in the direction of the Temple of Everlasting Harmony. 'I'm positive that someone noticed me sneaking out of the hotel at three o'clock this morning, and that word's already going about that I've got a lover – I swear Annette Hautecoeur has the hotel servants on retainer . . . If anyone sees us together while you're dressed like *that*, people are going to start saying I have a *Chinese* lover, and then I'll simply have to go live in Paris or someplace, though even in Paris that would be considered outside of enough.'

'I shall keep a respectful three paces behind you, ma'am,' responded Asher meekly, and he tugged his scarves a little higher up over the bridge of his nose. He had bathed at the bungalow – something that it had been simply too cold to do very often in the half-ruined courtyard on Pig-Dragon Lane – and Mizukami had provided him with a new *ch'i-p'ao*, *ku*, and cap. 'You could borrow Mrs Pilley's coat, couldn't you? And Ellen's skirt and hat?'

'I *could*, but that's the oldest trick in the book – I dare say Madame Hautecoeur has used it a thousand times herself. I could tell everyone you were conducting me to an opium den, though,' she had added, suddenly cheered. 'That would be perfectly acceptable—'

'It would be nothing of the kind!'

'Well, it would be understandable, and everyone would ask me what it was like . . . Which I'll have to find out before the story goes too far . . .'

But upon arrival at the Temple, the stout priest had informed them that Chiang had gone out begging – the occupation of all good priests – and would not return until dusk. Thus it was not until after nightfall that the experiment in hypnotism could be made.

'Voice in dreams,' repeated Chiang, and he brushed his

forehead with his fingers, as he had when speaking to Lydia in the hotel parlor.

The old-fashioned lamps in the building behind the Temple wavered in the drafts – desert wind blew down on the city again, the air fuzzy with dust. Shadows loomed, huge as the *kuei* in some old fairy-tale: a broken-down bed, a rack of scrolls, piles of books heaped everywhere. A thousand bottles and jars – ginseng, peony root, turtle plastron and rhinoceros horn – knobby ginger, and the bones and teeth of mice. A line of pestles in graduating size; a set of acupuncture needles like some strange, tiny musical instrument.

In the corner, the gleam of a halberd blade.

'You speak to voice?' asked Asher in Chinese.

The black eyes, bright as a squirrel's, turned toward him, and in the same language the old man replied, 'Sometimes I can. All my life I have spoken with spirits, you understand.' He gestured toward the scrolls, toward the line of tablets – slices of bamboo with characters carved into them – that hung on the soot-black-ened wall of the room. 'My mother also had this gift. When a family is in trouble, or in need of advice, I can sometimes reach out to the Great Beyond and ask an ancestor what it is best that they do. Or if someone is troubled with a hungry ghost, who cannot find rest and so returns to trouble the living: often these can be treated with and given what it is that keeps them from peace. But this – this cold thing that came to me as I slept . . . This was not a spirit.'

Asher said, 'No. Not spirit.'

'Yet nor is he a living man.'

Again Asher shook his head.

The priest frowned in thought, then rose and put a couple of pieces of coal in the brick stove which occupied one corner of the room. Asher guessed his age as in his seventies, but he could have been older. His hair, milk white, hung below his hips, not queued any more but tied in a simple thong; his thin beard and mustaches trailed down his chest. The Temple's other two priests – the stout little man and a taller, younger one – had seemed a little afraid of him, which made Asher smile inwardly.

Every one of Rebbe Solomon Karlebach's students – himself included – had been terrified of the old scholar.

'Perhaps he is a bodhisattva?' inquired Chiang. 'A saint who has achieved the Buddha-nature within himself – who has freed himself from the cycle of rebirths – but has lingered behind in this world to save others? Yet this coldness is nothing I have felt before. When a man's soul divides at death, and the upper soul is carried off to Heaven by the Spirit of the Dragon of Wisdom, the lower soul remains . . . but I understand that it usually disperses. Although, if one reads the writings of Wang Bi on the subject . . . Oh, yes, ten thousand pardons. You said you wished to speak to him . . .'

He returned to his stool, beside the bench where Asher sat. Closed his eyes.

Stillness filled the room, save for the keening of the wind around the Temple's eaves.

Then he whispered, 'Under the mountain.'

'You speak to him?'

Chiang moved his head a little, as if to say, *No*, then was still.

After another long silence he murmured in English, 'Mistress—'

'Are you all right?' Lydia put her hand to her lips the instant the question passed them, probably realizing, thought Asher, what a useless one it was. But, he thought, she couldn't not ask.

'I am well.' Even the timbre of that uninflected voice was the same.

'We're going to seal the mine –' Asher kept his tone deliberately matter-of-fact – 'after detonating cylinders of chlorine gas. Will that kill them?'

'Most assuredly. They are not immortal, James. Twelve entrances. The farthest two are ventilation shafts on the north-east flank of the mountain.'

'We know of all twelve.'

'There is a thirteenth you must also destroy, the worst. Below the level of the mine tunnels lies a natural cave system. The old mine entrance, on the far side of the mountain; follow the tunnel to the great gallery on the left, filled with slag and broken rock. From there the tunnel slopes down sharply and breaks through into the caves below. This tunnel must be sealed. They do not go there yet, but if driven they will. I know not how far those caves extend.'

'It will be done.'

'Thank you . . .' Lydia whispered.

'I assure you, Mistress, that had I known what this information would cost me, you would never have had it.'

'Could a vampire control these things?' asked Asher.

'*This* vampire cannot. Trust me, I have tried. The vampires of Prague have been trying for years.'

'What about a vampire who was infected with their blood?'

Into the long silence which followed this, Lydia added, 'Jamie found one of them. One of the old ones, it sounds like. He's being kept prisoner by a criminal family who's trying to get control of the Others.'

'Prisoner?'

'Tso—' Chiang flinched, put his hand to his head again, opened his eyes. 'A sound,' he explained in Chinese, looking at Asher. 'Something moving in the darkness. Where is this? Where is he?'

'Western Hills.'

'And you understood the words I said? Extraordinary.' Chiang's face was alight with fascination. 'Kuo Hsiang writes that it is possible to completely detach the mind from one's activities, to become utterly one with the Way; a most astonishing sensation. But he is afraid,' he added. 'Your friend. The things he fears, the things in the dark underground . . . I have heard stories of them. Now – since summer – when I go begging I hear of things here in the city as well, things seen in the night on the shores of the Seas—'

'You try,' asked Asher, 'bid these things come, bid them go? Listen to minds, as you listen for speech of spirits?'

Chiang tilted his head. There was something in his eyes that told Asher that he'd tried.

In time he said, 'No. There is nothing. Only madness, and hunger that cannot be assuaged.'

'Tomorrow, next day,' said Asher, 'come with us to hills? We destroy these creatures, *yao-kuei* in Shi'h Liu Mine. We need all help we can get.'

The old man was silent for a moment, studying Asher's face. At length he said, 'Yes. I will come.'

TWENTY-FOUR

On Monday, the eleventh of November, Asher, Mizukami, and Professor Karlebach took the noon train for Men T'ou Kuo. With them journeyed the bodyguard Ogata and four soldiers from the Japanese garrison, armed not only with rifles but with *flammenwerfer* – the new German flamethrowers – guarding a shipment of a thousand liters of pure chlorine. Two other soldiers, requisitioned – Mizukami said – on the grounds of a worsening infestation of rabid rats in the Shi'h Liu Mine, met them in the little town with horses, donkeys, and guns. They reached Mingliang Village shortly before nightfall.

'News of us will be all over the hills by moonrise,' surmised Asher as he checked the action on his borrowed Arisaka carbine, preparatory to taking the first shift at guard. 'We'll have the Kuo Min-tang and every gang of bandits this side of the Yellow River coming to have a try at them. And, unless we're really lucky, somebody will ride back to the city and let Huang and the Tso Family know there's something afoot as well.' Lydia had smuggled him his own clothes and boots from the hotel, so he no longer felt like a deserter from the chorus of *Turandot*. In addition to arranging for a squad of villagers to carry the cylinders of chlorine down into the mine, Dr Bauer had offered her clinic as a headquarters. But she was silent and uneasy, as if she guessed there was more behind the 'rabid rats' story than anyone was saying.

'This is beyond our capacity to alter.' Count Mizukami shut the small iron door on the *kang* that occupied a third of the room: their blankets were already spread out on the hollow brick platform that, in most Chinese farmhouses, served as both stove and bed. At the table, Karlebach said nothing. But every now and then he looked up from cleaning his shotgun, to regard Asher with a kind of aching wonderment, as if he couldn't believe that one of his surrogate sons, at least, had returned from the dead.

Knowing his old teacher incapable of disguising either grief or joy, Asher had kept hidden from him until they were on the train out of Peking. He'd had Mizukami break the news to Karlebach that Asher was in fact alive, before walking into the compartment himself, but still the old man had clung to him for a time in tears. His first question, when he could speak again, had been, *Does Madame know?* To which Asher had responded with a smile, 'Forgive me – but yes. She's a much better actress than you are.' This had lightened the air between them with laughter, but now Asher was interested to note that rather than ending Karlebach's grim resolve, the reunion had energized him. Once in their headquarters for the night, he had gone lovingly over every millimeter of his shotgun, and he was now checking each of its glinting brass shells, stuffed with enough solid silver deer-shot to blow a living man to Kingdom Come.

'Word could have gone out,' Mizukami went on reasonably, 'to Huang, or to the Kuo Min-tang, when Sergeant Tamayo arrived in Men T'ou Kuo yesterday and arranged for the porters and horses.' He removed his glasses and set them aside, but kept his sword beneath the blanket with him. 'If we set a guard openly, at least the small dogs of the hills will keep their distance for the night.'

With that, Asher had to agree, and in fact the night passed without incident. He returned from his watch at midnight to find his old teacher still awake, poring over the map which the priest Chiang had drawn for them the previous night in the Temple.

'You're sure this man's information can be trusted?' Karlebach looked up as he came in and brushed the map with his fingers. 'You say he is familiar with these hills. But after all, if he has not seen the Others, how can he be sure where it is that they sleep?'

'I know of no reason he'd lie.' Asher kept his voice low, for Mizukami slept under a pile of blankets and sheepskins on the *kang*, and the table had been drawn up close to it for warmth. He pulled off his gloves, held his half-frozen fingers to the *kang*'s iron door. 'For all I know he could be in the pay of the Tso Family, and this could be an elaborate trap to keep me from peaching on them to the British authorities about their nefarious deeds. In China you simply can't tell. But—'

The old man chuckled in the depths of his white beard and waved the possibility aside. Asher didn't want to tell him that Chiang had only been following Ysidro's thoughts, like a spiritualist wielding a planchette. *All vampires lie* was not a discussion he wanted to engage in just now.

Instead he brought out the map he and the Legation clerk P'ei had pieced together from the various mining company diagrams, turned it so that it was oriented in the same direction as Chiang's. 'The tunnels match,' he said. 'Look here – this is just where that gallery should be. There are cave temples in these hills, and Lydia tells me the ruins of one lie not far from that rear entrance. My guess is that Chiang served in one of them in times past and did a little exploring on his days off.'

If Taoist monks have days off, reflected Asher as he crawled into his own blankets on the *kang*, his cracked ribs aching under the plaster dressing that the Japanese Legation doctor had provided. Old Chiang had been thoroughly disconcerted at the thought of riding the Iron Dragon, as he had called the railway, and that morning had sent the hulking younger priest of the Temple to the station with a message in his stead. The speed of the train, the message had said, would so disrupt the geomantic alignments of his chi energy that it would be impossible for the earth to absorb the effects.

Thus, he said, he would walk to the mine. He hoped this would not inconvenience anyone.

Meaning we will have no one after all, reflected Asher, *who can listen through the darkness of the earth*. And in any case, Ysidro would be asleep.

Lying in the darkness and listening to the sob of the wind in the vent holes of the *kang*, Asher thought about the vampire, trapped in Father Orsino's silver-barred refuge. The vampire whom eighteen months ago he could have killed with swift mercy in St Petersburg. Ysidro might even have been grateful.

If the *yao-kuei* waked earlier in the evening than a vampire, and went to sleep later, then Father Orsino's refuge would indeed be a slightly larger version of a coffin, a prison inescapable. And soon it would be flooded with one of the most corrosive gasses known to man. With the *yao-kuei* dead, and the mine sealed, death would not even be an option for Ysidro – neither by being devoured, nor by the light of the sun. Only darkness eternal, and eternal burning pain.

Dante himself couldn't have come up with a more suitable fate. Asher closed his eyes, not wanting to think of it.

A horse snuffled in the courtyard. Liquid spots of reflected ember-light moved on the wall.

Somewhere a Just God is laughing, at one who decided he was willing to kill in order to live forever.

Had Ysidro not stayed at Lydia's side, one night in St Petersburg when the local vampire nest had attacked the house where she was staying, she would not be alive now. He would not have a daughter today.

Lydia would not, Asher knew, imitate those heroines of novels and go dashing off into the underground darkness to seek the vampire . . .

Still, he was glad she had not come.

Forty, he made himself think, taking refuge in planning and facts. *Not a great number. The first big gallery on the lowest level of the new part of the mine. A hundred and seventy feet down – too far to transport the gas cylinders, or run the detonator wires, but when the cylinders are blown up, the gas will sink.* This late in the year, even riding horses, there would barely be enough daylight hours to seal all its exits, to descend through the rear entrance to the opening between the mine and the cave system below, and to blow that up as well.

Twenty years in the Department had taught him precisely how many things could go wrong when one was working against a time limit.

In his mind he saw them as he sank into uneasy sleep: the Others, lying in the blackness like the trout that dozed beneath the shadows of the banks of the Stour when he was a boy. But open-eyed in the watery dark. Listening for their prey.

Asher and his party left the village as soon as it was light, to set charges in the cave that formed the mine's main entrance. A dozen villagers accompanied them, under the command of Dr Bauer. The moment Asher and the Japanese set foot in the cave, rats poured forth from both tunnels and up from the subsidence, as if some spigot deep in the mountain had been turned, and as Asher had suspected, the German *flammenwerfer* worked against them perfectly well. It was a hellish weapon to use even on rats – their squealing as the burning oil doused them was a sound he thought he would never get out of his head – and the thought that the flame-throwers had been designed for use against men in the war that everyone knew was coming turned his stomach. And it wasn't the rats' fault or intention, he knew, to attack these invaders, to die in agony . . .

But he was damn glad the compressed nitrogen threw the flames fifty feet down the tunnels. Even in flames, the rodents kept on coming until their bodies were consumed. The stink of charred flesh, burned oil, and scorched hair was horrific as they descended – through drifting smoke that almost obscured the light of their lanterns – to a gallery where, according to both maps and Ysidro's instructions, down-shafts led directly to the deep-sunk room where the *yao-kuei* slept.

'Have your porters stack the cylinders here,' Asher instructed the German missionary quietly. 'I'll wire a charge at the bottom of the pile but won't connect it to the detonator-box until all your men are out of the mine. It'll be perfectly safe. When the rest of the mine is sealed, we'll fire the charge to release the chlorine, then immediately detonate the charges on the main entrance.'

'And this is the only thing that can be done with them?' Bauer looked up into his face, her blue eyes filled with pity and regret. 'Kill them like dogs that have run mad?'

'Believe me,' said Asher, 'it is the only way. And it is necessary that it be done soon.'

She studied him for a moment more, then sighed a little, and nodded. 'Yes. I see that it is. And it shall be done.'

Karlebach lingered in the gallery as Asher set his charges, under the first of the growing dull-green mountain of chlorine cylinders. The only way to the lower levels from that long, dark chamber was a couple of rickety ladders, which the Japanese soldiers drew up for a little distance, then cut off and dropped back into the chasm. When it was time to go, Karlebach turned from the brink of the downshaft as if he could scarcely bear to leave it, his lined face set like stone.

Asher found himself remembering that he and Lydia were not the only ones tormented by the thought of someone who would be sealed in the poisoned abyss.

It would take, Asher guessed, until mid-afternoon for the villagers to carry all the canisters down the narrow tunnels. He showed Sergeant Tamayo how to affix the ends of the detonator wire into the box, listened to Mizukami translate his instructions:

the gas cylinders to be detonated at four thirty, the main charge to bring down the tunnels immediately thereafter. Two armed troopers would remain with the sergeant after the villagers left, to make sure there was no interference from bandits or anyone else.

'And if the President sends men to stop us,' Mizukami added as the rest of the little party nudged their scrubby Chinese ponies single file along the overgrown track toward the other entrances, 'Tamayo has instructions to hold them at bay and set the charges off immediately.'

'I doubt Yuan will authorize troops.' Asher scanned the brush-choked gully below the track, the queer, snaky ridges of the hills that closed in around them. His cracked ribs ached, and after the dark of the mines, the sunlight seemed queerly bright. 'He's sensitive about how he's perceived by the West. If there's trouble, he'll find his actions hard to justify. The ones we need to watch out for are the Tso. Though I wouldn't put it outside the realm of possibility,' he went on grimly, 'for us to meet Colonel von Mehren and some of *his* merry men – depending on who Madame Tso has chosen to sell information to.'

All around the rear flanks of the mountain, they stopped at the small subsidiary entrances and ventilation shafts of the mine – most barely more than holes in the ground, some centuries old – and blew them up as they went, burying in seconds the brutal labor of years.

Can he hear the explosions in his sleep? Asher wondered as the hillside jarred beneath him and thick yellow dust belched from the narrow pits. *Lying asleep a thousand and ten thousand and a hundred thousand black iron steps down into the earth . . .*

Is he counting them in his dreams? Twelve yet to go, then eleven, then ten . . . Until final darkness and an eternity alone with pain?

As he rolled up his wires, packed his detonator back on his shaggy little mount and then hauled himself – ribs stabbing him – into the saddle again, Asher glanced at Karlebach's stony face and wondered whether he thought the same.

But he could not bring himself to ask.

In its heyday, the entrance to the mine on the far side of Shi'h Liu mountain had been a workings in its own right. Asher traced the foundations of sheds and huts, small squares of brick and stone on the slope beneath the cave mouth, and a graded track that led down to what had been a worker's village, strung out along the trickle of a stream. Everything was gone now except for a few broken fragments of wall. This was a country where abandoned brick or cut stone did not go long un-scavenged. Rats swarmed forth – as they had at two other entrances – and Asher and the bodyguard Ogata swept them with flame. Then Asher checked his watch and wired the gelignite blocks into the decayed wooden props that held up the entrance to the cave. *Right on schedule, always supposing President Yuan hasn't sent an army to stop the villagers . . .*

He hid the detonator in what looked like the debris of a shed while Mizukami and one of the three soldiers, Nishiharu, scouted a few yards down the tunnel through the smoking carpet of dead and dying rats. Karlebach shouldered his shotgun, and the spare cylinders of oil and nitrogen, in case there were more vermin further down. Another soldier, Seki, carried in a satchel of explosives, wire, and a detonator box.

Asher signed Ogata and the third soldier, Hirato, to remain outside on guard over the ponies. Then he picked up his satchel and his lantern and followed the gleam of Mizukami's dim light down the tunnel into the dark.

It was then not quite three o'clock.

TWENTY-FIVE

Rats whipped among the rocks. Asher could hear the scrabble of their feet, their constant squeaking in the dark; their sweetish, fusty stink mingled with the scents of water and stone. In the abysses of the cross-drifts, tiny eyes glittered like malevolent rubies. Asher counted turnings, checked and rechecked both his maps by the lantern-gleam, and prayed that Ysidro's observations here had been correct, and that those lazy bastards at the Hsi Fang-te mining offices hadn't simply gone on hearsay of what was down here or, worse yet, just made something up – *who's going to go down to check, eh?*

Burn in Hell, the lot of you.

The ceiling barely cleared the heads of the Japanese and forced Asher and Karlebach to stoop as they walked. Mizukami whispered, '*Iei!*' and the light of his lantern fell on an X, scratched deeply into the stone of the left-hand wall. The scratches were fresh. 'What is this, Ashu Sensei?'

Asher checked his map. The tunnel beside the X was in the right place to be the one that led down to the gallery they sought.

'Who has been down here?' Karlebach asked hoarsely

'The priest Chiang,' lied Asher, 'said he recalled something like this. Let me go ahead.'

He raised his lantern, moved forward again. The tunnel sloped sharply, following an ancient coal-seam. When he touched the wall, moisture slicked his hand. After a time the walls widened out around them, the ceiling grew higher and the lantern-light showed them a few pillars still standing where the coal had been cut out around them. Wooden props had been installed to support the roof, gray and desiccated with age.

The whole thing will come down when we blow the tunnel . . .

Then the gallery narrowed again, and Asher had to turn sideways and brace himself against the steep angle of the floor. He held the lantern further out before him, then knelt and crept forward step by step.

Darkness dropped away before him. The ends of a ladder poked up over the edge, but he knew better than to trust it. He merely extended his lantern out over the abyss and glimpsed the faintest hints of pillars – stalactites aglitter with moisture and crystal – hanging from a ceiling somewhere not far above him, and undulating shapes of pale flowstone and stalagmites not far below. He called out, 'Hello!' into the darkness, and echoes picked up his voice, the distant ringing of vast underground space. Ysidro was right. The caverns would swallow any amount of chlorine, disperse it harmlessly in millions of cubic feet of air. The *yao-kuei* could probably follow them to some other entrance, miles away.

Asher edged back from the brink and scrambled, stooping, to where the others waited. 'The caves are down there, all right,' he said as he collected wires and gelignite from young Mr Seki. 'By the look of the ceiling here –' he raised his lantern toward the swagged-down rock, the age-grayed rotting props – 'an explosion will bring the whole gallery down, so I want the lot of you to go back up the tunnel.'

The detonator wires, extended across the gallery to the narrowing of the way to the caves, were some twenty feet short of the tunnel mouth. Asher wired the gelignite as close to the cave entry as he could, aware that only a few slabs remained to him in case they found some unexpected shaft or fissure that had been shown on neither map. 'Get back,' he said as he wired the lines to the box. 'I mean it.'

Mizukami put a gently-urging hand on Karlebach's arm, but the old man shrugged free. He was staring as if hypnotized at another X cut into the rock of the gallery wall. 'Is *he* down here?' he whispered in Czech, coming to kneel at Asher's side. His eyes almost blazed in the lantern-light. 'Not this priest . . . You know of whom I speak.'

'I don't know.' Asher met his gaze calmly. 'Chiang spoke of finding such marks—'

'Could they have been made by the Others? Or by the vampires of Peking, to lead us into a trap?'

Love and respect notwithstanding, Asher had to force himself not to snap, *Don't be such an ass!* 'He said they'd been down here for years.'

'And can he be trusted?' Karlebach's voice trembled with the violence of his emotions. 'Jamie, we hunt a thing which has no soul. A thing infinitely cunning, which can twist the minds and perceptions of even the good and the strong!'

From his pocket, Asher dug wads of cotton, handed two to the old scholar: 'Put those in your ears. Give these –' he unwrapped another from its blue paper – 'to Mizukami and his men, and don't forget to cover your mouth and nose as well.' He suited the action to the word, pulling up his own handkerchief, tied bandanna-wise over the lower part of his face like a Wild West badman. 'Now get back. God knows how much of this ceiling is going to come down.'

Simon, he thought, and cast a glance over his shoulder at the soldiers' retreating lantern, *forgive me . . .*

He shoved down the plunger, sprang to his feet, and ran for the tunnel as if the Devil of his father's worst sermons bit at his heels. He was still a yard short of it when the earth jerked under-foot, the world echoed with the trapped cataclysm of detonation, and a tidal wave of burning dust overtook and overwhelmed him, nearly throwing him to the ground. He staggered and stumbled on, mind focused on the tunnel and the distant lanterns as the lights vanished utterly in the murk. Behind him he heard rock falling – tons of it – as the gallery ceiling gave way . . .

He must have aimed dead on at the tunnel, for a sickly yellow blur showed almost in front of him. Men unrecognizable with dust – save for Mizukami's glasses and sword, Karlebach's height and beard – caught his arms. Ears ringing, Asher felt more than heard when silence fell behind them. He took the lantern, returned along the tunnel through what felt like a palpable wall of suspended dust, to find the inner end of the gallery roof had all come down, a bare yard in front of the detonator box. Dizzy with the shock of the explosion, his cracked ribs making him feel as if he'd been bayoneted, Asher nevertheless dragged the wires free of the rubble, wound them around his arm.

When he reached the soldiers again he had to put his watch almost up against the lantern to see the time.

Three forty. We'll still be on this side of the mountain when Sergeant Tamayo detonates the chlorine cylinders and seals the mine.

Karlebach's face was haggard in the grimy light of the lantern, and in his heart Asher heard him murmur, *Like a son to me . . .*

It was a blessing to smell air, even the cold, dusty air of the Western Hills. The daylight that Asher could glimpse beyond the tunnel mouth had the golden quality of the first approach of evening. Though his hearing was returning, Asher's head still ached, and Seki – whose nose had bled from the shock – looked like some gore-daubed creature of a horror tale.

Ysidro, in his sleep, would hear this next explosion – the one that would bring down the ceiling of the old rear entrance of the mine – and would know: *only one left.*

Don't think about it. In Asher's years with the Department, he had learned how not to think about things like that.

It was, in part, why he had left the Department.

The pain in his ribs when he coughed, the ache in every muscle and bone, was such that it was difficult to think about much of anything.

Then up ahead of him, beyond that round of daylight, he saw movement.

Men running toward the tunnel.

Too many men. Rifles in their hands.

Asher yelled, 'Back!' as the first bullets ripped into the cave.

Karlebach didn't have a soldier's reflexes. The private Nishiharu grabbed his arm, thrust him back down the tunnel. There was a cross-cut about thirty feet back – in its shelter Asher slid into the straps of his flame-thrower again, stepped out and sprayed the tunnel with fire. The five men just entering sprang clear; he saw they wore *ch'i-p'aos* and *ku*, with Western boots. Those behind them, the gray uniforms of the Chinese Army. A man in a Western suit – Asher recognized the American double-breasted jacket – stepped forward, hands raised.

'Asher!'

T'uan, he thought. *Chen Chi T'uan. Madame Tso's nephew.*

Even in the shadows he could see the bruises on the young man's face, the swelling where the deformation was beginning.

'Throw down your weapon, come out!' T'uan shouted. 'We got your wife!'

You're lying. The breath seemed to choke in his lungs.

He edged himself to the corner of the cross-cut tunnel, shouted, 'What do you want?' He repeated the words in Chinese, though T'uan had called out in English.

'We want you.' T'uan's English was clear, if simple. 'We want no trouble. Not kill you, not kill friends, not kill nobody. Promise. Swear on Holy Bible.'

And you want me to step out of cover and walk towards a dozen men with rifles on the strength of 'Promise'? You need to run for the government, friend.

'We got your wife, Asher,' T'uan repeated. 'Got her all safe. You come out, Japanese come out, nobody hurt. This mine our property. We—'

Shots cracked beyond T'uan. One of the bully boys in the mine entrance flung up his arms, pitched forward on his face. The Chinese soldiers sprang aside as a bullet kicked dirt among them. Then, as one, they and the bully boys ran forward into the shelter of the tunnel mouth—

Straight under the gelignite wired into the props beneath the roof.

Ogata. The thought came to Asher in the split instant before the explosion. *Driving them forward under the blast zone . . .*

He flinched back behind the shelter of the corner, clapped his hands over his ears. Thunder, blackness, dust in his lungs and the ground lurching underfoot. If the Chinese soldiers – or T'uan's enforcers – screamed, the sound didn't penetrate the booming horror of the explosion directly over their heads. Asher pressed his face to the wall and buried his nose and mouth in the crook of his arm.

Then stillness, terrible and deep. Blackness like the abyss of Hell. Through the ringing in his ears he heard one of the Japanese soldiers gasp a question and thought he heard someone say, *Ogata . . .*

It had been, Asher reflected, as neat a piece of tactics on Ogata's part as one could hope for, and the only way the two men left outside the tunnel could neutralize eleven well-armed enemies. The bodyguard knew the men in the mine had maps, to get them through the tunnels to the main entrance. At this very moment, he suspected Ogata and Hirato were riding hell for leather along those overgrown paths, to reach Sergeant Tamayo at the main entrance and tell him, *Don't detonate until they arrive . . .*

Which would make sense, Asher reflected, *if there were no reason not to delay detonation past fall of darkness.*

And if rats were the worst thing we're likely to meet in the mine.

Yellowish light smeared the dust-choked darkness behind him; he heard Karlebach's gasping cough. 'Is everyone all right?' Asher called out. 'Rabbi?'

'This depends,' croaked the old scholar, 'upon how one defines the words "all right".'

'We live,' Mizukami said. 'Ashu Sensei, the man cannot have known about Madame Ashu.'

'He can.' Asher coughed and spat up dust. 'We have forty minutes of safety to get to the front entrance of the mine – if Ogata can make it around the shoulder of the mountain that quickly. And if Tamayo and the others at the front aren't attacked—'

A gunshot cracked in the blackness, the bullet whining off the rock by his head. Dimly, in what seemed like a wall of solid dust, Asher saw the glint of catlike eyes.

T'uan can see in the darkness . . .

IT can see in the darkness.

The thing that used to be T'uan.

Of course it survived.

He answered the shot with a blast from his flame-thrower, then turned and thrust Karlebach and Mizukami ahead of him along the cross-cut. 'Go, forward! There should be a gallery ahead—'

Another shot. The air grew clearer as they plunged into the long chamber that ran before an ancient coalface. Asher uncovered his lantern again and stumbled toward the yellow gleam of someone else's; only by the height of the dim figure did he see it was Karlebach. The old man staggered, groped for the wall, and Asher caught his elbow, pulled him along. 'He can see in the dark! Don't close the lanterns!' The tiny glow showed huge heaps of waste rock all along the gallery walls, and they ducked behind the nearest one; Asher made a swift count of his companions, motioned for all to take hands, then signed for darkness.

It was pitchy, utter, and unspeakable, the silence horrible. Under the choke of dust, Asher smelled rats, heard them skittering among the loose rock of the slag heaps.

From the direction of the tunnel, nothing.

There was water on the floor. Could T'uan – and any of his men who might have survived the explosion – come near without sound? Or fool their perceptions, so as to remain unheard?

Beside him he felt Mizukami bend down a trifle, to reach the puddles . . . *Washing his eyeglasses,* Asher realized. The little nobleman had been stumbling along almost blind.

How sharp is their hearing? They were cousins to vampires, who could detect differences in the rhythm of breath in a crowded room . . .

He pressed his hand to his side, trying to will away the pain.

How far along is T'uan in his transformation to yao-kuei? How much did those 'herbs' affect the process? How much of his mind is left, and how long will that last?

Or would, in fact, the medicines allow the young man to retain enough of his human mind to command the *yao-kuei* – like figures on a chessboard?

We have your wife . . .

His heart screamed *that's impossible!* but the long-time field agent in him asked, *How did they do it, and where would they take her?*

Beside him Asher heard one of the soldiers jerk and gasp, and then the squeal of a rat as it was knocked to the floor.

Silence again.

At last he slipped the lantern cover a millimeter. 'Let's go.'

TWENTY-SIX

British Legation, Peking
Tuesday, November 12, 1912
Mrs Asher,
   Might I beg the favor of five minutes of your time? I would not dream of troubling you, save the matter is an urgent one, and of utmost importance.
      Ever your servant,
      Edmund Woodreave

'Please, ma'am.' Mrs Pilley clasped her hands over Lydia's, when Lydia would have torn up the note. 'The poor man looked so desperate when he stopped me in the lobby just now. I'm sure he wouldn't have waited half the morning here for you, just for foolishness.'

'Are you?' Lydia turned the note over in her black-gloved fingers. It sounded to her exactly like the sort of thing her most persistent suitor would do. She thought she'd glimpsed that tall, pot-bellied, awkward form scrambling up out of an armchair as she, Ellen, and Mrs Pilley had crossed the lobby with Miranda, after a morning spent walking with Madame Hautecoeur on the Tatar City's walls. At the sight of him she had quickened her steps to the stair.

The effort to keep her mind from what she knew had to be taking place in the Western Hills – from the thought of Jamie tangling with the Others, who might or might not be asleep; from the knowledge that Simon would be sealed into the mine with them – had exhausted her. Annette Hautecoeur, for all her gossipy slyness, had maintained a gentle flow of harmless commonplace as they'd looked out across that eerily impressive sea of gray and green and crimson roofs, and had made no comment about Lydia's distraction and silences.

A new-made widow, Lydia was finding, could get away with a lot.

Such forbearance would definitely not be encountered in Edmund Woodreave's company.

'Please.' The little nurse's voice almost had tears in it. 'He has a faithful heart, ma'am, and loves you so much.'

'He has debts of over five hundred pounds to his club, his tailor, his wine merchant, and Hoby's in London where he orders his boots,' returned Lydia astringently. 'And he loves so much the thought of an independent income which would put him in line for promotion.'

Mrs Pilley's face crumpled a little, her eyes pleading. Her own fondness for the clerk, she knew, would forever go unconsummated – without a marriage portion of some kind neither he nor anyone else could afford to look at her . . .

Unless, thought Lydia, with a sudden pang of mingled suspicion and pity, *he's courted her a little in order to get her help in delivering this.*

Another look at the nurse's face confirmed her thought. *Of course he has.*

She sighed, feeling a little sick, and inspected herself in the parlor mirror. She retreated to the bedroom and repaired the ravages wrought by an hour's sedate stroll under the protection of enough veiling to tent the grounds of New College – touches of rice powder, the tiniest refreshment of mascaro on the lids of her eyes (*I may be in mourning but there's no reason to look frightful . . .*), smoothing and readjustment of her coiffure . . . Then she tucked her spectacles back into their silver case, put on her gloves again, and made her way down to the lobby, steeled to be grief-stricken and polite.

Simon . . .

He'll find a way out somehow . . .

Woodreave was pacing the lobby outside the door of the smallest of the private parlors when Lydia came down the stairs. She noticed in passing a Chinese workman deep in argument with the manager at the desk and three laborers standing next to a number of rolled-up carpets nearby. Woodreave came forward and took her arm with a reverence that almost concealed the pre-emptory anxiety of the gesture. 'Madame – Mrs Asher – thank you for coming down! Truly I'm – I'm sorry for disturbing you this way, but I really had no choice . . .'

He conducted her into the private parlor with the blue curtains and closed the door.

Grant Hobart rose from beside the fire. 'Mrs Asher—'

Lydia turned sharply on Woodreave; his face was filled with anguish and guilt. 'Please, Mrs Asher, please forgive me! Mr Hobart needs very much to speak to you. He said you wouldn't answer his letters—'

'I wouldn't answer his letters,' responded Lydia, furious now, 'because I do not want to speak with him. The man who lied about my husband? Who drove him into the situation which resulted in his death, rather than have him reveal what he'd learned about the blood on his own hands?'

'Blood—?' Woodreave threw a pleading glance toward Hobart, who crossed the little parlor in two steps to Lydia's side. He looked frightful, Lydia thought, trying not to peer nearsightedly at him – haggard and feverish: *anxiety over Richard? When he knows perfectly well why Holly Eddington was murdered . . .*

'Ask him,' said Lydia coldly. 'Or was part of the money he offered you on the condition that you didn't ask him anything?'

She was so angry that it took her an instant to identify the smell that clung to Hobart's clothing. A breath of foulness, of fishy decay buried under nauseating French cologne . . . and something else, something chemical . . . *Chloroform—*

She turned to dive for the parlor door, but it was too late. Hobart grabbed her arm in a grip of terrifying strength and clapped a soaked rag to her nose and mouth. Lydia held her breath, kicked backwards at his shin—

And in the same instant, a Chinese man – respectably dressed in Western fashion – stepped from behind the curtains that half-concealed the alcove of the door, put one hand over Woodreave's mouth and with the other drove a foot-long steel stiletto at an angle up through the larynx and into – Lydia guessed – the medulla oblongata and the cerebellum behind it. Which was, she reflected with her last conscious thought before blacking out, truly excellent aim given the circumstances.

Asher smelled the *yao-kuei* in the darkness, some fifteen minutes before he and his companions were cornered. By the feeble glimmer of two of their lanterns it took all his concentration to keep count of turnings, and of the few landmarks that had been

noted on the map: did *stone pit* (or *dump*) really mean a disused
room filled in with broken 'gob', as it was called in Wales, or
was that something else that would be further along? Did a
hogback rise of the floor mean they'd come down the wrong
tunnel, or had the floor heaved up in the twenty years or more
since the map was made? Despite the chill in the mine he was
sweating, and he wondered how close they were to the detonation
site of the chlorine and how fast the gas would spread once the
canisters shattered.

Wondered where the sun was in the sky.

Ahead of him, Private Seki whispered, *'Nani-ka nioi desu ka?'*
and an instant later Asher smelled it, too. Fishy rottenness, the
human stink of unclean flesh . . .

Forty of them, Ysidro had said.

He checked the map. 'Back this way. There's a shaft down to
a gallery below this one, then a shaft up again—' *If we're in the
right tunnel.*

There was a shaft – a few yards down a cross-cut that wasn't
as the map had described it – and a ladder with rotten rungs that
cracked and whispered under the weight of the men, forty feet
down into utter darkness. A gallery, the entire ceiling of which
had sagged to within five feet of its floor, ankle deep in water
in places, a slippery, hideous scramble.

Then, like the warning rush of wind that presages the storm,
the skitter of claws on stone, the stink of rats.

Beyond the radius of the light Asher saw movement and a
river of glittering eyes. He quickly unshipped the nozzle of his
flame-thrower and lit the pilot (*six matches left* . . .), but when
he turned the flame on the creatures, the first wave of them was
already barely two yards from his boots. The rats shrieked, those
behind pushing the flaming leaders ahead, and the whole swarm
of them tried to fan out in a crescent around the men. Mizukami
and Nishiharu fired up their lights and swept the moving wings
of the army, the glare of the blaze blinding after hours of
darkness.

And God, I hope this swarm is only a single wave . . .

It was. The rodents scattered, squealing, the charred and dying
casualties a twitching carpet of stink and embers underfoot. They
gave squishily as Asher strode forward, praying that there would
indeed be the up-shaft that was supposedly at the end of the

gallery and that the ladder there would still be able to bear weight. Tiny feet splished in water behind them in the darkness, scratched on the stones.

'There!' Karlebach panted.

As the failing lantern-light touched the ascending shaft, a rat fell down it. Then two more.

Bollocks.

'Let me go up first.' Asher shifted the weight of the flame-thrower on his back. *Too light.* How much fuel remained?

He knew what would be at the top.

Rats lined the uppermost rung of the creaky ladder, rimmed the pit head, eyes a tiny wall of live embers in the dark. Asher fired a burst of flame up at them, climbed a yard – lantern banging awkwardly at his thigh where it hung from his belt – then braced himself and fired again, sweeping the top of the shaft. He sprang up the last few feet and fired once more as soon as he got his elbows over the edge on to solid ground, the yellow burst of flame racing for yards along the floor of the tunnel. Scrambled up and shouted, 'Come on! Now!'

Swept again, to keep the carpet of vermin at bay. The flame gave out with a sputter moments later; Mizukami swept the next wave of rodents while Asher shed the now-useless tank, reached down to haul Karlebach up the last few feet. The old man was gasping, struggling to hook his wrists over the rungs; in the dark behind him Asher made out Private Seki, pushing and guiding him from below.

'There's a tunnel leading into and out of this room,' panted Asher as he pulled Karlebach, then Seki up out of the shaft. 'We want the one that corners to the left.' The room was invisible beyond the glare of the flame-thrower. When the rats retreated, Asher led the way straight to the wall, which he knew would be close – on the map the room wasn't big. Slag and 'gob' heaped all around its walls – this part of the mine had been long abandoned as a dumping ground. The piled debris swarmed with rats. They followed the wall, but the tunnel they came to cornered right, and as Asher's lantern failed, and Nishiharu kindled his own to replace it, the yellow flare of the match caught more eyes in the darkness.

Not the eyes of rats.

Asher cursed, led the way along the wall toward where he

knew now the left-hand tunnel must be; behind him he heard Mizukami's quiet-voiced directions to his men. Asher guessed they had only a dozen rounds apiece, perfectly adequate to deal with bandits . . .

Four *yao-kuei* emerged from the left-hand tunnel when Asher was within two yards of it.

They were the first Asher had seen by anything brighter than moonlight, slumped shapes that moved like animals. Yet they came with deadly swiftness, fanged mouths gaping. He fired his pistol almost point-blank at the nearest one, and behind him one of the soldiers got off a shot with his rifle. One of the *yao-kuei* staggered to its feet again, the other – half its head blown away – crawled toward them until Mizukami hit it with the last stream from his flame-thrower. More *yao-kuei* emerged from the right-hand tunnel at the other side of the room, loped toward them, eyes flashing in the darkness, and very deliberately Rebbe Karlebach brought up his shotgun and emptied one of the barrels into the nearest creature at a distance of ten feet.

The result was shocking. The creature shrieked, staggered, tore at itself with huge, clawed hands. The bleeding wounds sizzled and blistered. The others backed a step, and in that instant the old man turned and fired the second barrel at one of the two that blocked the way to the left-hand tunnel. The thing collapsed to the floor, screaming and raking its own flesh around the smoking wounds. Mizukami stripped out of his spent flame-thrower and strode in on the attacking group, sword flashing, and in that same moment the tallest of the *yao-kuei* – even slumped it must have been nearly six feet – lunged at Karlebach, caught the barrels of his shotgun as if he would wrench the weapon from his hand—

And stopped, staring at him in the lantern-light.

And for an instant, Karlebach paused in his frantic scramble to reload, stared back.

There was nothing human left of the doglike face, but as Asher brought up his pistol and fired point-blank into the thing's head, his mind noted automatically that the few strands that remained of its verminous hair, as dark in the fitful glare as that of the others, were curly rather than straight and caught a mahogany-red gleam.

Asher's shot knocked the *yao-kuei* sprawling. He grabbed Karlebach by the shoulder of his coat, thrust him ahead of him into the left-hand tunnel. Nishiharu laid down a burst of fire to cover the other two, and Asher plunged forward, praying his recollection of what came after the room with the shaft was correct. An inclined corridor, the Hsi Fang-te map had noted. Ceiling bagged down with the weight of the mountain above and floor littered with broken props, another incline . . .

A gallery, this one high-ceilinged, with glimpses of scaffolding on the nearer wall. Asher pulled a hunk of it free of its rotting ties, fumbled for his map, swung around in shocked terror at the sudden flash of eyes a foot from his shoulder—

A white hand, cold as the grip of a corpse, blocked him from bringing his revolver to bear. Ysidro said, 'This way.'

'We blew up that tunnel this morning,' Asher gasped.

'You Protestant imbeciles!'

Karlebach shouted a curse, swung toward him with his shotgun—

And Ysidro was gone.

'They are down here too!' The Professor staggered, passed a hand over his eyes. 'I knew it! I knew it was a trap! I felt their presence—' Then, like the stroke of a monster drum, the ground underfoot jarred. The distant explosion was strong enough to send rocks slithering from the slag piles at one end of the gallery, and to make all the scaffolding rattle and sway. Dust rained from the ceiling. Then far off, and stronger, a second blast.

'That's it,' said Asher. 'They set off the gas – and sealed the mine.'

In the silence there seemed nothing more to say. *Lydia*, he thought. *Miranda . . .*

Far on the other end of the gallery, a light flickered. A shaky old voice called out, '*Na shih shei?*' *Who's there?*

And Asher shouted back, scarcely believing his ears, 'Chiang?'

The others simply stared as the distant blur of white resolved itself into the old man, hurrying toward them, surprisingly agile on the steep and slippery floor. In one hand he held his staff, a cheap tin lantern in the other, its glimmer turning his long white hair into trailing wisps of smoke. 'I thank the Yama-King and all the Magistrates of Hell for guiding me in this terrible place,' he said as he drew closer. 'The entrances to the mine have all been sealed up—'

'How you get in?'

'Ah, but there is a secret way, which lies in the crypt of the

Temple of the Concealed Buddha. I studied there after the death of my wife. It was built during the Sung Dynasty, when because of the growing strength of the Heaven and Earth Sect the Emperor decreed . . .' The old man looked from face to face of the fugitives. 'Those creatures that I saw—'

'Lead us,' commanded Asher. 'Poison gas, soon, quickly, now—'

Mizukami had gone to the edge of the lamplight, listening into the darkness; Karlebach and the two soldiers, without a word of Chinese among them, still stared at the white-haired priest as if he'd descended from the ceiling in a chariot of fire.

'Poison gas?' Chiang's white brows drew together indignantly. 'What a frightful thing! Mo Tzu, in the Spring and Autumn Period, wrote of the use of mustard to make toxic smokes to be blown at enemies, but it is a shameful use of man's wisdom and energies to—'

'Shameful waste *our* wisdom and energies,' said Asher tactfully, 'for us die with *yao-kuei* . . .'

'Oh, quite right, quite right!' The old priest nodded and led the way back along the gallery in the direction from which he had come. 'An excellent point. Yes, the *yao-kuei* . . . But surely the *yao-kuei* have their own path, their own place, in this world. The Buddha taught that even noxious insects have their own Buddha-nature.'

'Here they come,' Mizukami said.

Eyes glittered behind them in the darkness. Mizukami motioned Private Seki toward Karlebach, spoke an order; the young man handed his lantern to Asher, put his shoulder beneath the old Professor's arm. The floor ahead of them swarmed suddenly with rats, scurrying and dropping from the scaffolding; Mizukami snapped another order, and Nishiharu fired the flame-thrower.

'Fascinating,' murmured Chiang. 'In the Spring and Autumn Period, Sun Tzu wrote of such devices—'

Asher shoved him without ceremony toward the darkness: 'Run!'

They ran. The flame-thrower sputtered out, and Nishiharu slithered from its straps as he ran, then swung around to fire his rifle into the loping shadows of the *yao-kuei*. Asher smelled above their stink the distant reek of chlorine, growing stronger as it flowed into the mine. As he had observed on the shores of the

Peking Sea, the *yao-kuei* moved with the swift precision of a school of fish, dispersing themselves across the gallery. Some scrambled up on the rotting scaffolding, moved along it with terrifying agility, spreading out to keep from being shot into in a mob. To aim, the fugitives would have to stop, and to stop was to die.

'This way!' Chiang waved his staff encouragingly. The gallery ended in a steep tunnel, its walls marked with enormous, fresh chalk Xs – obviously Chiang's way of keeping from getting lost. Two *yao-kuei* dropped from the scaffolding in front of the entry to the tunnel, bared their outsize teeth. Asher didn't see how, but like an eye-blink, Ysidro was behind the creatures in the tunnel mouth: thin and rather tattered, skeletal in the lantern-light. He caught one of the *yao-kuei* with both hands around its head and twisted its neck. Asher heard the bones snap, but when Ysidro kicked the thing aside it got up again, staggered blindly, arms thrashing, still looking for prey. The second *yao-kuei* fell upon Ysidro, mouth stretched to bite, and Mizukami took off both its hands with one stroke of his sword, and then, as Ysidro dodged nimbly away, its head with the next stroke.

More of the creatures dropped from the scaffold, the main group – twenty at least – closing in from the gallery floor. Karlebach fired into the group as they approached, and a *yao-kuei* grabbed him from behind. Its claws tore through his thick coat, and it seized him by his white hair. The next second the thing was knocked sprawling by the tallest of the *yao-kuei* – blood clotting from the gaping entry-wound Asher's pistol had left in its skull – who flung the smaller creature aside, caught up the rifle Seki had dropped during the fray, and waded into the advancing others, swinging the weapon like a club.

The other *yao-kuei* fell back before it. It turned, for one second, and looked back at Asher, at Karlebach, at the small group huddled in the tunnel mouth in the lamplight.

Karlebach whispered: 'Matthias—'

It opened its fanged mouth like an ape and screeched at them. Then turned, and strode toward the others, holding them at bay.

'Go,' said Asher. 'Run!' He caught Karlebach by the arm, forced him along in the wake of Chiang's lantern, stumbling on the uneven floor. Another white X glimmered at the bottom of a shaft.

'Up,' urged Chiang. 'Hasten—' For indeed, the smell of chlorine was growing stronger in the shaft, and Asher began to cough,
lungs burning, ribs stabbing him, tears flooding his eyes.

'Go.' He slipped his satchel from his shoulder, with the last
two bars of gelignite. 'I'll be up—'

'You're a fool,' said Ysidro's voice in his ear as the others
disappeared up the ladder.

Asher was coughing so hard he couldn't respond. The pain in
his side made him dizzy.

'How do you set these?'

'Detonator – in the middle—'

Cold hands pulled the wires from his fingers. *All very well for
you to talk. You don't need to breathe . . .*

'Get up the ladder.'

'Lydia,' gasped Asher. 'Tso house— Said they have her—'

Ysidro swore hair-raisingly in Spanish. 'Go. And cover me
from that lunatic Jew before you touch off the explosion.'

Head swimming, Asher dragged himself up the rungs, endless
in the dark. Overhead, the lantern-light was a dim spot. It was
like trying to swim up out of a lightless well.

Hands grabbed his arms, pulled him up. He saw Mizukami
kneeling over the detonator box, gasped, 'Wait—' and staggered,
flung out his arm as if to catch his balance, and fell, knocking
lantern and detonator spinning away into the blackness.

The darkness was like being struck blind. Voices cried out,
scrabbled in the lightless abyss, and Asher lay on the stone floor
gasping. Aware that Ysidro had heard their voices in the mine
and come out from behind his protective silver bars and followed
them, once the Others were fully occupied . . .

Cold thin hands took his, pressed the hot metal of the lantern
into them. Long nails like claws. He managed to shout, 'I found
it,' and coughed again, almost nauseated, as he fumbled for
matches.

With the first flicker of the lamplight, Mizukami seized the
detonator and pressed the plunger home.

Deep, deep below them the earth surged. Dust erupted thickly
from the shaft, blurred the lamplight; filled what Asher saw now
was a small rock-cut room, its walls carved with column after
column of Buddhist scripture, engraved into the stone.

After the bellow of the explosion, silence. Karlebach dragged himself to the shaft's edge and knelt beside it, gazing down, crippled hands folded in prayer. The priest Chiang, standing behind him with the lantern, seemed to understand what had happened in the gallery, for he laid one skeletal hand on the old man's shoulder and over the shaft made a sign of blessing.

Of Ysidro, no trace remained.

TWENTY-SEVEN

must have fallen asleep at the Infirmary again.

Her feet were freezing, even in the sturdy hand-me-down boots that her friend Anne had sent her (which were too wide and had to be filled in with rags) after Lydia had walked out of her father's house. Her corset pinched her waist, and the hospital smell of chloroform had given her a splitting headache. When Dr Parton was on duty at the Radcliffe Infirmary Lydia was all right, for he treated her like any male orderly and understood that in addition to lectures, study, and practicum she was also tutoring students from the other colleges in science. The other physicians persisted in the belief that this unwanted 'bacheloress' (as they called her) could be pushed out of the male medical preserves by being given all the nastiest duties. So falling asleep in odd corners of the Infirmary was nothing new.

She'd dreamed she was married to Edmund Woodreave.

Dreamed she was tied to him inescapably. Was forced to stay at home and organize teas and pay calls on relatives in an endless round of hypocritical chit-chat . . .

Dreamed of wishing he were dead.

Dreamed of seeing his eyes as someone stabbed him before her . . .

Oh, God, that really happened—!

She woke. Slivers of twilight through shuttered windows showed her painted Chinese rafters overhead. She lay on a carpet. When she turned her head she made out the enclosing shape of a Chinese bed, like a little wooden room faintly smelling of cedar and dust. The carpet had simply been pushed on to the bare platform, and the whole room around her smelled of mustiness, and of something rotting nearby.

The carpet, she thought cloudily.

There were workmen with rolled-up carpets in the lobby. That must be how they got me out of the hotel, rolled up like Cleopatra in a rug.

And how they got poor Mr Woodreave's body out. She shuddered again, at that last sight of his eyes. *Ellen and Mrs Pilley won't know I'm missing. They'll think I went off somewhere with him.*

She moved, and somewhere in the room there was an instant scrabble and scurrying. Rats. She sat up hastily, groped for her reticule with her eyeglasses in it and had only to think of it to give the matter up in despair. Her money was in it, too, so the man in charge of the carpet-carriers had undoubtedly simply appropriated it as part of his pay. Her exploring hands found the protective silver chains gone from her throat and wrists. Her cameo, earrings, and necklaces of jet beads – suitable for mourning – were also gone. She pulled up her skirts and found the little roll of picklocks still buttoned to the bottom edge of her corset, and whispered a prayer of thanks to Jamie for suggesting she never go out of the house without it, even if it was only for a walk with Miranda.

Though if they've bolted the door from the outside I'm out of luck.

It was growing dark, wherever she was. Scratching at the wall somewhere close, tiny nasty little pink feet . . . Lydia struggled against panic at the sound. With the fetor in the room she wasn't surprised there were rats. *We must be near a midden or a garbage tip . . .*

No.

I'm at Mrs Tso's.

Cold swallowed her heart as the knowledge fell into place.

Hobart brought me here. He's working for them. With everything they know about him, of course they're blackmailing him. This must be the pavilion Jamie told me about: the pavilion where those two poor young men – or what used to be men – are being kept.

She got quickly to her feet. She was too nearsighted to see if there were rats in the shadows along the wall, but if there were, they weren't moving. Holding her skirts well up around her knees, she groped her way to the windows. They were shuttered, bolted on the inside, but when she unbolted and tested them, a hasp and padlock thumped softly on the other side of the thick wood. *Damn.*

Jamie, don't let them make you do anything stupid!

The door had a bolt on the inside but none on the outside. The room had evidently been an ordinary bedroom, and it opened into a larger chamber, likewise shuttered and padlocked, but scuttering with rats. The attic at Willoughby Court had been a haven of them, for both her mother and stepmother had had a loathing of cats, and one of her nanny's favorite threats had been that she would lock her up there. The smell in this room was stronger, too – one with which Lydia was profoundly familiar from her residency in a London charity clinic. Rotting flesh and human filth.

The door on the south side of the big room would lead into the courtyard, she guessed, given that the windowless wall of the bedroom where the bed stood was north. At least that's what the Baroness had said was true of all Chinese dwellings. The courtyard door was padlocked on the outside as well. In the other bedroom – the western one – the stench was worse, and the long table by the trapdoor near its west wall confirmed her fear. It was, as Jamie had described, stained, as if chunks of bleeding meat had been set carelessly down on one end of it, and there were spatters and dribbles of other substances, dark on the pale wood. Of the jars and bottles he'd seen there, all that remained were a sort of chafing dish and couple of small clay drinking-vessels stained with dark residue.

They must have cleared everything off after Jamie snooped through.

She took the candle from the chafing dish, hunted in the table drawer and found a box of matches. Whispered another prayer of relief. It was hard to guess how much daylight was left, but the thought of being in this place after full dark fell – completely blind – sickened her. She had Jamie's word that the poor wretches in the cellar were locked up in some fashion, but anything could have changed in the past two days. She lit the candle, descended the stair – also not locked nor even equipped with a lock. *Mrs Tso can't have had the scheme to use them for very long.*

She must have counted on keeping the pavilion itself under lock and key.

From what she'd heard of Mrs Tso, it was hard to imagine any member of the woman's household would dare go poking around in a place where they weren't supposed to be.

The stench at the bottom of the stairs was horrific, but still not worse than the yard behind the surgical theater of the charity hospital on a hot day after they'd been doing amputations. Lydia held the candle high up, squinting to see and not daring to go closer to the two men whose sleeping forms she could just make out.

They were chained to the walls at opposite ends of the little brick strongroom. There were buckets for drinking water and waste, but it was clear that both prisoners were beginning to forget that earliest of civilized behaviors. It was also clear, as far as Lydia could see, that the room was cleaned on a regular basis. They had blankets and quilts. Rats darted in the dense shadows, chewed on the half-eaten carcasses that lay on the floor nearby: what looked like part of a chicken and the half-picked leg of a goat.

She did this to them. Lydia backed carefully up the stairs, trembling and, despite herself, slightly faint. *Deliberately infected them, in the hopes of controlling the rest.* For a moment her mind flashed to Miranda, to what it felt like to hold her child in her arms.

What woman could do that to her own flesh?

Not someone whose power I want to be in.

She turned and climbed the remaining steps swiftly.

Grant Hobart was at the top.

Lydia gasped with shock and nearly fell back down the stair, but when he reached to steady her, she jerked sharply away. 'Don't you touch me!'

His face convulsed with anger, as if he would have shouted at her, and his hand flinched to strike. Then he stopped himself, panting. In the candlelight she saw his eyes glitter with fever.

And am I REALLY going to run back down into that room below?

'Don't blame me, Mrs Asher,' he gasped. 'I beg of you, don't think hard of me.'

'Don't think *hard* of you?' She knew she should pretend whatever he wanted, and couldn't.

'I couldn't help it! They forced my hand—'

'They didn't force you to get mixed up with them in the first place!'

He turned his face away. His breath had stunk of blood and decaying flesh, and she could see where his teeth had begun to sprout and deform, even since that morning when he'd seized her at the hotel. The telltale swollen bruising of his face showed where the frontal sutures of his skull had begun to loosen, to re-form in the characteristic shape of the *yao-kuei*. 'You don't understand.' He moved aside to let her step off the stair and into the room.

'I understand –' she kept her voice steady with an effort – 'that you brought me here so Mrs Tso and her minions can get hold of my husband, to keep him from interfering with Mrs Tso's efforts to control those things in the mines so she can sell them to President Yuan.'

'He's not going to be harmed! Good God, woman, you don't think I'd let Chinese harm a white man! They only want him out of the country!'

'They were waiting for him the night he fled,' Lydia pointed out. 'And what did you think the Crown was going to do with your accusation of treason when he got back to England? Say, *Oh, that's all right, what you do in China doesn't really count*?'

'Look, they – they've found a man who'll confess to the Eddington girl's murder.' He passed his hand over his face, like a man trying to scrub away sleep that is nearly overwhelming. 'Five hundred pounds – a Chinese, he's ill, dying, he needs it for his family.'

'And you *believed* that?' Lydia stared at him in appalled incredulity.

'I—' Hobart stammered. 'An told me . . .'

'And what a pillar of rectitude *he* is. All it means is that they found some man who'd confess, in order to keep *his* wife, or some member of his family, from being killed. That five hundred pounds is going straight into Mrs Tso's pocket . . . And did Mr An also tell you that the girls he'd bring to you *liked* being beaten up?'

The big man's distorted features contracted, and he looked away from her again. 'You don't understand.' He rubbed his face once more. Lydia could see where his nails were thickening, his hands deforming, bruised and swollen. *They must hurt like the very devil.* 'I'm not the only one in the Legations to use An's services, you know.'

Lydia forced herself not to shout at him, *And that makes it all right?* Instead she asked, in a quieter voice, 'What happened to you?'

'I came here Thursday night to give An the money. Your husband had fled; I prayed that would be enough for them. An was late, so I waited for him in . . . in one of the smaller court-yards . . .'

He shied away there from speaking of something – a lifetime of myopia and participation in the London social seasons had made Lydia very good at reading the inflections of peoples' voices when they were lying. *The pavilion Jamie saw, with the pornographic paintings? How does one go about ordering porno-graphic paintings when one is in China, anyway? Annette Hautecoeur would know . . .*

'I heard some kind of commotion and went out into the court-yard. This . . . this thing, this creature came out of the dark at me. I have a sword-cane, I cut it – one of Mrs Tso's nephews came running, and I didn't see – good God, what happened to them? I didn't see his – *its*! – face until it was close. T'uan and Yi – that's Madame's oldest boy – and their bully boys came and dragged them both away, and Yi told me I was not to speak of what I'd seen, of what had happened. *As I valued my own life and my son's*, they said . . . They can get a man into the Legation stockade, you know, to kill a prisoner there. But I could see T'uan's face was changing, too.'

'And you came back,' she said softly, 'when you started getting sick yourself?'

'I had to! I could see T'uan was all right, you see. I mean, he looked frightful, but he seemed to be in his right mind. He didn't have these – these terrible blank spaces, these horrible urges that come over me . . . When I came here on Friday night, the night of the riot at the Empress Garden, Mrs Tso told me, yes, they have Chinese medicine, Chinese herbs, that will control this sickness. They'd give them to me, she said, if I brought you here. They only want to talk to you, she said. She swore to me you wouldn't be harmed . . .'

'What did she swear on?' inquired Lydia, genuinely curious.

'The Bible? *Is* Mrs Tso a Christian? *Does* one swear on the Sayings of Confucius? I suppose one could—'

His hand jerked back again, and his mouth gaped suddenly, as if he not only would strike, but also bite. 'Shut up, you wittering bitch!' Lydia sprang back, got the corner of the table between them. 'I'm telling you you won't be hurt—'

'They didn't have any hesitation about hurting Mr Woodreave,' she said softly.

Hobart's head jerked sideways, like a horse tormented by a fly. 'What?'

'Mr Woodreave? The man you paid – I presume – to get me downstairs, knowing I'd come at his request but not at yours?'

'I – he shouldn't have . . .' By the blurred candle-flame she saw a tremor shake him, and he pawed the air near one ear. 'Excuse me?' He blinked at her, as if waking from a dream himself.

His mind is starting to go. Panic flooded her. *How long does it take to turn completely into one of those things? How long do I have before he turns on me?*

She took a deep breath and pretended she had a procedure to finish that had to be done correctly before the patient stopped breathing or went into shock. *There's plenty of time, but this needs to be done with delay . . .*

'Why did you come back here?' she asked. 'And how did you get in?'

For a moment he looked at her a little blankly, as if he'd forgotten again, then went to the corner by the open trapdoor, Lydia never taking her eyes from him as he moved. He picked up something he'd leaned against the wall, and she moved back away from the table a little. As she did, a whisper of icy air breathed on her from the total blackness of the room.

Moving air.

Door open. Window open.

'I don't know.' He held up a black rod. By the way he handled its weight it had to be a spanner or pry bar. 'Something . . . I had to come. I had to come here. It wants me.'

'Who wants you?' *If I run, will he chase me, as a dog will if you flee?*

'The ruler. The – The Lord of Hell – one of the Lords of Hell. Of this part of Hell. He needs me to— What?' His head jerked again, and in the near-dark, his stance changed, his hunched shoulders dropped a little. 'I – I'm sorry. This afternoon I dreamed – I slept, and I dreamed that I had to come back here. When I woke it was all I could think of. I didn't mean to, but . . . but it's as if I drifted off again for a bit, and then woke up and here I was.' He hefted the pry bar in his hand. *He's a big man*, she thought. *He can easily break a skull.*

'Did you break in through one of the gates?' she inquired, in the same tone of voice in which she'd have asked Lady Cottesmore where she'd got the shrimp for her buffet. *Thank you, Aunt Lavinnia, for all those lessons in speaking calmly and politely no matter what one feels . . .*

'Yes. There's not a soul in this part of the house, you know.' The words came out perfectly naturally. Then his head began to move again, as if he were disoriented, and he said something in Chinese. The candle in Lydia's hand flickered – she risked a glance down at it and saw it was burned nearly to its end in its little porcelain dish.

Hobart gasped and dropped the pry bar – it made a great, ringing clatter on the tiled floor – and clutched his head. Voices cried out in the room below: one in Chinese, the other simply bleating, a goatish sound that made Lydia's stomach turn.

Without a word, Hobart lurched away from her and vanished down the stair. Lydia turned at once and scanned the darkness, looking for anything . . .

There. A lighter rectangle in the blackness. He'd pried open a window.

She ran to it as soundlessly as she could, climbed out into the dark.

TWENTY-EIGHT

DAMN *those wretched gangsters for stealing my glasses!* Lydia strode along the side of the building to its corner in the darkness, one hand to the wall, trying desperately to remember whether Jamie had said anything about which way one went to get out of this particular courtyard. Both Jamie and

the Baroness Drosdrova had explained to her that in the larger
courtyard houses, only a few courtyards had gates or doors leading
out into the *hutongs*, and it would make sense that Mrs Tso
wouldn't imprison her son and her nephew in any courtyard that
fit that description . . .

So how had Grant Hobart found it?

Something was drawing him – the hive mind of the Others?

Whatever was happening – completely aside from the hostage-
for-Jamie issue – Lydia didn't want any part of it.

There isn't a soul in this part of the house, Hobart had said.

Moonlight painted the elaborate tiled ridges of the roofs,
but the courtyard remained plunged in shadow. A walkway
led away westward from the corner of the building, a blotchy
patchwork of darkness and deeper darkness. There might well
be more than one route out of the courtyard, but Lydia wasn't
about to stay and look for others. Hobart's pry bar would
make short work of the staples that held the *yao-kueis'* chains
to the cellar wall. The walkway led around two corners and
branched; she heard a woman's voice in one direction, and
the voices of children, and smelled cooking oil. The other
way took her into a deserted courtyard, and she made her way
slowly around its entire perimeter, searching for anything
resembling a doorway.

Two other walkways. It was like getting lost in the *hutongs*
that lay somewhere on the other side of all those crowding walls.
One led to a courtyard that was definitely occupied – the dim
glow of oil-light outlined windows showed Lydia goldfish-kongs
and laundry. The other opened into a longer walkway where the
light of a lantern bobbed, coming closer.

Lydia turned and walked away as if she were merely another
member of the family, but it didn't work. A man shouted at her
in Chinese. She broke into a run, dodged around a corner and
back along another walkway – or was it one she'd already
traversed? She fled across a courtyard, and two women emerged
from one of the rooms off it, shouting at her (presumably – for
all she knew they could be screaming about stains on the good
tablecloth the way her stepmother did). She tried to find another
way out, but the men with the lantern came running from
another corner of the court, shouting '*T'ing!*' One of them fired
a pistol, which knocked splinters of brick from a wall yards from

her, and both Chinese women immediately turned upon the guards and started to shriek at them.

Lydia tried to dart past them, but one of them seized her and twisted her arm brutally, and the other struck her in the face with force that took her breath away. The Chinese women still screaming at them, the men dragged her into the nearest room – empty, but obviously somebody's home, with blankets piled on a *kang* stove-bed and clothing of some kind hanging in the shadows on the wall. One of the men yelled a command to the women in the courtyard. There were shrieks of argument (*whoever said Chinese women were trained to be submissive?* Lydia wondered), and then running feet. *A child's*, Lydia thought as she was shoved into a battered bamboo chair. The way the women had moved, it was obvious that their feet were crippled.

She sat motionless, head throbbing from the blow. A more intrepid heroine, she reflected, would probably take on both guards with the chair. But one of them had the gun pointed at her, and she didn't see how being beaten senseless was going to help her flee later, to say nothing of the fact that even if she got out of this room and the courtyard, she still hadn't the slightest idea of which way the compound's single open gate was, if it *was* still open . . .

They need me as a hostage. They can't kill me, they need me as a hostage . . .

Only until they get Jamie.

The door opened.

There was only one person with Mrs Tso, a fat little Chinese man dressed in Western style, his hair cut short and smelling faintly of pomade. Lydia couldn't make out his features clearly but could see at least no sign of the horrors visible in Hobart's face and on the poor samurai Ito's. *Her oldest son?*

Mrs Tso swayed forward on her tiny stubs of feet, slapped Lydia hard, and poured out a tirade of furious Chinese at her. When the man hesitantly spoke to her – *she MUST be his mother!* – she turned on him, slapped him as well, then returned her attention to Lydia, black eyes flashing poison.

The man said, in halting English, 'My mother say you are foolish girl, you put self in danger, try to escape here. No harm come to you, if you wait and be quiet.'

Yes, and my Aunt Harriet's husband is descended in a true line from Henry VIII's secret marriage to Bess Blount and is the rightful King of England, too. Lydia looked meekly down at her captor's shoes and asked, in as timorous a voice as she could muster, 'Promise?'

Running boots in the courtyard. The door opened. More lantern-light, and a Niagara of Chinese from another guard.

Somebody must have discovered the prison door open and the two boys gone. Or else the gate into the street open, wherever it is—

Madame Tso went rigid with shock, then launched into several minutes of quick-fire questions and answers with the guard before turning back to Lydia, hand raised to slap again.

Lydia shrank back and covered her face. Those small, strong hands grabbed her wrist, pulled her hand aside. More questions shouted at her, furiously, as the older woman shook her by a handful of her hair.

Tso Jr. peered around his mother and asked, 'How you get out?'

'I heard someone moving about in the other room.' Lydia widened her eyes and looked terrified, something that didn't require a great deal of acting at the moment. 'Scraping and banging noises, as if the locks were being wrenched off the door. I hid until the noise got quieter, then I looked out. There was no one in the outer room, but one of the windows was open. I climbed out and ran.'

'You not go in other room?' He stood close enough that she could see his face: young and hard, with a wisp of mustache and brutal eyes. 'Not go down stairs?'

Lydia shook her head, eyes swimming with tears. 'No.' After having her hair pulled, tears weren't hard to summon, either, but any girl who'd had a London Season acquired the ability to weep at will, for purposes of either blackmail or self-defense. 'I was afraid, I didn't know what was happening—'

Tso Jr. – whose surname, Lydia recalled, was actually something else – Chen? – related this information to his mother. *Chen,* she thought, watching their faces. For his father, whom she now suspected had been eaten up alive by Madame in the fashion of spider husbands. *Definitely, they've discovered the boys have been freed . . .*

Madame stepped back, made a slashing gesture with one hand. Her son took Lydia's elbow, helped rather than pulled her to her feet. 'Please, not to do anything foolish,' he advised in a completely neutral tone as they led her from the room, across the court, down a walkway in the bobbing light of the lanterns. 'My mother—' He glanced at the woman who strode beside them, hanging on to his other arm but without the slightest sign of the pain which, Lydia knew, each step caused her.

Madame rolled her eyes, rattled off instructions as to what he was to say, and he obediently repeated, 'Courtyards guarded by dogs, big dogs. Wolves. Attack and kill. Tigers also.'

Funny, Jamie completely forgot to mention the tigers the other night . . .

She gasped and looked petrified.

'If you escape, we cannot save you. Stay where you are, all be well.'

They entered another courtyard, dust-drifted and deserted in the lantern-light, and Lydia gasped in earnest. It was as Jamie had described: the pathways beaten in the weeds before the shallow steps of the main pavilion, the nailed-up shutters, the western lock on its door. They pushed her through its main chamber and into its eastern room, which had no lock on it; Madame pulled a silk sash from the pocket of her *ch'i-p'ao*, threw it to her son with a brief command.

'Not to be frightened,' he said to Lydia as the single guard with them (*they must be short-handed tonight – why?*) dragged her hands behind her.

'No—' She struggled desperately as they thrust her against one of the pillars at the rear of the room, tied her wrists behind her and around it. 'Please, don't tie me—!'

'All be well.' He hesitated, then took one of the lanterns and hung it near the door. 'All be well.'

By the way he glanced at his mother as they filed from the room, he didn't believe this for a second.

Half a dozen horses stood saddled and bridled outside the half-ruined Temple of the Concealed Buddha. 'I found them in the gully, below the rear entrance to the mine,' Chiang explained. The tack was German, the blankets the five-colored stripe of the new Republic. 'I do not ride,' he added as Asher and the others

mounted. 'The philosopher Chuang Tzu, in the time of the
Warring States, wrote that to make a slave of an animal in that
fashion disturbs not only the Path of the animal, but the soul's
own path . . .'

'We not leave you.' The moon was barely a sliver, but the
night, though icy, was clear. Beyond the scrim of trees that
surrounded the temple, Asher could see the narrow track that led
back toward the Mingliang gully where the mine's main entrance
lay. They had, he now saw, passed the Temple itself on their
reconnaissance of that flank of the mountain, never guessing that
its crypt held a tunnel. Neither Ysidro nor the engineers of the
Hsi Fang-te Company had suspected – nor, presumably, had the
emperors who had condemned the Buddhist sects. 'Kuo Min-tang,
also bandits—'

'My son.' The moonlight – and his smile – turned the priest's
face curiously young. 'What can bandits steal of me? My stick?
I will then cut another. Go quickly now, and do not let an old
man's prejudice slow you down. I know the way back to the
City. I have walked it many times.'

Asher didn't linger to argue. He reined his horse around and set
off at a hand gallop down the track, as swift as the thin moonlight
would let him ride, the others stringing out behind him. *It could
have been a lie*, he told himself. *T'uan could have told you anything
about Lydia, without any way to prove it.* Yet the hair prickled on
the back of his neck. Lydia knew to stay away from Grant Hobart,
but at a guess, there were others in the Legations who had been
sufficiently careless, foolish, or unfortunate as to fall into the power
of the Tso to blackmail – and the recollection of what the Tso had
hidden in their house turned his heart to ice.

It would be two hours' ride from Mingliang Village before
they could reach the motor car Mizukami had left in Men T'ou
Kuo, even if they didn't encounter the Kuo Min-tang again.
Vampires could move very swiftly, either afoot or by using some
means of tricking or seducing the living into aiding them with
transport. But whether, once he reached Peking, Ysidro could
find the Tso house was another question, entirely apart from the
very real possibility that the vampires of Peking would kill him
before he reached the place.

They trust no one, Father Orsino had said.

Certainly not a *ch'ang pi kwei* vampire working in obvious

alliance with the living. Did they say of him what Karlebach did, that he could not be trusted and should be killed at sight?

As the horses topped the gully edge and the steep trail dropped away, Asher turned in the saddle. The Temple of the Concealed Buddha could still be glimpsed in the moonlight on the barren hillside, but of Chiang, no trace remained.

Lydia estimated that the lantern lasted an hour before it burned out. The fact that light could be seen in the room – even in the form of dull topaz needles through chinks in the shutters – filled her with horror, but when it finally perished, the absolute blackness was ten times worse.

Would Hobart – and the two Tso Others to whom he had now allied himself – be able to track her by the smell of living flesh, living blood, in the darkness?

She didn't know.

At least there were no rats here. Although the vampire Li, down in his cellar tomb, was – Jamie had assured her – utterly unable to move, still the antipathy that all animals had to those Undead predators seemed to persist. Even Simon's cats back in London gave the vampire wide berth, at least – Lydia suspected – until he had fed.

But the thought of that tall, narrow house on its nameless side-street – the street that had by coincidence been left off every map of London since the late sixteenth century – brought a desperate tightness to Lydia's throat, the sting of tears to her eyes. Every wall jammed with bookshelves, the carved graceful products of eighteenth-century cabinetmakers' art or simple goods boxes stacked on top of them . . . A desk of inlaid ebony, and a strange old German calculating-engine that grinned with ivory keys.

They are unable to reach me, nor I to pass them . . .

She remembered how cold his hands were when they touched hers; the journey in his company from Paris to Constantinople, long nights playing picquet to the swaying of the train coach ('. . . the representation in little of all human affairs,' he described the game, while beating her at it, soundly and mercilessly.) She still had a handful of his sonnets, hidden in the back of a drawer at home, a fact that she had never told either Simon or Jamie.

Remember me kindly, if we meet not again.

She leaned her head back against the pillar behind her. Her knees ached from standing, but she did not dare slither down to sit. The tightness of the binding on her wrists was such that, despite flexing and turning her hands as well as she could, her fingers kept going numb.

You don't understand, Hobart had whispered. A killer asking to be excused.

Simon had never asked that, nor pretended that he wasn't what he was.

Did that make him less deserving of being buried alive in a gas-choked mine?

No. No.

Then why are you crying?

The silence in the pavilion seemed deeper in the darkness. Then through that silence, dim and muffled, a voice lifted. Screaming. Words, Lydia thought, though the thickness of the intervening earth made it impossible to tell . . .

Does he scream every night?

Or just since they infected him with the blood of the yao-kuei?

Twenty years, Jamie had said. *Maybe longer.* Twenty years of lying propped on a little daybed with his long hair flowing down around him, unable to move. Had he trusted Mrs Tso, *beautiful as the sky with stars?* Had he let her know where he slept? Relied on her to do things for him, the way Don Simon Ysidro relied on her and Jamie? She had twice seen Ysidro asleep, sunk in the vampire trance of the daylight hours, from which nothing could waken them. On the second of those occasions, in St Petersburg, Jamie could have – should have, Karlebach would say – killed Simon where he lay, to save the lives of who knew how many thousands of men and women in the future.

And Karlebach was right! she thought despairingly.

But it had never – *would* never – have occurred to either of them to chop off his arms and legs and keep him alive to use his powers over the minds of others at their bidding.

And I suppose that's the reason I'm not the all-powerful matriarch of a gangster family.

But even that, Lydia reflected, was unfair. She had been born wealthy, a rich man's only child. God only knew where Mrs Tso had come from, or what had been done to her – other than crippling her feet to make her 'more beautiful' (and also more expensive on the market) – to turn her into a woman who would think of doing that. Who would use her son, and then her nephews, as pawns, so that she herself would never be that helpless again.

Deep below her, the vampire Li screamed in the dark.

Screaming? Or calling out?

Calling out for who?

TWENTY-NINE

A shot cracked the night.

Close. Lydia's heart lurched. *A few courtyards away . . .* In this part of the Tatar City gunplay could have nothing to do with the situation in the Tso compound tonight. Since the Emperor's fall, Peking had become a violent place, the gangs that controlled the brothels and *p'ai-gow* games, the rickshaw stables and opium dens all fighting for mastery, the soldiers of the President and of the Kuo Min-tang staging murderous battles in the taverns. Robbers, layabouts, and killers for hire hid out under the bridges and in the empty temples around the shallow 'Sea' and vastly outnumbered the new police-force.

But the shot filled her with panic.

Deep beneath the pavilion, Li had fallen silent.

For a thousandth time, Lydia pulled and twisted at the silken rope around her wrists, trying to at least get her fingernails on the knots.

Nothing.

Then, so softly she wasn't sure if the sound was actually in the ground beneath her or inside her head, Lydia heard Li crooning, a horrible mixture of words and throat sounds.

Oh, God, she thought, struggling again though she knew it would do her no good. *Oh God—*

Something – some*one* – pounded on the pavilion door.

Where are the wretched guards? They were every way I turned three hours ago . . .

Yet there had really been only a few. *Not a soul*, Hobart had said, and he'd been very nearly right; she remembered how

Mrs Tso had appeared with only her son for escort. *Had they heard that Jamie was going out to the Western Hills today and went out to prevent them blowing up the mine?*

And did Li know that?

Fists crashed on the shutters, a yard from her head. Lydia fought not to scream. Two of them – even in her terror she identified the sounds at the windows. Two of them, pounding on the wood with the violence of machinery. Hobart's face swam into her mind, distorted, fanged. The bloody mouth and sprouting teeth of the samurai Ito, the horrible thick claws of the things chained in the cellar . . .

More crashing, on the shutters of the main room this time, the pitchy darkness seeming to shake with the noise—

Jamie, Jamie get me out of here!

Gunshots again, right outside the pavilion. The things hammering at the front windows stopped, but the crashing at the windows beside her, in front of her, kept on, unheeding, and through the hammer blows she heard a man scream. Three more gunshots, with the speed of someone shooting wild in panic, and then the rending crash of wooden shutters tearing, and moonlight streamed into the room.

Two of them, black slumped silhouettes. One crossed the room to the door as if it didn't see her, but the other came straight for her, eyes flashing yellow like a cat's. After the blackness the dim blue moonlight seemed bright, and Lydia brought up one foot and kicked it in the stomach with all her strength as it reached for her.

It staggered back, bayed at her, a yawping animal sound, then drove in again. She kicked again and felt her skirt tear where it grabbed her, kicked a third time, and a fourth – it didn't seem to have any other strategy than to keep coming, keep grabbing, as if it knew that she'd tire long before it did. It leaned its weight on her, swung its arms, and her kick turned into a desperate shove, holding it away.

It howled.

Then it turned from her and followed its companion out the door and into the main room.

Lydia heard other things in that room and realized that the crashing in that direction had stopped. So had the screams and the shots. The smell of fresh blood came to her, and of cordite.

She heard them crashing and pounding on the door of the western chamber, drowning out the crooning wail of the vampire Li below.

Can he really control them, once he's brought them to him? Command them?

Or will they only see him as flesh that can't fight them when they go to eat it?

There was nothing on the floor around her – or nothing she could see, by dim moonlight without her glasses: no shattered glass or broken shards of wood. *There's got to be something . . .* Hesitantly, she bent her cramped knees, slithered down the pillar and squinted to get a better look at the floor. Distant and muffled, she heard Li's voice, shouting what sounded like commands . . .

Shouting them again, louder and then louder . . .

Then he screamed.

A slumped form loomed suddenly in the moonlight, huge as it staggered through the door. Lydia tried to push herself to her feet but it was too quick for her. She smelled the blood on its clothing, blood on the huge hand that closed on her arm as it dragged her up to her feet.

Blood on Hobart's breath as he stammered, 'Get you out— Get you out— Oh God, that thing down there!'

He must have had a penknife in his pocket. Lydia twisted her hand aside when he sliced her bonds. *Do not, DO NOT get a cut . . .*

He kept his grip on her arm, stared down at her with eyes that caught the moonlight like an animal's. In a voice that astonished her with its own reasonableness, she said, 'Let me go, I can walk,' just exactly as if he were Mr Woodreave trying to help her over a puddle.

It didn't work. His grip tightened.

'You'll run away.' His voice slurred over the swollen bloodiness of his growing fangs. 'Need you. Make them give me medicine.'

Dammit . . .

When he dragged her through the pavilion's central room she could hear Li screaming down below, hideous shrieks. *Dear God, they must be tearing him to pieces, eating him as he lies there . . .*

She tripped over the corpses in the doorway. Two of Mrs Tso's men, blood-covered.

'Dying in my head,' whispered Hobart. 'I feel it – I felt them all, dying, oh God! I'm going mad, and I can't go mad . . . I'll make her give me medicine . . .'

In the middle of the courtyard a third figure lay: a woman's, in a satin *ch'i-p'ao*. Bound feet in tiny shoes poked out from beneath her hem, and a gun lay near her hand.

Tell him who she was, or not? He barely seemed aware of her.

'You'll be all right. Swear it. Honor bright—' Hobart giggled suddenly and looked down into Lydia's face. 'Just – put you someplace safe for awhile. There's places under the bridges, under the palaces—'

'That really isn't necessary.' She forced her voice to be matter-of-fact. 'I can arrange—'

'No arrangement.' He dragged her to the walkway. 'Fed up to the bloody back teeth with goddam arrangements. Can't let them see me like this. She'll give me the medicine. I'll make her. They're all dying, I can feel them . . .'

More voices shouted in the courtyard, over the braying of the *yao-kuei*. Hobart stopped, and Lydia turned, to see in the moonlight indistinct figures rushing into the court as the slumped forms of the Others emerged from the pavilion. A shotgun roared. Lydia thought she saw the white blur of a beard on one tall figure, the flash of round spectacles and a samurai blade. She screamed, 'Jamie!' as Hobart seized her around her waist and lifted her from her feet, covered her mouth with a reeking hand.

And ran. Faster than she'd guessed the *yao-kuei* could run, down the walkway, across a court. Lydia kicked, writhed, nearly suffocated by the paw over her face, but he only tightened his grip. She heard him panting, almost in her ear, the hoarse, animal note of it terrifying. *His mind is nearly gone, and what then . . . ?*

Through a broken gate and out on to the sloping shore of the shallow lake, water scummed with dirty ice in the moonlight. A marble bridge where the northern lake ran into the southern, and broken steps leading down to blackness underneath. Hobart stopped, set her feet on the ground and looked around him—

'Remember this place,' he panted. 'Extraordinary—' And there was a lightness in his voice, like a man in a dream. 'Never been here in my life but remember it. They were here, there's a hole they went down, cellars – cellars into cellars . . . It's like I dreamed it.'

Then he flinched, put one hand to his head, face twisted with pain. 'They're dying. They scream when they die, inside my head. It's like pieces torn away bleeding from my brain. I'll put you there safe, then go back, talk to her . . . make her give me the medicine. It saved her boys, or would have, if they hadn't been killed—'

'She can't give you medicine,' gasped Lydia. 'She's dead. Back there. She's dead.'

He struck her, jerking her arm to drag her into the blow. Half-stunned, Lydia sagged against his gripping hand, and he pulled her up again, held her against him. The moonlight reflected in his eyes like mirrors. 'You're lying,' he whispered. 'Won't do you any good. You cunning little bitch.'

Then he grinned, with his bloody teeth, and put his palm to her cheek. 'But pretty—'

A second set of reflective eyes appeared behind his shoulder, and a long white hand wrapped around his chin, another braced on his shoulder. Hobart roared, spun, faster than Lydia had ever seen a living man move, flung her down on the broken steps and slashed at Ysidro with his claws. Ysidro strange and wraithlike, as she had seen him when he hadn't fed, weakened and stripped of illusion. He dodged, tried to twist free as Hobart grabbed him by the wrists—

And as if she'd rehearsed it a dozen times for a pantomime performance, Lydia stuck her foot between Hobart's legs.

Hobart went down like a felled tree on top of her, his weight crushing, and with a whispered oath, Ysidro reached down and neatly broke his neck.

'*Dios.*' The vampire rolled the horrible corpse away, held out his hand to help Lydia to her feet. His fingers were like frozen bone, his long hair hanging in his eyes. 'Mistress, I—'

In the same instant that Jamie's voice shouted, 'NO!' a dozen yards away, a shotgun roared.

Ysidro's body bowed under the impact of the blast, his white shirt starred suddenly with blood. For an instant his hand closed convulsively on hers, and their eyes met, as if he would have said something to her . . . She was aware of running footsteps, of Jamie and Professor Karlebach racing toward them, Asher tearing the shotgun out of Karlebach's hand—

Then Ysidro's eyes closed. His fingers slipped from hers, and he stepped back from her, his face relaxed into an expression of unearthly peace, and fell into the ebony lake without a sound.

THIRTY

'He was a vampire,' was all Karlebach would say. 'A murderer a thousand times over. How can you shed one single tear for such a thing? What kind of woman are you?'

Asher knew there was no hope of making him understand. Kneeling – cradling Lydia in his arms, her body shaking though she made not a whisper – he replied quietly, 'She's a woman who has just had her life saved and seen her rescuer killed before her eyes.'

Karlebach's face was the face of an Old Testament prophet, who speaks the judgement of God and is not moved. 'He was a vampire.' It was as if, for that space of time, he knew neither of them, nor anything beyond that fact.

The yellow light of flames sprang up behind the roofs of the Tso compound and showed Asher the trim little shape of Count Mizukami making his way down from the broken gate. 'Madame Ashu—'

'Is well.' Asher rose to his feet with Lydia held against him, all that exhaustion and the pain in his side would tolerate. Her face pressed to his shoulder, her hands gripped his torn sleeves convulsively, unable to speak or to meet the eyes of anyone around her. 'But I'm taking her back to the hotel. You'll tidy up here?' He glanced toward the spreading blaze now visibly licking above the roofs.

'It is done.' Mizukami must have used the spare petrol from the boot of his motor car, or else found lamp oil in one of the rooms near the vampire Li's prison. 'I even sent a man for the Fire Department.'

'Thank you.' Asher felt drained, emptied of every thought and feeling except that Lydia was alive and unhurt.

And that Ysidro was dead at last.

Young Private Seki, chalk-pale, brought the motor car around to the spot where Big Tiger Lane opened on to the lakeshore. Asher's boots crunched the icy sand as he stumbled up the short slope, laid Lydia gently in the back seat and covered her with the car rug. Rigid and silent, Karlebach got into the front beside the driver, his shotgun by his side.

And he has a right, thought Asher wearily, closing his eyes, *to be bitter. He did the right thing, by all the laws of God and man, and received no thanks for it. Not even acknowledgement for the death of the young man he loved like a son. Instead he was betrayed by one whom he's seen falling further and further beneath a vampire's seducing spell.*

No wonder he pulled that trigger, even as Ysidro saved Lydia's life.

Shooting Ysidro had been an act of salvation, to free both Asher and Lydia from servitude to the vampire's spells.

He is right. Asher leaned back into the leather of the car seat, Lydia's head resting on his thigh. Under his hands her tangled hair was wet silk. Lydia alive. Lydia unhurt. *He's right.*

In the dark behind his eyelids, Asher saw Ysidro's body buckle under the spray of silver buckshot. White shirt starred with blood, colorless hair like spider silk around the scarred and skull-like face. No expression, neither pain nor joy, anger nor regret, like a strange statue wrought of ivory, air and time.

Saw him fall backward into the near-freezing black water.

Into peace. Into death. Into Hell. A thousand and ten thousand and a hundred thousand black iron steps down . . .

The following day Karlebach informed him that he had changed his ticket home, and instead of traveling by the *Ravenna* with the Ashers at the end of the month, he would take the *Liliburo* out of Shanghai next week, alone.

On the night of the twentieth of November, Asher dreamed of Don Simon Ysidro.

He'd gone with Ellen and Miranda to see Rebbe Karlebach off at the train station, for his journey to Shanghai: Lydia still kept to her room. He'd offered to accompany his old teacher south on the day-long journey, and when Karlebach had refused – Mrs Asher, he said, needed her husband at her side – had arranged for the Legation clerk P'ei Cheng K'ang to go with him, and to see him safely on to the boat. On the platform the

old man had embraced him, and returning the embrace Asher
had felt how fragile his old friend seemed, stiff and brittle and
unyielding. Karlebach had whispered his name, and Asher had
said, 'Thank you, my friend.' He did not say for what.

They both knew – Asher felt this through his bones – that
nothing would be the same between them again.

It had been a week of nine-days'-wonders in the Legation
Quarter. The news that Sir Grant Hobart's body had been found
in the fire-gutted house of the notorious Mrs Tso ('I can't say
I'm wildly surprised,' had been Annette Hautecoeur's comment)
had been followed hard by Asher's resurrection ('No, no, haven't
the slightest idea what it was all about . . .'), and by Mr Timms's
gruff apology on behalf of the Legation police ('Telegram from
London informs us that the charge was all balderdash – no, they
said no more than that . . .').

'How astonishing,' Asher had said, with what he hoped was
a convincing look of baffled surprise.

Yet all these developments had been dwarfed by the appearance of five Chinese – presumably cousins of various Legation
servants, though there was no way of proving this – and a dilapi-
dated American artist named Jones, who walked into the Legation
police station and independently swore that they'd seen Richard
Hobart at various times on the night of October twenty-third
wearing a tie which in no way resembled the murder weapon.
Moreover, the rickshaw-puller who had brought Richard to
Eddington's put in an appearance, and testified in excellent
English – he'd been a professor of that language at the Imperial
Railway College at Shanhaikuan before the downfall of the
dynasty – that when he had brought the young man, incapably
drunk, to the gate, it had been to find Holly Eddington's body
lying already dead in the garden. His fare had, in fact, stared
down at the body, sobbed pitifully, 'Oh Holly, who has done
such a dreadful thing?' and had fainted. Mr K'ung had attempted
to revive him and had only run away from the scene when people
began to come from the house.

Asher wondered where the dead Mi Ching's cousins had
located an English-speaking rickshaw-puller for the purpose, not
to speak of an impoverished American artist. But, Lydia had
commented over tea later in the afternoon, it was a very nice
touch.

Lydia had been very quiet through it all.

Now Asher dreamed of the Temple of Everlasting Harmony. Lydia, guidebook in hand, was telling him about the various fearsome statues that stood along its western wall: 'This is Lu, Magistrate of the Wu Kuan Hell – I think that's the hell where sinners are fried in cauldrons of oil, only those poor people around his feet in the statue look like they're being steamed instead of fried . . .'

'Perhaps they're given a choice,' Asher suggested.

'Like the dumplings in a native restaurant?' She looked better than she had all the previous week, as if the horror of what had happened at the Tso compound, the grief at Ysidro's death, were beginning to loosen their grip on her. She still bore the bruises on her face where Hobart had struck her, and her glasses were her rimless spare pair, which she'd been wearing all week. Under his shirt, waistcoat, jacket and coat – the night was a cold one – Asher was conscious of the sticking-plaster dressing on his ribs.

'And this is Bao Cheng,' she went on, 'who was an official of the Sung Dynasty before he was promoted – I suppose you could call it that – to being Magistrate of . . . let's see . . . the Yama Hell. Is that the one with the metal cylinder they're supposed to climb with the fire lit inside it? Oh, and here's Chiang Tzu-Wen . . .'

They had reached the end of the Temple, and in the doorway beside the war god's banner-draped niche Ysidro stood, wrapped in the earth-colored robe of the temple priests, his pale hair tied back in their fashion. His arms were folded, as if against the chill, for indeed it had snowed that afternoon. A thin layer of it was visible beyond him in the disheveled garden – the pigeon-coops gone now, the garbage cleared away – glittering gently in the brightness of the moon. 'Mistress,' he said. 'James.'

Lydia gasped, moved an impulsive step towards him, then stopped herself, threw an uncertain glance at Asher. He took the guidebook from her hand and, freed of the encumbrance, she flung herself into Ysidro's arms.

Held him, tight and motionless, without a word, rocking a little in his arms. Face pressed to his shoulder, red hair like fire and poppies around the cold ivory spindles of his fingers.

'I'm glad to see you're all right,' said Asher.

'I trust, at my age, that a half-dozen pellets of silver in my shoulder aren't sufficient to discommode me from pulling myself under still water to safety.' The vampire put a hand on Lydia's back and added, in his soft, reasonable voice, 'Hush, Mistress, hush. What is this? Your husband will demand satisfaction of me. Has that lunatic vampire-hunter taken himself off for Prague?'

'This afternoon.' It was in Asher's mind to wonder if he would ever see the old scholar again.

'May his ship go down with all hands.' As he had in the mines, Don Simon looked thin and haggard, and very unhuman. The scars on his face and throat, which he generally used his psychic glamor to cover from living eyes, were shockingly visible. Asher wondered whether this was because this was only a dream, or because of the silver that had scorched his flesh.

'I suppose the thought has never crossed his mind that, had he followed his own dictates and simply destroyed that precious student of his the moment he became infected, rather than giving him the wherewithal to travel and spread the virus, all this might have been avoided.'

'On the contrary,' said Asher, 'I think the thought was very much in his mind. This journey for him was penance – and redemption.'

'At someone else's expense,' said the vampire with a sniff. 'And without asking those he would "help" if they wanted his interference. Like all the Van Helsings of the world, who must become a little mad in order to pursue such phantoms as we. Obsession with us destroys them – as obsession with our own safety destroys us, in the end. I am only grateful,' he added as Lydia stepped back from him, 'that 'twas no worse. Is it well with you, Mistress?'

She smiled a little and straightened her glasses. 'Thank you,' she said softly.

'Yes,' said Asher. 'Thank you – more than I can say.'

Ysidro's eyes touched Asher's – asking permission, as gentlemen do. Asher nodded, and the vampire took Lydia's hand and brushed the ink-stained fingers lightly with cold lips. He released his hold at once, and when Asher held out his own hand to him, took it – a little gingerly – in a skeletal clasp.

Behind Ysidro, in the shadows of Kuan Yu's statue, Asher

became aware of the priest Chiang, curiously young-looking in the moonlight, his eyes gleaming reflectively, like a cat's.

And deep in his dreaming, Asher wondered how he could possibly not have noticed that the old Taoist was a vampire.

Did he always look like that? Asher had the impression that the man's coloring had been warmer, not silk pale as it was now. He had no recollection of noticing before that the old man didn't breathe, nor had he ever taken note – and he couldn't imagine he had been that unobservant – that the long nails of his hands, like Ysidro's, were hard and shiny as claws. Moreover, he had the impression somewhere at the back of his mind that he'd seen the old man in daylight. Whether the psychic illusion did not hold in dreams, or merely because Chiang wished to make matters more clear, Asher saw him now.

He said, 'Chiang Tzu-Wen. One of the ten Magistrates of Hell. You were an official in the Han Dynasty and later worshiped as a god in the Moliang District—'

His Chinese was much better in his dream than it was in real life.

'Long ago.' The old vampire responded to him in Latin and inclined his head. 'We all of us – Professor Gellar – have lives which we once lived, once upon a time.'

He rested his hand on Ysidro's shoulder, the black claws curving like a dragon's against the skin of his throat. 'I will say that I was surprised – and not pleased – to learn that one of those whom I summoned here to deal with the Filthy Ones turned out to be a vampire. We had enough to deal with, my kindred and I, without the concern about a newcomer making alliances that would shift the balance of things here in this city.'

'Without his assistance,' replied Asher, 'we could not have destroyed them – if they are indeed destroyed.'

'They are. I – and my kindred – have gone out to the mine and have walked by night among the bridges and temples on the shores of Peking's five Seas. No trace of the things have we found. Li had summoned to him all those few that dwelled in the city, and all perished together in the flames. We have gone to the place: nothing of them remains.'

Through the door behind him, in the moonlit garden, Asher was briefly conscious of other shadows among the bare wisteria, the timeless stones: a woman with the unbound hair of a shamaness, a great sturdy man who stood like a warrior, a cold-faced mandarin in the robes of a dynasty long perished. They kept their distance from one another, their eyes like pale marsh-fire, wary and ancient and indescribably alien, more like dragons than human souls.

And Lydia, who had been listening with difficulty – her Latin being limited to medical texts – stepped forward and put a hand on Chiang's ragged sleeve. 'He risked his life to learn of them,' she said. 'And he didn't have to come here.'

The old vampire regarded her with a dragon's inhuman gaze. 'It is so, Lady,' he said. 'And as I said, I was surprised. It is not often that the *chiang-shi* –' the pronunciation was completely different from that of his name – 'display interest in anything but the hunt and their own immediate safety.' He shared, in part, in Ysidro's quality of stillness, but Asher detected the momentary flicker of a derisive glance at the vampires in the courtyard beyond the door. 'We *all* owe you thanks.'

The Magistrates in the courtyard – among whom, Asher was interested to note, Father Orsino was not present – did not look as if they thought they owed the *yang kwei tse* anything, living or dead, but evidently nobody was going to argue with Chiang Tzu-Wen. After a moment they too inclined their heads, then stepped back and dissolved into the moonlight. Their reflective eyes seemed to linger on for a moment more.

'Much as my heart longs to say that it was our pleasure,' remarked Ysidro, 'I can assure you, my lord, it was not.'

'Even so.' Chiang's hand tightened slightly on his uninjured shoulder, then released him. 'Yet you did it nevertheless. The Tso woman has been put out of the way, along with poor Li: as you will have observed, the living who meddle in the affairs of the dead are far less dangerous to all than the dead who meddle in the affairs of the living. One hopes that a lesson was learned by all –' he glanced again toward the now-empty courtyard – 'and that the matter will not arise another time.' The last gleam of lingering eyes flickered away.

Chiang made a move to step away, and Lydia – always insatiably curious – lifted her hand again, as if to stay him. 'Sir,' she asked diffidently, in her careful Latin, 'when Li summoned the Others – the *yao-kuei* – to him, was it to get him out of there? Or might he have known that they would destroy him – might he have known he couldn't control them . . . but only wished to end his life in the only way that he could?'

Chiang considered her for a moment, half a smile touching his mouth. 'This I do not know, Lady,' he said. 'Perhaps Li did not know either. But assuredly, he has gone on to Hell—' He stepped back into the shadows of the war god's niche, so that, like the Cheshire cat, only the glimmer of his eyes and the ghost of his voice remained. 'Not as a Magistrate, but as a humble client, as we all shall one day be.'

'*Domine salvet me*,' Ysidro whispered, and from the darkness, Chiang's voice replied.

'No doubt He will, when He has a use for your services.'

Waking, Asher laid his hand on the pillow at his side. Swathed in a heavy quilt, Lydia sat beside the window that overlooked Rue Meiji. But she was looking at her hand, and as Asher sat up, she brushed the back of it with her finger, where Ysidro's cold lips had touched. At his movement she turned her head and her eyes met his.

She looked at peace.

He went to her, and she opened the quilt, to wrap him as well. 'Did you dream about him?' he asked.

'In the Temple of Everlasting Harmony. You spoke to Mr Chiang in Chinese . . . I've never dreamed in Chinese! And then in Latin, of all things. And Chiang—'

'Chiang is a vampire,' said Asher quietly. 'By the sound of it, I suspect he's the Master of Peking.'

'Well, he had no business getting sniffy about the dead meddling with the affairs of the living,' said Lydia, 'if he was getting the other priests in the Temple to work for him.' She pushed her rimless glasses more firmly on to her nose. 'I think his coffin must be one of those crates in the strongroom below the Temple . . . What did he mean, he *summoned* us here? We came here because—'

She broke off, calculating back in her mind how it was they'd happened to journey to China. 'Chiang killed the thing whose body Dr Bauer found in Mingliang, didn't he?'

'I think he must have,' said Asher. 'With fewer than a dozen vampires in Peking – one of them missing for the past twenty years, and who knows how many of them insane, as Father Orsino is – the Master of Peking may have felt in need of Western help. The Prague vampire nest has never been able to make headway against the Others, and they've been there since the fourteenth century. I think Chiang Tzu-Wen must have lain in wait by the mines until he was able to kill one, which he left where a Western doctor would find it. He knew she'd write it up in a journal somewhere. He knew someone would come. I'm guessing he's dealt with vampire hunters before.'

'*The Van Helsings of the world*,' quoted Lydia softly. 'When Ysidro was trapped in the mine, he said he dreamed of him . . .'

'I think it more likely that Chiang went to the mine himself. It was certainly Chiang who helped me escape from the *yao-kuei* – and the rats – when they cornered me on the lakeshore. Even at the time I thought my escape was . . . providential. The fact was that he still needed me.'

Lydia's hand closed tight on his.

After a long time she asked, 'Did Ysidro say in your dream – he didn't in mine – where he's going, when he leaves Peking?'

Asher shook his head. His eyes met those of his wife, troubled behind their thick glasses, afraid for that strange friend whom neither of them had any business speaking to, let alone serving now and again, no matter what the cause. In *her* dream, he wondered, had she thrown herself into Ysidro's arms? In *her* dream, what had Ysidro said to her?

What kind of woman are you? Karlebach had asked, almost spitting the words.

And what kind of man am I?

She wrapped her arms – carefully – around his ribcage, rested her head on his shoulder.

There's an answer to that question somewhere. But God only knows what it is.

Neither dreamed of Don Simon Ysidro again before they left China, nor for a long time thereafter.

But as he and Lydia walked up the gangplank of the *Ravenna* at Tientsin a week later in the freezing winter dusk, Asher did notice, among the trunks being loaded in the hold, a massive one of tan leather with brass corners.